"Taboo, breathtaking, and scorching hot! I freaking loved *Welcome to the Dark Side.*"

—Skye Warren, *New York Times* bestselling author

"This book stole my soul and gave my heart a beatdown! This book was hot, suspenseful, and emotional. A perfect read! You get me?"

—K Webster, *USA Today* bestselling author

"Giana Darling weaves a sexy and addictive story that's unlike anything I've ever read before."

—Ava Harrison, *USA Today* bestselling author

"A love story like nothing I've read before. Beautifully written and perfectly executed, as is Darling's style. I give it ALL the lionhearted stars. A new all-time favorite."

—Haley Jenner, author

"Giana Darling at her absolute best. A raw, gritty, emotional read that draws you in, page by page, until you're utterly consumed with Priest and Bea. Beautiful characters, emotional storyline, and steamy scenes to fulfill all your dark romance needs. Five peachy stars!"

—Dani René, bestselling author

"This book is decadent and delicious, and I devoured it. I love everything Giana Darling writes, but this takes the top spot in my favorites of hers. The romance is outrageous, unapologetically blood pounding. The action is gorgeously choreographed. One click, and then prepare to get lost in the pages of this five-star BANGER! I can't recommend it enough."

—Dylan Allen, *USA Today* bestselling author

MY DARK
FAIRY TALE

OTHER TITLES BY GIANA DARLING

The Fallen Men Series

The Fallen Men is a series of interconnected, stand-alone, erotic MC romances that each feature age-gap love stories between dirty-talking alpha males and the strong, sassy women who win their hearts.

Lessons in Corruption

Welcome to the Dark Side

Good Gone Bad

Fallen Son (a short story)

After the Fall

Inked in Lies

Fallen King (a short story)

Dead Man Walking

Caution to the Wind

Asking for Trouble

King of Iron Hearts (a Fallen Men companion book of poetry)

The Evolution of Sin Trilogy

Giselle Moore is running away from her past in France for a new life in America, but before she moves to New York City, she takes a holiday on the beaches of Mexico and meets a sinful, enigmatic French businessman, Sinclair, who awakens submissive desires and changes her life forever.

The Affair (The Evolution of Sin Book 1)

The Secret (The Evolution of Sin Book 2)
The Consequence (The Evolution of Sin Book 3)

The Enslaved Duet

The Enslaved Duet is a dark romance duology about an eighteen-year-old Italian fashion model, Cosima Lombardi, who is sold by her indebted father to a British earl whose nefarious plans for her include more than just sexual slavery . . . Their epic tale spans Italy, England, Scotland, and the United States across a five-year period that sees them endure murder, separation, and a web of infinite lies.

Enthralled (The Enslaved Duet Book 1)
Enamoured (The Enslaved Duet Book 2)

Anti-Heroes in Love Duet

Elena Lombardi is an ice-cold, brokenhearted criminal lawyer with a distaste for anything untoward, but when her sister begs her to represent New York City's most infamous mafioso in a murder trial, she can't refuse, and soon she finds herself unable to resist the dangerous charms of Dante Salvatore.

When Heroes Fall (Anti-Heroes in Love Duet Book 1)
When Villains Rise (Anti-Heroes in Love Duet Book 2)

The Dark Dream Duet

The Dark Dream duology is a guardian/ward, enemies-to-lovers romance about the dangerous, scarred black sheep of the Morelli family, Tiernan, and the innocent Bianca Belcante. After Bianca's mother dies, Tiernan becomes the guardian to both her and her little brother. But Tiernan doesn't do anything out of the goodness of his heart, and soon Bianca is thrust into the wealthy elite of Bishop's Landing and the dark secrets that lurk beneath its glittering surface.

Bad Dream: A Dark Dream Prologue (free)
Dangerous Temptation (Dark Dream Book 1)
Beautiful Nightmare (Dark Dream Book 2)

The Elite Seven Series

Sloth

Coming Soon

The Impossible Universe Trilogy
Fallen Men Book 9

MY DARK
FAIRY TALE

GIANA DARLING

Published by Montlake, Seattle

www.apub.com

Amazon, the Amazon logo, and Montlake are trademarks of Amazon.com, Inc., or its affiliates.

ISBN-13: 9781662527579 (paperback)
ISBN-13: 9781662527562 (digital)

Cover design by Hang Le
Cover image: © FTAPE LIMITED; © NatalyFox / Shutterstock; © Adrien Olichon / Unsplash

Printed in the United States of America

To Georgana Grinstead, who is my real-life fairy godmother, making all my wildest dreams come true. I'll love you forever and always.

These violent delights have violent ends.
—Shakespeare, *Romeo & Juliet*

CHAPTER ONE

Guinevere

The Tuscan hills rolled in endless gold-and-green waves into the horizon, where the setting sun glowed as orange as an egg yolk, split and spilling tangerine light into the bowls of the valley. There were the sharp tang of cypress and musk of hay on the sticky breeze wafting through the open window of the little Fiat I'd rented for my trip and the sound of some random Italian pop song playing through the radio. My belly was full of the *cacio e pepe* pasta I'd devoured in a small corner restaurant in Rome I'd had bookmarked in my browser for years before I'd departed for the apartment I was renting in Florence, but I had a few fresh plums in the cup holders in case I needed a snack.

It was the first day of my long-anticipated, desperately needed trip to Italy.

And it was *paradise.*

I didn't take a moment for granted, because this trip had been a lifetime in the making.

I thought every child grew up idolizing something. A film star, a book series, an older sibling's best friend. It wasn't that strange to obsess over the idea of something until it became a part of you, a dream stitched into your soul, a fantasy carved into your psyche.

Mine was the vision of Italy.

My father had emigrated before I was born from some small town in the Tuscan hills. He didn't speak about his history or ancestry much at all, no tall tales or shared customs. It was as if he'd stripped himself of all cultural identity the minute he stepped foot on American soil. I often wondered if it was because he had a traumatic past there he didn't want to share or notions about his native land he didn't want to pass on to his children.

Maybe it said strange things about how much I admired and adored him that I wanted to get to the heart of his magic, and my childish mind had latched on to Italy as its source. Maybe it was because I'd spent so much time in the hospital staring at the same walls for hours on hours, wishing for escape. Imagining a fantasy world with goblins and unicorns had seemed too intangible for comfort, but a real country across the world, filled with history and cultural richness, was the perfect vehicle for escapism.

For whatever reason, I started my Italian-trip fund when I was seven years old. At first, it was selling lemonade at our plastic kids' table on the side of the road at our lake house, but it morphed into making babysitting money and busking during the summers, then working at the local movie theater when I was a teen. I also interned for my dad's wealth management firm during my summer breaks between college semesters at the University of Michigan, but it didn't pay much, and I supplemented with evenings working at Mancini's restaurant. I didn't have time for boyfriends or parties when I was on a mission to spend the entire summer after college graduation in the land of my dreams.

My parents didn't know I was going to Italy because I wouldn't have put it past them to lock me in the basement for the duration of the summer. The way John Stone hated his home country was almost biblical. The only things he let slip over the years were a handful of expressions he'd mutter that couldn't be properly translated and the general area his family had originated in. When I expressed interest in anything to do with Italy, he shut me down and told me that we were American and that I should be satisfied with calling such a great country my own.

And I was, but whether or not it was because I was a child, his hatred and refusal to indulge my curiosity only stoked the flames of my intrigue even higher. I was desperate to visit his homeland and determined to discover if we had any remaining family there, despite having very little information to begin my search with when I arrived. In the way of most parental disapproval, my father's aversion to Italy only made me lust after it more.

So when I declared I was going away for an entire summer as a graduation present to myself, I told them I was backpacking through Europe. England, France, Spain, the Balkans. Anywhere but Italy.

My father had gone so far as to make me promise on his ancient leather-bound family Bible. It was stamped on the inside of the cover with a lion holding a shield embossed with a fleur-de-lis. The symbol of Florence and the principal reason I'd decided to spend my summer in that particular Tuscan city. I'd hidden my wince, crossed my fingers, and thanked my lucky stars I was an atheist.

My parents had made it clear to me all along that they wouldn't financially support my trip, and even though they could well afford it, I didn't argue. They were happy for Gemma to go on a trip to Denmark with her friends after high school and to Aspen for ski trips every year, and the summer she'd passed away, she had been doing a year abroad in Albania.

They didn't treat me the same way they treated Gemma, because I'd been born with a serious health defect that meant I'd spent most of my childhood in and out of the hospital. They cared about us both, but they never got over their fear for my safety. They didn't want me gallivanting around the world or going out with boys. They wanted me wrapped up at home on a path they set out for me so they could have some sense of control in a situation where they'd felt hopeless one too many times.

I got it, I did.

But it didn't stop me from making my own plans.

By the time I walked across the stage at Michigan to get my diploma from the Ross School of Business, I had $10,000 saved for my trip.

Ten thousand.

Which was nothing to sniff at, especially considering I also had a normal savings account to set myself up for my future.

Because Italy wasn't my future.

It was a beautiful blip in time where I could explore the country of my dreams and my true self at the same time.

My future had been set for me a long time ago by my father.

And it was only solidified when we lost Gemma last year. Only twenty-six, healthy and beautiful, and suddenly gone thanks to a spontaneous coronary artery dissection.

I would spend the summer in Italy on my own dime and return to start working for my father so eventually I could take over his wealth management firm.

Thrilling stuff.

But that was for future Guinevere to worry about.

Now I was literally living my dream.

I sang along to the song on the radio in my passable Italian and tapped my hands on the hot steering wheel as I enjoyed the open road leading me through the scenic route to Florence.

As if offended by my lack of singing talents, the car let out a sudden, ferocious growl followed by an ominous bang. Black smoke belched out of the hood and curled through my open window.

"Dammit," I cursed, pulling over to the side of the road as the engine sputtered and made a series of tumbling noises.

The music cut off as soon as I turned off the car, leaving only a quietness that existed in every countryside the world over: crickets, birdsong, and the shush of the breeze through long grass. No sounds of cars.

And no sight of them either.

I could see most of the road in either direction, losing sight in sections as the hills dipped and swelled.

But there was nothing.

I was alone in the Tuscan countryside, where I knew absolutely no one, and with only a textbook understanding of the Italian language.

"Why?" I whispered, closing my eyes to beat back the sorrow that seemed to shadow every waking moment of my life since Gemma died.

"*Why?*"

The first day of my dream trip had already devolved into a nightmare.

I sucked in a deep breath to brace myself, then coughed as the noxious fumes from the car scorched down my throat.

There was nothing for it, though.

I couldn't just wallow there as the sun set and night threatened. Even though Italy was fairly safe for tourists, camping out on the side of the road was not safe for anyone, let alone a twenty-three-year-old foreigner.

So I rubbed the tears lurking in my ducts with a fist and then marched to the trunk for the tool kit the rental representative had assured me was inside. I wasn't sure if there was anything my meager knowledge of cars could do with a smoking Fiat, but my only recourse was to try.

Twenty minutes later, I threw the oil-coated rag to the asphalt and dropped to the gravel with my sweaty forehead in my hands. My skin was tight across my face, a sure sign I was getting a burn from the hot sun even though it was dipping low over the horizon and casting long, slightly sinister shadows now. I'd checked the coolant system, as my trusty internet search had suggested, and the oil, but it was hard to tell which might be the problem. The car wasn't smoking anymore, but I wasn't confident I should drive any longer.

Still, if someone didn't come along soon, it was either drive a hazardous car or sleep in it in the middle of the countryside, a plum prize for any human traffickers that might be lurking in the night.

I told myself to stop being so paranoid, but it was my father's voice in my head, and it was hard to quell.

Italy isn't safe, he always said whenever I spoke of my trip. *Go to England or France, Spain even, if you want some heat. Italy isn't a good place for a young woman. Promise me you won't set foot on that godforsaken land.*

I winced as I thought about him seeing me then, half smeared in grease, with a burn on my forearm from the overheated engine.

My phone battery was at 18 percent, and I cursed myself for not charging it on the plane ride over. I looked up my location on the map and nearly threw the phone into the golden grass field in frustration when the page wouldn't load.

"Okay," I said slowly, leaning my head back against the warm car to stare at the cerulean blue sky, its beauty mocking me. "Don't freak out."

I was beginning to freak out.

Of course I'd just *had* to take the road through Val d'Orcia instead of the highway straight through to Florence. Of course I'd just *had* to rent the little red Fiat because it was so cute and totally matched my lifelong vision of driving through Italy.

Of course this would happen to me.

I tried to manifest, to stay positive, but I'd always been unlucky.

My parents and Gemma even called me Jinx because if something could go wrong for me, it usually did.

Gemma said I must have been very, very bad in a past life.

So I tried to be good in this one. I volunteered at the suicide helpline, went to church, bought groceries for my elderly neighbor in Ann Arbor, always left change for the homeless, and tried to say only kind things when I said anything at all.

It didn't make a single bit of difference.

And honestly, sometimes, watching Gemma live her happy-go-lucky, responsibility-free life, I'd often wondered if it was worth it.

Being the good girl.

It was one of the reasons I was even in Italy. My parents had practically begged me not to go on my trip, still too rattled by Gemma's passing to deal with having me so far from them, especially when I had health concerns of my own.

But I felt it was a fitting tribute to Gemma to finally do something I wanted for a change. She had encouraged me for years, but particularly those months she'd been living abroad, to branch out from under my parents' shelter and discover the world for myself.

I knew with bone-deep certainty she would approve of my duplicitous holiday.

Distantly, a humming vibration sounded.

I perked up against the side of the car, cocking my head to strain my ears.

Yes, a car.

I shot to my feet, slipping slightly in the gravel, and then ran around the car to the roadside. A nondescript blue sedan was descending the hill before this one.

Without really thinking through the ramifications, I threw myself into the middle of the road, jumping up and down, waving my arms, and crying out.

When the car crested the hill, it slowed instantly, the driver probably unused to seeing a crazy American in the middle of a country road.

"*Ciao*," I called, dropping my arms as it crept to a standstill just in front of me. "*Parli inglese?*"

Do you speak English? I asked.

My Italian was passable, but not when I was in panic mode.

I moved closer to the open window and noted that the driver was a middle-aged gentleman with weathered tan skin in workingman's clothes. We were surrounded by vineyards, so I had to wonder if he was one of the men who worked them.

"My car broke down," I explained, waving an unnecessary hand at the cute and inoperable Fiat.

He blinked at me, almost like he couldn't be sure I existed. "Broken?"

"Yes," I exclaimed a little too enthusiastically. "Yes, broken."

"I can look," he offered, a slow grin taking over his swarthy features.

I beamed back at him. "That would be great, honestly. I know next to nothing about cars."

He nodded, indicating for me to move so that he could pull off the road behind my car. I went to wait near the Fiat, fiddling with my phone because I'd been taught to text my dad if I was ever in trouble, but he was all the way back in Michigan, and texting him would just make him worry.

I startled a little bit when the gentleman got out of his car. He was a big man, broad through the shoulders and at least six feet. Given I was five foot three on a good day, my heart started to race.

"What's your name?" I asked him, trying to establish a connection because I'd read once somewhere that people were less likely to harm you if you shared details about your life with them.

He grunted as he grabbed a tool kit out of the back of his trunk. "Galasso."

I'd never heard the name before, and it made me think he was making it up, but I told myself to chill out. It was still light out, though the sun was only a sliver of molten orange on the horizon behind the vineyards and the sky was sprayed with pink-and-purple clouds. I remembered the number for emergency services in Italy and typed it into my phone even though I didn't have great service, ready to press the call button if the need arose.

"Thank you for this," I said as he walked over to the Fiat and started his inspection under the hood. "I'm in Italy with my entire family just twenty minutes from here, but of course I had to wander off on my own. They'll be so worried about me if I don't get home soon."

Galasso's mouth twitched, the first sign of true humanity in him. "I have daughter a little younger than you," he admitted in thickly accented English.

Instantly, I felt relief sluice through me like cool water on this hot summer's night.

He had a daughter.

Good, not a predator, then, but a helpful father who envisioned me as his own daughter stranded on the side of the road.

More at ease, I grinned at him and ducked into the car to grab two plums, then offered one to him.

He shook his head and indicated the engine with a jerk of his chin. Right.

Well, I leaned against the side of the car and took a bite of the succulent plum.

"I have more in the car if you change your mind. The produce here is so divine," I praised, wiping juice from my chin with the back of my hand. "Do you work in the vineyards nearby?"

"For a man who owns vineyards, *si*."

Okay, so not a talker. Not a problem.

I could be chatty with just about anyone. My father called it "the curse of the Midwest" when he was teasing my mom about making friends with everyone everywhere we went. I didn't think Galasso would be friendly given his gruff nature, but he listened to me babble as he worked on the car. The sun had gone completely, the sky an electric shade of blue before true dark descended, when he finally closed the hood and wiped his hands on his dirty jeans.

"*Bene*," he told me. "Is finished."

"*Bravo*," I exclaimed, clapping my hands together. "*Grazie mille, Signore.*"

"*Prego.*"

When he extended his hand, I frowned at him and then remembered I'd offered him a plum if he changed his mind.

"Of course." I opened the driver's door and bent inside to grab the last stone fruit sitting in the console.

As I did, a firm hand landed on my hip.

The touch hit me like a thousand watts through a cattle prod. I jumped, banging my head on the roof of the car. Before I could jostle away, his other hand landed on my opposite hip and gripped tight. A moment later, he was pressed hard against my bottom, his erection obvious through the layers of cloth between us.

Panic pulled the plug on all rational thought, and the only thing left in my mind was *no no no*.

I lurched away from him, scrambling farther into the car because I knew I'd have no chance of getting past his bulk behind me. He wasn't expecting that. I'd made it to the passenger seat, the door handle in my hand, when a big hand caught my ankle and tugged.

"NO!" I screamed, kicking back with all my strength to dislodge him.

His nails carved into my skin like fire, but he was forced to let go with a curse when I knocked him partially out of the car.

Static buzzed in my ears, spots dancing in my vision because I didn't realize I was holding my breath as I threw my whole body at the passenger door and spilled out the other side of the car. My shoulder and knees hit the gravel hard, stones embedding in my skin, but the pain only cut through my fear like a hot blade.

I needed to *run*.

My cute sandals lost purchase on the gravel as I tried to push myself into a run from my sprawl, but I quickly gained my feet and booked it into the tall yellow grass beside the road. Through the hard bass of my heart thumping against my rib cage and the billow of breath through my nose, I could hear him behind me, giving chase.

I picked up the skirt of my long dress in one hand and used the other out in front of me to push the grasses from my face as I sprinted through the wheat without a clue of where I was heading.

I just knew if I didn't get away, I'd end up like those newsclips you saw on TV where a traveler in a foreign land took a wrong turn and ended up dead too young.

I'd never been more grateful for my love of long-distance running.

Even with the oppressive heat, it only took ten minutes for the sound of him crashing behind me to diminish into nothing. After fifteen, I risked looking over my shoulder to see his murky outline in the dark grasses behind me at a standstill, hands on his hips.

I kept running.

All my things were back in that unlocked Fiat.

My passport, my luggage, my wallet.

Only my phone was with me. Thank God for dresses with pockets. But what did material things matter in the face of being raped, beaten, killed, or taken?

The sky was darkening rapidly now, the hand in front of my face a dark-gray smear in the inky press of grass all around me. I tried not to think about the snakes and mice and other critters that might be living in the wheat fields and pressed on, hoping to find a house or a town at the other end of this.

I didn't expect to tumble out of the field straight into another road, one with a car careening too fast down the asphalt straight at me. The headlights blinded me, leaving me frozen in the middle of the road as the car barreled toward me.

Oh my God, I thought with sudden clarity, *I'm going to die, and my parents will have lost both their children in one year.*

I closed my eyes and wished fervently that my parents would be okay.

There was a sudden shriek of tires against the road and the acrid scent of burning rubber. I braced for impact, and a moment later, something clipped my hip hard.

Hard, but not brutally.

Hard enough to throw me to the ground, but not enough to kill.

I knew, because I lay there on the road, staring up at the stars blinking into existence in the black bowl of night as pain ricocheted through my left side and the back of my skull and my breath streamed through my nose, that I'd never felt more alive.

A car door slammed, and shoes pounded over the pavement seconds before a body loomed over me.

"*Vaffanculo, sei uno stronzo!*" he shouted down at me.

Hysteria bubbled in my belly and emerged from my mouth as a high, panic-edged giggle. Once I started, I found it impossible to stop. The combination of relief and adrenaline was simply intoxicating.

There was a mumbled male curse, and then someone was crouching beside me, a large hand tapping lightly at my cheek.

"First," I gasped through my laughter, "you hit me with your car and then with your hand. I really am the unluckiest girl in the world. Out of the frying pan . . ."

"And into the fire," he finished in a rough, Italian-accented voice. "You are American. This explains the idiocy."

I winced as I tried to sit up, pain sinking sharp teeth into my side. "Well, I've been in Italy for less than twenty-four hours, and one person has already tried to rape me and another has hit me with his car. What does that say about Italians?"

He seemed a little shocked by my audacity but recovered quickly. His face was all in shadow, backlit by the headlights, but he was a large man, and I was suddenly acutely aware of the position I was in, sprawled across the ground.

When he reached for me, I flinched, dragging myself back across the pavement. My dress tore with an audible rip, but it was the least of my concerns.

"I mean you no harm," he assured me, as if the idea was preposterous. "Beyond having hit you with my car, obviously. Let me help you to your feet."

I ignored his hand and awkwardly pushed myself to my feet, swaying a little when I stood up. My head pounded ruthlessly, and my vision grayed out around the edges. A hand on my elbow steadied me as I took a deep breath and closed my eyes to let the dizziness pass.

"*Tranquillo*," he murmured, and even though his voice was still rough, there was a softness to it I knew was meant to soothe me. "Take a moment, *idiota*. You have just been hit by a car."

"Your car," I reminded him, snapping my eyes open to fix him with a glare.

In the murky light, I could just make out the shape of his small smile.

"*Si*, my car. I have damaged you, and you have damaged her. I am inclined to believe a Ferrari is worth more than an American tourist, but I am feeling gracious tonight, so why do we not call it even?"

I snorted before I could stop myself, my ribs aching a little at the effort. My hand pressed to my side, and I winced.

"You most likely have a concussion," he mused blandly. "Maybe bruised ribs and a painful contusion on your hip."

"Are you a doctor or something?"

There was a light pause that felt almost like I'd pressed on a bruise beneath his skin. "No," he said finally. "I am more prone to hurt than heal, which is why helping you is so oddly out of character."

I rolled my eyes, slapping at his hand to release my elbow so I could retrieve the shoe that had been knocked off when I was hit. "You have an even odder definition of helping someone if you think running them down counts."

He let me go, but only so he could bend down to pick up my broken sandal.

"You mentioned someone tried to . . . hurt you," he said, so darkly a little shiver dragged nails down my spine. "Where did this happen?"

"Across the field." I gestured vaguely to the black abyss beside us. "I left my car, my luggage, my passport . . . everything."

"Nothing is worth the price of your life or sanity," he declared, as if I shouldn't worry about all my material possessions and my means of leaving the country being lost to me. "You say you are unlucky, but from where I stand, you should count your lucky stars."

"And how is that?" I asked, limping toward the side of the car just so he would be forced to face the light. After the events of the evening, I wasn't comfortable with a faceless stranger.

He didn't turn to me at first, his head dipped to look at the snapped strap of my sandal in his big hands. When he finally turned to face me, the light slapped across his features almost violently, sending them into stark relief.

I gasped and took a step away from him.

"Because," the beautiful man before me practically purred. "Tonight, I feel like playing the hero instead of the villain."

CHAPTER TWO

Raffa

If there was ever a night not to hit an American girl stumbling into the middle of a country road on my way back to the house in Toscana, it was tonight.

My week in Rome had been arduous, to say the least.

I disliked being away from home, even though my best friend and soldiers were more than capable of protecting my mother and sisters. It didn't seem to matter. Ever since I'd received the call that changed my life four years ago, I'd been on the knife's edge of fear. I refused to let it conquer me, but in order to control it, I had to have my finger on the pulse of every aspect of our operations in the region.

If I knew what was coming, I could head it off at the pass.

I'd been successful at doing just that with the head of the Roman Mafia Capitale, yet unsuccessful in avoiding this slip of a girl who'd appeared like a deer frozen in the headlights of my speeding car.

The irritating truth was, I couldn't just leave her there, as much as my cold, dark heart assured me it would be the easier option. The man I'd been before taking over my father's criminal organization still lingered in my soft tissues, reminding me that she was just a girl like any of my three sisters.

Would I want a stranger to leave them alone to fend for themselves in a foreign land, without anything to their names?

The frustrating answer was, of course, no.

So I sighed heavily and walked toward the American girl, who flinched at my approach. I raised a brow as I slowly opened the passenger side door.

"Get in," I ordered. "I will circle around to where you have left your car and see what can be done."

She bit her lip, and I noticed for the first time that though she was young, she was fairly pretty for an American. Petite in a way that made me feel as if I towered over her, but with a femininity that cut through my annoyance like a knife, eviscerating it with a single look from those long-lashed eyes. In the harsh yellow light cast from the Ferrari, they seemed dark as ink and filled with feminine mystique.

"What's your name?" she asked finally, as if knowing it was the key to lessening her fear.

I understood, in theory. It was much easier to trust a face with a name.

"Raffa," I said, but offered no more.

She peered up through those lashes, a streak of dirt painted along her sharp cheekbone and a cut on her chin. "Guinevere," she said, sticking her hand out between us. "It's good to meet you."

My other eyebrow joined the first high on my forehead, but I decided to indulge her silliness and clasped her delicate hand in my own. It was cold, the palm badly abraded from her fall. I could feel the wet smear of her blood against my skin.

Without thinking, I turned her hand over in my hold and retrieved my pocket square with my other hand so I could use it as a makeshift bandage for her wound. She gasped as I tightened it but otherwise didn't protest.

"I think you just ruined your designer hankie," she pointed out.

"It is a pocket square," I corrected, because a grown man did *not* carry a . . . hankie. "Now, get in the car."

She moved gently, face pale and tight with pain. A hiss streamed through her clenched teeth as she lowered herself sideways into the low car. Before she could spin forward, I crouched down and grabbed her slim ankle. She tried to jerk away, but I only hushed her as I slipped the broken sandal over her foot and deftly tied the leather pieces together.

"It will do for now," I declared.

She swallowed thickly and whispered, "Okay."

I straightened, nudging her to face forward so I could close the door before I crossed to the driver's side. The damage to the Ferrari was nonexistent, but then, Guinevere could only have been 110 pounds soaking wet, so that wasn't a surprise.

What was surprising was the little bubble of tenderness that had taken up residence in the hollow casing of my chest.

This girl was not my family.

She was not a friend.

She was an inconvenience I could barely afford, given the contents of my trunk.

Yet I felt moved to help her.

Not just that, I felt moved to avenge her.

Because what kind of *bastardo* would take advantage of a woman in trouble?

I was the last person to pretend at having a moral conscience, but *Madonna santa*, women and children were sacred.

My mouth watered at the idea of finding the man who'd chased her through the countryside, and my imagination took a merry romp through the dark, picturing exactly how I'd punish him.

Composing myself, I got into the Ferrari and immediately started the engine without looking her way. I figured in the tight enclosure she would enjoy some semblance of privacy.

"You said it was the other side of this field?" I confirmed, expertly spinning the car back onto the proper side of the road before taking off into the night.

"Yes, I'm sorry I can't be more helpful."

"I grew up in this region. Each vineyard and valley might look the same to you, but not to me."

"How do you speak English so well?"

"We do have schools in Italia," I pointed out dryly.

Her sigh was beleaguered, and despite everything, it made the edges of my mouth curl.

"I lived in London for some time," I explained, though I usually didn't allow myself to think about those years of my life.

"This is my first time out of the United States," she admitted softly, gaze fixed outside the window as if she wanted to absorb the scenery even in the dark. Her fingertips touched the pane of glass separating her from the countryside almost reverently. "But I've dreamed of visiting since I was a girl."

"I am sorry we have done little to meet your expectations." I wasn't sorry, but it seemed the thing to say. Part of me wanted to explain that the Italy of her dreams was a romanticized version.

For every lavish villa, there was a *baraccopoli*.

For every Romeo, there was someone like that man who wanted to harm her.

It was, like any other place on earth, a country of steep contrasts.

She sighed. "It's my own fault, I guess. I probably should have taken the main route to Florence, but I was excited to see the famous Tuscan countryside."

We turned onto the road lining the other side of the field, and after a moment, a Fiat appeared on the side of the pavement, its interior lights on because the doors were open wide.

"Dammit," she muttered, leaning forward with a wince. "I hope the bastard left my passport at least."

"Did he give you a name?" I asked as I pulled onto the shoulder behind the Fiat.

"Galasso." Her pretty face screwed up with self-loathing. "He was a father, so I thought he'd be less likely to hurt me."

"Even monsters procreate," I quipped drolly, thinking of my own father as I got out of the car. "Stay here."

I closed the door on her protest and walked around the Fiat, surveying the damage. Galasso had left her purse on the passenger seat, open and empty, and a quick look in the trunk showed he'd taken her suitcase as well.

Cazzo, this girl was entirely alone and without a penny to her name.

"What am I going to do?"

I startled at the quiet voice behind me and glowered as I turned to face Guinevere. "Did I not tell you to stay in the car?"

She ignored me to lean stiffly into the driver's seat beside me. "What's the point in even leaving my purse and wallet if he was just going to take everything inside it?"

I didn't have an answer for her, even though I felt enraged on her behalf. I'd never heard of Galasso, but it shouldn't be hard to find the man. I had contacts throughout the region, and it was a fairly uncommon name.

A sniffle drew my attention back to Guinevere, who had one hand braced against the side of the car, eyes squeezed shut and torso swaying. "What am I going to do?" she whispered before collapsing to her knees and vomiting into the gravel.

Without thinking, I crouched beside her to hold back her hair as she emptied the contents of her stomach. When she was finished, she slumped heavily to the side, and I used my body to prop her up.

"I'm sorry," she whispered, voice cracking slightly. "I'm a mess. I promise I'm not usually a damsel in distress. I can hold my own. If you could just give me a ride to the nearest town, I can file a police report a-and call my dad to wire me some money to tide me over until I can get new credit cards. I-I just need . . ." She sucked in a huge, wet breath through her mouth to steady herself. "I just really need you to drive me to the next town, if that's okay?"

The man I had spent the last four years honing myself into like the sharp edge of a blade shattered into pieces. The contrast of her chin-tipped, trembling-lip bravery against the dark, tear-glazed vulner-ability was simply impossible to guard against. Some part of me wanted to think she was pathetic, crumpled on the ground beside her own sick, having lost everything because of girlish naivete. But I couldn't force it.

I found myself admiring her gumption, moved by her tenacity.

I wanted to curl her tight into my side and use my body to shield her from all the horrors of her Italian dream turned nightmare.

For the first time in my life, I wanted to be someone's knight in shining armor.

"No," I found myself saying. My fist was still loosely wrapped in her hair, but she didn't pull away, and I liked the silk texture against my palm.

She deflated slightly, and I paused to see if she would finally fall to pieces. Instead, she sucked in another bracing breath through her teeth and pulled her shoulders back like she was preparing for battle.

Something in the fallow soil of my heart germinated and threatened to take root.

"No," I repeated, softer, my hand sliding from her hair so I could stand and offer her my hand. "You will come home with me and stay until you are on your feet again, *capisci*?"

She blinked up at me with those large dark eyes, and for a moment, I couldn't push air through my lungs.

"Are you serious?"

"Deadly," I said with a grin, the edges sharp enough to hurt my cheeks.

She didn't seem intimidated by the offer, which made me irratio-nally furious with her. Where was her sense of self-preservation?

If she so much as looked in my trunk, she would know I was not the kind of man anyone should accept help from.

"I don't think I could impose on you," she said, worrying her lower lip as she took my offered hand and let me lift her from the ground. "You seem like a busy man."

Her gesture encompassed my car and the three-piece suit that had become rumpled beyond belief.

I shrugged one shoulder. "I am. But no matter what I am, I refuse to be the kind of person who leaves a girl alone in the dark on the side of the road to fend for herself. Now, get in so we can get you cleaned up and checked out."

"You're sure?"

I narrowed my eyes at her. "Is this an American tic? I have said I am sure, and each time you ask, it merely delays the inevitable. Now, are you coming with me, or am I leaving you here to enjoy the quiet countryside?"

Her answer was to move, haltingly because of her side, to the passenger door of the car.

"I thought so," I muttered.

Before driving off, I decided it would be prudent to check the contents of my trunk, so I unlocked it and opened the hatch.

The man within was still knocked out cold, his hands and feet locked tight with zip ties, a black hood over his head and a gag in his mouth. I checked his pulse to make certain he was still alive and then gave his cheek a little tap.

"Not to worry," I murmured to him. "As soon as I get the girl situated, you will have my full and undivided attention."

CHAPTER THREE

Guinevere

I woke up groaning.

Not in the way I'd dreamed in my fantasies of meeting a handsome Italian and being caught up in his strong arms, but in the way of my entire body pulsing like one giant bruise. My eyelids were crusted together, and my head felt so heavy on the pillow I was almost surprised it didn't fall straight through the soft down and mattress to the floor. Instantly, I wished I could go back to sleep, but the pain was too vibrant to ignore.

"Oh God," I croaked, my throat parched and sore.

"You should not take the Lord's name in vain."

I lifted a weak hand to rub my eyes so I could pry them open to look at the man sitting on the edge of my bed.

Or not my bed.

His bed.

In his house in Florence.

It wasn't really a house, though. Not like we had in the US.

Raffa had flippantly called it a palazzo last night as he led me blurrily through the massive home to a bedroom on the second floor.

I was sleeping in a literal *palace*.

My life had become some seriously messed-up Italian version of a Grimms' fairy tale since I'd arrived in Rome.

I swiveled my gaze over the high ceilings and stone walls, the modern furnishings a stark but attractive contrast to the old architecture. There was an actual marble sculpture in the corner of the room beside open French doors and a painting I was fairly sure, even with my blurry vision, was a real Botticelli.

"It was built in the sixteenth century, but I assure you, we have running water," he drawled in that decadent Italian accent.

Even though the effort made me wince, I barely turned my head on the pillow to squint at him in the honeyed light spilling through the sheer curtains.

The sight of him in full daylight stole my breath straight from my lungs.

He was . . .

I scrambled for words to define him and wished fruitlessly that I had a better grasp of Italian. It seemed the only language romantic enough, beautiful enough, to fulfill any accurate description of him.

It wasn't that he himself was soft or romantic.

No.

His face was all planes and angles, with the hard jut of a square jaw and slightly pronounced chin that made him seem imperious, especially matched to the arrogance of those thick brows, arched over eyes that were brown but pale. Light as sunlight caught in maple syrup, clear and completely unmuddied. It felt almost wrong to call eyes like that brown, as mine were.

They were piercing, cutting through me as I lay there, like hot knives pinning me to the bed.

It should have been terrifying, that level of intense, unwavering attention from a near stranger who was broad enough and tall enough to finish what Galasso had tried to begin the night before.

But I felt oddly settled by it.

Intensity was exactly what I had been searching for in Michigan, what I'd been yearning for my entire young life. I had a voracious appetite for life that urged me to crack it open with my bare hands and suck out the marrow, messy and violent with satisfaction. It was a kind of savagery I'd always had to temper back home.

That was the way my Italian stranger looked at me then.

Like a meal he was impatient to eat through to the bones.

"Oh," I said without thinking. "You're beautiful."

His expressive brows slammed down over those clear eyes. "A man is not beautiful."

"You are," I insisted. "Not like someone from a Renaissance painting. Like, well, like Dante's angels, maybe."

"Nothing about me is heavenly," he argued again, crossing his arms defensively, but there was a tiny curl in his mouth that said he was enjoying this.

Enjoying me.

"A fallen angel," I corrected.

"Dante's fallen angels are monstrous looking," he retorted. "Your youth is revealing yourself. Have you even read *The Divine Comedy*?"

"Yes." I winced. "Could we blame it on the potential concussion?"

He made a sound like a snort that was only an exhalation of breath through his nose. "In fact, I am certain you have one. The doctor is waiting downstairs to give you an exam. This is why I woke you."

I tried to sit up and winced when my entire side crackled with pain. "I don't think I can sit up."

"No," he agreed. "*Dottor* Pesci will make sure you do not have anything emergent because I would like to avoid a trip to the hospital while you do not even have identification. At most, I think you could have some broken ribs, but there is nothing to be done for that but time."

"Time I can't waste. I need to go to the consulate and figure out what to do about money and buy clothes because otherwise I'll just have a dirty, torn dress to wear, and the consulate might not even let me *inside* wearing that, looking like a—" I stopped abruptly when Raffa's large hand gently covered my mouth.

"*Abbastanza*," he ordered, not unkindly. "You have been threatened, chased, and hit by a car. You need rest."

"But—" I mumbled beneath the weight of his palm.

"No. We do not know each other, I understand that. But the first thing you should know about me is this: Once I make a decision, I am loyal to it no matter what. I knew what I was signing up for when I invited you into my car last night. Do not make me regret my uncharacteristic show of kindness by being timid. You are here, you will remain here until you are healthy and reestablished, and that is the end of the discussion."

He stared at me for a long moment as if to punctuate his point, but it wasn't necessary.

His offer—no, *declaration*—of help was unexpected. In the light of day, he didn't seem like the kind of man to care about the well-being of a stranger. He was wearing another expensive suit, this one a rich, textured brown that perfectly matched his wavy hair, and a wristwatch that winked diamond bright back at me. He owned a palazzo in central Florence and drove a Ferrari.

So it might have been out of character for him to offer help, but he could also definitely afford to do it.

When he slowly pulled his hand away, I worried my lower lip with my teeth as I considered my situation and noticed how his furrowed brow tightened while he watched the gesture.

"Thank you," I said finally. My throat ached like I was also coming down with a cold, which seemed in keeping with my perpetual bad luck. "I can't really express how grateful I am."

He shrugged one shoulder slightly, a flippant, arrogant expression that suited him.

"I took the liberty of plugging your phone in because it was dead. Why do you not text whoever you must to tell them you are safe and start the process of canceling your cards? I will send the doctor up."

He stood up abruptly, passed me my cell phone, and then strode to the door. It occurred to me that he was tall, not only compared to my measly height, but in general. His wide shoulders filled the suit jacket perfectly, and his long legs ate up the floor in athletic strides.

If I'd been feeling better, I might have ogled him a little.

Who was I kidding?

I could ogle him just fine, even with a concussion.

He was so gorgeous, I couldn't really believe he was real and this wasn't all some kind of fever dream.

"Raffa?" I called as he opened the door. He hesitated, shoulders visibly tightening at the sound of his name. It tasted good in my mouth, chocolaty and rich. "I promise I'll be out of your hair by the end of the week."

He gave a clipped nod and shut the door behind him.

But as it turned out, I was a liar.

The doctor's exam passed in a hazy, exhausted blur. He confirmed I had a mild concussion, bruised ribs, and the beginnings of a bad illness that made my throat feel tight and swollen. He recommended sleep, fluids, over-the-counter pain meds, and bed rest until I could stand without feeling dizzy and pained. When I told him about my condition, he clucked his tongue at me and declared he'd be back to check on me the next day in case I needed to be hooked up to an IV to replace my fluids and replenish my vitamin B.

Raffa stood over his shoulder the entire exam after I gave him permission to stay, his arms crossed and brow furrowed in a way I was beginning to think was his trademark stance and position. He watched the doctor with hawkish focus, as if afraid I'd be triggered by the man's clinical hands on my body after what happened last night.

It was strangely sweet from a man who seemed determined to refute any softness or kindness in himself.

After the exam, I fell asleep and didn't wake up until it was dark again. I attempted to move, needing the restroom, but my entire body had seized up, encased in cement that refused to budge without considerable effort. I whimpered as I shifted one leg to the edge of the bed and began dragging the other over the mattress.

When both feet were dangling above the floor, I tried to twist and raise my torso into a seated position. Sharp blades of pain slid between each of the ribs on my left side, and a cry of pain escaped my lips before I could curb the urge.

Seconds later there was a knock on my bedroom door, which immediately opened to reveal Raffa in low-slung black pajama pants and an open black robe. Without hesitation, he strode across the room and to my side, winding an arm around my waist gently to lift me out of bed and to my feet. He held me while I swayed, searching for my equilibrium.

"*Costante*," he murmured, curling me closer into the bracket of his strong arm and warm side.

I noticed vaguely that he smelled like oakmoss, smoky and earthen. An aroma that made me want to lean closer, cuddle up, and inhale that warmth until the fuzzy, awful haze in my brain faded clean away.

"Bathroom," I tried to say through the swollen, hot confines of my throat, but the word emerged as only a mangled whisper.

Without hesitation, he started to lead me toward the door, but two steps in, a small cry left my lips because my side screamed in protest. Raffa made a displeased noise and very carefully bent to gather my legs over one arm and prop my back delicately against the other so as not to jostle my ribs. I pressed my stuffed nose into the short hair on his hard chest and squeezed my eyes against the tears that sprang up behind them.

The simple kindness was too much to handle after the sheer terribleness of my first day in the country.

"Sorry," I croaked.

"*Stai zitta.*"

That I knew well.

Shut up.

My father still muttered it under his breath sometimes when one of us was being particularly obstinate.

I obeyed, but only because I needed to save my energy for when he put me down in the bathroom. The hallway outside my bedroom was narrow, dotted every couple meters with chandeliers that glittered dimly on a low setting. When we reached the bathroom door, Raffa gently lowered me to my feet, hands on my forearms as I steadied myself. I tried to look up at him, but the effort made my head ache sharply, and I could barely open my eyes to see him anyway.

"Call if you need me," he demanded.

I shuffled around without saying anything because I'd be damned if I asked this gorgeous stranger to help me in the bathroom. As it was, it took me way too long after closing the door on him to lower myself to the toilet and do my business. I thought briefly about checking myself out in the mirror, but I knew turning on the light would only hurt my eyes. By the time I reached the doorway again, I had to lean my entire body against the door for a moment of reprieve.

For one clear, brutal second, I wanted to cry.

I wanted teleportation to exist so I could wish myself back to Michigan with one click of ruby-red slippers.

My mom would coo over me and make sure I was fed, watered, and cuddled to within an inch of my life, while my dad would go all over town to get my favorite treats to brighten my day. I was twenty-three years old, but I felt so young, so unprepared to be sick, alone, and without money or ID in a foreign country, at the mercy of a man who'd hit me with his freaking car.

Gemma had been the one to call me Jinx for the first time when I fell through a rotted board in a friend's treehouse as a girl and broke my arm. My parents had joined in soon after when it became apparent that karma had a grudge against me.

I'd felt lucky recently, though, that I was not the one who'd died in my twenties like my sister.

Now I wasn't sure if being lucky or unlucky really mattered.

The truth seemed to be this: As soon as you were comfortable, life found a way to kick you straight in the teeth.

"Guinevere?" Raffa's voice filtered through the door. "Do you need help?"

I sucked in a breath and pushed off the door so I could open it. He stood to the side, arms crossed, naked torso framed by that black robe.

"I wish I felt better to admire you properly," I admitted as I braced myself against the doorframe.

I was too out of it to control my impulses, so I wasn't even embarrassed when Raffa surprised me by grinning slightly, a wolfish expression that should have been threatening.

"You will have the opportunity when you are better," he quipped before stepping forward to pick me up again. As he adjusted me in his arms, he added, "You have a fever."

"Mmm," I agreed, pressing my nose shamelessly to the column of his throat in search of the warm scent. "Cold."

He cursed softly but took me to my room and gently laid me back in bed. I shivered as he tucked the bedsheets in around me, then watched through slitted eyes as he retrieved another blanket from the cabinet in one corner. Before he left, he took up my phone, held it to my face to open the screen with the facial recognition, and then typed away at something.

"My number," he told me, placing the phone by my hip on the bed so I wouldn't have to strain to reach it. "Text if you need the bathroom or anything else, *si*? Do not be an *idiota* and suffer needlessly."

"Aye, aye," I said, sucking in a wet breath before continuing, "Captain."

He stared at me critically, then pressed the back of his hand to my forehead with a shake of his head. "If this does not come down by the morning, I will call the doctor back. And you must drink, if you can. A kidney condition is not something to fuck with."

29

"'M fine."

He ignored me, pushing a lock of hair off my brow when he'd finished taking my temperature. *"Sogni d'oro."*

Sweet dreams.

"Not as sweet as I thought they'd be," I confessed in a slur as sleep rushed up to meet me like a slap to the face.

"Not yet," he agreed before I fell into slumber. "But they will be again soon. *Prometto.*"

I promise.

That continued for the next four days. Raffa was around whenever I texted, at all hours, to help me to the bathroom, to bring me medication and cool cloths he pressed to my forehead. He never lingered, but it was soothing to know he was so close, so watchful. Between the horrific cold I'd probably caught on the plane, which led too quickly to dehydration, and the bruises from the accident, I'd never felt so ill in my body before, not even after my kidney transplant, when I'd been dosed up on painkillers. It was enough to give me nightmares that meant I woke up with croaking screams, tears wet on my face, ribs so painful they burned like fire.

And Raffa was there by the side of my bed like a sentient shadow, with cool, soothing hands and quiet Italian words my muddled brain couldn't process. There were hazy memories of his big hand cupping the back of my head to support me while he tipped a cold glass of water to my lips and the salt of his fingers against my lips as he forced me to eat small morsels of bread and sweet slices of peach.

The doctor came back and hooked me up to an IV so I could get proper fluids, which was a godsend, because otherwise I would have had to go to the hospital and try to explain, while I was in agony, what had happened to my money and ID.

On the fifth day my fever finally broke and left me as hollow as a dried weed. I slept for nearly a full day after that, waking on the sixth day feeling marginally better than I had in what felt like years.

There was a tray beside me on the bed holding sweet Italian *cornetti*, toast, a pot of hazelnut-chocolate spread, and a few ripe Italian plums. I pushed myself into a seated lean with gritted teeth, even though the pain in my ribs and hip was duller than it had been. On the tray there was a folded piece of notecard I picked up with shaky fingers.

Ragazza,
Eat. You were too skinny before this sickness. Now you make a very pretty skeleton. I will be back in two hours. Call if you need me.
RR

"Bossy even in absentia," I murmured, shocked by the rough texture of my voice.

Still, I was ravenous because I hadn't eaten more than broth, focaccia, and peaches for days, so I slathered a triangle of toast in chocolate spread and shoved it into my mouth.

Which was when, of course, the door to the room opened and a stranger appeared.

She was a small woman but clearly athletic, muscles evident in her shoulders and arms through her tight black T-shirt and black cargo pants. Though she was pretty, her makeup-free face was severe, her outfit stark and almost military.

"*Bene*, you're up," she declared, moving to the closed curtains to toss them open unceremoniously, yellow light piercing through the room and my eyes.

I shielded them in the crook of my arm so I could adjust, and when I opened them again, she was at the side of my bed, staring down at me.

"Now I understand," she mused.

"Um, understand what?"

"Why Raffa picked up a girl on the side of the road," she offered condescendingly, as if it was obvious.

I guessed it actually was.

"You look like shit," she told me.

My hand flew to my hair, and I winced at the greasy, ratty mass of it.

"You smell too," she informed me helpfully.

"Thanks," I muttered. "I've been sick for days. What's your excuse?"

She blinked at me, then threw her head back to laugh from her belly, deep and loud and long. When she recovered, dashing a tear from her eye with the back of her hand, she grinned at me. "*Si*, I understand now. My name is Martina."

"Guinevere," I said.

"Raffa told me not to bother you," she said, and I got the feeling she didn't often follow orders. "But I had to meet you. Also, I thought you might want a shower."

"I'd love one, but . . ." I wasn't sure I was up to it energetically, which was incredibly sad.

"We can leave the door open slightly, and I'll wait in the hall. If you need help, I'll be there in a second," she proposed.

I bit my lower lip as I considered her offer. It was just so . . . strange to be relying on strangers when I felt so vulnerable and unwell. But there was nothing for it, and I decided to be grateful instead of suspicious. Most good midwesterners would have treated me the same in this situation, I was sure, so it shouldn't be weird that Italians might too.

"Thank you. I do feel disgusting."

Martina nodded emphatically to make it clear that I also *looked* disgusting.

"Finish your food while you tell me about yourself," she suggested, but it was more like an order, and I had to wonder if she was in the military or something. She just had a commanding aura, like you'd rather die than disobey her, and if you still managed that somehow, she'd kill you herself.

So I grabbed the *cornetto* and tore off the sugar-sticky end to pop in my mouth. "What do you want to know?"

"How old are you?"

"Twenty-three."

She seemed to find that amusing. "Oh yes."

"Is twenty-three an exciting age for some reason?"

"Not really." Her grin was sharp and wicked. "If you're curious, Raffa is thirty-four."

"Hmm," I hummed noncommittally.

I hadn't thought about his age or occupation or really any pertinent details about the man who'd become my reluctant rescuer. My injuries and illness had thrown me into a survival-state fugue that I was only now emerging from.

But I could admit to curiosity.

To thinking that an age gap that large was probably *too* large.

I was a naive girl in a foreign land freshly graduated with my MBA from U of M, and Raffa was a man with a job and a *palace*.

Yeah, talk about out of my league.

He was helping me out because he felt sorry for me, and even though he was gorgeous and gracious enough to be a walking, talking heartthrob, life had taught me better than to hope for the impossible.

"He's been very nice to me," I admitted. "Not everyone would have helped me the way he has."

"Not even Raffa would have helped someone the way he has helped you."

I frowned at her quip. "Are you implying he isn't usually a nice person? Aren't you friends?"

Martina laughed that barrel laugh again. "He's my boss, I guess you could say. And he can be . . . kind. He's just not known for it outside his family and small circle of friends. You are the exception, it seems."

I thought she meant it as a compliment, but it only planted a small seed of unease in my belly. If Raffa wasn't usually this nice a guy, who was he really?

CHAPTER FOUR

Raffa

Bruno Cardona hung from his hands in the damp, wine-musk-scented cellar of Tenuta Romano like a sprig of drying rosemary in my mother's kitchen. He was currently unconscious, head limp between his shoulders, hair dull with old sweat, and face covered in blood from a gash above his forehead and another through his lower lip.

Two weeks ago, he'd been a trusted *soldato* in my organization. He had worked down in Naples with the Camorra outfit under Damiano Vitale for years before coming north to join my ranks, and he'd come highly recommended. He was in possession of a special skill set I needed for my operations up north, someone with experience in olive oil harvest and fraud, and ties to the Corporazione Mastri Oleari, one of the entities that verified extra-virgin olive oils. He had helped my outfit rake in millions of euros over the last four years from our agromafia pursuits alone.

Then, on a Thursday night when I was waiting for my driver to pick me up in Rome, someone on a Vespa had sped up the straight in front of the restaurant I was waiting beside and opened fire on me with a semiautomatic.

I'd ducked behind a Lamborghini almost immediately, but one of the bullets had taken a chunk out of the meat of my bicep. Shouts from inside the restaurant sounded the alarm, and the *figlio di puttana* took off without getting the job done.

The job being my murder.

It had been a very long time since someone had tried to take out the capo of the Toscana Camorra. Four years, in fact. When someone had successfully put a bullet between my father's eyes.

It seemed my brief era of peace had ended.

Unhappily for Bruno, I had recognized two important details about my shooter.

He was left handed, and he was wearing a black jacket with an SSC Napoli football team logo on it.

Little things, but didn't they say the devil was in the details?

It meant my would-be assassin was from Naples, the heart of Camorra Mafia territory.

My territory, if only by proxy.

While Damiano ruled Campania, it was my family who reigned supreme in the north.

Oh, tourists thought the Mafia only existed in Sicily, maybe in the heart of Naples, but no farther. Even Northern Italians loved to bury their heads in the sand, claiming the camorristi were a disease of the south.

We were not.

We were everywhere inside the country, with branches extending all over the globe.

New York, London, Buenos Aires.

We'd just gotten smarter than the gold-chain-wearing, swaggering mafiosi of the eighties and early nineties who thought they were invincible. We'd learned from the crackdown on the Cosa Nostra in Sicily and adjusted.

I ran a multimillion-euro business out of the heart of Tuscany, and I'd never personally had any issues with the carabinieri. It was almost unbelievable what a few well-greased palms would buy you in local politics.

We might not have had any trouble with the police, but rival families were another matter entirely. Every criminal syndicate wanted a foothold in Italy's north, with its bustling industries to launder money through, its countless tourists to scam and extort, its thriving ports.

But only one could rule.

And that man was *me*.

Something I had been certain Bruno understood until I'd seen that SSC Napoli patch and known in my gut it was my rabid-fan *soldato*. A man who had also known my schedule in Rome.

"Wake him up," I ordered Renzo.

My cousin stormed forward with a bucket of icy well water and tossed it over Bruno's limply hanging form.

He came sputtering to life, thrashing and gasping for breath like a fish out of water.

I took a drag of my cigarette, studied the long line of ash at its end, and flicked it to the floor.

"*Bastardo*," Bruno cursed when he gained his bearings, hurling insults at me as if they were knives.

They weren't, and they did nothing to hurt me.

"Bruno, Bruno," I scolded lightly, strolling forward to the edge of the dirty puddle pooling beneath his bare feet. "Do not bite the hand that can kill you."

"I don't deserve this. I am a good man," he countered. "A good man for you. Haven't I made you money?"

I arched a brow, studied the butt of my cigarette again, and then lashed forward with my free hand to grip Bruno hard by the throat. The tip of the lit tobacco sizzled satisfyingly as I pressed it to his wet cheek. He hollered and jerked, but I had a good grip on him and did not let go.

"Understand something," I suggested mildly. "I may not have wanted to become a made man, but fate saw fit to take that choice from my hands and anointed them in blood instead of ink. I do not fight fate. So here we are. You and me. They call me the Gentleman Mafioso, but that is misleading, is it not? You know me better than that."

I wrenched his head toward me, a scream slipping from his contorted mouth as the pressure seared through his shoulders.

"You know the secret," I whispered as I flicked the damp butt to the floor and exchanged it for the knife from my belt, pressing the blade into Bruno's anxiously jumping Adam's apple. "You know I might not have wanted this life, but I am very, very good at it. I like to get creative, bending the law to my whims. I enjoy looking for new ways to make money. But what I really love?"

I cut a long, thin slice across his neck just to watch him bleed. Not enough to kill him.

Not yet.

Just enough for him to come to the inevitable conclusion that if he did not turn on whoever paid him, he would die.

In a way that I would find long, slow, and highly enjoyable.

"I love to kill those who would come after me and mine. And I like to do it in a way that sends a message to everyone else who has ever thought to try."

I stepped back, dropping my hold on him abruptly so his body swung on the chains like a macabre church bell, heralding my kind of communion.

"What do you think, Bruno? Are you ready to talk, or would you like to be my messenger?"

In the end, it turned out he was both.

"How is she?" I asked Martina the moment I got through the door of the palazzo later that day.

Even in the midst of skinning a man alive, I'd thought of the small American girl back at my apartment.

There was no reason she should have inspired such curiosity in me.

She was just a girl.

Not more than twenty-five and not at all my type.

I liked my women tall and curved, soft edges and round handholds. I liked them mature and independent, almost detached, so they would ask no questions and I would have to tell no lies.

But . . .

There was something about Guinevere.

Perhaps her helplessness called to my baser self.

I didn't think that was it, or all of it, though.

I found myself intrigued by her contrasts: She was a silly girl who trusted strangers but one who quite literally laughed in the face of danger after being chased by a man and hit by a car. One who teased me, a grown man, a stranger, like she had the right to when grown men who had known me for years would never dare.

It was an irreverence, a charming one, like she knew the world had big teeth, but she was going to explore it anyway. Armed with a mocking self-deprecation and keen curiosity that made her a glaring beacon for bad men.

Like me.

Because it made me wonder—if she saw my big teeth, would she run away scared or stare into my eyes and ask me to take a bite?

"I just helped her into bed after her shower," Martina replied as she sharpened her knife on a whetstone with a repetitive hissing rasp. "She finally noticed she was wearing one of your shirts. I gave her a new one that did not smell."

I raised an eyebrow at her tone and in question.

My friend grinned. "She offered to have it professionally dry-cleaned."

Laughter bubbled inside my throat, but I swallowed it down.

Still, Martina saw my amusement, however guarded, and smiled wider. "Yes, she's an interesting girl for an American."

I inclined my head in agreement, already moving through the living room toward the stairs to check on her.

"You know," Martina called after me in a bland voice that warned me she did not intend to let this go. "There are other options for the girl. You could loan her some money and send her on her way. Suggest a hotel, if you feel responsible for her. Maybe call Cesar and get her a fast appointment at the consulate."

I didn't respond because I didn't want to acknowledge her words.

Only three more steps toward the stairs and she said, "Or your mother would take her. If you really care that much about helping her until she's well. You're not exactly a natural-born caretaker, and you have better things to do than play nursemaid."

A snarl lodged in my throat, and I was grateful to be facing away from her so she could not see the sneer contorting my features.

Nursemaid?

Cazzo, that was not who I was playing.

But I could not—would not—tell her that my role was that of the shining knight. A role I'd last wanted to play as a boy fighting with sticks as swords against my best friend, Leo.

A role I had banished from my mind completely since picking up the mantle of my father.

The ruler of the underworld did not get to be the good guy in any scenario, I'd told myself as I laid it to rest.

But then, Guinevere had appeared in front of my headlights, a startled deer so ready for slaughter.

And I felt the tug of that nostalgic longing.

To do something *good* for the first time in a long time.

To feel like a good kind of man again.

"It is not your business," I said to Martina. "I asked you here because you are the only woman I trust in Firenze."

"I'm honored," she annoyed me by saying, walking forward to place a soft hand on my arm. "And I won't judge, Raffa. I only meant to tease you. She's a very pretty girl."

"It is not about that," I snapped, and truly it wasn't.

She could have been a troll, and that same part of me would have yearned to help her. It wasn't even *about* her.

It was about me and the kind of man I was and could no longer be.

Guinevere was giving me the fleeting chance to live out a different side of myself, and I was going to take it. And that was a secret I'd take to my grave.

"You know Angela has become obsessed with setting me up with Stefania, which has convinced Stef she has a chance with me. Being seen around town with another woman will deter both of them from thinking I would ever go through with such an arrangement."

It wasn't exactly a lie, but then over the last four years I had become very adept at skirting the truth. I was annoyed with Mama and Stefania for their mechanisms. I was a grown man capable of finding my own wife when and if the desire struck me. Taking Guinevere out to one of my usual haunts meant the word would spread through Firenze in a matter of hours that I had a new woman on my arm, and hopefully Stefania would take the unsubtle hint after a series of subtle rebuffs.

"*Va bene.* So you're just using her as a beard until you can get rid of her," Martina surmised, but her voice was too dry, and I knew she was challenging me.

"My actions do not require an explanation to you or anyone," I reminded her. "I have something more important for you to focus on. Bruno sang a very beautiful song before he died at Tenuta Romano. I want you to find out who the fuck San Marco is."

"Like the piazza in Venice?"

"Like a man," I corrected over my shoulder. "Bruno said he is the man Rico Pietra introduced him to for the job."

Her mouth dropped open. "You think the Pietras tried to kill you?"

I shrugged one shoulder as I headed for the stairs again. "It was four years in the making, Tina. There was no way they would not look for revenge one day. Maybe it just took them this long to get their shit together. Maybe they were just the go-between. Or maybe Bruno was lying through his teeth. At this point, we are shooting in the dark."

She didn't respond after that, which was good because I was done with the conversation for now. Martina was ex-military and shockingly efficient, but her corruption and decommissioning were rooted in rebelling against authority. She ignored my orders five times out of ten, but the 50 percent she did obey yielded incredible results.

Usually that level of insubordination would have been dealt with swiftly, but Martina had been my boyhood friend, and that was the kind of loyalty you didn't grow out of.

She would die for me, and she had almost proven it one too many times.

So I knew she wouldn't speak of the American girl to anyone, not only because it would expose too much about her capo but also because she cared for me. She would help me find the *stronzo* with enough awareness of my operation to target Bruno and come after me because she would want them dead just as much as I did.

In the Camorra, trust was measured in blood, and Martina had anointed herself with enough to be in my innermost circle.

Upstairs was quiet, as it always was.

I rarely spent time in this house because I preferred the estate in the countryside, and my mother and sisters only ventured into town for concerts or shopping trips. It was a luxurious home to be so infrequently used, but my father had been a frivolous man, and this had been his purchase.

I'd never been fond of it, but when I walked through the open door of the bedroom I'd given for Guinevere's use and saw her seated against a mound of white silk pillows in one of my old white button-down linen shirts, her dark, wet hair turning the material transparent over her breasts, I thought it was the perfect backdrop to her kind of romantic beauty.

She seemed like something straight out of an Arthurian legend in the four-poster bed with the sheer curtains billowing in the warm breeze flowing in from the pushed-open French doors. Like something a man would have to earn the right to win.

When she looked up at me in the doorway, I was shocked by her smile. It was wide and without insecurity, as if she'd looked up at me with that same smile for years, always happy to greet me. It hit me in the chest like a fist and made me hesitate in the doorway.

"*Ciao*, Raffa," she greeted me, her voice still strained from her cold but much better than the painful croak it had been the last few days. "How are you?"

I leaned against the doorjamb and crossed my arms as I regarded her. "I think that is my line. You are the one who has been injured and ill."

"I'm a bit better, thank you."

"You told the doctor that you had a condition." I gestured to the IV that was now unhooked and pushed against the wall. "You needed more water than you could drink?"

She winced as she adjusted herself against the pillows and moved her hair off her chest to rest on the top of the cushion behind her head. It left her breasts shockingly apparent through the wet linen, her nipples hard and pink.

I didn't tell her to cover herself, but I tried not to stare too much lest I gave myself away.

"I have a genetic disorder," she admitted. "Primary hyperoxaluria type 1. It doesn't usually cause issues if I take care of myself. Basically, my body produces too much of a substance called oxalate that can affect the kidneys, liver, and urinary tract, so I have to manually flush them by drinking copious amounts of water every day, watching my diet, and taking my medicine." She gestured to the side table, where the doctor had left her a series of pill bottles. "I was born with it, but it took them a few years to figure out why I was smaller and sicker than other kids."

I frowned. "It is dangerous?"

"Not really. I mean, it can be." She looked into space for a moment. "I was matched with a buddy through the medical center in France, and she passed away after a failed liver transplant when I was eighteen. But it's not . . . I mean, I'm healthy right now."

Something twisted in my gut and went rancid. It felt a lot like guilt, even though I had nothing at all to do with this girl. Even though I wasn't responsible for her illness or her well-being.

"Your parents let you travel to Italy alone when you are sick?"

"I am *not* sick," she insisted, some of that bite she'd exhibited on the roadside coming back. "I was born with a genetic disorder. I am not sick, and I am not dying. I'm a healthy young woman capable of traveling alone, taking care of herself, and having adventures, despite what my first horrible day here might make you believe."

I opened my palms in surrender, trying not to let the smile loose on my face because I had the feeling it would make her even more indignant, and I was already finding her wildly endearing.

"*Bene*, I meant no offense. You are obviously feeling better if you are ready to go for the throat of the man who saved you."

Her scowl disappeared as she rubbed a weary hand over her mouth. "God, I'm sorry. It's just, the whole topic is a little triggering for me. I have overbearing parents."

"Italian." I gestured to myself. "Tell me about it."

She smiled again, the shy curve of her mouth making me take an involuntary step into the room to be closer to her.

"I'm sorry about this." When I rolled my eyes at her, she laughed. "I know you aren't a fan of apologies, but I'm from Michigan and it's basically cultural, so don't get mad at me. I just wanted to say, thank you again. I know I've been an awful imposition. But I'm feeling better." A cough racked her entire frame and then made her wince as it irritated her bruised ribs and side. "I'll probably be okay to leave tomorrow—"

I held up a hand to stop her, and her mouth snapped shut with an audible click.

"I do not believe I have ever had a woman try so hard to get away from me before," I mused, and watched a mixture of horror and amusement wash over her expressive face. It was rather entertaining. "Now, stop trying to run away. You are still sick, and having you occupy one of my eight bedrooms in this giant mausoleum is not an inconvenience.

I know how much you Americans like to sue. I am really just covering my own ass so you do not come after me for hitting you with my car."

Her laugh was throaty. "I'm not sure I'd have a case to make, seeing as how I ran out into the road like a madwoman."

"I have a man on it. On finding this Galasso character," I informed her.

I had not intended on sharing that, not just because I did not want her to guess at what kind of man would or could "have a man on it" but also because I did not want her to think I was forming some kind of . . . attachment to her. I would find this *stronzo* so he did not hurt any other woman ever again, not because he had hurt this particular girl. Unfortunately, it was impossible to look at her in that bed, vulnerable and sweet enough to make my damn teeth ache, and not want to offer her something.

A present.

A tribute.

Something of meaning ripped straight out of my skin.

Her pink mouth parted in shock. "*Oh.* I didn't . . . I mean, to what end? Do you think he'll still have any of my things?"

No, I thought, but I could make him pay for taking them.

"*Forse.*" Maybe, I allowed.

"Well, thank you." She tried to gather her hair again, sucking in a pained breath as she moved to push it out of her face.

"Let me help you," I offered before I could think it through, moving briskly around the bed to her side.

There was a hairbrush on the marble nightstand and one of my sister's hair ties Martina must have found for Guinevere in the bathroom. I pushed aside the mountain of pillows from behind her back so I could balance a knee on the bed behind her.

"What are you—?" she started to ask and then shivered when I gathered her wet hair in one hand and laid it down her back.

The tension in her shoulders loosened the moment I passed the brush through the strands, careful of the tangles. The sound of bristles passing through the damp silk and her slightly raspy breath from the lingering cold were the only noises in the entire house. It made the scene oddly intimate even though I meant for it to be perfunctory.

When I started to collect her hair into three parts and braid it, she shifted in surprise.

"You know how to braid?"

"I have three older sisters," I divulged in answer. "This is the least of the things they taught me."

She giggled. An honest-to-God, bright, bubbling giggle that passed through my armor like vapor.

"French, Dutch, crown," I continued, listing the ways my siblings had forced me to plait their hair. "My backup profession could be being a hairdresser."

She laughed again, softly because it clearly still hurt her. "I'm impressed. Even though it feels odd that the only things I know about you are that you own a literal palace, your first name is Raffa, and you're very good at braiding."

I slid a lock of rich brown hair through my fingers as I considered that. She knew nothing about me. Nothing.

How fucking freeing.

"Well, I love my country and consider myself an amateur historian. I like to cook, but I hate to clean up after myself, so I have a cook for when I am too lazy and a cleaner for when I am not. If I do not work out every day, I am a *brontolone*. A . . . grouch, I think the word is. I am allergic to kiwis. And until I met you, I was not very fond of Americans."

She shivered as my warm breath wafted over her ear. I pretended not to notice, tying off the braid and then getting off the bed to stand beside it.

She lifted a hand gingerly to feel over the braid and offered me that shy, sweet smile like a present she'd wrapped just for me. "*Grazie mille*, Raffa."

"*Prego*. Now, you are probably tired. I will leave you."

"No, I mean, *yes*. I am tired, but if you wanted to stay . . . it's kind of boring laying around without anything to do. I'm not allowed screen time, and I'm not allowed to read, so . . ." She shrugged limply.

I had work to do. Two men to find and, hopefully, kill.

What I did not have time for was caving to the whims of a girl with wide brown eyes and hair like silk.

So why was I crossing the room to the bookshelf near the fireplace and picking up the book I knew I'd find on the second shelf?

I lifted the cover to show her as I crossed back to her bedside and pulled up a chair to get comfortable.

"*The Divine Comedy*," I said with a raised brow. "Should we refresh your memory about Dante's fallen angels?"

I knew I was royally fucked the moment she twisted slightly to pull a pillow behind her back and then faced me with a beaming smile that brought out dimples in both cheeks.

"'Have pity on me,' unto him I cried, 'Whiche'er thou art, or shade or real man!'" I began, skipping straight to this line because it occurred to me that it eerily echoed our own meeting.

And how Guinevere made me feel.

Not like the shade of my father I had postured as for half a decade, but like the man I'd once been. It was a dangerous allusion, but one I found myself reluctant to cull even if it was for my own good.

And her own safety.

CHAPTER FIVE

Guinevere

Eight days after the incident, I finally woke up feeling good again.

In fact, I woke up and still felt as if I was dreaming.

Light filtered through the sheer curtains and pooled on the white linen bedcovers like liquid gold. Raffa had left the doors open slightly so the faint sounds of city life streamed in, the staccato of Italian conversations and the toy car honk of a Vespa. It was so idyllic I had to pinch myself to make sure I was truly awake.

Stretching the vestiges of sleep from my body, I noted I was still sore and stiff, but not nearly as crippled by the accident as I had been even two days ago. My throat was tender like a healing wound, but I didn't feel pain when swallowing anymore, and my thoughts were unmuddied.

It was time to get organized and out of Raffa's space.

There was accepting kindness from a stranger and then exploiting that kindness, and I felt dangerously on the verge of the latter. Raffa had fed me and given me shelter, but he'd also carried me to the bathroom when I was too sick and in pain to walk, read to me from Dante's *Inferno* because I couldn't entertain myself with a concussion, and even braided my hair.

God.

The feeling of his big hands moving gently over my scalp and hair had been the single most romantic and erotic experience in my life.

Which was depressing, really, but it was one of the many reasons I was on this adventure. To learn about myself in every way, including my sexuality. It embarrassed me a little to be a twenty-three-year-old virgin, but I'd never had time for boys. I was either too sick or working too hard.

Now I was free to fall for anyone I wanted, but of course I had to set my sights on the gorgeous Italian man eleven years my senior and wildly out of my league.

I sighed as I slipped out of bed and wiggled my toes in the plush Aubusson carpet. A full-length ornate gold mirror in the corner of the room showed my skinny legs beneath the tails of Raffa's borrowed linen shirt. I raised the cuff to my nose to inhale the delicious scent of air-dried laundry and wondered what the material might smell like after a day spent pressed to his skin.

"Concentrate," I scolded myself as I headed to the bathroom to take care of my morning business.

When I was finished, I tiptoed down the hall to the staircase spiraling up and down to other floors, straining to hear if anyone was awake and inside. A faint clatter of dishware from the first floor had me moving down the stairs, taking in the interior of the palace properly for the first time.

It was magnificent. Like something from a Disney movie. There was even an intricate fresco painted on the ceiling of the main floor that extended from a formal living room through a huge dining room and music room. Artwork I recognized from history books and museums lined the walls, along with some marble statues that had to be authentic antiques. Finally, I found the kitchen and, through two sets of open doors, a huge terrace where Raffa sat at a ceramic-inlaid table, drinking an espresso while he read the local paper.

I took a moment to study him in the rich morning sunlight because it was my first opportunity to really look my fill. And look I did because he was simply too lovely not to admire.

Even though I'd mostly seen him in dismantled businessman finery, he was obviously fit, with the kind of quilted muscles that left seams in his skin I wanted to trail with my fingertips. The sun turned his dark-brown hair to bronze and caught the pale maple of his eyes so they glowed like a predator's, narrow and intent on something written in the newsprint. Those same big, tanned hands that had braided my hair made my throat dry as I watched them flex, the tendons in his forearms popping as he folded the paper impatiently and dropped it to the table with a dark glare.

For one insane moment, I thought getting chased through a wheat field and hit by a car was worth it to see such a man sitting there, as beautiful as any piece of art I'd ever admired before him.

"Something unpleasant in the news?" I asked as I moved forward into the doorframe. "How shocking."

He looked up at me without surprise, as if he'd known I was there the entire time. The expression on his face was too bland to be called a smile, but there was amusement there.

"This is universal, I think," he agreed, gesturing for me to sit across from him. "Help yourself to fruit and bread, but do not eat too much. We have things to do today."

"Yeah, I was going to have a bite to eat and then go to the bank. I researched, and there is one in this neighborhood." It was only a fifteen-minute walk, which I could manage easily even with a stiff hip. "I just have to call my parents to ask them to transfer me some money. Then I guess I'll go to the police and file a report. It seems like I'd have to do that in order to get an appointment at the consulate for a new passport."

Raffa crossed one ankle over the opposite knee, and I noticed he was wearing leather loafers without socks. The sight of his olive-brown ankles shouldn't have been shocking or sexy, yet it made my pulse pound. I wanted to reach out and touch the knob of bone and the plum-thin skin to see if he'd shiver.

"No."

I blinked away the fantasy, heat rushing to my cheeks as I stared up into his implacable gaze. "Sorry, what?"

"No," he repeated clearly. "I have a better idea. You will finish your breakfast, and then we will go get you some clothes. As tempting as you are in my shirt, I do not think it is appropriate attire for a police station or the consulate."

I winced because somehow I'd forgotten that little detail.

"Maybe I can borrow a belt?" I suggested.

Raffa's full mouth twitched. "That will do until we get to the stores, maybe. Do not worry about money, Guinevere. You may have noticed I am not exactly worried about it myself."

I sat back in the wrought iron chair with a slice of melon in my hand and sighed. "I just feel like I've taken a lot from you."

"Is it taken if I have given it freely?" he asked imperiously.

He should have been condescending, speaking like that, *looking* like that, but there was an unmissable warmth I couldn't pinpoint to any one mannerism. It was obvious he liked helping me. That maybe he even liked me.

"I'll pay you back," I insisted. "My father raised me to believe it's vital not to be in debt to anyone."

"Smart man."

"He is," I agreed. "And I still need to call him . . . I sent a text saying I was under the weather, and they've been checking in on me. I didn't want to worry them unnecessarily."

They would have been on the first flight out if I'd told them what had happened to me, especially if I'd been forced to admit I was in Italy, and not France as I'd told them. It would have meant the end of my trip before it even had a chance to begin, and after everything—my illness, the years of anticipation, the loss of Gemma—I found it was the final straw I couldn't allow myself to lose.

"You are their child. It is their right to worry."

"Hmm, well I guess you have a point there." Only, I'd never thought of it quite like that. I'd always been vaguely annoyed by, though always accepting of, my parents' concerns and hovering.

They'd almost lost me twice to brutal kidney infections when I was a child and then had to watch as I underwent major surgery for a kidney transplant at sixteen. Then we'd lost Gemma, and whatever gains they'd made in giving me some autonomy had diminished like smoke in the wind.

"I'll call them," I told him, feeling properly chastised.

He shrugged a shoulder. "Do what you want. I was merely telling the truth from my experience. I do not have children, but you cannot grow up with an Italian mother without hearing how difficult it is to raise and love your children, then let them go off into the world on their own. She is always happier when we are all under one roof, and all of us are grown."

I plucked a clementine from the fruit bowl and picked at the peel anxiously. "They're going to flip out."

His expressive, slashing brows rose. "Well, their daughter was almost raped and then hit by a car. Can you blame them?"

"No. But they'll want me to go home immediately."

Another flippant shrug as if he didn't see the problem. "So? You are a grown woman, are you not?"

"Of course!"

"Then, you can do as you wish." He sighed at my flat look and leaned closer so that the sunlight caught both of his eyes and turned them to burnished gold. "There is a difference between respect and blind obedience, *capisci*? You can respect them by telling them the truth about what has happened to you, but you do not owe them submission to their desires. I do not know why you are in Italy, but does one not usually spend time abroad to discover oneself?" When I nodded somewhat woodenly, a little cowed by his wisdom, he leaned back in his chair and opened his palms. "Then, do what you want and only what you want. This time and this place are for you. It is rare we get so much freedom. Do not squander it before your adventure has even begun."

I blinked at him as I chewed a piece of bright citrus. It was both eerie and wonderful that his thoughts so closely aligned with my own. Maybe it shouldn't have surprised me, given that he was almost a perfect stranger, yet I felt more comfortable sitting there that morning with him on a terrace in Florence than I'd felt in most other places with most other people in my life so far.

"Are all Italian men so wise?" I teased finally.

Raffa's slow, curling grin was wicked. "You have not seen anything yet."

"Okay, Yoda," I quipped, then hesitated. "Sorry, do you know *Star Wars*?"

"I am Italian, not an alien," he drawled. "Of course I understand the reference, young Padawan."

My grin was so wide it hurt my cheeks, dimples digging trenches into my face.

Raffa got up with a murmur about making me an espresso, and I tipped my face into the sun, closing my eyes to smell the jasmine blooming in the flower boxes along the terrace's stone railing. I let myself wonder what it might be like to live this kind of life every day, waking up in a palace and having breakfast on the terrace in Florence's most exclusive neighborhood. Instead of going to work at my father's financial firm every day, I would bike through the streets to the Uffizi Gallery, where I could give tours to English tourists on the bevy of art and artifacts on display. I could come home every night to Raffa, tie discarded, buttons undone to his sternum to reveal the crisp black chest hair I'd pressed my nose into while I was too delirious with sickness to truly enjoy it. We'd cook dinner and listen to jazz and dance under the moonlight.

I snorted at my own silliness, shaking my head to clear it of those childish fantasies.

There was an Italian saying my father had told me, *vivere nel mondo della luna*, which kind of meant living with your head in the clouds.

My entire life, I'd been dreaming of traveling to other places and being a different kind of person. I wasn't going to waste my opportunity now that it was here by fantasizing about something that would never happen.

Of course, that was easier said than done when Raffa drove us to Via de' Tornabuoni, which I knew from researching Florence inside and out was the most exclusive shopping street in the city. I gawked out the window as we pulled up outside a large boutique and watched a uniformed valet move toward the car.

"When you said *shopping*, I was kind of expecting a Forever 21 or something," I murmured as a gorgeous older woman strutted by in a pencil skirt and high heels that should have made it impossible for her to walk at all.

Raffa huffed something like a laugh but otherwise didn't respond, getting out of the car to hand his keys to the eager driver. Before I could pull myself together to leave the car, he was at my door, opening it and then offering me his hand.

I blinked up at him dumbly because no one had ever opened the door for me, let alone helped me out of my car. My father didn't even do it for my mother because she said it was antiquated and she knew damn well how to open the door of a car herself.

And sure, even recovering as I was, I could have levered myself out of the low Ferrari with minimal effort and much less grace.

This was just a much lovelier alternative.

I slipped my hand over his calloused palm and allowed his strength to pull me gently out of the car . . . and into his body. The hard length of his chest pressed against my small breasts, and the heat of him seared me through to the bone.

My mouth dropped open in an inaudible gasp as I tipped my head back to look up at him. He was staring down at me almost somberly, those copper eyes tracing my features. I was close enough to notice how square his chin was, the nick of an old scar white against the tanned skin at the corner of his jaw.

"Do not be embarrassed when we go in," he ordered. "You are not the kind of woman who should wear cheap American cloth, and I am not the kind of man to buy it for you. We will go inside together, and you will let me buy for you what I want simply because I want to and it will bring me joy. You understand?"

I pursed my lips and narrowed my eyes at him. "You know, you're really bossy, but it's hard to take umbrage at it when you're also being insanely generous."

He gave me that one-shouldered shrug, like my concerns were beneath him and he knew he would get what he wanted in the end.

Why was that brand of arrogance so sexy?

Without another word, he shifted a hand to my lower back and pressed me forward to walk slightly in front of him toward the store.

"Signore," a woman greeted him instantly when we walked in. She smiled beatifically as she moved toward us, hands open in greeting. "It has been too long."

"Maria Lucia." They exchanged brief kisses on both cheeks before Raffa presented me with a little push to the base of my spine. "This is my friend, Guinevere . . ."

"Stone," I supplied, offering my hand to Maria Lucia. "Nice to meet you."

She blinked at my outstretched hand and then dissolved into a warm smile, grasping me lightly by the shoulders to kiss the air beside both my cheeks.

When she spoke, her English was flawless. "Hello, Guinevere Stone. I see you need some clothing?"

Her gaze trailed over Raffa's shirt, which was belted at my waist with a Gucci scarf and paired with my hastily repaired sandals. A blush warmed my cheeks like a sunburn, but before I could open my mouth to explain, Raffa was taking my hand to lead me to the nearest display.

"*Si*, she needs a new wardrobe for summer. Is Maria Teresa working with you today?" When she nodded, he went on. "Good. When you have picked out some outfits, tell her I will pay her extra to go gather shoes and accessories for Guinevere while she wraps everything up here."

"Raffa," I started to complain when I lifted the tag on a linen dress and saw it was €1,500. "Please, I can't afford—"

He lifted his buzzing cell phone from his pocket and raised a single finger to hush me. "I must take this. Maria Lucia, please ignore whatever protests Signorina Stone gives you, and if she is reluctant to shop, choose for her, *capisci?*"

Before either of us could respond, he turned on his heel and strode for the door, answering the phone with a short, sharp "*Pronto.*"

I blinked after him, then turned with a little wince to face Maria Lucia again.

She was grinning at me conspiratorially. "It is best, I've found, not to argue with Signore Romano."

Romano. Well, at least I knew his last name now. Maybe I could google him from the changing room to find out who exactly my fabulously wealthy benefactor was.

"He's a little overbearing," I agreed with a sigh, trying to think about how much money I could afford to give Raffa for this designer wardrobe he was insisting on.

I had the ten grand saved for my trip, but some of that had already been spent on the apartment I'd rented and still hadn't seen, and the few excursions I'd booked, including a day trip to Volterra to see the Etruscan ruins.

Now that Raffa had made an appointment this afternoon to expedite my replacement passport, I'd have access to my accounts again by next week, which was frankly a massive relief. Because it meant I didn't have to divulge the details of my trouble to my parents.

I agreed with Raffa to a certain extent. They deserved to know I'd been really sick and maybe even hurt, but I wasn't going to tell them enough to jeopardize my trip.

For the first time in twenty-three years I was doing something for *me*, and I wouldn't give that up without a fight.

"Don't stress," Maria Lucia encouraged me with a gentle pat to my forearm. "Signore Romano is a very successful man. He can afford to spoil his *ragazza*."

"Oh, I'm just a friend," I corrected, awkwardly moving my hands as if I could erase the question from the air between us. "Not even a friend, really. He's just helping me out."

"Of course," she soothed, but the creases beside her smiling eyes said otherwise. "Let's get to work, either way. He is not a man who likes to be kept waiting. You are a size forty, I think? Yes. Do you have favorite colors?"

"Maybe just neutrals. I don't usually wear bright colors."

"Red."

I jerked my head around to see Raffa coming back into the store, his phone still pressed to his ear, one hand covering the microphone.

"I don't really . . ."

"Red," he repeated. "It is my favorite color."

Oh.

He turned away from us to speak into the phone again, pacing the front of the store.

I didn't know what to think about him wanting to see me in his favorite color. It felt somehow inappropriate.

Intimate.

Like he'd imagined me in shades of red and found himself pleased with the image.

"Well then, we better find some lovely shades of red," Maria Lucia said with a wink before gently leading me deeper into the store, chattering away about Gucci's new summer line and Valentino's to-die-for poppy patterns.

I let her compile an excessive number of outfits, all of them hanging together in the spacious changing room at the back of the store when she practically pushed me inside to try them all on. I wasn't a fan of shopping on the best of days, but only because I'd never really gone shopping with friends or even my mother or sister growing up. Being ill so much had barred me from those little pleasures, and I hadn't realized until now, trying on a slightly sheer black tank dress, how much I wished I'd had that time with Mom and Gemma.

Maria Lucia and Maria Teresa both cooed and exclaimed over me each time I emerged from the room to show them my outfits, fussing over me as they pinched the fabric at my waist and tried to prop my small breasts up more appealingly in low-cut tops. They'd pulled things for me I'd usually never wear in a million years: a citrus-yellow maxi skirt and white silk cropped shirt, a sunset-orange midi dress with a sweetheart neckline, and a long, form-fitting dress that made me look like I was dipped in liquid gold silk. Everything was too bold, too extravagant, utterly inappropriate for my simple life back home in Ann Arbor.

But even I had to admit, as I twirled in an almost backless white linen shift dress, that it was the perfect wardrobe for a summer in Italy.

Raffa appeared at one point, leaning against the wall across from my changing room with his arms crossed, a small scowl fixed to his face as if his features had been molded that way since birth. At first it made me self-conscious, but the Marias' excitement was contagious, and when Maria Lucia took my hand and twirled me around in a red Oscar de la Renta, I laughed with her, spinning until I was dizzy.

When I stopped, wavering on my feet, breathless and smiling, it was Raffa who stood before me, the Marias silently disappearing back into the front of the store.

His hand was on my elbow, hot and firm, balancing me so suddenly I felt as if I'd slammed both feet on the ground.

"I knew it would look like this on you," he said, and it was an intimate whisper, as if he didn't want the shopgirls or other shoppers to know.

It was declarative. Bold as the shade of red cupping my breasts and brushing against my thighs.

"Like what?" I breathed, a little embarrassed that my nipples were pebbling just from his sure, platonic touch on my arm.

His mouth didn't flex, but I noticed a softness around his eyes that was a microexpression of a smile. My mouth went dry as he moved his hand up my bare arm to the bow tied over one shoulder. There was a whisper as he tugged on one end of the fabric and it fell apart, the straps falling free, the bust of my dress dipping dangerously low over my left breast.

I wanted to say something, but I had no vocabulary for the shame and desire and protestations swirling inside my belly.

We were in public.

We were strangers.

This was not the way Guinevere Stone would act.

But wasn't that exactly the point?

Hadn't I yearned to feel the kind of fire I felt then, standing in a cool designer boutique in the heart of Florence with a man who looked like a real-life Adonis? Didn't I secretly love the way that single brush of his fingers over my skin had razed my inhibitions to ash and resurrected a voracious hunger for him in its wake?

A deep, forbidden part of my subconscious longed to shrug the other strap off my shoulder and bare my breasts to his predatory gaze. To cup my flesh in offering, lifting each nipple so he could worship or torture it with his mouth, with the teeth that flashed strong and white when he flashed an infrequent, wicked grin.

Raffa's hands slowly gathered the edges of the fabric and pulled tight, redoing the bow so it lay beautifully against my skin.

"Uneven," he explained calmly, but his eyes were fixed intently on his tanned fingers tracing the edge of the red fabric against my pale skin.

"Thank you," I said thickly. "But honestly, Raffa, I can't accept even half of this. I just can't pay you back for it."

"You will not," he said simply, dropping his hand as his brows dropped over his eyes. He stepped back, and I was both relieved and annoyed by the distance.

"You said yourself my father was a smart man for teaching me not to be in debt to someone," I pointed out.

"*Si, certo,*" he agreed. "But I intended for you to pay me back, just not with something so silly as euros."

I fisted my hands on my hips and leveled him with a cool glare. "I'm not a prostitute."

A reluctant grin claimed his mouth, pink against the dark stubble all along the curve of his jaw. "Do not insult us both. I only meant I have a fundraiser at the Pitti Palace next Friday evening and no date. If you are willing to bear the tedium, you would be repaying me with your company."

I snorted, forgetting my nerves and attraction in the silliness of his request. "Oh c'mon. You're *you*. I'm sure you could have any girl in Tuscany with one snap of your fingers."

Slowly, he raised his hand between us and snapped his fingers. "Oh look. It is the only girl I want in Tuscany."

His deadpan delivery made me laugh, releasing some of the giddy bubbles floating through my belly.

"You know, your friend Martina confessed to me you're never this kind to strangers," I said, and told myself I wasn't flirting, but I could practically feel the hearts in my eyes.

He leaned a shoulder against the wall beside us and crossed his arms again, muscles bulging beneath the blazer. A lock of wavy dark hair fell over his forehead, and my fingers itched to push it back.

"I am not," he agreed easily.

I dragged my toe against the plush carpet and looked up at him through my lashes. "Why do I seem to be the exception, then?"

He actually considered the question, rubbing a hand over his lower lip as he studied me. Finally, he reached out and adjusted the bow he'd just retied over my shoulder, observing as my skin broke into goose bumps.

"Because the kindness does not stem from the good of my heart," he admitted, voice rough and textured enough to abrade my skin. "The moment I saw you like a deer trapped in my headlights, I saw you with the eyes of a predator."

I swallowed thickly. "Predators usually hunt their prey."

"*Si*, but I do not intend to kill you, *cerbiatta*." His finger traced the strap down to the sweetheart neckline and tracked daringly over the edge of my breast exposed above the fabric. I watched up close as his eyes went from amber to bronze, dark with hunger. "I only intend to *eat* you."

I tried to swallow and almost choked at the dryness of my throat. "Are you hitting on me?" I asked, just to be sure, because this entire trip was dreamlike in a way I couldn't shake, for good or ill.

A tiny smile cut into one edge of his mouth. "How old are you?"

"Twenty-three."

"*Allora si*," he said, curling his hand around my throat, using his thumb to tip my chin up. "*Ci sto provando.*"

Then yes, he said, I am.

Before I could truly process that, he was moving closer for a kiss. I pursed my lips slightly, eager to test the texture of his mouth against my own. But to my slight shame and disappointment, those lips only tipped into a grin and then pressed first to one cheek and then the other.

How could the simple brush of his mouth against my skin liquefy my spine?

When he stepped away with low-lidded eyes and a smug smile, I was as breathless as if he'd kissed the air right out of my lungs.

CHAPTER SIX

Raffa

Shopping was not an aphrodisiac.

Nor was visiting the police station and the American consulate, where I pulled strings to get Guinevere seen to immediately while I waited outside, working from my phone.

Yet by the end of our errands, my blood felt like it had been boiling on low heat for hours.

Impulse control had always been one of my greatest assets. I was not besieged by lust, avarice, gluttony, or envy like so many other capos and *soldati* whose hunger was never sated. Being a criminal was not something I would have chosen for myself, but now that I was firmly entrenched on the wrong side of the law, I found I relished the mental challenge of it. How to bend the rules into angles that worked for me without breaking them completely. How to rule the underworld of the north without drawing attention from the wrong people as *capo dei capi*. It was about checks and balances, problems reduced to easy mathematical equations I could solve with simple logic.

I had been top of my class at Oxford in math and economics and gone on to work on Lombard Street, in the heart of London's financial district, for years before I was called by duty and honor to come home.

Emotion and hedonism did not factor into my life.

Blasphemy for an Italian, but it was one of the reasons I'd always been drawn to Britain and to finance.

My father had made excuses all my life for his behavior.

I am a man. I have needs.

She was so beautiful, I had to have her.

Yes, the palazzo was too expensive, but we need to show others we are rich and powerful.

He dared to speak to me like that, so I was forced to cut out his tongue.

Pathetic, I had always thought, to be so ruled by his baser instincts.

Yet I found myself oddly incapable of refraining from touching Guinevere when she emerged from the changing room wearing my favorite color just because I'd asked her to. There was an ethereal quality about her beauty, something in the large, luminous eyes and the small, full red mouth, the sharp chin and all that thick dark hair swinging in waves to her waist. She was delicate, almost dreamy, but also elfin, and everyone knew never to underestimate the dangerous appeal of the fey. In that dress the color of freshly oxidized blood, Guinevere would have looked as perfect in a Tuscan field of poppies, twirling like she was doing under Maria Lucia's arm, as she would have spinning to slip a blade neatly between the ribs of some hapless victim.

The duality of the fantasy—of her—wrote itself into my bones. Soft and sharp, naive and witty, untried but strong.

For the first time in a very long time, I gave in to my reckless impulses and undid the bow at her shoulder just to watch that dress dip dangerously low over one pale breast. I thought of biting that white skin until it was the same color as the fabric, until that sweet mound was ringed in teeth marks.

I could have too. Her desire was obvious in the stain of her cheeks and the hitch of her breath. She wanted me, and she wasn't afraid of it. Her chest pushed slightly into my hand, and when I bent to kiss each of her suede-soft cheeks, I caught the pucker of her mouth ready to meet my own, and I was charmed by it.

What I could teach her, I thought, and was almost scared of my own desire to do so. To take her in hand and show her how to please me exactly as I wished. To introduce her to pleasures her sweet, shielded brain had never even thought to dream of.

I had stepped away from the temptation, but it had taken a surprising strength of will to do it. And even then, throughout the mundane, frankly irritating errands we accomplished the rest of the day, I found myself struck by the contours of her bow-shaped mouth, wondering if that incredibly soft skin extended to the tender curve of her inner thigh.

When the police officer took her into a room to speak with her alone and they came out laughing softly together, I made sure to remember his name—Riccardo Grassi—and had to fight the urge to stop her from giving him her phone number.

When we went to the consulate and my friend, Giuseppe Diati, told me in a congratulatory way that she was very beautiful, I did *not* fight the urge to tell him to keep his eyes to himself.

She seemed to awaken an oddly intoxicating mix of protectiveness and arousal in me that I hadn't felt before in any of my thirty-four years, despite having countless partners.

So it irritated me that Guinevere Stone, this slip of an American girl who looked unfairly like a princess from a medieval Italian romance, could set my regimented life on its head.

It had been my intention to take her for dinner at Trattoria Marione because I knew she would fucking delight over their Florentine *ribollita*, but by the time we finished at the consulate, I felt as if I were coming out of my skin with a mixture of desire and irritation.

So I set our course for home and turned up the volume on the jazz filtering through the Ferrari. Despite my ignoring her, Guinevere's presence was impossible to overlook. She shone with her own light, even sitting in the tight confines of the sports car. I watched the play of expressions over her face from my peripheral vision as we passed sights she had clearly read about and lusted over for years. The way her fingers touched the window so reverently made me wonder how they would touch me. Would that same worshipful light enter her eyes as she slowly undid my zipper, metal tooth by metal tooth? Would that same shocky gasp leave her lips when I took the tip of one of her small breasts between my lips?

"*Madonna santa*," I cursed under my breath as we finally pulled through the automatic gates to the courtyard of my palazzo on the south bank of the Arno River.

If I had to spend one more moment in a confined space with this siren, I was going to lose my infamous cool and do something we'd both regret.

Like press her reverently to the window and kiss her until she trembled.

"Servio will make you whatever you want for dinner," I grunted as I unbuckled and opened the door. "I have to work the rest of the evening."

Before she could respond, I was levering myself out of the Ferrari and stalking across the pavers to the side entrance. The gym was on this lower level, and without skipping a beat, I tore off my suit jacket, kicked off my loafers, and rolled up my sleeves before stalking over to the punching bag hanging idle in the corner.

When I looked up countless minutes later, sweat was beading in my hairline and dripping from my jaw. Martina stood in the doorway, affecting my normal pose in silent mockery.

I blew a lock of wet hair out of my eyes and steadied the bag with my gloved hands so I could start my combinations again.

"So," she said, when it became clear I would not indulge her. "Fun day?"

My answer was a jab-hook-uppercut combination that set the bag vibrating on its chain.

"I know men don't enjoy shopping much, but I thought you would have at least enjoyed the company."

Martina was like that, a bloodhound with the scent of vulnerability in her nose, ceaseless until she hunted it down and pinned it beneath her notice.

Her laugh filtered through the quiet room when I did not respond. "Are you ready for me to call in your mother? Angela would love to take in a pretty stray. Your sisters would probably throw her a welcome party."

The idea of Guinevere meeting my family was almost horrifying. They were not cut from the same cloth, but there was a synchronicity that I inherently knew existed between them. The big, boisterous family obsessed with living in each other's pockets and knowing every single person's business and a girl who was so clearly a little lost and lonely, and entirely too lovely. They would stitch together beautifully. Mama would harness Guinevere's enthusiasm for Italian culture and teach her how to cook every Tuscan dish. Delfina would take her through the olive groves and vines, showing her how to test the fruits for readiness, educating her on Tuscany's famous Sangiovese grapes, while Stacci and Carlotta would enfold her in family duties, pushing babies into her arms and laughing with her as she played with the young boys in the grass.

The vision was so vivid it took my breath away the way punching the *merda* out of the punching bag had failed to do.

"No," I said curtly, but there was a wealth of reasons behind the syllable.

At the moment, I could convince myself this strange fascination I had with the American was lust. Heady. Dangerous. But acceptable. I was a red-blooded man faced with a gorgeous woman who needed my help. There were very few men who would not feel as I did in the same situation.

But if I saw her in my true home with the people I had given up my lifelong dreams for, I was aware that passionate intensity could morph into something entirely too heartbound.

"A hotel, then?" she offered sweetly, as if she was the kind of person who lived to be helpful. "She is so *young*—you'd want to make sure she was somewhere safe. As a concerned older guardian."

I shot her a glare and caught the wide, shameless grin pinned to her face. *"Vai a quel paese."*

Fuck off.

Her resulting laugh was bright and long. "Oh, Raffa, I only wish Leo was in town to see this."

Cazzo, I was grateful he was at the villa with the family. Martina was pushy, but she had nothing on Leo, who would level me with one amusement-filled look and offer to be my best man at the wedding.

"Was there a reason you decided to bother me?" I demanded, and turned my focus back to the punching bag and the burn in my torso as I beat into it at a steady, punishing pace.

Jab, jab, right hook, uppercut, jab, jab.

"Oh, not really," she mused blandly, pretending to check her fingernails as if she gave a shit about their appearance. "Probably nothing you'd be interested in because you don't care much for the girl either way."

"Spit it out, Tina," I ordered as sweat dripped into my eyes.

"*Va bene.* Ludo found the man, Galasso."

Immediately, my hands fell limply to my sides, and I turned on Martina with a snarl. "You tell me this *now*?"

She shrugged. "I didn't know you'd be so . . . invested."

"Cut the shit," I demanded before tearing off my gloves with my teeth and shucking them to the floor. "Where is he?"

"They have him at Trattoria Umberto, in the cellar."

"Why so public?"

"Ludo found him in town skulking around, and it was the closest place."

"They will be in full dinner service upstairs," I pointed out.

Another shrug. "It's loud with the live music, and the cellar is beneath layers of concrete. No one will hear them. Or you, if you decide to deal with him yourself."

I ignored her, already stalking out of the room to shower and change for the reckoning with Guinevere's would-be assaulter. A human head was much better than a punching bag for relieving stress anyway.

◆ ◆ ◆

The trattoria was in Santa Croce and filled with locals who tried to stay away from the chaos of central Florence during the summer months, when tourists descended on the streets like locusts. We had owned the restaurant for twenty years, since the proprietor Ambrigio's wife was diagnosed with cancer, and they had no money to pay for the bills and her treatment. My father had stepped in with an offer of help, plenty of strings attached, and the trattoria had made us a tidy profit from its legal business as well as hundreds of thousands of euros in laundered money. It was also where I met with the odd local capo to discuss business over Ambrigio's delicious *bistecca alla Fiorentina* and a bottle of Chianti or, on occasion, where I doled out punishment to rats and other bottom dwellers who interfered with my business.

Obviously, this visit was about the latter.

When I descended the steps into my own hellish dominion, Galasso was sitting at a wobbly old wooden table against a rack of wine. Carmine stood behind him with his arms crossed, his whipcord-lean frame made threatening by the sheer number of weapons discernible on his person: a gun in his shoulder holster, brass knuckles on one fisted hand, a row of knife handles visible above his waistband. Next to him stood Renzo, his younger brother, who made up for his age by being the biggest man I'd ever known, towering over even me at six foot six, with a neck as thick as a leg of prosciutto. Ludo, the third in my trio of trusted personal *soldati*, greeted me at the stairs, his heavy brow and slightly undershot jaw giving him a primitive appearance that was inherently threatening.

Sometimes, people made the mistake of underestimating me because of my good looks, which I always found utterly amusing. If I was attractive, it was because generations of my mafioso ancestors had been affluent enough to attract beautiful women despite their own lack of beauty until the end result was someone like me.

Beautiful and dangerous, as so many mythological beings.

Galasso muttered something behind the tape over his mouth and tried to stand up as soon as he saw me, but Renzo clamped a hand over his shoulder and forced him back down.

I ignored him completely, heading to the wine rack to pick a nice bottle of Brunello di Montalcino to share with my guest. It was the kind of expensive bottle that needed to breathe, so I moved to grab a vintage Murano decanter from a cabinet and transferred the red liquid into the glass with my back to Galasso. He watched me with wide eyes as I slid out the chair across from him and settled comfortably into it before placing the wine between us on the table. I sniffed the cork, then accepted two short glasses from my friend and poured Galasso and myself some of the fine vintage.

Sliding the glass across the table with one finger, I nodded slightly at Renzo, who reached forward to tear the tape from Galasso's mouth.

"*Figlio di puttanna*," he cursed viciously.

"Watch your mouth," I encouraged him calmly, observing the play of the low cellar light in the garnet-red wine. "You would not want to ruin our civilized conversation by insulting my mother, would you?"

He glared at me, chin lifted pugnaciously. "What do you want with me, Gentiluomo?"

"Ah, so I see I do not have to introduce myself. That makes things easier. Though I do not know you, Galasso. Perhaps we should start with your introduction?"

When he didn't immediately speak, I flicked my gaze to Renzo, who used the butt of his gun to pistol-whip the man.

He let out a cry, blood flying from his broken nose, but quickly after he murmured, "Galasso Pagano."

"From?" I encouraged with a thin smile, as if this was just a polite interview.

Sometimes it was fun to play with your food before you destroyed it.

"Napoli." He spat a wad of blood onto the floor beside the table. "Originally."

"Ah, and how long have you been in our lovely Toscana?"

"Four years."

Premonition skittered down my spine. Four years ago my father was killed. Four years ago I became a man I'd never intended to be.

"Where do you work?"

"With the vines. Up near Pistoia."

"What car do you drive?"

He blinked but answered easily enough, caught in the tide of rapid questions. "A 2012 Lancia Ypsilon."

"Color?" I asked, deceptively calm even though my blood was surging through my veins, thirsting to spill some of his. I had armed myself with more information about him over breakfast with Guinevere, so I was ready to catch him out.

"Blue."

Chi vince piglia tutto.

We have a winner!

"Well, Galasso, I am sorry my men bothered you. We have had trouble with rats, you see, and you have the distinct look of one." I shrugged and gestured to his broken nose with my glass. "Maybe it is the nose? Either way, please accept my apologies. They acted without thinking as sometimes soldiers do."

Galasso peered at me through his small brown eyes, brow furrowed as he chewed furiously over my words, testing their merit. I merely returned his gaze calmly.

Eventually, he sighed, and the tension in his shoulders dissolved a bit. "Thank you. I thought being brought in front of Il Gentiluomo had to be a mistake."

"Yes, yes. Please, lift your glass and drink with me. It is a very fine vintage befitting an apology."

Galasso was clearly not a clever man, because though he had heard of my reputation enough to know what they called me in the underworld, he raised his glass with a barely shaking hand and clinked it against my own.

"*Salute*," we said in unison, and each brought the wine to our mouths.

I watched over the rim of the glass as Galasso took a deep draught of the Brunello di Montalcino red and then, finding it exemplary, he took another, longer taste.

When I lowered my glass without drinking, he did not notice.

"It is good, no?" I asked with a bland smile when he downed the wine like a heathen and set the empty glass heavily on the table.

"Excellent," he admitted. "We make good wine in Pistoia, but it is mostly Vernaccia. It is nice to have a decent red."

"You like wine, then."

"Mmm, what Italian doesn't?" He laughed, and the line of his shoulders loosened completely, his thighs spreading wider beneath the table. Getting comfortable.

"Of course. Wine, cars, and women."

Understanding made his wizened brows lift. "This is why you asked about my car. Ah. I admit, it is not a fancy one. I bet you drive something slick. A Lamborghini."

"Close." I dipped my head and poured him another glass of wine. Watched his thick fingers close around the glass and imagined them closing around Guinevere's thin ankle. "A Ferrari."

"Aha!" he exclaimed, as if he had guessed correctly from the start. "I knew it. I love the Ferrari. What I wouldn't give to drive one someday."

I let the moment settle. Watched as he drank down more of that fine red wine.

"You know," he said with a sly look. "It would be a good way to forget how your men treated me. That one with the face like a pig's nearly put out my shoulder."

In the corner behind me, Ludo grunted softly.

"Now, that is an idea," I murmured, then looked up at Renzo over his shoulder. "You do not think my offer of wine is enough?"

He had to tread carefully to avoid further insulting me, but there was a sly cast to his gaze that intrigued me. "I have powerful friends, Signore. Not so powerful as you, but still, they are old school. They do not like one of their own to be mistreated."

"What friends would those be?" I asked softly.

"Leonardo di Conte."

I fought the smile that pulled at my mouth, but Carmine had to hide his behind a hand.

"Well, we would not want to upset Leonardo di Conte, would we?" I said somberly, even though the man he spoke of had been my lifelong friend, as close to a brother as I had ever had.

Obviously, Galasso knew enough to know about the mythical Il Gentiluomo, but not about my outfit.

"Will you get the keys, Zo?" I told Renzo. "The least we could do is let this poor man take a ride."

Galasso's eagerness leaked through the air, gaseous and nauseating. The charade was almost over, and I was finding it harder and harder to pretend.

"So you like red wine and vintage Ferraris. What kind of woman do you enjoy, Galasso?"

His name hissed through my teeth, a threat he was too inebriated to notice.

"Smooth," he said, like the pervert he was. "Young and sweet. Ask any real man, he'll tell you the same."

I waited until his chuckles settled and then slowly got up out of my chair. "Come, let us go to the car."

Galasso stumbled getting up but smacked Carmine's hand when he tried to help, muttering a curse under his breath as he moved forward when I waved him down the hall ahead of me.

"I like them with eyes like a doe's, wide and lovely brown," I told him conversationally as we walked slowly down the winding, dark corridor carved into the ground. "Long dark hair soft as mink, and *fast*. So fast, you cannot catch them if you give chase."

In front of me Galasso missed a step ascending to the next room and stilled, shoulders hunching slightly.

"Do you know such a girl, Signore Galasso?" I asked softly as I stepped too closely behind him, looming over his shorter frame. "A *cerbiatta* so enchanting you could not stop yourself from trying to hunt her down."

"I don't," he argued until he felt the tip of the hunting knife in my hand pressed hard enough to draw a bead of blood, as red as our shared wine, against his neck. "H-how did you know?"

"Because that little fawn stumbled into the path of an even bigger predator as she fled from you."

"You can have her!" he almost shouted, the words bouncing off the close walls. "I-I didn't even touch her."

"Oh, but I think you did. I think you touched her hip and then her ankle. I *know* you wanted to touch a lot more than that. Did you never learn, Galasso, that all women are too good for the likes of you? And unluckily for you, this woman in particular is so far above your thick head that now you must lose it for attempting to keep her for yourself."

The door opened before Galasso so quickly, he didn't have time to orient himself before I was shoving him over the ledge onto the black tarp Renzo had laid across the floor. The older man fell to his knees with a wailing moan for help.

Of course, there was no help to be had.

He'd trespassed into my underworld, where I was judge, jury, and executioner. Some capos relegated the blood work to their soldiers, but not me.

Especially not now.

Before Galasso could straighten from his unbalanced lean, I was on him. My fists were slightly sore from the beating I had given the leather bag in my basement, but that did not numb their efficacy at all.

One strike to the side of his head, already muddled by the drugs I'd slipped into the wine.

Another to his broken nose when I flipped him over and straddled his torso.

A trio to the cheeks—left, right, left—like the number of kisses Italians bestowed for good luck.

I thought of Guinevere alone in a foreign country, helpless and vulnerable on the side of the road, desperate for aid that came in the shape of this man beneath my knees. I thought of the half-moon smile and the low-lidded gaze peeking out beneath long lashes as she smiled shyly at me and the surprising edge of her bladed tongue.

Slowly, methodically, with an audience of three, I beat Galasso Pagano to death.

And when I was done, I carved "*stupratore*" into his forehead with the edge of my knife and watched as Ludo lifted the body in his gloved hands to transfer it to my vintage Ferrari waiting in the back alley, driven there by Carmine. He would take them into the countryside and stage a car crash somewhere deep in the valley. With his blood alcohol content high thanks to the drugs and the wine, there would be no doubt the accident was of Galasso's own making.

Except for those letters across his forehead deeming him a rapist.

The police would not have enough to make a case for homicide, but those who lurked in the unlawful shadows would know a message had been sent from the Gentleman of the Camorra, and they'd live in fear of receiving it themselves.

Do not fuck with me or mine.

When I'd decided that Guinevere was mine, I was not sure and didn't linger on. The point was, it had happened, and I wasn't the kind of man to worry about why.

CHAPTER SEVEN

Guinevere

I sat for all of sixty seconds on the edge of the bed Raffa had lent me in his Florentine palace, feeling confused and downtrodden by his sudden cold dismissal after a lovely day together, before I told myself to stop being an *idiota*.

Raffa may have rejected whatever bond I'd felt growing between us, tenuous but sticky like the first tendrils of a spider's web, but that didn't mean all of Florence wasn't waiting outside these doors for me to explore. I had money (from Raffa) and clothes (also from Raffa), so what was stopping me from setting off on my own adventure?

Raffa, really, or the thought of him.

After such a short time, I shouldn't have been able to factor him into my Italian fantasies so easily, but dreams floated across my consciousness like scenes from a much-loved film. Twirling in that field of poppies, in that dress he seemed to love, only to tumble into his strong arms, the two of us then crushing the delicate blooms beneath our bodies as we had sex in the grass. Sucking aged Modena balsamic off his thumb while we shared a meal in the city, and laughing with him when he teased me for enjoying everything with a little too much enthusiasm.

Exploring alone seemed desaturated now, but I wouldn't let my trip be derailed by a moody Italian.

So I grabbed the big raffia YSL bag Maria Lucia had thrust into my hands at one point that morning, along with the thick handful of euro notes Raffa had given me, and set off to take in the city.

Just as I was opening the front door, Martina appeared, silent and terrifying with a cleaver, of all things, in one hand.

"Going somewhere?" she asked with a raised brow.

I eyed the knife and swallowed. "Yes, I thought I'd check out the city because I've been cooped up indoors for too long. I'm sick of waiting around for adventure to come to me."

For some reason, this seemed highly amusing to her. "*Si, capisco.* Have fun, then."

"Do you have any suggestions for a nice place to grab dinner?" I asked after a brief hesitation.

"Where are you headed?"

"I want to see the Duomo," I admitted, a little sheepish because I felt like such a tourist admitting I wanted to see the most famous site in the city.

But Martina only nodded. "Of course, why don't you try Trattoria Umberto? It's on the way to the Duomo, across the river. Eat first and see the Duomo for the first time under the lights. Something tells me you will like it better at night."

I wasn't so sure about that. Walking around Florence after dark made me apprehensive after my encounter with Galasso, even though I'd looked up safety in Florence at least a dozen times before I'd left Michigan. It was safe to walk through the center at night, even as a lone woman, as long as I stuck to the main thoroughfares, which would be thick with tourists. I just had to watch my belongings and stay away from dark corners.

Which was easier said than done, really, when I'd always been drawn inexplicably but inexorably to the shadows.

I thanked Martina, ignoring her manic grin and the gleam of the cleaver, and pushed into the hot evening air. It was thick and stagnant, but I could smell garlic and cooking meat from the little restaurant down the street, and on cue my stomach rumbled.

As I headed toward the Arno and the famous Ponte Vecchio, my phone buzzed in my purse. I pulled it out to see the screen lit with two missed calls and three text messages, one from my mother and two from my father.

I chewed on my lower lip as I scrolled them.

Dad: Why haven't you called? I know you said you were sick, but surely you're better now.

Dad: Guinevere Luisa Stone, if you do not give me proof of life in the next 24 hours, I will be on the next flight to Paris to find you.

Mom: He means it.

Damn.

I'd been texting them almost every day, except those few days when I was so sick and concussed I could barely open my eyes, and they still worried about me. I was twenty-three years old with a master's degree, and they still couldn't stop worrying.

As I hesitated, another text came in.

Mom: Are you taking your medicine? Don't forget, the humidity will dehydrate you quicker than you're used to!

My sigh unwound like a spool of thread over my tongue. I looked around and saw a building that could pass for something in Paris. It made my chest ache to perpetuate this lie to my parents, the first of my life, but it also felt necessary. A rebellion against a totalitarian parenthood. I smiled into my camera phone and took a photo.

Jinx: I'm alive and well if a little pale from being stuck inside. Don't worry about me if I don't check in every day. I missed a whole week to sickness. I want to soak it all in!

I sent the message and the photo, then resolutely stuffed my phone deep into my purse and quickened my pace as if I could leave the past and my reality back in Michigan in the dust.

A moment later, my worries faded to nothing as I took in the bustling, stunning sight of Ponte Vecchio ahead of me. The famous bridge was built up on either side with stores, most of them tourist traps, I knew from my research, but the effect was still unlike anything I'd ever seen. Tourists milled between the narrow bridge walls, looking at overpriced jewelry and licking fast-melting cones of vibrant gelato.

A giggle bubbled up in my throat as I took my first steps onto the bridge, and even when a tall man bumped into me, I just beamed up at him in response.

It hit me all at once, a week after I'd arrived.

I was *here*.

I'd made it.

Five weeks in Italy stretched out before me like a red carpet lined with bright lights. I was so excited it was hard not to get ahead of myself and imagine how I might feel when I returned stateside to my predictable life and boring self after what had already been a fairly life-changing trip.

But that was a future-me problem.

In that moment, I had nothing to worry about but luxuriating in the setting and finding authentic Toscana food to fill my hungry belly.

I took some time to look through one of the arches in the middle of the bridge with a fabulous view of the Arno. The sun was a huge golden medallion kissing the edge of the horizon, the river blushed pink from the embrace, and the sky tinged tangerine. I took a photo, but I knew nothing would ever capture this experience for what it was.

Total freedom and the realization of a dream I'd first conceived of in a hospital bed as a child.

"I'm here," I whispered, perhaps a little foolishly, to the spirit of my sister I imagined I carried with me on my travels. "I made it, Gemma. And I think you'd be proud of me."

I let the swell of tourists push me gently forward over the bridge onto the opposite bank and then turned right instead of heading straight to the Duomo. According to my phone, Trattoria Umberto was a little restaurant with rave reviews off the beaten track deep in the Santa Croce neighborhood.

There were other restaurants I had in the typed itinerary on my phone (I'd lost my physical laminated copy along with my suitcase), but I was trying to be more impulsive and a little less uptight about everything. Control had always been my favorite method to combat the uncertainty of being ill. When your own body acted against you, it was easy to cave into helplessness, and while I wasn't immune from bouts of rage and frustration, being organized and disciplined was its own kind of balm.

Besides, I figured a local would know the best places to eat, and I was ready to make a fool of myself over a proper plate of Italian pasta.

The restaurant was nothing special from the outside. A wooden overhang with the restaurant name written in golden paint and two small windows filled with hanging legs of prosciutto to either side of the door. There wasn't a line, but when I entered the dark, fairly cool interior, it was packed with diners, most of them speaking fluid, loud Italian.

I grinned at the bustle, noting the crooked art and photographs on the walls, the way the building seemed to be a collection of varying rooms at slightly different elevations, the wood dark and the beams exposed.

It was gorgeous.

A curvy older woman with iron-gray hair and sharp creases beside her mouth bustled up to me and asked me something in rapid-fire Italian.

"A little slower?" I asked in my own timid Italian.

Her smile softened a bit, but she didn't switch to English, which I was grateful for. "Table for one? We only have space in the back."

"Yes, please."

She nodded briskly and turned to weave her way efficiently through the tables. Even though I wanted to hesitate over the fragrant plates of food at the tables and eavesdrop on some of the louder conversations, I followed quickly so I wouldn't lose her in the maze of rooms. She dropped me off at a table in the very back where the room opened up to allow for a second wooden bar and a small band playing live music in the opposite corner.

"*Bene?*" she asked me, already setting down the menu.

I nodded, turning my smile on her. "*Grazie mille, Signora.*"

She laughed, a short, sharp exhalation. "It is my job."

Within moments of my sitting down, an older server swept up to my table with a charming smile and exaggerated politeness.

"Signorina," he said in Italian. "I am deeply pleased to welcome you here tonight."

I laughed, charmed despite his obviousness. "Thank you. I'm really happy to be here."

"American?" he asked in English. "Ah, but you look Italiana to me!"

"My father," I explained. "He was born somewhere in the area."

"Of course, this is why your beauty caught my eye from across the room," he said shamelessly, but there was a twinkle in his eye that said he was just having fun.

It felt good after Raffa's obvious rejection to have a little admiration.

"I'm sure you tell that to all the ladies," I countered.

"Not her," he assured me, gesturing to the woman who had seated me as she power walked through the room.

I muffled my laugh behind one hand, but the server didn't bother to hide his.

"I'm Guinevere," I said, because it felt wrong not to introduce myself somehow.

"Nicola. Now, what can I get you to drink?"

"What do you suggest?"

His face lit up even more, creasing the skin beside his eyes and cheeks handsomely. "Will you let me have the chef prepare a true Toscana meal for you tonight? We will start with a beautiful bottle of Sangiovese and a *panzanella*. It is bread salad, very good."

"Just a glass, please," I corrected, because I had to limit my alcohol intake as much as possible with my kidney transplant and condition. Transplants typically lasted twelve to fifteen years if you took good care of them, and I didn't want to have any more surgeries than necessary in my lifetime.

"*D'accordo.* You have allergies?" When I shook my head, he clapped his hands together and whisked my menu away without my having opened it. "*Bene, bene.* Prepare yourself for culinary delights."

I was still laughing when he spun away from the table toward the bar.

Even though it was my first time taking myself for dinner, I found I wasn't embarrassed at all. The room was too filled with happy people and the vibrancy of live music, cliché jazz crooners that reminded everyone of Italy and made my foot tap along to the familiar beats. I wasn't alone much, anyway. Nicola lingered by the table between courses and sent over some of the other servers when they weren't busy to keep me company. Every dish came with an explanation about its origins—*panzanella*, a good use for stale, leftover bread, used by farmers for generations; potato tortellini drenched in a butter-sage sauce; and Tuscany's famous pecorino cheese.

By the time Nicola insisted on serving me a plate of tiramisu on the house, along with biscotti and a glass of Vin Santo, a sweet, nutty dessert wine, I felt like I'd roll through the streets back to Raffa's.

I was midlaughter when the hairs on the back of my neck stood on end, an electrical current pulsing over my skin. My hand stilled halfway to my mouth, my glass of sweet wine arrested as I searched the room for danger.

I found it staring out from the golden-brown eyes of a man I'd come to know too well in such a short time.

Raffa stood in the open archway, torso turned toward the hostess who had ushered me, but his head tilted my way, eyes fixed on me so intensely I felt physically restrained by his scrutiny.

"Guinevere, *va bene?*" Nicola asked, blocking my view of Raffa as he bent closer, his features suffused with concern.

"I-I just thought I saw someone I knew," I admitted, lowering my slightly trembling glass to the table without taking a sip.

But when Nicola moved, Raffa was gone, and I wondered if some part of my wistful imagination had conjured him out of thin air.

I turned my attention back to the live band and noticed a man with some friends at a table near an empty space around the musicians. It was as if he'd been waiting for me to look over for some time, because his brows lifted and his mouth pulled wide into a generous smile.

He was handsome, but I couldn't help thinking of Raffa, with his dark hair threaded through with hints of copper and those metallic eyes glinting as cool as bronze coins. He was so beautiful, it hurt to think of him as anything but a dream, something that would dissolve as soon as I tried to touch it.

But my skin tingled over my left breast, where his fingers had made contact earlier that day. I was still wearing that same dress, the bows tied neatly by his hand.

When the stranger came over, I wasn't surprised, but it did shock and warm me to see Nicola hovering with a frown, as if he was protective of me.

"You look as if you want to dance," the stranger announced, leaning a hip into my table so he could beam down at me comfortably. He spoke English with a mild accent that seemed more French than Italian. "I thought I had better ask you."

I forced thoughts of Raffa away and tried to think of Gemma, who could flirt and enjoy men with a kind of irreverent joy I'd always been envious of.

"Was that a question?" I teased.

His smile loosened into something more genuine, and he offered his hand. "It was, if you'll say yes?"

Instead of answering, I pushed out of my seat and took his warm, smooth palm. He led me to the empty space before the band and held me dramatically at the end of his arm before spinning me into his arms, his chest to my back.

It was intimate for strangers. Intimate for *me*. I couldn't remember if I'd ever been held like that before and decided I hadn't. It made me feel sad and determined in equal measure. As much as my instincts told me to pull away, to hide from the many eyes turned to us over their dinner plates and fold myself against the wall like a preserved flower, I made myself stay inside the embrace.

I'd come to Italy on a quest to find myself, and wasn't romance the ultimate adventure?

I thought about offering him my name, but I liked the mystery of a dance with a stranger, of being nameless and mysterious, how I'd always imagined Italian women to be, instead of the plain and straightforward American I was.

Before I could even swing my hips with his in time with the music, the warm bracket of his body disappeared from behind me, and my arms were left wrapped around my torso, hugging my body as if in consolation.

I stood there for one interminable moment, alone on the dance floor in front of an entire restaurant of people, frozen in humiliation.

Just as I turned to see what had happened to my dance partner, he pressed against my back, his arms sliding around my waist to pin me even more aggressively to his front.

When I wiggled, trying to find some space, a familiar whisper wafted hot across my neck, breaking my flesh into goose bumps. "*Placati, cerbiatta.* It is only the man you wished to dance with from the very start."

A shiver sluiced down my body like a bucket of cool water dropped over my head.

"Raffa," I breathed, even though I meant it to be an accusation. "What are you doing?"

"It should be obvious," he drawled, spinning me away and then pulling me gently, inexorably against his body so we were sewn tight from chest to thighs. He was so much taller than me, even in my heeled sandals, that I had to tip my head back and expose my neck to look into his coolly amused gaze. "We are dancing."

"Why?" I demanded, ignoring the way his eyes dipped down to the line of my throat and darkened noticeably. "A few hours ago, you couldn't get away from me fast enough."

"A few hours ago, I did not think you were foolish enough to entice a room of Florentine men to seduce you."

"Don't be ridiculous," I snapped, trying to pull away from the artful way his body led mine in an easy series of steps around the small dance floor. No one had joined us, but I wasn't surprised. The way Raffa held me was deeply possessive, his large palm pressed to the bottom curve of my spine, his bigger body curled over mine as if he could shield me from view. As if this dance was private and not an exhibition. If he could not make them cease to exist, he would pretend anyway.

"Men have been circling you like carrion all night." In the low golden lights of the restaurant, Raffa seemed like a bronze statue come to life, his dark edges softened and blurred, his skin a warm olive.

"Are you saying I'm dead meat?" I demanded, trying to pull away using all my force.

I only succeeded in tripping slightly, but Raffa dipped me seamlessly, as if it was intended, and rolled me up and across into his opposite arm before carrying on.

"I am saying you could be, if you bat those obscenely beautiful lashes at the wrong man. You are not in America anymore, little fawn. You must pay attention to your surroundings."

"The most dangerous man in this room seems to be the one forcing me to dance against my will," I countered.

"Like my little *bambolina*?"

His little doll.

"I am not a fawn or a doll," I said between my teeth, tossing my heavy hair over my shoulder as sweat started to bead down my back from the closeness of our bodies. "I have *teeth*."

I was surprised by the gentle amusement in his smile, even though I should have found it condescending. The hand clasping mine placed it on his chest so his fingers were free to glide up my bare arm, tease my shoulder, and slide up my neck until his thumb trailed over my mouth. "Yes, but no one has taught you how to use them. Though I have wondered what it would feel like to be bitten by you."

His thumb dipped between my lips to test the edge of my front teeth and then retreated before I could remember myself.

"Dream on," I scoffed, but I knew the flush warming the skin of my cheeks and chest would give away the truth.

I'd never been so turned on in my life.

The way he touched me, as if he had a right to but was still a little wary, coaxing and respectful simultaneously. I realized that I didn't have to try to be atavistic with him or charming; our flirtation was as sharp edged and pretty as a medieval blade, but it was still flirtation, and with Raffa it came easy.

Too easy, even.

The music swelled to a crescendo, and Raffa pulled me into a quick rhythm, the steady rattle of a tambourine snakelike, a dangerous temptation woven through the staccato song. Raffa moved me faster, twirling me under his arm, tugging me this way and that so seamlessly and forcefully it felt as if I was flowing like a river between rocks. When the music came to a crashing halt, Raffa tugged me hard toward him, and I allowed impulse to push my hands into his shoulders as he gripped my hips and lifted me into the air. A giddy, breathless laugh escaped me as he spun me in the air, and I let my arms rise like sails, wishing foolishly that I could float there forever.

Applause exploded into the quivering silence left by the song, some diners calling out "*Bravi!*" and "*Ben fatto!*"

But everything was muted in the rushing of blood in my ears as Raffa slowly, inch by excruciating inch, lowered my body to the floor, pressing it intimately against his own. I was damp and panting, but so was he, and it intensified the smell of him. That rich, oak-and-smoke scent I dragged into my heaving lungs like a drug. My mind seemed to swim, high off him the way I'd never been off anything before.

I wasn't prepared for a man like him.

Raffa stared down into my face, skin glistening, and I realized when his brows lifted in surprise that I had spoken aloud.

"*È appropriato,*" he murmured. "Because I have no context for a girl like you, and therefore, it seems, I have no defenses against you."

"You don't need to defend against me. I am just a *cerbiatta*, remember?" I taunted, but the self-mockery hit too close to home.

Just a fawn, common, foolish, untried.

"Ah, but even a fawn is a wild animal and dangerous when provoked," he reminded me, using two fingers to push a lock of sweaty hair away from my forehead. "So I had best not provoke you."

Too late, I thought.

I am provoked.

You have awakened the beast inside me that was always hungry for more, eating at my bones when I wouldn't feed it anything of value.

And now it had found something—someone—to sink its teeth into, and I was worried what kind of woman I could become if I gave in to that ever-gnawing need to devour.

Not just Raffa, bones and all, but life itself.

It was as I was contemplating this that I noticed the spot of red on his white shirt collar. At first, I thought it was lipstick, and feminine rage scoured through me, scorched earth in its wake. I didn't pause to consider the vehemence of my jealousy because the next second it occurred to me it was *blood*.

"You have blood on your shirt," I said.

And Raffa?

He smiled that movie-star villain's grin that curled the sides of his mouth and bared his sharp teeth in a way that felt like a threat.

"I had red meat for dinner," he explained casually, but there was something buried in his tone that dared me to dig deep and excavate the secrets hidden there like bones. "I like it still bleeding."

"Practically still beating," I joked, but his face was solemn when he pulled me toward my abandoned table with my hand tucked into the crook of his arm.

"No," he said. "Very, very dead."

CHAPTER EIGHT

Raffa

"Haven't seen you let go like that in a while, boss," Ludo mentioned the next morning as I was sitting on the terrace, eating the breakfast Servio had laid out for me.

It was early, the sun still a pale, unsaturated yellow leaking through the streets of Florence, highlighting the locals who populated San Niccolò and guarded it zealously from the tourists across the Arno. I watched a teenage couple press into each other in an empty doorway, kissing like fools and dressed in disarray as if they were both making their way home after a night of shared debauchery.

I had not even kissed her, yet I felt the way I did the morning after a night of particularly feral fucking. Energized and exhausted all at once. I had not slept more than a handful of hours after we returned home from the restaurant. Murder and dancing with a shockingly erotic slip of a girl were a potent cocktail that left me buzzing inside my skin, as if it were too tight to contain my insides.

I lay awake for hours, imagining all the ways I wanted to have Guinevere Stone and all the reasons I shouldn't.

The former far outweighed the latter.

Because the only real reason I could cling to was that having a holiday romance with a well-known mafioso was dangerous, even if she did not know I was *nella mafia*.

But looking into those wide eyes as rich as the earth after fresh rain, I saw too much trust and innocent curiosity to let the ruinous longings in my chest taint such a thing of beauty.

"That asshole deserved it," I told Ludo finally with a shrug, as if I hadn't been filled with rage as I beat into Galasso's ugly mug, leaving it irrevocably uglier than I had found it.

"You know I don't care much about the why of things," Ludo admitted. "But what did the poor bastard do?"

I cracked the top off a soft-boiled egg with one strike of my spoon. "He tried to take a woman against her will."

The sound Ludo made was lupine, a snarling kind of whine like he was both distressed and enraged by the idea. This was why he, Renzo, Martina, and Carmine were my closest *soldati*. They had a moral compass; it just didn't point to the usual true north. We had internalized rules, a code adopted from the Camorra but skewed by our judgments.

No harming women or children. No stealing from the old.

These two tenets alone were almost unheard of in our world. The 'Ndrangheta were infamous for abusing their women, but it happened across every clan, and the Mafia made tens of millions of euros every year off scamming the elderly.

We stuck to what I was comfortable with: agromafia business, money laundering, and transportation of every kind of illegal good. These activities were relatively easy to hide or fob off as someone else's error if we were ever caught, though that had only happened once, in the beginning, when one of our shipments was seized by the Pietra clan on the coast of Pisa. Barrels of cocaine in shipping crates of textiles imported from the United States.

We had blamed it on a scapegoat in the Pietra clan itself and never smuggled goods in that way again.

We had moved on to small electric submarines that came into port at night nearly undetected.

This was the modern Mafia. We avoided warfare in the streets and bragging, obvious symbols of our trade—such as the color red or gaudy gold jewelry—and lived instead like quiet, officious white-collar gentlemen. We rarely met in large groups and communicated through codes that were rewritten every year to keep the Direzione Investigativa Antimafia (DIA) from deciphering our inner workings if they were ever successful at hacking our systems.

So it was not a surprise that Ludo took umbrage at Galasso without having to understand the reason I'd wanted him killed.

That was the kind of trust and loyalty you could not buy with money.

Its only currency was blood.

And once, as a boy, I had saved Ludo from a group of teenage thugs much older than us who decided to attack him for being ungainly and slow thinking. They did not realize, as I had from the start, that a slow processor did not equal stupidity.

Ludo was worth more than fifteen other capos from my territory.

"I would have beat his face in with a hammer," Ludo told me earnestly, "if I had known."

I waved away the sentiment. "I know, *fratello*, but this was for me to do."

"Because of the girl?" he asked, and when I raised my brows at him as I sipped from my double espresso, he grinned lopsidedly. "Renzo and Carmine watched you in the restaurant. They said you put on quite a show. They said she was pretty like something in one of your expensive paintings."

I would not mention that I had already searched local auction houses to see if there were any worthwhile paintings of Guinevere's namesake for sale. It was disgustingly sentimental, but I knew I had to have one for the day when she would leave. If I could not have her, the house could benefit from a symbol of her beauty and innocence.

"She is captivating," I admitted, staring into the dark coffee the same luxurious shade as her eyes and all that heavy hair. "She makes me curious."

"About her?"

"Yes," I mused, almost to myself. "And about me."

"*Buongiorno*," her light voice called from the kitchen a moment before Guinevere appeared in the doorway, dressed in a loose white linen shift dress that seemed precariously close to falling off her shoulders and exposing her entirely. When she turned slightly to face Ludo, I saw the low dip exposing half her unblemished back.

My mouth went dry as dust.

"*Buongiorno*," Ludo greeted her, getting up from his lean against the balustrade to cross to her, offering a big, square-fingered hand to her. "Ludovico. Call me Ludo."

"Guinevere," she echoed with a jaunty smile, her hand entirely engulfed in his. "Call me Guinevere."

"You don't like Gwen?" he asked, dropping her hand and extending his toward the empty chair across from me.

"Not much," she confessed, walking almost on tiptoe over to her seat. I had noticed she had a way of doing that and wondered if she had been a ballerina or if it was simply to add some height to her short frame. "My parents always corrected anyone who called me that grow-ing up, and my full name kind of stuck."

"What about Vera?" I asked casually as I plucked a ripe plum from the fruit bowl and cut it neatly into segments with a sharp knife. She watched me intently, tracing the line of the blade as her tongue traced her lips, as if she was seduced by it.

"No one has ever called me that," she admitted, sitting on her knees on the chair cushion so she could lean across the table to grab the freshly squeezed orange juice. "Is it a popular name in Italy?"

"No," I mused. "It is mostly used as a word. It means 'true.' I thought it was fitting."

She paused, arm extended, heavy pitcher wobbling slightly in her grip, as she stared at me for a weighted moment.

When she moved again, she poured the juice so quickly it splashed over her fingers, and I had the frustrating joy of watching her lick them clean.

"I'll allow it, then," she decided with an impish grin.

I inclined my head, but it only made her laugh.

"You would have continued to call me that anyway, wouldn't you?"

It was my turn to grin, a curling lift of one side of my mouth.

She clucked her tongue, but when I handed her the bowl, she accepted the fruit I'd cut up for her. I kept one piece for myself, but she leaned across the table to make a swipe for it, so I held it out between two fingers for her to take. I pulled it back when she tried to grab it with her fingers and lifted a brow in silent command.

She rolled her eyes, but there was a tiny grin tucked into the edge of her mouth when she leaned forward on her knees to grasp it between her teeth. Her lips closed over my thumb, plush and damp.

I wanted to see them wrapped around so much more than just my fingers.

"This is how they eat fruit in America?" Ludo asked in his usual monotone way that made it difficult for strangers to understand his sense of humor.

But Guinevere laughed lightly and sank back on her heels, happily munching on the fruit from the bowl. "Sometimes, between friends."

"Is that what we are now?" I asked, thinking about the fact that I had never danced with a friend the way I had with her last night.

"I think people who dance together so well must be friends," she quipped, looking at me with an air of deliberation. "What kind of dance was that, by the way? It seemed traditional, somehow."

"It was, a bit. Not the way we danced it, but the song. It is the 'Tarantella Napoletana' from Campania, where my family is originally from."

I ignored Ludo's eyes on me, hoping he would leave it alone, but of course he felt compelled to add, "It is a courtship dance."

I scoffed lightly as I took the last sip of my coffee, but Guinevere's smile was radiant as she looked into her bowl of fruit.

Why was her shyness so beguiling? Was it that every emotion seemed purer because I knew it had to fight through her natural reserve to shine through? That it felt hard won when so much in my life had come easy?

"Stefania won't like it," Carmine said as he swept onto the terrace in a three-piece brown suit with his hair carefully slicked back from his forehead, emphasizing his widow's peak. He grabbed an apricot from the bowl on the table without even looking at Guinevere and hopped up to sit on the stone balustrade. "She'll have heard of the American now and already be plotting."

"Do not be dramatic, Carm," I ordered. "I know you like life to mirror those absurd dramas you watch on daytime television, but this is not that."

Ludo grunted. "Stefania makes those women look like sheep compared to a wolf."

He was not wrong, unfortunately. And there was some merit to her aggression. As the daughter of a Camorra capo in Lombardy, she had been raised around men with blood inked into their skin. It was not fair to assume she would remain untainted by it. It was not right to want her to be either.

But her aggression seemed hollow, a thin armor over an abyss of insecurity that could be easily manipulated.

She did not interest me.

Across from me, Guinevere had lost her smile and was staring into her empty bowl of fruit as if searching for answers.

"I would like to go check into my apartment today," she said abruptly. "I emailed Signora Verga that I was ill, but I'm better now, and it's time I got things in order."

"Order?" Carmine laughed. "Aren't you on vacation?"

"Yes."

"Well then, what does order have to do with it?" He spoke English well because his father was a Canadian who had moved to the region years ago after meeting his mother while she was studying abroad in Halifax.

Guinevere sniffed at him in such a haughty, catlike way, I could not help but smile.

"I want to be sure I get to everything I want to do. I'm only here for six weeks, and I wasted one of them being sick and in bed."

"Ignore Carmine. It is what I do. What is on your list, then?" I asked, disregarding her original entreaty.

For whatever reason, I did not want her to leave the shelter of my roof. Even if I had convinced myself to resist her temptation, I was not immune to this strange, celestial connection between us. It felt like *fortuna*, like fate. The hand of some greater force playing us both like *burattini*.

I could not stop wondering if I was meant to know her.

There was this inarguable sense that I had known her before. Or, maybe, that I had been waiting for her all this time without knowing it.

Could a stranger feel so immediately like a friend?

"I want to visit a winery, climb the steps of the Duomo, watch the sunset from Piazzale Michelangelo, spend hours at the Uffizi, eat my weight in gelato, explore the Etruscan ruins at Volterra, visit Siena and San Gimignano and Montepulciano—"

"*Bene, bene, basta!*" Carmine said, laughing as he held up his hands in surrender. "You have a lot to see and do. I agree."

"It's a good thing you have Raffaele," Martina announced as she joined us on the terrace in her workout kit, glistening with sweat from her morning exercise. Renzo followed closely behind, wet with perspiration too. "He is the best tour guide."

Carmine snorted orange juice out his nose, and Ludo barked out a laugh.

"I hate to ferry out-of-towners around," I admitted to Guinevere, who focused on smearing a gob of Nutella on top of a cream-filled Ringo cookie.

"Well, no pressure. I came here alone, and I am happy to travel alone. You don't need to be forced into my company just because you hit me with your car."

Renzo laughed into the back of his hand.

"*Di classe*," Carmine drawled.

Smooth.

"It is the least I could do, I suppose, after hitting Bambi," I teased with a flash of a smile that bared my teeth.

I'd noticed that whenever I did that, a flush spilled down her front like spilled wine. It was no different now, the white of her dress emphasizing her blush.

"I wouldn't want to bother you," she insisted between her teeth, her gumption fighting through her conservatism.

I felt as I had when I was a boy pulling a girl's pigtails, giddy and mean.

"Well, I think we are past that, do you not?"

She glared at me.

I glared right back.

Until Martina laughed and clapped her hands. "*Perfetto*. Today is a good day to show her the wines. You promised Imelda you would visit Fattoria Casa Luna today, anyway. Guinevere can visit while you do business."

"Fine," I agreed.

"Can we swing by my apartment first?" Guinevere asked, standing up and fruitlessly trying to brush the wrinkles from her dress.

No.

"Fine," I repeated, colder than before.

She bit the bottom of her lip, gaze skirting mine before she made her way inside.

My *soldati* barely waited until she was through the kitchen before bursting into laughter. Even Ludo.

"She is stunning, boss, I'll give you that," Carmine said through his chuckles, wiping at his leaking eyes.

"Evil," I told them in Italian. "Swine."

"Genius," Martina quipped, pointing to herself. "Matchmaker. Just promise me when you marry the girl I can be your best man."

"I believe you all have business to get to? I want to know who the hell this San Marco is by the time I return tonight. And Ludo? Did you find any of Guinevere's things at Galasso's residence?"

He shook his head. "Only a photo of her family, I think. Parents and sister."

I frowned, surprised that the *bastardo* had sold or thrown out everything that wasn't of value from her car but kept a silly photo.

"Did you take his hard drive?"

Ludo only blinked dispassionately at me, because of course he had.

"Tell me what you find tonight," I said as I stood from the table. "He mentioned Leo's name. Someone call him and find out how well he knew the *stronzo*."

"Aye, aye, boss," Martina agreed. "Now, you have fun on your date!"

I rolled my eyes and went into the cool depths of the house to get ready for my outing, ignoring the way they started gossiping about me before I'd even left earshot.

"Where is the Ferrari?" Guinevere asked when I took her to the garage and led her toward my matte silver Bugatti Chiron.

She eyed the Maserati, the two Lamborghinis, and the Ducati motorcycle almost suspiciously and muttered under her breath, "You could feed a starving nation with the money from these cars."

"Unfortunately, I do not have an altruistic bone in my body," I said, unashamed of my excess.

It was not something Italians were made to feel guilty about like they seemed to be in puritanical-leaning America. I worked hard for my fortune and ill-gotten gains. Why should I feel embarrassed about it?

"You helped me," she reminded me as we got into the leather-scented interior. In the deep bucket seat, her dress rode up to scandalous heights, revealing that while she was short, she had long legs for her proportions.

I wanted to suck bruises into the tender, pale skin of her inner thighs like stepping stones leading toward her sweet *figa*.

"Exception, not rule," I said as the car rumbled to life and I pulled briskly out of the garage and through the open gate into gentle mid-morning traffic. "As you seem to be for all my rules."

"Is that a compliment or a complaint?"

"Both," I decided, sliding a look at her to see the way she bit the edge of her smile.

"So the Ferrari. What happened to it?" she asked again, much to my annoyance.

"You, if you will remember that night last week when you hip checked it."

She rolled her eyes so exaggeratedly I worried they would get stuck that way. "Har har. Was the damage really so bad? I mean, I did have a mild concussion, but I remember it looking fine, and we drove it yesterday."

"Fine is not perfect."

"And it's perfect or nothing for Raffaele Romano?" she asked, pronouncing my name like a local.

It shouldn't have been so attractive, the sound of my name in her mouth. But she rolled her *r*'s as if tasting fine wine, savoring the taste of each syllable.

"You say that like it is a bad thing."

She shrugged in my periphery as I followed the direction system to the address she'd given me across the Arno for her rented apartment.

"You must find yourself disappointed a lot," she said, her gaze pressed to the side of my face the way her fingers were the other day to the glass separating her from Florence's wonders. As if my secrets were just under the skin.

"My definition of *perfect* is different from yours, perhaps. To me, it does not mean 'flawless.' It means 'enticing,' so vibrant you cannot help but find it beautiful, flaws and all."

"And what would you consider a flaw?"

I hummed over that for a moment because too many came to mind, but I did not think she would enjoy my flippancy.

"Stupidity. Willful ignorance. A lack of loyalty to family and friends."

She flinched as if I had hit her, turning toward the window so I only caught a fleeting glimpse of the self-recrimination on her face.

Uncharacteristically, I did not know what to say. I had not been deliberately insulting as I sometimes meant to be when we bantered, and I was strangely . . . unsettled that my words had hurt her.

The tension in the car mounted as I maneuvered us silently through traffic to the other side of the city.

"*Chi sta bene da solo, sta bene con tutti,*" I said finally, pushing the words out into the dense quiet between us. "Have you heard of this saying?"

"No," she said softly without looking at me.

"It means something like 'If you feel good about yourself, you will feel good about everyone, and they will feel the same way about you in return.'" When she didn't fill my pause, I sighed. "I did not intend to insult you, Guinevere, and I am sorry that I did nonetheless. I am sorrier, though, that you were so ready to believe I would. That I *should* even."

"You were the one who called me an *idiota*," she pointed out with a sharp look from the corner of her eye.

I wanted to smile at her show of teeth but refrained. "That was before I knew you. Now I do not think you are stupid or willfully ignorant or disloyal. Naive, certainly. New to Italian culture, clearly. But I cannot think poorly of you in any sense, *cerbiatta*, and I have only known you for a week. I shudder to think how grand my impression of you will become if I know you any longer."

She bit her lip to downplay her grin, but there was a noticeable shift in her energy, like sunshine slicing through a dense cloud.

"That was probably, in a very roundabout sort of way, the sweetest thing anyone has ever said about me," she confessed.

"You should find better company, then," I said mildly as we waited for the crowds of tourists to cross the street a block away from our destination.

"Sweet," she echoed softly, turning her pleased expression to the window.

Of course, no one in my life had ever called me sweet. Not even my mother or sisters, who adored me. Even as a boy I had been calculating and brutally honest. I could remember making Delfina cry on her first day of high school because I told her that her perm made her look like Valeria Golino's ugly sister.

Guinevere was the type of person to look for the good in everything. Even made men with very bad intentions. It didn't make her stupid exactly, but it did make her easy prey to dangerous men and poor decision-making.

This was especially evident when I pulled in front of the apartment building where she had rented a flat for her six-week summer vacation and found a group of three young men dealing drugs just to the left of the doorway. It wasn't surprising. Though there weren't any seriously unsafe areas in Florence proper, the street behind Fortezza da Basso was an open secret with locals who wanted to buy anything from pharmaceuticals to hard-core street drugs.

"Hey, people my age," Guinevere said happily, perking up from her lean against the window. "That's nice to know."

"If you like drugs, perhaps," I drawled, twisting to raise my brow at her. "You do not look like the average user, but maybe I was mistaken."

Her mouth dropped into a comical little O of shock. "They're dealing *drugs?*"

She whispered the last word as if she could get in trouble just for speaking it.

I was torn between hilarity and rage. "Guinevere, please tell me you were not raised in a convent."

Her frown was fierce, and she crossed her arms, unconsciously mimicking my own pose. "*No.* I grew up in a college town, so I'm aware that people do drugs. I've never seen a drug deal before."

Madonna santa, she was so young and unblemished.

So what did it say about me that I wanted to dirty her up with sin?

"Did you research this neighborhood before you booked the flat?"

The knot between her brows tightened. "Yes, Raffa. I'm not an idiot, as you yourself just announced. This area is safe."

"Says who? The internet?"

"I read like forty forums and blogs from locals," she retorted.

"Well, one of them should have mentioned this has become a popular spot for drug deals," I snapped. "With your self-proclaimed bad luck, how long do you think it will take for you to be in the wrong place at the wrong time?"

She rolled her eyes dramatically. "This is Florence. Compared to most other cities in the country, it has a really low crime rate. And don't even get me started on comparing it to big cities back home in the States. You're being silly."

"Silly?" I echoed.

"*Sì,*" she said with a sharp nod. "*Sciocco.*"

"She ridicules me in my own tongue," I murmured, once again shocked by her gumption. "You know, most women would thank me for looking out for them."

"Maybe you should spend the day with them instead." She smiled sweetly, tossed her hair over her shoulder, and got out of the car.

It gave me time to lock down my grin before I followed suit and joined her at the door to the flats.

"I can meet Signora Verga without your help," she groused.

I ignored her, but when the buzz sounded and the door unlocked, I did not immediately follow her into the building. After catching the door before it could close, I wedged a loose brick into the jamb and then turned to face the cluster of young men a few yards away.

They did not notice me approaching at first. Probably because they were high.

But when a skinhead caught sight of me, he glared and nudged his friends with his elbows.

"Hey, asshole," he called in Italian, thin chest puffed out, a fanny pack worn crossed over it in the style of trendy teenagers. "What the fuck do you want?"

It was an easy mistake to make. A young man thinking he could prove himself by throwing words like knives at a well-dressed civilian walking down the street. An easy mark for an unprovoked attack that would make him cool to his friends in crime.

Only I wasn't a civilian.

I was a camorrista, a *capo dei capi* of my territory.

I had the satisfaction of watching his bravado crack down the middle when I continued my quick, strong strides toward him. It crumbled completely when one of his friends turned, saw me, and gasped before muttering quickly, "*È il gentiluomo mafioso.*"

The Gentleman Mafioso.

Such a stupid nickname, but one my best friend had given to me the first time I killed a man in cold blood. It was my eighteenth birthday, and my father told me if I wanted to be allowed to leave the country for college, I had to prove my loyalty to the family.

And *nella mafia*, the only way to prove anything was to write it in blood.

To this day, I have no idea what the poor *bastardo* had done to cross Aldo Romano, but that was the point. A loyal member of the Camorra followed orders without needing context.

I was dragged out of bed at dawn by my father, still in boxers and bare feet as we crossed the courtyard into the rows of vines separating the main house from the barn. A man was waiting within, tied to a chair, wearing a stained, ruined suit that had once been worth a lot of money. My father's consigliere, Tonio, was there, and, shockingly, my best friend, Leo.

It was Leo, stern faced, who handed me the gun.

"Kill him," my father had ordered as he sat in a wooden chair at a table near the back wall set with a moka espresso maker and a hand-painted ceramic cup and saucer.

He proceeded to pour himself an espresso and ignore us entirely, looking over documents someone had left for him to peruse.

"You have to," Leo told me in a quiet murmur before Tonio reeled him to his side with a hand on his shoulder.

"Please," the man who had wronged my family begged as I stepped closer. He was much older than me, his skin sallow and flaccid from too much drink. There was a fine sheen of grease on his flesh from old sweat merging with new, and a dribble of blackening blood on his mouth. "Please, I have a family."

I could still remember the weight of the gun in my hand, how warm it was from Leo's grip before mine. I'd been taught to shoot almost as soon as I could walk, so it felt natural in my hand, the way a glove might feel to a sportsman.

Except this was the only sport I'd ever been trained at.

Before I killed him, I took the tie from around his neck. I loosened the knot and stuffed the Gucci silk inside his mouth so he'd stop his pleading.

It meant nothing to me because it meant nothing to Aldo and Tonio.

He thought I had the power to change his fate when I was already struggling to swim upstream against my own.

I took two steps back and shot him through the forehead, right between the eyes.

My father wasn't pleased.

"Too easy," he muttered in disgust as he narrowed his eyes at me. "What kind of message is this to send our enemies?"

To appease him, because I wanted to go back to the big house for breakfast with my mother and sisters, I yanked the hunting knife from *zio* Tonio's belt and carved a message into the dead man's forehead.

Traditore.

Traitor.

When Tonio, Leo, and I carefully staged his body back in his apartment, I took care to clean him up and set him perfectly behind his desk. Aside from the lurid red gouge marks in his forehead, he could have been sleeping.

Some reporter called the killing almost gentlemanly for a Mafia hit. Unfortunately, the moniker stuck.

"Good," I told the thugs as they tensed for flight, sensing a bigger predator in their midst. "You know who I am. So you will understand how serious I am when I say if any of you so much as look at the small brunette who just entered Signora Verga's apartments, I will skin you alive and then play mix and match with your flesh until you are each dressed in another man's face. Do you understand me?"

The skinhead's mouth had fallen open on the broken hinge of his jaw. "Yeah, yeah, man. No worries."

"D-do you need us to like . . . look out for her?" an acne-faced boy worked up the nerve to ask me.

I considered it for a moment and shrugged. "If you want to, it would not go unforgotten."

Though I was one fucking mishap away from telling Guinevere she was spending the next five weeks under my roof.

The kids stammered their agreement and skittered away with one wave of my hand. I shook my head as I made my way back to Verga's building and pushed through the door. Kids like that were usually prime pickings for *soldati*, but not in my outfit. We played sharp and smart, which meant teenage wannabe badasses were exempt from our ranks. I let Damiano pick them up in Naples and put them through the wringer before I ever thought about accepting them into the fold. The Romano family had more college graduates than a prep school. It was the key to our success and our subtlety.

The soft lilt of Guinevere's American accent reached me in the foyer, and I followed it up two flights of stairs to the open doorway of an apartment. The entire thing was visible from my position in the frame: a small kitchenette with a half fridge to the right, a tiny table for two, a lumpy blue love seat and ancient television with rabbit-ear antennae to the left, and a double bed with a brass headboard at the back of the room beside a hand-painted chest of drawers. The postage-stamp size, along with the lingering scent of heavy Middle Eastern spices from the shawarma place down the street, lent it a distinctly unappealing air.

Guinevere, though, seemed to think it was fabulous.

"It's fabulous," she crowed, clapping her hands together as she stood in the middle of the room with a bright smile, as if Signora Verga had shown her the wonders of Michelangelo's *David*. "I can't believe I get to live here."

Signora Verga smiled at her widely, caught up in Guinevere's enthusiasm as it spilled out of her like sunlight. "*Si, si*, very lucky. You be happy here."

"I will," Guinevere agreed, touching the windowsill gently, giving it a caress as if it were sentient. "Thank you for renting it to me. I'm so sorry I wasn't able to get here sooner."

"No, you explain," Signora Verga said, waving off the apology.

"Signora Verga," I said in Italian, startling both women who turned to face me with hands over their hearts. "I assume you know about the boys who loiter outside your apartment selling drugs?"

The older woman's finely lined face creased like a crumpled silk scarf. "They aren't bad boys."

"Oh?" I asked, crossing my arms as I leaned into the frame.

"Not like your kind," she said, brave in the way of all older people, close enough to death to disregard danger.

"My kind? Hmmm." I looked at Guinevere, who was frowning slightly as she struggled to keep up with the conversation. "My kind saved this girl from a worse kind of man and kept her safe this last week."

"Then you know not all men who do bad things are rotten in their hearts," she rebutted smugly, sniffing in triumph.

Amusement tickled the edge of my mouth, but I kept it firmly pressed shut.

"I like it here," Guinevere told me, crossing her own arms to stand off with me. Given she was five foot nothing and light as a feather, it was laughable but oddly endearing. "I searched for ages until I found somewhere this cute that I could afford in the center of Florence."

I leaned forward to inspect the lock on the door, lifting the latch and then dropping it to hear the squeal of the rusted hinge. Without saying a word, I looked back at her with a raised brow.

Her arms tightened protectively over her chest. "If Signora Verga is safe here, I'm sure I will be too."

"Signora Verga isn't an exquisitely beautiful young woman with more courage than sense," I drawled.

"Raffa," she gasped. "Don't be rude."

I almost laughed at her outrage when I had just given her one of the nicest compliments to ever leave my lips. She had all the indignation of a wet cat, and I found myself ridiculously attracted to that stubborn nobility.

"It's true." Signora Verga allowed with a dirty look my way that shifted to a sweet smile for Guinevere. "I am old now, not young and pretty like I once was."

I turned my snort of disbelief into a short cough, but Guinevere saw through my ruse and leveled me with a glare.

"You're lovely," she declared. "And so is this apartment. I can't wait to settle in."

Something strange happened in my gut, hooks ripping up the lining of my stomach as if something was being forcibly dislodged.

"You are not staying here tonight."

She pressed her lips into a flat line at my tone, which I could admit was the same one I used when ordering my *soldati*.

"Why not?" she asked in an excessively reasonable manner. "I'm no longer sick, I have clothes, and you kindly lent me some cash that I'll be able to pay you back for next week when I get my expedited replacement passport. In fact, forget about taking me on your work trip to the winery. I can go another day by myself to one of my own choosing. You'll be happy to be free of the American *idiota*."

Wasn't that the million-euro question.

Why didn't I *want* to be free of her?

I hadn't been home to Villa Romano in two weeks, the longest stretch of time I'd spent away from my family since the death of my father. The Pietra scum were peeking their ugly mugs out of the ground with their sights set on revenge and taking over my territory. Mama and Stefania were convinced an arranged marriage between Stef's family and my own would solidify my power base and provide long-awaited babies.

I was a capo with real-life fucking problems.

So why did I want to continue this farce of playing Prince Fucking Charming with this American girl?

"*Lasciaci*," I told Signora Verga.

Leave us.

She sniffed at me again, shot a look at Guinevere like she was tossing her a lifeline, and then shuffled out of the apartment in her slippers.

I didn't close the door behind me, but I didn't need to.

Instead, I held Guinevere's long-lashed brown eyes and stalked slowly toward her. She held her ground, tipping her chin up when I loomed over her so she could maintain eye contact.

She opened her mouth, no doubt to use her sharp little teeth to take a bite out of my bossy ass, but I silenced her by pressing my index finger to her mouth.

"I have gone to great lengths to take care of you, *cerbiatta*," I murmured, moving my hand from her closed mouth to trace the line of her cheekbone up into the loose hair over her ear. She shivered slightly when I hooked a lock with my finger and pressed it behind the delicate shell. "I find myself . . . invested in your well-being now."

"Financially," she quipped, but the word was too breathless to be punchy.

"I have invested more money in many more things, and they could go bankrupt tomorrow without me giving a single fuck," I admitted.

"A rich man."

"Yes, and oftentimes, a bored man."

"I'm not a toy, you know." She rolled onto her tiptoes, but she was still so short she had no hope of intimidating me. "I'm not . . . some *bambolina* you can just dress up and play with."

I smirked a little because it was cute she was so excited to spit my words from last night on the dance floor back at me.

"No?" I murmured, sliding my entire palm under the heavy mane of hair against her neck, my thumb placed intimately over the thrum of her pulse. "You would not like to be my doll, sometime? Dressed in red, all this hair spread out on my pillow, your thighs spread for the weight of me between them? You did not enjoy being pressed against me while I led you through a dance that made your nipples bead behind the fabric of that pretty dress?"

An almost violent shiver rattled her slim shoulders, but she set her teeth against the physical mark of her desire. "I told you, I'm not a prostitute."

"Did I say you were?"

"You implied it by saying you've invested in me and now you want a return."

"I do not know the kind of men you have in America, but in Italy, a man is honest about his attraction. I find you . . . *incantevole*. Do you know what that means, Guinevere?"

"No," she whispered as my thumb stroked gently back and forth over her thudding pulse point.

"It means *beguiling*. Enchanting. And for a man like me, that is dangerous. I cannot afford distractions, but here I am in this ugly apartment feeling . . . unsettled because you are suggesting I will not see you again when all I want is more of you."

"In the biblical sense?" she asked, a little lost and entirely aroused.

I didn't leash the grin that spread warm and dark across my face. "*Si, certo*, one day. But until that day, I want to see you in a field of poppies as red as that dress. I want to take you to dinner at my favorite trattoria because I can imagine the face you will make when you try true *bistecca alla Fiorentina*. I want to finish reading Dante's *Inferno* to you before we walk through his house together here in Firenze. I want to witness you falling in love with my country because I think you could make this bored man fall in love with it again too."

"Oh," she mouthed, searching my gaze for something I both wanted her to see and desperately wanted to hide.

See the me I used to be, I thought, the young college Raffa with charm and swagger and a zeal for life that entranced people into his orbit.

Don't see Raffaele Romano, the cold, dark metal of a man made into a weapon.

"What are you asking me, exactly?" she asked, reaching up to gently grip my wrist below the hand framing her throat.

When she pressed her thumb to my pulse, it felt as if a loop closed between us. Our hearts, when I took a moment to observe, beat in perfect bass-note harmony.

"I want to know you," I admitted, even though it felt like a confession and I had stopped going to church for those such a long time ago I could not remember. "Will you let me?"

"Will I get to know you too?" she asked, and if I had thought she was clever before, I knew it for certain then.

Because it was not a given this knowing would go both ways.

In fact, it absolutely would *not*.

But I'd avoided indulging in anything for so long, the temptation to do so now was physically overpowering. It burned in my gut and quaked in my bones. It echoed in the beat of my blood knocking against Guinevere's thumb.

Do something for yourself. Take something for your own.

Know her and let someone, just one person, know you too.

"*Si*," I whispered, as I pushed her hair behind her back, leaving her neck warm from my grip but bare for my lips as I sealed my promise with a kiss. "You will."

CHAPTER NINE

Guinevere

I practically vibrated in my seat the entire way to the Chianti region, where Raffa's business associate Imelda had one of the country's best wineries. It was impossible to sit still when I felt carbonated with giddiness and anticipation.

Raffa wanted to know me.

Why was that so much more alluring than simply saying he liked me? *Liking* seemed so juvenile and inconsequential next to *knowing*. One was surface shallow and the other bone deep.

I was tempted to lie supine before him and hand him a scalpel. Dare him to do his worst. Because I had the sense that in allowing someone like Raffa to know me, I would inevitably learn more about myself.

It was probably a good idea to play it cool. Act like I wasn't about to burst out of my skin with eagerness to really start this *thing* between us, strike against it—against him—until all that delicious friction lit into flame.

But even though I was trying to be a different version of myself—bolder, braver, fearless—I was still *me*, so I couldn't curb my enthusiasm and decided not to try.

Even after a week and a half, Raffa had to know I had an over-zealous hunger in the pit of my gut that demanded more now that I'd started to feed it.

"Who were all the people on the terrace today? I thought it would be rude to ask in front of them, but it was strange to have them just walk out like they lived there. Wait." I paused. "Do they live there? God, am I that unobservant that I just haven't noticed before now?"

"*Calmati*, Vera," he said on a small huff of laughter. "They do not live with me, though they each have rooms if they ever want to spend the night. They work for me. You could say they are my executives."

I considered the motley crew gathered around the breakfast table. Ludovico was a big, quiet man with a crudely carved face and ears that stuck out too far. I'd found myself liking him right away, though. There was something in his manner that said he was the type of man to trap a spider under a glass and transfer it outside rather than kill it. A form of innate kindness that showed through his dark eyes.

Carmine I did not enjoy after my first impression, even though I thought our differences might have been cultural. It was rude not to introduce himself and then to mock me when I was just a stranger to him.

Martina had told me he was harmless when she'd dropped by my room after the meal to chat, but she had also said that about Renzo, who was the largest man I'd ever seen, quilted in such dense muscle I wondered how many hours a day he spent in the gym.

I could have bought Raffa and Carmine as typical businessmen, but Ludo and Renzo didn't have that look to them. They had to have physically demanding jobs, and for Raffa, I figured something solitary would be best.

"What is it that you do exactly?" I asked as he drove fast along the country roads with one hand on the wheel and the other braced on the edge of the open window.

The breeze ruffled his slightly wavy hair away from his face, and the sun lit the hair on his corded forearm to blue black. His navy blue linen shirt was unbuttoned to the top of his sternum, revealing a wedge of tanned skin feathered in that same dark hair I wanted to tug between my teeth. My eyes drifted down to his strong thighs beneath the gray trousers and the subtle but honestly mouthwatering ridge of his dick at the apex.

"I can feel you touching every inch of my body with your eyes," he said, startling me from my survey. His voice was low and rich with sin, something too decadent to indulge in without adverse effects to your health. "Do not be afraid to touch with your hands too."

I laughed, but it was a little shrill. "You are imagining things in your old age."

"Says the woman who is so attracted to this *old man* that she is squeezing her thighs together to quell her ache for me."

I gasped, but it wasn't indignant the way I thought it should have been. It was soft, an exclamation like I'd heard actresses make in love scenes on-screen.

"*Si, cerbiatta mia*, I told you I am attracted to you. I told you I want to know you, and that includes the place between your thighs that is growing wetter as we talk. One day, I will taste how sweet you are down there with my tongue. Would you like that?"

I swallowed, but there was no moisture in my mouth to ease the way, so mostly I choked.

His smile was small, but he switched hands on the wheel and moved one to squeeze my bare thigh comfortingly.

"Have I shocked you?"

"We haven't even kissed yet," I reminded him a little primly despite myself. "And you're talking about kissing me *there*."

"Your pussy?" he confirmed with a roguish grin.

I rolled my eyes but repeated, "My pussy, yes."

"*La figa*," he said in Italian.

I echoed him.

His eyes were sparkling as they slid to me before looking back to the road. "Should we spend our drive having a sexy lesson in Italiano?"

I laughed, and my nerves shattered like broken glass. "Yes, that sounds fun."

"Mmm," he hummed. "It does. *Mi fai eccitare. Potrei guardarti tutto il giorno.* You turn me on. I could look at you all day."

My head thunked back against the headrest, my mouth parting on a sigh.

"Repeat after me, Guinevere," he demanded, and that cold edge made me hotter than his compliment.

"*Mi fai eccitare. Potrei guardarti tutto il giorno.*"

"*Grazie tante,*" he teased, thanking me for my compliment. "Very good."

I squirmed but didn't stop his hand as it traced languid designs on the skin of my thigh, moving slowly higher and higher up under the fabric of my dress.

"*Scommetto che hai una bella albicocca,*" he said, so husky it was almost a growl. "I bet you have a pretty pussy."

"*Albicocca?*" I repeated, more than a little breathless. "Apricot?"

"*La figa* is the most popular, but a pussy can be as sweet as *albicocca* or *fragola,* as lovely as a *farfalla* or *passerina.*"

Fig, apricot, strawberry. Butterfly or sparrow.

"Everything is so beautiful in Italian. *Pussy* and *cunt* sound so much coarser," I admitted, gripping his wrist not to stop him but to ground myself in the moment as his fingertips brushed the tender skin beside my groin.

"*Sì,* something so sweet and juicy and pretty pink must be spoken of like poetry," he agreed, but his eyes were dark as they left the road to watch his fingers ruck my skirt up to my hips.

The pale blue of my panties was exposed to the heat of his gaze, and every molecule in my body seemed to buzz with its own electrical current.

We still hadn't even *kissed.*

Why did that make this sensual Italian lesson so much more erotic?

"*Che bella,*" he said, and he didn't have to translate for me.

What beauty.

I blushed so deeply I worried the color would be tattooed on my skin. There was a squirmy sensation in my gut that was an intoxicating mix of arousal, daring, and lingering shame. A small noise like a whine leaked from my throat as I struggled to voice any of my desires.

"Slide your hips down for me," he murmured.

I obeyed without thinking, settling deeper into the seat so I could spread my legs wider.

This was the kind of encounter I'd dreamed of late at night in my bed back home in Michigan when the winters seemed as endless as my loneliness. Warm summer air and the heavy weight of a man's hand on my skin.

I sucked in a deep breath when Raffa brushed his thumb down the center of my fabric-covered groin, pressing into the damp spot at the apex. When he pulled away, I almost protested, but my words died on my tongue when he pressed the tip of his damp thumb into his mouth and sucked it clean.

"*Hai un buon sapore come immaginavo,*" he said. "You taste as good as I imagined."

"Like apricots?" I teased, surprised by the confidence I felt, half lying in my seat with my wet underwear exposed and my taste on Raffa's lips.

"Like sin," he corrected. "It is addictive."

There was a brief pause that felt like a prelude to something dangerous. I held my breath.

"Tell me, Vera, have you ever tasted yourself?" he asked finally in a low purr.

"No," I said on an exhale of shocked laughter.

He groaned then, lowering his hand to adjust the huge ridge in his trousers to lie down one thigh. "You are killing me."

"How?" I licked my dry lips, wishing we were somewhere he could turn the full weight of his attention on me and my curious, aching yearning.

"Imagining all the things I could teach you. The ways I could corrupt that pure mind of yours. I want to feed you the seeds of a pomegranate from the underworld even knowing you can never go back after tasting them."

"I prefer to think Persephone chose to stay half the year with Hades," I said, finding the courage to reach between my thighs to cup my sex. "I think she couldn't live any longer without knowing what it was like to taste the dark."

Raffa shot a quick glance to my hand and rumbled low in his chest. "Do you want me to teach you how I like my cock to be sucked? Show you how many times I can make you come on my tongue? You wanted adventure, and I am happy to be your guide."

"You hate being a guide," I quipped, even as I rubbed lightly at the growing damp spot on my panties, blushing as the smell of my arousal filled the car.

"I truly cannot imagine anything better than guiding you through this," he admitted baldly as he abruptly swerved the car, and I realized we had driven into the gravel parking lot at the winery.

Before I could fully remove my hand, Raffa's large palm was pushing it back against my pussy.

"Seal our deal with your first taste," he coaxed, splitting our fingers over my mound to dig beneath the edge of my panties.

I gasped, neck going limp as my fingertips dipped into the hot well at my entrance. Raffa pressed his forehead to my temple, his breath hot on my neck, his eyes fixed to our connection between my legs.

"*Bellissima*," he muttered.

Beautiful.

I panted as he moved our fingers through my wetness, wondering if he would make me orgasm right there in the car. We were hidden behind some kind of shed and surrounded by linden trees on two sides, so there was privacy, but the threat of exposure made me so hot I burned.

Instead, he pulled our hands away, two fingers glistening with my juices as he raised them to hover between us. He brought his hand to his mouth, painting the wetness along his bottom lip. His eyes seemed to stare straight through me, glowing like banked coals as, slowly, I followed his silent order to echo him and traced my mouth with my essence.

My tongue peeked out to touch the gloss, and I shivered delicately as the flavor bloomed on my taste buds.

"Mmm," I hummed, but before I could say any more, Raffa's clean hand was sliding through the back of my hair and tugging hard. My torso twisted toward him, head canting back to alleviate the strain, and my mouth parted on a gasp.

A moment later, he ate that sound and the taste of my *figa* out of my mouth with his tongue.

I groaned shamelessly at the invasion, hands flying up to curl over his shoulders so I could cling to him as he rocked everything I'd known off its axis. He tasted like me but also like him, dark and male, his scent heady in my nose and the heat of his mouth the epicenter of my universe.

I thought, *So this is what it's like to be kissed.*

This is what it's like to feel lust like a lightning bolt, electricity fizzing through every vein.

Without thinking, I pulled him closer, trying to kiss him even deeper.

His moan was my reward, vibrating from his mouth to mine. In that moment, I thought I would have done anything to earn that sound from him again and again.

In that moment, I had never felt so alive.

When Raffa finally pulled away, forehead pressed to mine, breath wafting across my wet, swollen lips, soothing the stubble burn he'd left on my skin, I found my eyes mortifyingly damp.

"*Cerbiatta,*" he murmured, releasing my hair to cup the entire back of my skull in one big hand.

It was a question and consolation without making me feel foolish or too young.

I laughed as a single tear dislodged and rolled down my cheek. "I've never done that before. I always wanted to. Always dreamed of kissing and . . . more. But I was sick or too sheltered, and the opportunity never came. This, well, it was better than I ever imagined. I'm sorry for crying. It's silly."

"*Non sciocco*," he corrected firmly as his other thumb caught the tear and brought that to his mouth too. He paused to lick the salt from his skin in a way that was startlingly hot. "I understand wanting something for so long and believing you will never have it."

"What do you want?" I asked, stripped of my usual shyness by our proximity and the simple but devastating act of sharing the taste of me between our lips.

His eyes shuttered, but when I cupped his cheek in one hand, he answered, "To be the man who deserves that look on your face."

"What look?" I asked, afraid of the question—and the answer—but not enough to take it back.

"Like I could pull the stars from the sky for you if only you asked me to."

"And would you?"

His sigh sounded almost resigned as it feathered over my mouth. "*Troverei un modo.*"

I would find a way.

Fattoria Casa Luna was a stunning sprawl of golden stone buildings arranged around a pretty garden and patio that were elevated over a vista of hills lined with wine grapes. I squinted against the sunlight, raising a hand to cover my eyes as I tried to see where the vines ended three hills and valleys deep from where I stood.

"Incredible," I breathed, tipping my head back and dropping my hand to soak up the sunlight on my face.

Raffa had shown me the bathroom at the entrance to the main building and then gone off to find Imelda with a promise to meet me on the patio. Washing my hands and staring at myself in the antique mirror without his presence to muffle my senses had been its own kind of enlightenment.

My cheeks were flushed, my hair tousled from his tight grip, and the skin around my swollen mouth was pinked from the roughness of his cheeks as he'd kissed me.

I looked slightly debauched and ridiculously proud of it.

My smile was close lipped and smug, a coy expression I'd seen before on Gemma's face when she'd returned home from a date with her boyfriend, but never on my own.

God, she would have loved this for me.

Thinking about how she would have crowed in delight and teased me about the mysterious Italian stranger who had swept me off my feet stole my breath for a moment. I rested my hands against the counter and blinked the tears from my eyes.

Who would have known kissing could be so emotional?

But then, I could acknowledge it wasn't just the kiss.

It was the entire adventure laid before me, not the one I'd so meticulously planned from the comfort of my home in Ann Arbor, but a new future entirely. One elevated by the presence of Raffaele Romano.

He would have appealed to any woman with a pulse, I was sure, with his beauty and wealth, but there was something intangible about him that had appealed to me almost from the start.

A mirror image of the tension I felt inside myself, maybe, between who we were and who we wanted to be.

I didn't know why Raffa struggled with it or how it manifested itself, but the divide was subtly clear.

He was kind with me, thoughtful and tender, which seemed uncharacteristic given his gruff, exacting manner. Martina had said how he related to me was unusual, and Raffa himself had said I was the exception to every one of his rules.

Maybe that should have been a red flag, but I couldn't deny it made me feel special. Secure, even. If he had never experienced the kind of chemistry we had together, I could rely on it to feel just as real to him as it did to me.

Still, the idea of embarking on a true holiday romance was so surreal, I giggled to myself in the bathroom. Guinevere Stone, American virgin, licking the taste of herself out of someone else's mouth.

No one back home would believe it.

Then again, Gemma and my parents had always been my best friends, the ones who knew me best, and it wasn't like I could have ever told them the secret, kinky fantasies I touched myself to at night. Talk about awkward.

And now I had the perfect opportunity to explore them without embarrassment. Because I didn't know Raffa that well, not really, but I knew in my bones I could trust him to teach me about pleasure without any judgment or shame.

It wasn't easy to realize that my parents and I had been so afraid of my death throughout most of my life that I'd let fear wrap me in chains and keep me anchored to the safe banks of banal mundanity.

Didn't survivors deserve more than just what they could eke out moment to moment? Didn't they deserve to thrive and rejoice in every single second? Suck the marrow from the bone, juices dripping down the chin, gluttony not a sin but a privilege after the barren, hungry times of survival?

I would always have to mind my health. It was as much a fact of life as taking my next breath, but it did not mean I couldn't take chances and indulge when opportunities were worthy.

I'd first started to feel this when Gemma died. Healthy, robust Gemma who was beautiful and young and at the beginning of her whole life. How could she be gone between one minute and the next when there was no indication she had ever been ill? The randomness of it had not just shaken my reality, it had cracked it, and from that crack had grown an abyss I was finally able to crawl out of.

And here I was free to live my life for myself as I hadn't been able to do the last twenty-three years.

What was I going to do?

Before I could think about it too long, I ducked into a stall and pulled off my damp silk thong, one of many that the Marias had picked out for me at the boutique and that I never would have bought for myself. I rolled the material into a ball and put it in my purse, feeling the heat in my cheeks as I thought about slipping it into Raffa's pocket at some point, the look on his face when he realized I was naked beneath the shift.

I'd seen how he looked at me when I came out in the dress that morning, and I knew he wouldn't try very hard to resist.

I smiled as I thought about it, opening my palms to get the sun on as much of my skin as I could. The scent of gardenia, freesia, and honeysuckle from the garden was undercut by the woody notes of herbs.

Minutes later, Raffa was still nowhere to be found, so I decided to walk the grounds myself. The patio edged a fragrant garden filled with the faint hum of fat bumblebees hovering between stalks of lavender and white-faced gardenias. I followed the flagstone path through the maze of plants toward the sound of trickling water and found a fountain with a small cupid spitting water from its pursed mouth.

I trailed my fingertips in the cool water for a brief reprieve from the July heat, feeling so at peace it was hard to believe my surroundings were real.

The sound of harsh yelling reminded me they were.

I straightened, hesitating, before following the sound of the angry voice toward some kind of industrial warehouse to the left of the main wine-tasting building. The voice grew clear, shouting in a way that conveyed anger but also a contrary desire to be quiet.

I hovered behind a line of cypress trees separating most of the garden from the behind-the-scenes setting of the vineyard, peeking between the gap.

"*Calmati!*" Raffa's voice found me before my eyes found him; he was facing away from me and toward the man who had been yelling. "*Che cazzo fai?* Do you want the entire staff to hear you, Wyatt?"

The man in question switched to British-accented English, but his posture remained on guard, a finger raised like a weapon at Raffa.

"This is not how we do business, Romano."

Raffa cocked his head. "This is how *we* do business in Italia. This is how *I* expect things to go, *capisci?* I command and you obey. There is no other option."

"There is always another option," Wyatt retorted, but his anger had transformed into something closer to agitation and a healthy dose of fear.

"You do not want another option," Raffa murmured so quietly I almost couldn't hear him.

I gasped when he uncoiled like a snake, striking out to grab Wyatt by his shirtfront to push him up against the stone wall. If I had stumbled upon them just then, I might have thought they were lovers for how closely they stood, but I knew, after Galasso, that closeness could be used for intimidation too.

I couldn't hear what he said then, catching only the low timbre of his voice like a bass note to the cicadas' song as they nested above me.

It should have been alarming to see him so cold, so absolute in his totalitarianism. He was obviously not a businessman afraid to get his hands dirty by confronting his misbehaving staff. My father would have forbidden me to see him anymore after a scene like this, always wary of men's anger.

But it was yet another thing I had no true experience with that I found curiously arousing. The cold snap of his voice like a whip. The power of his body unleashing quick and lethal.

It spoke of a masculinity and rare power that I hadn't seen in any of my university classmates back home. A kind of virility, like he could take care of himself and *me* if he was called on to do so.

It made me feel safe and just slightly afraid of what that voice could make me do if that tone was leveled in my direction.

"Guinevere."

My head snapped to my left, where Raffa was standing at the entrance to the path with his arms crossed—muscles coiled like rope beneath his skin, visible under the thin knit of his shirt—staring at me like I was a naughty child.

"Were you eavesdropping, *cerbiatta?*" he asked me.

I pursed my lips. "Is it eavesdropping if there is yelling? I could hardly *not* listen."

"*Faccia tosta,*" he said with a click of his tongue. "Come here."

"What does that mean?"

"'Cheeky.' Now, come here."

I paused a moment, only because it was part of the game I was coming to understand we both liked to play. It made me feel bold even when I acquiesced to him.

I walked on my toes until I was a foot away from him, grinning slyly. "Are your ears still ringing, old man? You need me closer to hear what I have to say?"

"I need you closer," he said with a mock snarl, lashing out the way he had done to the Brit, but only to reel me in with an arm around my waist so I was pressed belly to belly with him. "So I can kiss you."

"If I don't kiss you back, will you be angry with me like you were with that man?" I tested, not because I was afraid of him but because I *wasn't.*

I knew what his answer would be.

He would have dropped me off at a hospital or a police station after hitting me with his car if there hadn't been something about me that spoke to him in a different language than he was used to.

Raffa sensed my playfulness, eyes flashing as they caught the sunlight before dipping down so he could tip my chin and bite at it. "Angry? No. You would have to do much worse to win my temper."

I made a noise in my throat that sounded to both of us like disappointment.

Understanding flickered in his expression as he collected my hands and pulled them behind my back, collaring them in one of his so that my back was arched. My balance was entirely dependent on him anchoring my front and providing a counterweight at my wrists. It was erotic, a makeshift bondage.

My lids felt heavy, and my heart thrummed too quick in my chest, heating my blood to a low simmer.

"You do not want my rage, *piccola*, but you want something like it?" he asked low, speaking the words directly into my ear before nipping my lobe with his teeth. "Do not worry. I will teach you the words in any language for what makes your blood hum, *d'accordo?*"

"How can you know the words I need when I can't even speak them?" I asked, bitterness on my tongue. My naivete felt more constricting than his hand around my wrists.

"I will know," he promised, running the bridge of his nose down my chin and along my jaw until his mouth hovered over mine. "As I know now that you want me to kiss you the way I might bite into a plum. All tongue and teeth. Devouring."

Instead of replying with words, I leveraged his hold on my hands to tip my face forward to claim his lips for myself. His chuckle tickled my mouth a moment before he slanted his head and did as he promised.

Devoured.

None of the gentle exploration from the Bugatti. Only an attack of ownership. Tongue behind my teeth, plundering, seeking new corners yet undiscovered.

I surrendered myself to the kiss, to his hold, and felt like I existed only in the frame of his body, pinned against his mouth. There was a freedom in it that soared through me along with pleasure.

When he'd finally had his fill, he broke away to look down into my face, studying me to catalog the effect he'd had on me.

"Wow," I said, a little shell shocked.

I was rewarded with a full smile, completely unguarded, almost as if I'd surprised him into an honest expression.

"*Che bello*," he agreed. "Now, as much as I wish I could kiss you in this garden for the rest of the day, I think you mentioned wanting to see how a vineyard works?"

I laughed, and it came from my belly. "I did."

His smile had narrowed, softened, but it was still there, and when he pulled me toward the main building again, he did it holding my hand.

CHAPTER TEN

Raffa

How do you shield yourself from sunlight?

Even when you wear a hat, glasses, sunscreen, you can still feel its warmth beneath your clothes, taste its humidity on your tongue, see the bright cast of its light through your lenses.

How do you defend yourself against the kind of sunlight that leaked from Guinevere Stone's every pore?

I realized it would be difficult when she smiled at me in that red dress. Knew it was dangerous exposure when I danced with her at the trattoria. Surrendered to it completely when she parted her slim thighs, trusting me to teach her to know a completely new part of herself without any hesitation, as if I deserved that faith.

Wondered if I might kill and die for another taste of her as soon as we kissed.

Ero fottuto.

I was fucked.

It was just lust, and maybe an inkling of admiration, but the kind I had never experienced before. I wanted to drag her into the bushes and fuck her against a linden tree. I wanted to paint a necklace of bruises around her throat like a collar so that everyone would know she was taken.

The civilized man I'd tried to become before my father died seemed to be crumbling into primitive urges under the regard of those beautiful doe eyes.

I watched as she walked ahead of me down the row of vines with Imelda, her face animated with enthusiasm as she listened to the history of the vineyard and its wine-making process. Imelda seemed just as taken with Guinevere, touching her arm, encouraging her to pluck a grape from the vine and cut it open with her teeth to see its insides.

They didn't need my interaction, but it was obvious Guinevere was still highly aware of me. Her gaze seemed to slide to mine like a magnet meeting another, our eyes locking together for long moments before she refocused on Imelda.

I wondered what she might look like wandering the vines on my family's land near Montepulciano.

"Raffa? He is an investor," Imelda caught my attention by explaining. "We wanted to expand to meet the increasing international demand for our wines, and Raffa was there with the money. A godsend."

My old friend grinned at me, swarthy face creasing into folds. She had been a friend of my mother's since I was a boy and had watched me grow, and while she had always rejected offers of investment from my father, she was eager to work with me when I took over the business. In fact, investing and laundering through Fattoria Casa Luna had been the first deal I'd made as capo.

"You were doing just fine without me," I reminded her. "Winning a gold medal at the IWSC awards was only the beginning."

"True," she agreed. "But I was facing pressure from other potential investors, and you cannot imagine my relief when they fled at the sight of Raffa coming into play."

She laughed lightly, but I only glowered at her, and Guinevere looked thoughtful as she gazed between the two of us.

"Is his reputation for being a grump so well renowned?" she asked laconically.

Imelda laughed, this time from the belly. "Something like that. He is a wolf in business. Always getting what he wants, always making money. His mother always said he was touched by fortune."

Guinevere grinned, an edge of self-deprecation in her expression, and I was reminded that her own family called her Jinx for being so unlucky in life.

Well, that had changed since she ran into the side of my car. I had more than enough fortune to share with her.

"Perhaps that is why I am so impatient with the product that has been misplaced this month," I suggested smoothly, the very casualness of my tone relaying to Imelda that I was *not* impressed with her new manager, Wyatt.

He was Imelda's sister's boy, born and raised in England but in love with Italian wine. When she offered him the job, it was made explicitly clear that he would be reporting to both of us. It was easy enough to keep higher management out of the loop about our money-laundering activities, so he wasn't made aware and he would never be, given he seemed to have some innate problem with me. Whenever I visited, he took umbrage at something I suggested for the company, and his latest rebellion had resulted in three shipments being lost en route to China, one of our biggest markets.

Imelda looked at me sidelong, the irritation in her gaze not directed at me. "You and me both, Raffa, I assure you."

Guinevere looked between us with a little crease between her brows. "What's the problem?"

I hesitated but decided being honest was the least suspicious course of action. Beside the fact that our issue stemmed from gross negligence and not Mafia-related activities.

"It seems there has been a mix-up with shipments of fourteen crates of our premium wine to Shanghai. Our Chinese business associates are not pleased, obviously, and if we cannot find the product, we will effectively be out tens of thousands of euros," I explained dryly.

"Yikes," Guinevere murmured, and a flare of warmth lit inside my chest at her adorable sincerity. "Well, I'm sure you have people looking into it, but I have an MBA with a concentration in finance, and I have kind of a knack for pattern recognition if you want me to take a peek at the manifests?"

I blinked at her, surprised by her audacity but also unwittingly entranced by it. This young woman really thought she could make a difference in a mess Imelda's very expensive accountants and managers could not put to rights.

Something perverse in me liked the idea of testing her. If she failed, as I believed she would, the exercise would still give her insight into my work in a way that wouldn't lead to uncomfortable questions, and it would give me some peace in my own mind.

That she was just a girl, however beguiling, and nothing to be over-concerned about.

If she succeeded, well, it would be impossible not to admire her even more than I already did, which would be alarming, but it would also solve this multi-thousand-euro issue.

"Fine," I decided. "If you think you can handle it."

She tucked a dark lock of hair behind her ear and shot me a withering look. "Just because I'm younger than you, Raffa, does not mean I'm not capable."

A reluctant grin tugged my mouth before I looked over at Imelda, who was watching us with knowing, sparkling eyes. My expression flat-lined at her expression.

"Lead on, Imelda," I requested flatly, indicating she should lead us to her office. "Let us see what the American girl can make of things."

As it turned out, the American girl could do a lot.

I left her with Imelda's shipping manager and accountant, confident that she would be preoccupied while I dealt with the rest of my business at the estate, but I was not expecting to return over an hour later to any kind of breakthrough.

Let alone a complete rundown of the issue.

"They're trying to commit fraud," Guinevere told me, her face lit with the kind of enthusiasm I'd previously only seen targeted at Italian cultural phenomena and history. "Erasmo and I noticed that they have been disputing shipments for the last six months. Product allegedly arriving broken. Bottles were corked, and a crate here or there had gone missing. Isacco told me it's company policy to refund based on these claims without any kind of investigation. Which makes sense from a customer-relations perspective, but not when it becomes a pattern of taking advantage of the winery."

She sucked in a deep breath, as excited as a child on their birthday. "Zhang-Liu Imports *is* receiving the product, and it seems to be in fine condition."

"But how can you verify that?" Imelda asked, rounding her desk to see what Guinevere, Isacco, and Erasmo had spread out across the table and three different computer screens. I followed, hands behind my back, expression blank as I processed this new information.

"Here," Guinevere said, pointing at a list of numbers in an Excel sheet on the screen. "When we noticed the claims, I looked through the financial logs between your two companies. If they were experiencing that many issues with the winery, it would stand to reason they wouldn't make more purchases from you, but their imports have increased during that term. So I thought, *Why?*"

"And then she did something I do not understand," Erasmo, who was in his late seventies, admitted with a wince.

Guinevere laughed, lightly placing her hand on his arm as if they were old friends. "It's something we do at my father's firm to assess financial risk when investing in a company. I applied the same principles to Zhang-Liu, and on paper, their business is booming. China is the eighth-largest importer of wine, with the numbers only continuing to grow, and Zhang-Liu is the second-biggest high-end-market wine company in the country."

"So the only feasible conclusion is that they have received our product every time they have said they have not or that something is wrong with a shipment and they are profiting off of it," I surmised, the cold words clicking against my teeth like chips of ice.

"Yes," Guinevere agreed with a sympathetic nod, the brightness of new discovery fading from her eyes as she realized the very real implications. "I'm afraid they're swindling you."

I did not laugh, but there was something about the combination of shrewd intelligence and sweetness in her gaze that made me want to.

"Well, for the first time in years, I am happy to be proven wrong, *cerbiatta*," I confessed, pulling Guinevere up from the chair. She came willingly, stepping to my side as if the space had been tailor made for her. "Thank you for lending your expertise."

The smile she gifted me was soft, small only because it was almost shy, as if accepting praise from me was too much happiness to bear. "Thank you for letting me check it out."

"I will not hesitate next time," I quipped. "Though I do hope there will never be a next time."

I slanted Imelda a look, and she nodded over Guinevere's head. We would be dealing with this transgression by Zhang-Liu *my* way. The odds were high that they were doing the same thing to countless suppliers in the country, but they'd picked the wrong winery when they chose Fattoria Casa Luna to steal from.

By the time I was done with them, they would not exist to do so anymore.

"Well, that is done, then. Shall we go inside and try the wine?" I suggested mildly, but Imelda knew there was no more information I wanted to discuss in front of polite company, so she quickly took Guinevere's other arm to lead her back to the tasting rooms.

"Oh! Okay, well, *ciao, Isacco e Erasmo!*" Guinevere called over her shoulder as she was ushered from the room. When we were in the hall with the door closed behind us, she peered up at me with flushed cheeks. "What are you going to do about everything?"

Raze their company to the ground and cut out the CEO's tongue so he never tells another lie again.

"I will pursue justice through the proper authorities," I said calmly.

The only authority was *me*, but I did not need to clarify that for her.

"I'm sorry, Raffa," she said, leaning heavily into my side in a gesture of comfort. "I hope I haven't ruined your day."

"Far from that," I assured her, staring down into that beautiful, almost angelic face and wondering how such a creature could not only exist but also be so drawn into my orbit. "You have saved it. And now, you will distract me by drinking some of our very fine wine with me."

We were crossing the main lobby when a familiar sight made me pause midstep.

"Leo?"

My best friend turned from speaking animatedly to that British *stronzo*, Wyatt, to stare at me stupidly for half a beat before collecting himself with a wide grin.

"Raffa!" He walked toward me with his arms open, slapping them over my shoulders to press his cheek to mine in greeting. "*Fratello mio,* what brings you to the vines today?"

"I could ask the same of you. You should be minding the house, no?" I asked, trying to keep the edge from my tone because Guinevere was behind my shoulder, watching the entire exchange with keen eyes.

Leo had opened his mouth to answer when a shrill feminine squeal pierced the air.

"Raffa!"

I had one second to brace myself before my sister Delfina was in my arms, pressing kisses to both my cheeks. When she was done, she cupped my face in her hands to study me thoroughly.

"Why do you look so content when we have not seen you in weeks?" she demanded in rapid Italian.

"You do know I am a busy man, correct? You know, running an empire to keep you in clothes and Diet Cokes."

She laughed, turning to Leo to say, "Do you see who I found?"

"I think I found him first," he countered, but he was smiling the kind of relaxed grin I hadn't seen on his face since my father died.

"Technically, I found you," I retorted. "And you were just about to tell me why you were not at the villa with the family."

"We are not birds you can keep in a cage, Raffuccio," she decreed, pulling out of my arms to fist her hands on her hips. "I wanted to speak with Mario about the satellite GPS system. Ours is on the fritz, and they have the same model."

"Telephones have existed for decades now," I reminded her, crossing my arms.

"That is not the best way to do business," Leo chimed in, stepping closer to Delfina's back to support her. "As you always say."

"That is a different kind of business. One that requires discretion," I told them both sternly.

"Hello."

Leo and Delfina startled as Guinevere stepped up beside me, much the way Leo had just done with my sister. When her hand gently found the small of my back in a gesture of obvious support, I had to bite my grin. *Mio dio*, she was sweet.

"I'm Guinevere," she continued into the silence with a small smile.

In tandem, Leo and Delfina looked from her to me for an explanation.

I sighed wearily, pulling Guinevere to my side with an arm around her waist and gesturing to my family. "This is Leonardo di Conte, my childhood friend, and my sister Delfina."

"I forgot you have a sister," she murmured, looking up at me. "Two, right?"

"Three," Delfina supplied happily.

"You do not know me very well," I reminded her, my voice cool. "It is understandable you would forget."

I felt the tension settle into her bones and hated that I had made her feel other when we had just shared such an intimate morning. But this was not the time or place for the Raffa I could allow myself to be in the safety of her orbit.

I was Raffaele Romano here, standing in a place of business with my right-hand man and sister. The armor I donned was instinctual, camouflage as a matter of survival.

"How did you meet my brother?" Delfina asked to fill the awkward silence.

Leo was scrutinizing Guinevere with a curiosity that had my hackles rising. She was gorgeous, of course, but Leo was a playboy through and through.

He wasn't getting within another foot of her if I could help it.

"Are you Italian?" he asked, before Guinevere could respond to my sister.

"Through my father," she admitted.

"What is your last name?"

She frowned at his intensity, pressing her hip into me. "Stone."

"And do you have any family in the region?" he pressed.

"*Basta*, Leo," I ordered, because he was interrogating her without cause. "We met, if you must know, Delfi, when I hit her with my car."

Delfina blinked and then burst into laughter. "You're kidding?"

Guinevere lifted the hem of her short dress higher on one side to show the lingering yellow bruise on her hip. "No, we literally collided."

"So you did not know who Raffa was before you *ran* into him?" Leo asked, his tone uncharacteristically hard.

He was one of the most ruthless bastards I knew, but his public persona was almost debonair, flirtatious with women and chummy with men.

"Leo," Delfina and I both scolded at the same time.

Guinevere offered him her own cool smile, an expression I found wildly attractive. "I am an American traveling from the Midwest. I'm more likely to know U of M college football stats than I am to know about some random Italian businessman."

"Not so random," Leo countered. "One of the richest men in the country."

"Leo, *basta*," I told him.

Enough.

"I'm just making conversation with your . . . friend," Leo protested with a plastic smile. "What did you say you do when you aren't traveling? Or are you old enough to work?"

A growl worked itself out of my throat, and I dropped my arm around Guinevere to step in front of her, blocking his view. "I said *enough*. Speak like that to her again, and you will not like the person I become."

"To defend her against *me*?" he asked in Italian, eyes blown wide with shock. "I'm your brother."

"That does not mean you can speak to her like she is an enemy. I hit her with my car after she was nearly sexually assaulted on the side of the road. She is more Bambi than hunter. Let her be and leave her to me."

"Leave her to you," he echoed, trying to process my words. "Who is this girl, Raffaele?"

"No one to you," I declared.

But someone to me, I didn't say.

We stared at each other for a long moment, two predators snarling over prey, but finally Leo looked away with a grimace.

"Apologize," I suggested, unafraid to rub dirt in his wounded pride.

Leo's expression was sour as he spoke slowly in English, like Guinevere was stupid. "I am sorry. You just look like someone I once knew, and it took me by surprise."

"An unpleasant one, obviously," Guinevere noted, and I was not sure how much of our Italian argument she understood, but I had to admire her grace as she inclined her head at him. "It's forgotten. From what I understand, Raffa isn't known for his kindness, so it's probably strange to see him with a woman like this."

"It's not at all strange to see him with a woman," Leo muttered.

"As his *friend*," Guinevere corrected with a saccharine smile.

He snorted under his breath, but I decided we were done with him.

"Take Delfina back home when you are done with Mario," I told him before turning to my sister with a much softer expression. "Delfi, I will see you soon."

"Very soon," she vowed, an implied threat that if she did not get the details of my *friendship* with Guinevere within twenty-four hours, she would show up at my doorstep.

I nodded, kissing her goodbye. *"Ciao, sorella mia."*

"It was lovely to meet you," Guinevere told my sister when I pulled away, offering her hand to shake.

I hid my smile behind my hand at the typically American gesture and watched as Delfina pulled her in for kisses.

"Very good. I am sure I will see you again," she promised before turning to follow after Leo, who was already stalking through the lobby away from us.

I was certain she would not, if I had anything to do with it.

These worlds colliding only strengthened my conviction that they could not coexist. The man I could be with Guinevere in the sanctity of our own bubble was not that man I'd honed myself into carefully and meticulously, like the edge of a blade. She was happy to believe she had done a good service today in showing me the winery was being stolen from, and I did not want to test what she might think if she discovered the only compensation I would seek from the thieves would be paid in blood.

I could have this, I told myself as I wordlessly took Guinevere's hand to lead her to the cellar and our private tasting room, but this fantasy had a deadline, and after five weeks, our relationship would turn into a pumpkin and I'd be left right back where I was before.

More metal than man.

CHAPTER ELEVEN

Guinevere

I was worried the intimacy of our day would falter after we discovered someone was effectively stealing from the winery and had an awkward run-in with his sister and best friend, but Raffa proved me wonderfully wrong. If anything, he seemed filled with intent, his attention keen eyed as he showed me the *fattoria*'s well-organized cellar suffused with the sweet musk of aging wine and barrel wood. Imelda had made herself scarce after setting up the wine-tasting table for us, and Raffa himself seemed determined to be my sommelier.

"I am beginning to think you have a kink for teaching me," I teased him as he poured a splash of Chianti Classico into my glass after explaining the specifics of its bouquet to me.

"Maybe," he admitted, watching with dark eyes as I placed my nose at the top of the glass to breathe in the scents and then breathed in again through my mouth before taking a sip that I aerated with my teeth. "It seems in this I do not have to."

I laughed and admitted, "My father is Italian, remember? He taught my sister and me about wine well before we could drink it."

Gemma had loved the science of viticulture and was studying to be a sommelier herself. One of the reasons she had decided to live abroad in Albania for a year was to study in one of the oldest wine-making regions in the world. It made me feel close to her, tasting wine in an Italian cellar, knowing she would have loved it like I did.

"More evidence that we do not know each other very well," he chided with a cluck of his tongue as he leaned against the table across from me. "You have not spoken much of your own sister."

"She died," I confessed softly, staring into the garnet liquid so he wouldn't see the agony in my face. "Last year. It was a really rare form of heart attack. She was living abroad when it happened, and we just . . . weren't expecting it. Of the two of us, it always seemed more likely I would be the one to die young because of my illness."

"*Mi dispiace*," he said softly, reaching across the table to draw two fingers down the back of my hand. "I lost my father four years ago, and it still feels fresh."

"You were close?" My curiosity sprang like water from a tapped well. Raffa had shared so little about himself in contrast to how comfortable I felt in his company. I was eager to know more, especially after his best friend had been rude to me and Martina had seemed shocked he would've played the white knight for anyone.

"In some ways," he mused. "In others, we were at odds. It is often the way with parents, I think."

I winced a little, hiding my reaction behind the glass as I raised it to take another sip. After swirling the wine around my palate, I spat the liquid into the silver spittoon.

When I looked up, Raffa had a brow raised. "I will not think less of you if you want to actually drink the wine."

A blush fired my cheeks. "I didn't think so. I just have to be careful with alcohol."

His other brow joined the first. "Because of your condition."

"Yes. I would have to watch my intake anyway, but I had a kidney transplant when I was sixteen, so I have to be doubly cautious." I hesitated. "My sister was the donor."

He made a noise in the back of his throat that was somehow sympathetic without being coddling. "It is not such a bad thing. As much as most Italians are loath to admit it, alcohol is not exactly a health food."

I laughed, shocked that he continually found ways to put me at ease. "That's true."

"But you enjoy it?" He nodded at my glass.

"I know Chianti is made specifically to pair with food, but it's lovely."

"Lovely," he murmured, coming around the table to my side, where he seemed to reach for me before crossing my body to grab another bottle of wine to pour into two clean glasses for us both. "That is not a word I would use for wine, but for a woman."

"I think it works for both," I breathed, my nipples pebbling from the brush of his forearm across them as he replaced the wine.

"Both," he mused, wickedness slowly pulling his mouth into a crooked grin. "I cannot say I have tasted both to know if you are right."

"No, not together," I started to correct him, but my words were lost to a gasp when Raffa picked me up by the hips and placed me on the table. "What are you doing?"

"This is a wine tasting," he said drolly. "I am tasting my wine."

I opened my mouth to say something but forgot entirely when he lifted my glass to my nose so I could smell the red before he tipped it against my mouth.

"Open," he coaxed, a light flush on his pronounced cheekbones. "Taste."

I shivered as cabernet sauvignon pooled on my tongue, all red fruits and a shadow of oak.

"Do not swallow," he ordered in that domineering, faintly cold way that made my skin flush.

I waited obediently, instinctually, and had the gratification of his wide smile, white teeth and pointed canines almost lupine and entirely too gorgeous.

"*Molto bene*," he praised before stepping in close between my thighs so my dress rode up almost all the way to my hips. One hand rose to grip my chin, tilting it slightly so that when his mouth descended on mine, we fit perfectly.

At first it was closed lips, just the trace of his tongue against my lower lip and then pushing beyond to touch my teeth. Then he was slipping inside, drinking the wine from my mouth. When it was gone, he languidly sucked the taste from my tongue until I moaned around a full body shiver.

"Mmm," he hummed, pulling back an inch to stare at my wine-stained lips. "Perhaps *lovely* is *not* the word for either. *È ambrosia. Divino. Come una droga.*"

It is ambrosia. Divine. Like a drug.

Unwittingly, I squeezed Raffa's lean hips between my thighs, trying to relieve the ache he'd placed at their center. His answering expression was low lidded, one corner of his full bottom lip depressed by a sharp tooth.

"Do you agree, *cerbiatta?*" he asked me in a husky drawl.

"Well," I said, my voice choked off with desire. "I can't say for sure after only one taste."

"Ah, fair," he declared softly, and I realized we had both been speaking quietly as if in a confessional, making the miles-long cellar feel close and intimate, a space just for us. "Shall we try again?"

I nodded too enthusiastically, and his smile only flared wider in response, as if he found me endearing. I had no defenses against a man like this, and I knew it had little to do with my lack of experience and more to do with the fact that he was as near perfection as any man I'd ever known.

Devilishly handsome, powerful, kind, and complicated enough to keep my mind busy like a Rubik's Cube, with endless combinations of enticement.

When he raised the glass this time, it was to his own lips, and I watched as his strong, tanned throat worked, Adam's apple bobbing. Why was that so wildly attractive?

After taking his own sip, he sank a hand into the back of my hair to cup my skull and tilted me back slightly so my weight rested in his hand. It was a habit he had, I realized, of wanting me to trust him to balance me.

When his lips sealed over mine, slowly releasing the rich wine into my mouth, I drank it down greedily so I could taste the remnants on his tongue and teeth. A dribble of wine leaked down my chin, but Raffa's tongue was there before I could do anything, tracing the spill up my neck, jaw, and chin and back behind my teeth.

I was so wet that a draft of the cool cellar air teased my bared pussy like a feather. It made me realize Raffa still didn't know I'd taken off my underwear.

He kissed the edge of the smile I hadn't realized I'd been wearing. "Well?"

"*Divino*," I said back at him, feeling emboldened by the press of the thick erection I felt against my thigh. "Almost as delicious as me."

I was close enough to see the way his sunlit-whiskey irises thinned to frame blown-wide pupils, black holes of desire I wanted to throw myself into.

"Not quite," he protested. "But we just began our experiment . . ."

He trailed off to grab the bottle of wine, forgoing the glass entirely to hover it over my chest.

"Raffa," I warned. "This dress cost you hundreds of euros!"

He shrugged, gaze intent on my breasts. "I have wondered all day if I could see your nipples through this dress if it was wet, and I intend to find out."

I didn't have a good argument for that, and my wetness was seeping down my pussy to the fabric beneath my bottom, so I figured the dress was beyond redemption already.

In response, I leaned back on my hands to expose my chest entirely, hair shifting down my back, breasts raised.

His gaze flickered up to mine, warm with pride. "Do you know how delicious it is to watch you be brave and bold like this? It makes me want to worship you on my knees."

My mouth went bone dry at the thought of his dark head feasting between my thighs, big hands pinning me open for his hungry mouth.

Cool wine broke my flesh into goose bumps as Raffa splashed some at the base of my neck to watch it pool against my collarbones and trickle down my skin into the white linen, saturating it until the fabric was a wet pink press against my breasts.

"*Che bella*," he murmured almost to himself before ducking his head to sip the wine from my neck, licking down my chest until he hit fabric and then blowing cool air on my wet-wrapped breasts. My nipples furled so tightly they ached.

Raffa made an appreciative noise in the back of his throat and then thumbed one peak, tweaking it in a way that felt like pure electricity. His mouth followed, a welcome heat after the cold and the pain, his tongue curling around my nipple and his mouth pulling hard. The suction and abrasion of the rough linen made my pleasure arch down my belly to my shamelessly wet sex.

"*Ambrosia*," he said against the curve of my breast before sinking his teeth into the roundness to test its bounce.

I cried out, one hand clutching his thick, lush hair to keep him pinned to my chest.

He cooed something soothing before going to work on my right nipple, giving it the same treatment. When he was done, the fabric over my peaks was paler pink than the surrounding linen, almost sucked clean by his mouth. His lips were swollen and vividly red against the black stubble lining his jaw. But it was his eyes, dark, dangerous, and glinting like a predator's in the night, that made me physically tremble with want.

I wanted him to devour me, bones and all.

There was no fear or shyness, no trace of a virgin's mindset. The hunger that had lain dormant in my gut for so long was fully roused and ravenous.

"Raffa," I told him, breathless, chest heaving. "I think you should know . . . I'm not wearing anything under this dress."

The growl that rumbled through his chest was the sexiest thing I had ever heard. He tugged me closer to the edge of the table and dropped to his knees, unthinking of the hard ceramic tile. He didn't even wince, though, the full weight of his focus between my thighs as he pushed them open with his palms and stared at my bare *figa*.

I could feel my blush in my scalp and my toes, but the embarrassment only amplified my desire, compressing it from burning coal to something clear and diamond bright.

"How do I say 'lick me'?" I asked him, playing into his teacher kink.

He bit sharply at the soft flesh of my inner thigh to watch me squirm before lifting his black eyes to mine. *"Leccami la figa."*

"Leccami la figa, prego, Signore," I said.

Lick my pussy, please, sir.

"Such a good girl," he praised, and his approbation was headier than any amount of fine Italian wine. "Hand me the wine."

I did so without hesitation and watched with my lip between my teeth as he poured some at the crease of each thigh. After placing the bottle on the floor out of the way, he refocused his attention on my pussy, and it felt like a physical touch. Like a promise.

Suddenly, his tongue was on me, lapping up the alcohol from my thin-skinned groin without really touching my core. I thanked Gemma for gifting me sessions of laser hair removal for my eighteenth birthday, because the feel of his tongue against my bare skin was so exquisite I had to curl my hands around the edge of the table to resist pushing his head closer to the leaking center of me.

"Look at how wet this pussy is," he mused, resting his cheek on one inner thigh to stare intimately at my folds, using the thumb of his other hand to lightly trace from beneath my aching clit to just before my ass. When he raised his fingers to show me, they glistened as if with dew.

I started panting when he slid them into his mouth and sucked them, cheeks hollowing.

"*Come una droga*," he repeated, this time about my taste.

Like a drug.

Without hesitation, he wrapped his arms under my thighs, lifting me to his mouth, his hands pinning my hips still so he could attack me with his lips, teeth, and tongue.

I shouted, head dropping back between my shoulders as if my spine had been cut like a thread. Sensation exploded so sharply through my entire body, emanating from his magical mouth, that I felt like I would come out of my skin. His tongue found my clit, testing it with slow, languid strokes before increasing the pressure, wrapping his lips around it and *pulling*.

Under any other circumstances I might have been embarrassed by how quickly I came, hips juddering uselessly under his strong hands, pussy spasming like an open-and-closed fist around an ache even the pleasure couldn't quench. But the entire day had been a prelude to this. A slow-burn seduction of my body and mind that left me as wanton and ready as a seasoned courtesan in the historical romance novels I loved so much.

This was so much better than anything I had ever read about it.

Raffa licked me through the climax, moving away from my throbbing, sensitive clit to tongue at my entrance. The sound of his mouth licking up my cum was shameless and unbearably hot.

My hands wove into his hair and pulled tight.

"*Voglio di più*," I told him in Italian, because it seemed like the only language that could hold all this desire without breaking under the weight.

His response was a muttered curse and a sharp bite to the meat of my thigh. My hips jumped at the pain before it transformed into something with roots that dug deep into my pelvis and thighs.

"*Ancora*," I cried, needing his mouth on me but also his teeth, his pain like a punctuation mark of ownership on my skin.

Instead of biting me, he moved his mouth back to the wet slick of my pussy and reached up with both hands to pinch my nipples hard between his fingertips.

I cried out, voice breaking, pleasure shattering, vision whiting out with pinwheels of bright color popping through. His name was in my mouth like a prayer, a hymn I would never forget even long after I went home and left him behind forever.

Raffa, Raffa, Raffa.

I wanted to tattoo the word on the inside of my mouth because it tasted just as good as that wine and my sex.

My arms collapsed, dropping me to my elbows on the table, my bare feet—sandals long dropped to the floor—pressed to his broad shoulders. I was more exposed than I'd ever been in my life, and as I fought to find earth again, I wondered vaguely if my slight curves and skinny ribs could be attractive enough to him.

But then he was rearing up, wiping his glistening mouth with the back of his hand before he tore his belt open, his zipper down, and pulled out his cock.

I'd only ever seen one in porn or anatomy classes, and they certainly didn't look like this.

Vivid purple red at the broad, leaking head. The shaft so thick and long even his big bare hand seemed insufficient to handle it. The skin looked soft as silk, the precum pooling in the head creamy.

My mouth watered, and before I could think to stop myself, I begged softly, "Can I taste it?"

Raffa's groan vibrated his entire tensed body. "*Certo, piccola.*"

His thumb swiped over the head as he stepped closer. One hand pressed down on my belly to lay me flat against the low table, and the other, salt slicked, painted my panting mouth with his seed.

My tongue darted out instantly, tapping the sharply saline, faintly bitter taste of him. He was watching me with burning eyes, one hand fisted at the base of that big dick like a vise, precum leaking down onto my thigh as he loomed over me.

"*Come una droga*," I told him honestly. I licked my mouth clean, already thinking about drinking straight from the source.

"*Sei un sogno erotico*," he rasped. "You are already covered in wine, but I want to make you filthy with cum."

It was an expression of desire and a question. His entire body was coiled tight enough to snap, the muscles in his exposed abdomen and forearms corded, tendons and veins popped. If I told him no, I thought, he wouldn't. If I told him he was scaring me, that this was too much, he would put that painfully hard erection in the cage of his zipper and belt and walk away.

It made something real, something that had lain in the center of my chest since he'd taken care of me through my sickness and concussion, germinate and take tentative root.

I reached for him, wrapping my fingers in his shirt to tug him down so he had to brace a hand on the table, his hair falling from his forehead into his eyes, tangling with his long lashes.

"Come for me," I said as I pulled the front of my dress down, the loose straps sliding down my shoulders so most of my breasts were exposed. "*Vieni per me. Vieni su di me.*"

Come for me. Come on me.

Raffa loosed an animalistic rumble as he started to jack off his dick over my torso, his eyes pinned to my face as if the sight of *me*, Guinevere Stone, was enough to make him climax. Not my body, even. Just my eyes, locked to his blown black gaze as he furiously striped his cock and then came a minute later with a muted roar. His eyes squeezed shut, his full, kissed-pink mouth falling open as he came all over my skin.

I could have climaxed again from the sight of him and the feel of his hot seed marking my flesh like a brand.

I'd never felt so connected to anyone in my life, and for the first time in a long time, I was grateful for my virginity so I could have this first experience with him.

In the cellar of a vineyard in a €1,000 dress we'd destroyed because it was fun and sexy to do so.

I laughed, a high, bubbling sound that trickled out of me like water from the cupid fountain in the garden. Raffa opened his eyes, looking down at me as they creased at the corners with his small smile. In answer, I shook my head and pulled him down so I could share the laughter on my tongue.

"Tears after our first kiss, laughter after our first orgasms together," he murmured against my mouth, but his tone was playful. "You could give a man a complex."

I laughed again, then framed his impossibly beautiful face in my hands just because I *could*. Just because I somehow had license to touch this man all over.

"Well, I think you've destroyed mine," I admitted with a cheeky grin. "Goodbye, Madonna. Hello, whore."

"Vera," he said, eyes flashing. "I will not have you saying that. Enjoying pleasure should be a fact of life, not a sin or an insult."

"No," I agreed. "I'm saying I see that now. Thank you. You made me feel invincible even as you took me apart. I'm not sure how you did it."

He nosed at my cheek before pressing a kiss there. "In English or Italian, you are nothing short of brilliant. So bright, I could not ignore your light even when I wished to. If I made you feel that truth for a moment, I am happy."

"Sweet," I told him as I had in the car earlier that day.

He grunted a rejection, but I noticed, as he pulled away to reach for a hand towel meant for the wine-bottle condensation and started to clean me with it as best he could, that there was a smile tucked into one cheek.

"Um, Raffa," I said after he'd wiped the cum from my belly and helped me sit up. "What are we going to do about my dress?"

We both looked down at the wine- and cum-stained garment and burst into laughter simultaneously.

CHAPTER TWELVE

Raffa

"Absolutely not."

"Raffa!"

"At what point in our acquaintance have I given the impression that I can be moved once I make a decision? I am an immovable force, Guinevere, unless *I* am the one deciding to move."

"Oh my gosh, I can't believe I spent most of the day thinking you were so dreamy," she scoffed, crossing her arms in an approximation of a pose she'd adopted from me.

It was not nearly as effective, given she was five foot nothing and looked like a woodland sprite, but it was endearing nonetheless.

"Dreamy?" I asked, letting my amusement leak into my tone.

She sighed dramatically. "Yes, Raffaele, I *thought* you were dreamy. I've since reconsidered my position because you are being very annoying and stubborn."

"I prefer *obstinate*. It is one of my favorite English words," I offered helpfully.

Her response was an exasperated groan. "Is that the secret to being a successful businessman in Italy? Annoying your subordinates into obeying your orders?"

"First, Guinevere, you are *not* my subordinate. I make a point of avoiding entanglements with employees." Not to mention that most of the women I worked with were terrifying in their own right and married or related to me. "Second, for future reference, pouting is not the way to sway me. Though you do look *molto carina* when you do it."

"You're mocking me now," she declared. "Wow. And I thought I was supposed to be the younger one here."

"Trust me, you are."

There was a moment of quivering silence before we both laughed. I hadn't felt so at ease and happy in years, but the reason for my contentment wasn't something I was going to worry about now. I was still riding the high of making Guinevere come on my tongue twice and the sight of her pinned beneath me, asking me to paint her in my cum. Even though we were arguing, the atmosphere in the car was warm and intimate, our own little universe traveling seventy miles per hour under a clear summer sky.

There was something about being with her that insulated me from the normal demands of reality. Something stronger than a bubble, something with resiliency, because it made both of us feel safe to let our guards down. A snow globe of some idyllic fantasy world I never wanted to leave.

Our silence was undercut by the humming purr of the Bugatti as I drove us through the dark streets of Toscana after dinner at Fattoria Casa Luna. Imelda had asked no questions when I texted her to bring me a spare change of women's clothes, and she had even managed to keep a straight face when Guinevere emerged from the cellar wearing an oversized green T-shirt with the logo of the vineyard embossed on it in gold and a long tan linen skirt she had to roll three times at the waist so she did not trip over it.

Imelda was a good friend.

The winery was closed to tourists on Sundays, so she had invited us to have dinner together with her husband, Mario, on the patio. Their chef was almost as good as Servio, and I had the good fortune to watch

Guinevere try boar sauce for the first time, the way she smiled around her fork and hummed a random tune that spoke to her simple joy in the food.

It was a good day.

Maybe the best I'd had since I was too young a boy to know the evils of my world, playing games like *bocce*, *morra*, and *mosca cieca* with my sisters in the olive grove beside the barn.

There was an ache in my chest when I thought about taking Guinevere to Villa Romano, to the setting of those happy days. How she might bring them back to life for me after my father had tainted that place for most of my adulthood.

"Can I please explain why I think it's important that I go back to the apartment behind Fortezza da Basso?" Guinevere asked softly, turning in the seat to face me. Her hands were twisted loosely in her lap, but her thumb rubbed back and forth over the opposite knuckles almost frenetically, like she was nervous.

I dipped my chin for her to go on.

"I don't really know how to say this without making a mess of it, but I'm going to try because it's worth it. I mean, this"—she gestured between us—"is worth it. I know we've only known each other for like ten days, and I know I have to leave in just over a month. I know I'm probably going to sound crazy and scare you away, but you told me that the name Vera suited me because I'm honest or true, right? So I'm just going to say it." She dragged in a deep breath, held it for a second, and then let it rush between her lips. "I've never known anyone like you before, and I really don't think I ever will again. You say you aren't sweet or kind, but in the last ten days you've shown me more kindness and generosity than anyone ever has. Today was one of the best days I've ever had. I wish I could keep it perfectly preserved between the pages of a book forever and pull it out when I'm old and gray and boring again, but I know I'll never forget a moment of it."

She inhaled sharply, and I took a moment to glance at her even though I knew it would be hard to pull my gaze away from the sincerity in those thick-lashed eyes.

"All this is to say, this—*you*—are important to me. So even though this is inevitably a fling, I want to do it right. I want you to know that I am spending time with you because I like the man I am getting to know and not because I like the fact that you buy me Dolce & Gabbana or that you live in an actual palace. And I want the independence I was seeking in coming here. Living with you and relying on you, while it's been a godsend, just doesn't feel right in the long term. I want to stand on my own two feet so I can meet you halfway. Does that make any sense?"

I blinked as the last of her words sank beneath my armor and took root somewhere so deep inside me I wasn't sure I'd ever be able to dig them out.

"You know, I do not believe I have ever heard you say so much at once," I mused and then mock-winced when she hit me on the shoulder.

But her laughter was my reward. She had been so brave, my fawn, standing on those shaking legs but unwilling to back away. She knew what she wanted, and she wasn't afraid to stand up for herself. It was such a compelling combination, that tangle of innocence wrapped around a curious mind and a steel spine.

More intoxicating than any of the wine we'd drunk that day or any woman I'd ever wanted in all my thirty-four years.

"You are such a jerk," she said, but there was a soft smile on her face, and she reached over to squeeze my thigh as if she couldn't help it.

"You make a good argument," I said, tone somber now because she deserved that. "I am older, wealthier, and local here. The power skews in my favor, and I would never want you to feel . . ." I made a face. "As if you did not have a choice in this."

"For the record, I don't feel that way. At all. Remember earlier when I said you were dreamy?"

I chuckled. "*Distintamente*. Still, I hear you, and even though I do not like the idea of you sleeping across the street from a drug deal, I am not in charge of you, and I respect your decision to stay there." I hesitated before adding, "For now."

Her only response was a light laugh as she relaxed back into the seat, curling up her legs to hug them to her chest as she tilted her head to look out the window at the watercolor blur of the landscape passing by.

"*Grazie*, Raffa."

"You do not have to thank me," I said. "Just call me if you hear or see anything that is not right. *Prometti?*"

I did not think I would sleep knowing she was alone in that place and decided that one of my *soldati* could be spared to keep surveillance on her, at least for the first few nights, to make sure it was safe enough.

"*Prometto*," she swore.

Minutes later, she was asleep against the passenger door.

When I parked in front of her building, I took a moment to study her in the yellow cast of the sodium streetlights. Even bathed in unforgiving shadows, she seemed ethereal, some *fata* who should be curled up in a woodland grove instead of a Bugatti Chiron. I caved to temptation and pushed her hair back over her shoulder. It was heavy as brocade silk, fine and thick. I thought about braiding it again and was surprised when arousal pooled warm in my gut.

I had given up on this. On moments such as these, strung together like beads in a rosary, something only the pious could hold and find comfort in. The day of my father's funeral, faced with the eradication of my entire remaining family if I did not step into his shoes, the boy I had been and the man I had tried to become had died a swift death. Laid to eternal rest in the ground beside *capo dei capi* Aldo Romano. A man who, the last time I'd seen him, had branded me with the Romano family crest with the iron we used on wooden wine boxes at the vineyard. I had promised him I would never live under his rule again, and in a sense, I was right.

Instead, I took over it.

A reluctant mafioso if ever there was one.

Leo had teased me at first, wondering if I could stomach the responsibility after years in England living as a student and financial analyst.

To prove him wrong and keep my mother and sisters safe from the tradition of new capos eliminating the old reigning families, I buried who I was six feet deep inside my soul.

Somehow, an American foreigner had stumbled upon the gravestone. And instead of fleeing like any sensible, sheltered girl should have, Guinevere had sunk to her knees in the dirt and started excavating.

I did not want to take her inside that *appartamento di merda*. I did not want to leave her alone in my city. I did not even want her to leave my car.

But I appreciated her speech, both for the courage it took to speak so candidly and for her solid logic.

So I got out of the car, rounding the hood, and opened the door softly so I could catch her body as it slumped without the support. I unclipped her seat belt and carefully took her into my arms the way I had done so many times when she was sick. Only now, I could appreciate the way her hair smelled of the rosemary shampoo Martina had bought her and the lingering undercurrent of wine I knew would probably arouse me at inopportune moments for years to come. Her hair tickled my cheek as I curled her into my chest and locked the car. The key was in her purse, zipped into a compartment, and the door buzzed loudly when we entered, but she was out like a light.

The apartment still smelled faintly of za'atar spice and slow-cooked meat from the restaurant next door, but I could admit it was clean enough as I laid her in the thin, rough sheets of the single bed. It was easy to tug off the oversized skirt, but I left her in the winery shirt and arranged her aura of inky hair on her pillow so it wouldn't fall on her face. I itched to braid it but resisted because I realized I was just making excuses to stay.

It took effort, but I pressed a kiss to her smooth forehead and stood up to survey the apartment properly before I left. The lock was pathetic, so I used the butcher's knife from the kitchen and wedged its blade through the frame over the door as another layer of defense before I climbed out the window, closing it securely behind me and then dropping to the wooden overhang over the first floor. I dangled from my fingertips and fell to the cobblestones to find one of the skinhead thugs from that morning watching me with a cigarette hanging loosely from his gaping mouth.

"She sleeps safely every night, I'll give you one hundred euros a day," I told him, smoothing my shirt as I moved to the Bugatti. "If she has even one bad encounter, I will gut you and feed your innards to the rest of your crew."

CHAPTER THIRTEEN

Raffa

I did not see Guinevere for four days.

It was unacceptable but seemingly unavoidable.

I had neglected business for too long to take care of her when she was sick, and both my desk and my inbox were stuffed with items that needed immediate attention.

After my weekly security brief with Ludo, I was even more on edge.

When I had taken over the outfit, I had moved our focus from trafficking mostly drugs to prioritizing imitation products. The counterfeit trade was a wildly lucrative market with huge audiences in Asia, Europe, and America, and none of the other clans had monopolized it yet, so it was rife for the dominating. In the last four years, we had made over €250 million from that part of our portfolio alone. It seemed everyone wanted knockoff designer handbags and garments. Since we'd opened five factories run by Clan Riva and Clan Burette in Lombardy, our profit margins had doubled.

So why was Ludo reporting that the anti-Mafia police force was looking at the Camorra for the influx of street drugs through the port of Livorno?

"When was our last drug shipment?" I asked, tossing my pen to the leather desktop in exasperation.

Carmine and Renzo were both in attendance, too, the former seated beside Ludo across from me and the latter standing by the window with his arms crossed.

"Over a month ago. We were finishing out our agreement with the Albanians. We're scheduled for one last delivery in two weeks, but with the DIA looking into us, it's a risk," Carmine admitted.

"*Porca puttana*," I cursed, driving both hands through my hair. "How the fuck did this happen?"

"The Albanians?" Renzo suggested. "I know Carmine said they didn't seem aggrieved about finding someone new to work with, but they're fucking crazy. They could have turned rat out of bitterness."

"No," Carmine argued. "Yeah, they're nuts, but they've got their own sense of honor, same as us. Ratting on a former business partner is just not their style."

"Are you only saying that because you're sleeping with Drita Hoxha?" his older brother asked with raised brows.

"Fuck you," Carmine snapped, but before they could get into it, I raised a hand for silence and waited until I received it.

"Not the Albanians," I mused, chewing over my thoughts. "But who are they working with now that we have cut ties?"

When no one answered, I sighed. "Fine. Ludo, find out who they have moved on to. I do not like any of this. Why have we had relative peace for years, and now we have police interest in Livorno, which will fuck up our counterfeit production and transportation, an assassination attempt on me in Roma, and what?" I looked at my tablet. "Three cyberattacks on three separate holdings. Whoever our enemy is, he knows too goddamn much about our business."

"A traitor," Ludo said baldly.

The silence seemed to echo around those words.

I flashed back to first carving that word into the forehead of one of my father's enemies and wondered if I would be forced to do the same again.

"Signore Romano?" My housekeeper, Signora Angelucci, knocked on the door. "Signora Imelda Sabitini is here."

"Let her in," I ordered.

Imelda appeared in the doorway looking unusually haggard, her salt-and-pepper hair collected into a haphazard bun and her mouth pulled taut and pale like stretched taffy.

"What has happened?" I asked, moving to take her arm and help her to the empty chair between Ludo and Carmine.

She sat and let out a shaky sigh. "Mario caught someone in the laboratory last night. He will be okay, but they hit him over the head with a gun."

"Why am I finding out about this now?" I demanded.

"Be calm, Raffa. It has happened before that someone comes sniffing around to learn our secrets. You do not become one of the top wineries in this country without inviting espionage."

"Yes, but this is a pattern," I muttered as I shared a quick glance with my *soldati*. "These are obviously not isolated incidents. They are coming at us from all sides, trying to sense where we are weakest."

I checked the brief Ludo had emailed me again and noted that in the last month, ten of our top-grossing vineyards had been victims of either attempted cyberhacking or on-site breaking and entering.

That was *not* normal.

And it lent itself to the growing picture I was puzzling together.

Someone was coming for Clan Romano, which could only mean someone wanted to be *capo dei capi* for themselves.

I thought through the most dominant families in the region and concluded that three of them were the only real threats.

The obvious choice was the Pietra clan, which had feuded with my family over control of Tuscany for decades before they'd killed my father. The détente had lasted almost half a decade, but perhaps they had regrouped enough to make a serious comeback. Renzo and Carmine had urged me to wipe out the entire clan, but my life outside the Mafia still lingered in my soft tissues and made me weak.

The Riva family was headed by the matriarch Pamina, who was as bloodthirsty as they came and known by *la mafia* as Vampira because of it. They were located to the west and focused mostly on drug trafficking through the port of Rimini to and from eastern Europe. We had a good relationship, but her voraciousness made her fairly unpredictable. An argument could be made that she was setting her sights on the eastern ports as well so she could dominate the entirety of central Tuscany, Emilia-Romagna, and much of Marche.

The next were the Grecos in Liguria, who made no bones about lusting after total control of the north, but who I had always thought to be too stupid to make a go of it. Still, idiocy wasn't really the deterrent it should have been, and they were ridiculous enough to think they could take over now that Aldo Romano was dead.

The question was, Why hadn't they tried before now?

I'd been in power for four years, and while I'd faced assassination and coup attempts in the beginning, they had ceased after four or five prudent and public messages had been sent to our enemies, written on corpses.

It seemed so . . . random that they should come for me now.

Imelda was bright enough to see my mind working and suggested, "The Clan Romano of today is not what it was under your father. It's taken you time, but you have changed the outfit fundamentally, Raffa. You must see others could be threatened by that."

"Success is success. People will be threatened by it no matter how it happens or who it happens to." It was disgusting, but a truth I'd faced countless times. Even friends I'd had at Oxford had begrudged me my sudden inheritance, though it meant the death of my own father. It was easy for outsiders to get caught up in the glamour of success, to be ignorant of the way it corroded over time.

"Maybe. But you have brought so much modernity to a staunchly traditionalist society. Even at *la fattoria*, we are scoffed at by old wine-makers who say the use of technology on our scale is basically sacrilegious. My husband manages the grapes, but I manage the money. A woman. And I am not the only one you have empowered, Raffa."

"It is the twenty-first century, and I was raised by a strong mother and three older sisters. We have a female prime minister, for fuck's sake."

"And even she doesn't declare herself a feminist," Imelda pointed out. "We are not talking about national politics, anyway, but Mafia politics, which are so far stuck in the past, I am surprised the men don't insist on wearing togas and being fed grapes by hand. All this to say, you might not have police eyes on you, but you have the eyes of the underworld watching and scrutinizing your every move."

I crossed my arms over my chest and sank back into my chair. "I knew it would seem to weaken my position when we stopped focusing so much on drug smuggling, but money laundering, agromafia operations, and counterfeiting make us more money than we made under my father, with half the risk."

Imelda held her hands in the air, her wrists bony and covered in bangles that chimed as she gestured. "I know, Raffuccio, but this is the world you live in."

"She is right," Renzo added, moving from the window to stand over my shoulder, where he usually resided, like a permanent symbol of support and a giant deterrent to my enemies. "The capos have quieted, but many of them were unhappy when you made Pamina capo after she killed her husband."

"He nearly killed *her*," I said, but I was exhausted by this subject and had been for years. "The women in this organization are some of the best minds we have."

"You made it clear Martina will be consigliere when Tonio dies, and he only occupies the position still out of respect for your father," Carmine pointed out. "Martina already does most of the legal legwork."

"Enough. I know my faults, but bringing the Camorra into the twenty-first century is not one of them. New York's *capo dei capi* Dante Salvatore would agree with me, as would Damiano in Napoli. The issue here is that someone is coming for us, and I will not have peace until I know the face of our enemy." I stared each of my men in the eye. "Find me names, and do not show your faces to me until you do."

Renzo clasped me on the shoulder on his way out, taking my words as the dismissal they were. Carmine kissed Imelda on the cheeks before following Ludo and Renzo out of my study, closing the door behind them.

"I am sorry," I told my mother's best friend, "that Mario was hurt because of this."

"It is not because of you directly. All the top wineries contend with such things."

"I will increase security," I promised.

She shrugged and waved the words away with one hand, but her eyes were shrewd on me. "You look half-elated and half-exhausted. Does either have anything to do with the lovely Guinevere?"

I hesitated, rubbing my overgrown stubble as I considered telling her anything about my conflict around Vera. How much I already ached to see her. How these new risks made me afraid for the first time in a long time because I did not want my dangers to become hers.

My family was insulated at Villa Romano with staff and soldiers to tend to their every need and protection. Guinevere was just a foreigner trying to have an adventure on her own in a new place, and unwittingly, she'd run into the arms of the worst monster in Tuscany.

"Once you said you would never enter into a deal with the family," I reminded her, then asked the question I had always wanted answered. "Why did you, in the end?"

"You have made me a very wealthy woman. I think, in this country, we have a strange relationship with the Mafia. We hate them and revere them in equal turn. You are terrifying and horrible so often, and yet you can change generations of lives in an instant. The investment you made in Alfonso took it from a local pizzeria to an international chain. My nephew is at school in London and told me he had a slice of home from their first location there." She sighed, toying with a marble wolf figurine from my desk as she searched for the words. "What is the saying? *A femmena bona, si tentata e resta onesta, nun e stata bona tentata.*"

A good woman, if tempted, remains honest, but that means she was not well tempted.

"You are a complicated man, but not a bad one by any means. Your father delighted in his cruelty when it was necessary, and I believe you see the Mafia as a game, one of life and death, but with calculation and an eye to the stakes. If you can manipulate a situation to suit your needs without death, you will do anything in your power to make it happen. I suppose I wanted to indulge my greediness and avoid my fear of death."

She ended with a joke, but I was not in a laughing mood hearing those words.

I had always struggled with my definitions of *good* and *bad*, *righteous* and *evil*, and how these words could be applied to me. I had killed, stolen, and lied and would continue to do so for the rest of my life with little compunction.

But there was a soft spot in my heart I couldn't seem to harden no matter how much I tried. I was not empathetic, exactly, but I could be moved by beauty in all its forms and sought valiantly to preserve it.

I had purchased the crumbling church in the town next to Villa Romano simply because it had once been beautiful, and I wanted it restored instead of demolished for housing. I had helped to fund the continued excavation of the gladiator training grounds outside the Colosseum in Roma, even going so far as to buy a block of buildings in order to demolish them for the sake of discovering and preserving our history. I had killed Martina's husband because he was eroding her day by day in front of my eyes and I could take it no longer, and I had allowed Pamina to become capo of her territory after killing her own husband for the same kind of abuse. I had helped Guinevere because I could not resist such a beautiful woman lost and alone with the odds stacked against her.

Not much of a moral code, one founded on keeping beauty intact instead of one of honor or justice, but it was the only one I had.

"I wanted a good life for my family long after I am dead," Imelda added, peering at me with cunning gray eyes the same color as that marble wolf. "Isn't that why you are where you sit today? *Capo dei capi* of everything you swore you'd never touch?"

"It is easy to have good intentions when the stakes are low," I conceded. "There is nothing I would not do for my mother and sisters. For my chosen family in the Camorra."

"Yes," she agreed. "This is our way, I think. Family before all else. It is not something foreigners understand well."

That was true, but I considered Guinevere and wondered if there was another exception there. The dead sister who had given her a kidney, the mother and father she lied to in order to give them peace of mind so she could have some freedom. The future she was intent on following because it was what they wanted for her even if she did not want it for herself.

"You care for her," Imelda said, a note of awe in her words.

Frustration wrapped a firm hand around my throat and squeezed. "She is . . . interesting."

"Interesting and lovely."

I chuckled, because that word would never be free of the memory of Guinevere's wine-soaked skin and breathy, surprised moans of pleasure.

"Yes, lovely."

"You deserve such loveliness. I know you do not agree, but it is true. Everyone needs happiness, Raffa. And if you are worried that you are too much the villain to deserve it, consider that unhappiness will only drive you further into the dark. I know that is not the kind of man you wish to be in thirty years. The kind of man your father was." She got up and came around my desk to press her cheeks to each of mine. *Chi non risica non rosica.*

He who does not risk does not get the rose.

It was an Italian proverb my mother had used my entire life, so it was fitting that her best friend would use it now to taunt me to take a chance on Guinevere.

"There is no future if I tell her, and there is no future if I do not," I admitted as she pulled away. "She is going back to America in a month."

Imelda shrugged one shoulder and walked toward the door, stopping only to throw back, "Is she?"

CHAPTER FOURTEEN

Guinevere

I spent the rest of the week at the apartment and threw myself back into my original plan for my vacation as if I was not missing Raffa nearly every moment I wasn't with him.

Even though I had almost nothing to go on, I endeavored to find records of my father and his relatives in the area. I knew his given birth name—Mariano Giovanni—even though he had changed it to John when he moved to America, and I remembered that he once mentioned going to the Uffizi on a school trip from his village, so I knew he had been raised in the countryside close to Florence. I did as much research as I could on online genealogy sites, but there was absolutely nothing linking John Stone to anyone in the country. So I went in person to the state archives office, and then, when that failed, I met with a priest at the Basilica di Santa Croce to ask about getting access to church records, which I had read were much more thorough. Though he was kinder than the official at the state archives, the priest informed me that unless I had a last name, there was almost no way he could help me. Mariano and Giovanni were both incredibly popular names, especially for the generation of men born during my father's time.

A dead end.

One that didn't surprise me but still hurt somewhere deep inside, where the longing to truly belong to this magical culture and country throbbed like a beacon.

Still, I found other ways to absorb and assimilate. I took a weeklong language class that I almost forgot I'd signed up to take, each session four hours in the morning and afternoon. It was an immersion class, and I left every day feeling as if my brain was stuffed with Italian cotton, verbs and conjugations coming out my ears. I had a mind for math and patterns, and I made the entire undertaking easier by breaking down conjugations into simple formulas and tessellations. All that work was worth it, because when I met Raffa for dinner after class on Tuesday and again on Thursday, he was shocked by my progress and insisted we spend both meals speaking in Italiano.

Outside of our two dinners, we only found time to take a joint run through the city to the top of Piazzale Michelangelo to watch the sunset. We were both sweating profusely in the thick July heat, my fancy running clothes so saturated from my running the hilly steps that I might have been embarrassed if Raffa hadn't led me to the stone railing overlooking the city center and wrapped his arms around my waist. He pressed his nose into the hair behind my ear and licked a stripe up my salty neck.

"*Divino*," he murmured.

And just like that, I felt somehow radiant.

It was a kind of magic that he had to make me feel like he only saw the best version of me, even when I was at my worst.

There had been live music in the piazza, and artists splashing colors across canvas to replicate the famous view as the sun broke open on the rooftops and spilled rose gold light through the streets.

It was magnificent.

"I saw the real *David* today," I told him as we stood looking out over the Arno and the glowing red rooftops.

"And what did you think of Michelangelo's most famous creation?" he asked, even though he seemed more preoccupied with nibbling on my ear.

"Eh, I think the sight of you naked would be much more appealing," I admitted.

He laughed softly right into my ear, and it was the loveliest thing I had ever heard.

"I will have to see what your verdict is after you have seen me as David is," he teased in that smoky voice. "But in case you did not notice in the wine cellar, I am much better endowed than that poor *bastardo*."

I laughed so hard one of the tourists beside us glared at me, but Raffa only shot them a glower and made a rude gesture only Italians would understand.

I had planned to go back to his palazzo for dinner, but he got a phone call on our run back into town and reluctantly asked me for a rain check.

As much as I wanted to spend more time with him, his business gave me plenty of time to explore on my own terms. Armed with my new passport and access to my own money again, I set out to enjoy everything Florence had to offer. I ate a sandwich from the famous All'antico Vinaio while I strolled through the Piazza della Signoria to look at the many statues in the Loggia dei Lanzi and concluded that the theme of female rape was a little too dark to be enjoyable. I walked through the leather market and laughed as various shopkeepers hit on me with a kind of irreverent jolliness that was endearing. I finally saw the Duomo in all its splendor, climbing the 463 ridiculously narrow steps to the innermost point of the dome to see the ornate ceiling mural *The Last Judgment*, painted in the 1500s. It was just as breathtaking as I'd always assumed, and not only because I'd just taken a steep climb.

A few classmates invited me out one night to have dinner at a pizzeria down the road from our little school, and I delighted in talking with people who felt a similar *passione Italiana*. The people of so few countries spoke Italian, yet our instructor had told us it was the fourth-most-taught language in the world. A German student wanted to learn because she was a fashion addict, a Guyanese couple because they had become passionate about Italian cooking, and an older Scottish man professed he was obsessed with Italian football and wanted to be able to speak the language of the players he spoke about on his podcast.

I truly believed that the ability to speak other languages was an attainable superpower. The first time I had an entire conversation with a shopkeeper in Italian without them switching over to English, I bought myself a gelato in triumph.

The only blight on my week, other than not seeing Raffa daily, was the fact that my father was entirely too nosy about my experience and upset about my lack of communication.

"How is France?" he asked me Friday afternoon over the phone. "You should video call us in front of the Eiffel Tower one day. Your mother would love that."

"I'm trying to save on data," I explained, but there was an ever-growing knot of toxicity in my gut each time I lied to him. "But how are you and Mom doing? Enough about me and my adventures."

"Enough about them? You've barely told us anything."

I could hear the frustration in his voice and the underlying edge of worry. I knew it was hard for them to give me this space, that they had tried to discourage me in every way they knew how—no financial support, emotional manipulation, incentivizing a summer off in Michigan by promising to rent a cabin on Gun Lake—but I knew it all came from love and loss. They had come close to losing me so many times when we were struggling to figure out my diagnoses and when my left kidney started failing, only to lose their other daughter when I was finally in a stable place. It was the kind of thing that changed a person fundamentally, and the tectonic plates in the foundation of our family had been shifting uneasily ever since.

"I told you I've made friends with people in my language class," I repeated, keeping my calm even though I wanted to end the conversation and go back to my fantasy life. "About Greta and Fergus and

Bibi and her husband, Ramesh. I told you that I love the food and the history, and I've already been to all the museums. What else do you want to know, Dad?"

He made a frustrated sound before silence fell, as heavy and smothering as a thick blanket.

"I miss you and Mom," I told him honestly, letting the emotion that had simmered on low in my belly all day long surge painfully to the surface. "I miss you both so much that I try not to think about it because it makes me want to cry."

His breath whooshed out in stark relief. "We miss you, Jinx. I'm having trouble sleeping wondering what could happen to you over there."

"I am in France, not Syria. I got really sick from the plane, but I'm fine, Dad. Truly, I am happier than I've been in . . ." I couldn't say "my entire life" because it felt mean somehow, so instead I said, "A long time. I feel like I was always meant to do this."

I knew I was. Meant to be in this country, in this city. It filled something that had been vacant in my chest since childhood, a sense of belonging amid the summer-toned buildings with streets named romantic things like Via dell'Inferno and the wine windows where you could pass money through a small slot and receive a glass of wine to drink while you strolled. It was vibrant and loud and filled with so much history and culture I could live there forever and never know it all.

And it felt like home in a way that Ann Arbor just never had.

But how could I explain that to my father when he would have a heart attack knowing I'd even set foot in Italy?

"Dad," I ventured carefully. "You know, you've never told me why you left Italy and renounced your citizenship."

Silence.

"Dad?"

"Why are you asking about this right now?" he asked, weary and annoyed. "I have to be at work soon. I should let you go."

"No, Dad, please. I'm asking because I've wondered all my life what could have driven you away from your home."

Another pause, the edges of this one so sharp it felt like teeth at my throat.

"I suppose I could ask you the same thing," he said finally, each word a bullet shot through the phone line. "Have a good day, Guinevere."

I stayed frozen with my phone to my ear for five minutes before I could unfreeze my muscles enough to set it down. The small pile of postcards I'd started collecting from my explorations caught my eye, and I pulled them apart with my fingertip to stare at the images: Cathedral of Santa Maria del Fiore, Pitti Palace, Michelangelo's slightly underwhelming *David*.

I flipped that card over with my fingernail to read what I had written that day.

> Gemma,
> Even in the tomblike hush of the museum, I know you would have burst out laughing seeing *David* in real life. He is just a boy, curly haired and slim, with fabulous definition because Michelangelo is a genius, but still, just a boy. And yet people come from all over the world to see him. After seeing so much of the art this city has to offer, I think I will stick to my appreciation of its food, architecture, and living—and much more handsome—men.
> Xoxo,
> Jinx

The postcards were new. But I had started writing to Gemma the day after my parents told me she was dead, and I wasn't sure I would ever stop. She had emailed me throughout her own travels through Europe, and I still had the message she'd sent the day before she died.

Just as she had been in real life, writing to her was a direct link to my sanity. She was still my cheerleader, urging me to experience life, to make mistakes and get messy because even when it hurt, you had a good story to tell.

And Gemma had been a masterful storyteller.

Which was what made her such a fucking good liar.

It hurt to know I was channeling that part of her along with her more admirable characteristics, but I was ruthlessly unable to give up on this dream.

Especially when it now included Raffaele Romano.

There was a quote by the Italian poet and translator Petrarch that I had written into every journal I had kept for the last few years: "The more we live, the more constellations we discover."

The more I grew to know Florence and Raffa, the more questions I had about each and the farther down this path I felt compelled to travel.

I wasn't sure anything could stop and make me turn back now.

A horn honking outside my window drew my attention away from the postcards. I checked my phone screen and winced because I'd had a short run after my last day of language class, and I needed a shower before I could get ready for the charity event at Pitti Palace with Raffa that evening.

Another honk, this one a long, obnoxious blare.

I stopped halfway to the bathroom, something drawing me toward one of the big windows so I could lean out and look at the street.

Laughter frothed over when I saw Raffa's Bugatti out front, illegally parked in a way that took up almost the entire narrow street. He had his suited forearms crossed over the roof of the car as if he had been waiting for me for ages, and he checked his watch dramatically at the sight of me.

"About time," he called up to me, amusement tamped down in his tone. "*Vieni, Cenerentola!* Your carriage awaits."

I laughed again. "If I'm Cinderella, does that make you Prince Charming?"

"Mmm," he pretended to muse, uncaring of the two cars piling up behind him and the small crowd of people watching our interaction. "In that case, perhaps it is better to say that you are Kore and I am Pluto."

"I like that more," I agreed, crossing my arms over the wrought iron railing of the Juliet balcony. "I don't suppose you have any pomegranate we could have for dessert?"

His grin creased the tanned skin beside his eyes and mouth, those uncharacteristically sharp canines flashing in the sunlight, his hair as darkly bronze as that of a sculpture of the god of the underworld excavated from the past.

He was the most beautiful thing I'd ever seen, and I was currently living in the most beautiful place in the world, so that was saying a lot.

"I think something could be arranged," he said. "Now, come. We do not have much time before we have to arrive."

"Clearly, I am not ready," I told him, gesturing to my damp tank top and running shorts.

Carmine had showed up with most of my things the day after I'd moved into the apartment, though I noticed not everything had made its way from Raffa's house. It was hard not to hope that it was because he still expected me to spend a lot more time there.

"No, but you cannot prepare properly here. Just take your phone and come, *cerbiatta.*"

"Bossy," I called as I turned into the room to grab my things.

"I *am* a god," he retorted, making me snort.

When I met him at the car, there was a backup five cars deep behind him, and someone at the end of the line was yelling obscenities at him in Italian.

"Let's go," I said, opening the door to slip inside.

But Raffa was suddenly there, pressing me into the door so that it closed again. He spun me by the hip to face him and then slid one hand under my hair to cup the back of my skull and the other to lift my leg up around his hip. Again, I was balanced only by his grace, wrapped like a vine around him.

I didn't complain even though we were in public, watched by those drug-dealing teens who had actually been quite sweet to me, and yelled at by angry drivers. It all faded away the moment his hands were on me. All I could see were those pale-brown eyes, luminous as sunlight trapped in amber.

"Is that how you are going to greet your consort, Kore?" he asked me, the words winding around me, another form of bondage.

"Kore was a virgin maiden stolen from a field of flowers by Pluto," I reminded him. "If you want me to greet you like that, I think a slap might be more appropriate."

His chuckle was all smoke. "Proserpina, then. How would she greet her husband?"

I tipped my chin up just as he curled over me, shielding me from the crowd.

"Like this," I whispered, before closing my lips over his and sliding my tongue into his mouth.

He tasted like dark chocolate, rich and slightly bitter. I hummed at the flavor and plastered myself even closer to him until I was trying to climb him like a tree.

Finally, he broke away with something that was half chuckle, half moan. "That is exactly how I expect to be greeted from now on, *capisci?*"

"*Pidocchio!*" someone yelled from right behind us. "*Che cazzo fai?*"

Scumbag. What the fuck are you doing?

I jumped, but Raffa was already turning, pressing me back into the car like a human shield. I peeked around his shoulder to see a balding, middle-aged man with hairy knuckles gesture rudely at us.

Seemingly unperturbed, Raffa crossed his arms over his chest and coolly asked, "*Ma perche non ti fai i cazzi tuoi?*"

Why don't you mind your own business?

"Jesus, Raffa, let's just *go,*" I hissed, tugging on the back of his expensive blazer.

He did not move, not even when the angry man stormed right up to him and drilled a finger into his chest.

"*Faccia di merda, vaffanculo!*" he shouted, spittle flying as he glared up at the much taller man.

"*C'è una signora presente*," Raffa told him calmly, but I could see that somehow he'd grabbed the man's finger and had twisted it nearly back to his wrist. "*Bada a come parli.*"

There is a woman present. Watch your mouth.

"Raffa, it's fine," I insisted, but broke off when the man spat, "*Chi? Quella puttana? La pagherò cinque euro.*"

Who? That whore? I'll give you five euros for her.

I closed my eyes for a second.

Oh no.

I opened them again when Raffa abruptly moved off my body. He had the other man by the throat of his shirt, pushing him a few feet to press against the wall surrounding the Fortezza da Basso. I could see the corner of his mouth moving even though he spoke too quietly for me to hear. Before I could blink, his hand was in the man's pocket, wrenching out a wallet and then a card from within it. He shook it gently in the man's purpling face and then pocketed it himself.

He stepped back, and I heard him say, "*Capisci, Enrico?*"

The man, presumably Enrico, nodded, the color draining from his face as he stared unblinking up at Raffa. "*Mi dispiace, signore. Mi dispiace.*"

Raffa gently slapped his face. "*Ricorda solo quello che ho detto.*"

Just remember what I said.

He turned on his heel, waved at the few locals gawking at him, and then whistled as he walked back toward the car. When he caught my eye over the hood, he inclined his head.

"Should we go, then?"

I nodded, struck dumb by the display, and slid bonelessly into the interior.

It was only when we were well on our way to Raffa's palazzo that I found the words to say, "Well, that was intense."

Raffa's mouth was flat, and his hands were white knuckled on the wheel.

He didn't respond.

"Do you usually deal with conflict like that?" I teased, but the joke fell to the floor of the car in the heavy air.

His fingers squeaked as he curled them tighter around the leather. He flinched just slightly when I gently placed my hand on his tensed thigh.

"Raffa," I murmured. "Are you okay?"

"What he said to you was not *right*," he said through gritted teeth, eyes flashing to mine just long enough for me to see the anger still burning there.

"No," I agreed. "But I am not a whore, and him saying the words didn't make me believe them."

He made a noise of frustration in his throat. "Maybe in the US men do not deal with insults like this, but here? It is the worst insult for a someone to say such things about a man's mother, sisters, or *ragazza*."

"*Ragazza*," I repeated, because it could mean "girl," but in this context it usually meant . . . "Is that what I am, your girl?"

He let out a sharp, almost barking chuckle before most of the tension dissolved in his big frame, his thick musculature no longer like granite beneath my hand. When he reached for my fingers, I offered them to his hold and watched as he placed a kiss in the very center of my palm.

"You are not an *idiota*, Vera. Do you think I buy new wardrobes and carry sick women to the bathroom if I do not want them to be my girl? If a part of me had not already considered you mine?"

I smiled, because the compliment was so him. Condescending to start, with the sweetest finish tinged in primal possession. It was an addictive cocktail I wanted to drink until the end of time.

"I like the sound of being yours," I told him boldly, running my thumb over his bottom lip, loving the contrast of the silk against his stubble, almost a short beard now. "But for the record, I do not need you to protect my honor."

"For the record," he countered as we pulled through the automatic gates into the courtyard of the palazzo, "I will protect you from anything that comes for you in any way that it comes." When I opened my mouth to protest, he placed our joined hands over it. "No, Guinevere. This is the kind of man I am, so this is the kind of man you must accept." He paused, mouth flatlining. "For at least the next four weeks."

I stared at him for a long moment, and he let me, his own gaze unwavering on mine. There was a scar on his chin, white beneath the black stubble, that I wanted to trace with my finger, and a cowlick in his wavy hair that constantly caused an errant piece to fall over his forehead in his eyes. Only two weeks of knowing him and I felt as if I had memorized every beautiful aspect of his face, the exact color of those maple-brown eyes and the curve of each thick, slashing brow, the mobility of his smiles and the variation of his glares.

Yet I did not know much beyond the facade.

I did not know what he did for a living, exactly, or where he had grown up. I knew he had sisters and a best friend named Leo, along with a motley crew that seemed to cycle through his palazzo as they pleased, each one a hybrid of friend and employee. I knew he could be cold and domineering but also secretly, achingly generous and kind.

I knew that if I let myself see beyond the beautiful veil of his face, I could fall in love with this man.

Even if what I found was darker than what I'd known.

Hadn't he called himself Pluto instead of Prince Charming?

Did it matter that the hero who had saved me my first day in Tuscany could be so much more complicated than a two-dimensional stereotype?

There was a huge gap between the hero and the villain, and most people occupied the gray space within.

In fact, I couldn't delude myself into ignoring how arousing it was to see him stand up for me like that. To know that one insult against my honor could bring him to such violence was almost intoxicating. That he could curb that same tendency with me and be so tender only multiplied its effect.

"Okay," I said, curling my hand around the sharp edge of his jaw, fingers digging into the hinge to bring him toward me for a kiss. "I can accept it for four weeks or four decades. It actually makes me feel safe."

When I pulled away from our brief embrace, his eyebrows were raised and his tone wary when he said, "I broke the man's finger."

I winced. "I figured by the sound it made. And the angle."

His eyes were narrowed, and one thigh jittered up and down in an anxious motion. "I threatened him."

"Yes," I agreed, wondering why he was pressing on this bruise, thinking it was my wound when it was clear it was his own.

One hand went into his pocket to grab the card he'd stuffed there. He held it up so I could see that it was a driver's license of one Enrico Tornei.

"I told him I was taking this in case I changed my mind and decided that a broken finger wasn't enough of a lesson."

I blinked. "Um, just out of curiosity, what would have made you change your mind?"

Raffa put the license back into his pocket before reaching out to palm my throat, thumb rubbing over my pulse point. I'd never been held like that before. It felt proprietary. A necklace of ownership.

My pulse kicked into a sprint, and my chest tightened.

I *liked* it.

"Your reaction," he said. "He is lucky you are made of sunshine. If you had shed one tear or voiced one misgiving, I would be dropping you off and going to pay Signore Tornei a visit."

"Raffa," I said, my tone a mangled mess of amusement, exasperation, and a little awe. "You can't just . . . assault people."

"I can if they hurt your feelings."

I shook my head. "Who are you, even?"

Finally, the edge of his firm mouth curved slightly into the little lopsided smile I was growing addicted to, the look of reluctant amusement more attractive than most people's full-blown grins.

"Raffaele Romano, the god of Firenze's underworld, remember?"

I laughed, leaning into his grip on my throat in a way that made my nipples hard as I sought his mouth. "All hail Rex Infernus," I teased.

He frowned, hand shifting so he could lift my chin. "Latin?"

"Another name for Pluto," I said with a little shrug. "It was always my favorite. It means 'King Below.'"

"King Below," he echoed. "Fitting. *E stasera sarai la mia regina.*"

And tonight, you will be my queen.

CHAPTER FIFTEEN

Raffa

"Stop pacing," Martina said through her laughter. "A woman cannot be rushed."

I checked my Rolex again as I turned on my heel and walked back along the path I had been tracing for the last fifteen minutes. There was being fashionably late, and then there was being *late*. But that wasn't the entire reason I was anxious.

Guinevere's reaction to my aggression that afternoon had both eased and excited something inside me. I had acted instinctively, as I would have if he had insulted Mama or my sisters or Martina. No one insulted the women in my life and remained unscathed.

Apparently, Guinevere was now among their ranks, and truthfully, it was hard not to question if I would go to the same lengths for her that I had and would go to for my family after knowing her for all of two weeks. It was so unlike me and so wildly *stupid* that I could not quite digest it.

But I knew it was the truth.

Especially in the car, after she'd questioned me. When she had blinked those luminous dark eyes, filled with their usual curiosity but also a notable degree of acceptance and even a little arousal. When she had taken my face in her hand and kissed me in a way that felt like a stamp of approval.

"Okay," she had said, "I can accept it for four weeks or four decades."

I rubbed a hand over my eyes as a fantasy of those four decades unfurled like cinema roll behind my lids.

Enough.

It was one thing to indulge in this affair. To enjoy Guinevere while I had her. And quite another to dream of any future.

She was as bright and hopeful as a shooting star across my dark galaxy, and I had to remember that. Fleeting, but lovely to behold.

"The dress fit?" I asked Martina, even though I had asked her twice already.

That was the other reason I was pacing.

I could not wait to see Guinevere in that dress.

It was one she had seen in the window of a boutique we'd passed on our run to Piazzale Michelangelo the other night. Midstride, she had halted and turned to the window as if drawn by gravity. I had stopped immediately and then followed behind her silently as she crossed to the display and raised her fingers the way she had in the car our first day out in Florence. There was reverence in her face as she stared at the gown, and when she finally realized I was beside her, she startled as if awaking from a dream.

"Sorry," she'd murmured, that gorgeous flush spilling from her cheeks to her chest. "I've never seen something like this before."

"A dress?" I asked with an arched brow to tease her gently.

A little shoulder shrug any Italian would be proud of. "It looks like art."

I sent a soldier out to buy it the next day.

"It fits," a voice said, slicing my thoughts to ribbons. "And it's gorgeous."

I followed the sound up the grand staircase leading from the second floor to the marble-floored foyer.

And there she was.

Italian writers had coined the term *sbigottimento*, which referred to a phenomenon that had no direct English equivalent but meant the profound and arresting feeling of being confronted with the object of your desire. It was almost sickening in its extreme. I lost my breath to it, heart knocking too hard at my breastbone as if it was fighting to escape my chest and go to her.

Guinevere.

Gliding down the stairs toward me in a diaphanous dress of sheer layers hand painted with vague impressions of flowers in light pastels. It made her look like a nymph shrouded in fog, picking up petals as she walked through dew in some blooming spring pasture. All that thick dark hair had been loosely curled, some caught up at the back of her skull where I liked to cup my hand. I imagined the end of the night when I could take out the clip and watch the heavy fall of mink around her bare shoulders.

Proserpina, indeed.

Without my consent, my hand had found its way to my chest, where I was pressing it as if I could force my heart back inside the cage of my ribs.

Too fanciful for a capo. Too dangerous for a man in my position, and yet there I stood.

Struck by *il colpo di fulmine*.

A lightning bolt of passion so acute it felt like it could be love.

"You haven't said a word," Guinevere noted as she took the last step and floated toward me, made taller with her heels but still so much shorter than me I had to bend my head to maintain eye contact. "Don't tell me you hate it?"

"I hate myself for agreeing to take you as my date," I admitted caustically. "Because I will be the one having to fight off a room of admirers."

Her laugh was delighted, the antidote to the angst burning like acid in my gut.

"We must stand as a united front, then, because you look absolutely . . ." She drifted off as her gaze dipped to my polished dress shoes and rose up the length of my black Dolce & Gabbana suit. Her fingers ran lightly up the velvet lapels to the open throat of my black dress shirt. I swallowed against the press of her touch and watched the way her mouth fell open on a little sigh. "Stunning."

I grasped her fingers and brought them to my mouth. "Thank you, but it does not hurt my pride to know that I pale in comparison to you. You are lucky—otherwise I would be angry we are late."

"He has a thing about time," Martina inserted helpfully from her seat on the antique velvet sofa. "You get used to it."

I leveled her with a cool look that ordered her to be quiet.

She mocked zipping her lips and then throwing away the key like the insolent *soldato* she was.

"I have a present for you," I told Guinevere, reaching into my pocket for the gift I'd found in a small shop in Santa Croce the other day on my walk home from meeting with my man at the local bank.

"Raffa, *no*." She was suddenly fierce, pushing my hand back into my pocket. "Equals, remember? I'm not here for gifts and palaces."

I stared at her implacably, waiting for her to take her hands from mine.

"I'm here for the sex," she declared loud enough for Martina to snort Peroni through her nose. "If you must know."

I pursed my lips to hide my smile and merely raised my brows until she sighed and let go. Only then did I lift my closed fist between us.

"This is a gift I bought for fifteen euro in a local shop," I told her dryly. "But it is something I thought would be fitting for a girl whose nickname in America is Jinx."

I turned my fist over and opened my palm to reveal the red coral pendant attached to a gold chain.

"This is a *cornicello*. In the south, where my father was from, it is a good luck charm. There are many stories about how people came to wear them that date back to the Neolithic period, but my favorite is that it was first derived from a crescent moon, for the goddess of the moon. She is also the goddess of the hunt, and her symbol has always been the deer. So what better lucky charm to give to my unlucky little fawn?"

Guinevere reached out tentatively, mouth open in a little moue as she touched the twisted coral horn with her pinky. "It's beautiful, Raffa. And very, very sweet," she teased, looking up at me with black-velvet eyes strewn with glitter.

I turned her around, so she would not see the way she affected me, and efficiently clipped the necklace around her throat. When she faced me, I could see that the pendant rested in the hollow of her throat.

"It's your favorite color too," she murmured, touching it against her skin. "I love it."

I crossed my arms over my chest and stared at her with blatant displeasure. "Really? I could not tell. Did we not talk about how I expect to be greeted just a few hours ago?"

She rolled her eyes, but there was no curbing her wide smile. She practically *sparkled* with happiness.

"Oh, I think I remember something about that. Let me . . ." She braced a hand against my chest and rolled to the tips of her high heels, using her other hand to tug me down by the back of my hair when she still couldn't reach. When her lips touched mine, I could feel the shape of her smile.

"Better?" she murmured.

"No."

When she opened her mouth to speak, I sealed it shut with my own and kissed her the way I'd wanted to for the last two hours. I cupped her neck instead of her head so I did not ruin her hair and pressed my other hand to the base of her spine so I could tip her slightly over my arm and absolutely plunder her mouth. I could feel her knees weaken at the onslaught, the feathery moans of her pleasure like a siren's song urging me to take her right there in the middle of the foyer.

It had been almost a week since I'd last really touched her, and every inch of me burned to teach her more, show her how explosive I knew it would be between us.

A harsh cough splintered the moment.

"Ah, now you are *really* running late," Martina called out with faux helpfulness.

"Togliti di torno." I told her mildly to fuck off, and both Martina and Guinevere laughed.

"So," Guinevere asked after I'd helped her into my Lamborghini and she had rolled her eyes at my excess. "What is the charity we are raising money for tonight?"

"For the museum itself. There are ongoing construction and restoration for a building constructed in the sixteenth century."

"Fair enough. You don't seem like the kind of man who would enjoy events like this."

"I am not." In fact, I tried to send Martina or Carmine in my place whenever I could. I rarely even visited Florence proper, running most of my business from Villa Romano and traveling through the north as needed.

"Then why are we going to this one?"

"Two reasons. The first is that I have not made an appearance in Florentine society in some time, and it is a beast that requires at least infrequent feeding. There will be many people there I should rub elbows with. Even then, I might have canceled last minute if it were not for my second reason." I slid a hand over her thigh and squeezed. "Seeing you in that dress, and later, seeing you out of it."

Her laugh was light and as frothy as overflowing champagne. "Raffa, trust me, you do not need to take me to a gala to see me naked."

"No?" I arched a brow.

"No," she said firmly, linking her hand with mine. "Honestly, I think if you snapped your fingers and looked at me in that way you do sometimes like I am prettier than Botticelli's Venus, I would do almost anything you asked."

"Even though you are a virgin?" I asked, despite never having explicitly spoken about her sexual history.

Her blush was obvious even in the dim car. "Maybe because I am. It makes me feel wanted and confident to have your attention. To earn your praise like I did in the car on the way to the vineyard the other day. I've always been very goal oriented."

I laughed, startled by her endearing honesty although I should have been used to it. "Well, I am happy to oblige. Tonight, you will come back to the palazzo with me."

"Yes," she agreed. "But I'm afraid I don't have any pajamas at your place."

Cazzo, her coquettishness was making me hard just as we pulled up to the valet drop-off for the gala.

I put the car in neutral as we waited in line for the valet and slid my hand under her hair to pull her close.

"You can sleep in my cum," I offered graciously and then ate the little gasp straight off her tongue.

◆ ◆ ◆

I had not worried about how Guinevere would act on my arm, despite knowing the event brought the cream of Florentine society out of their villas, palaces, and penthouses in enough finery to feed a third world nation for years.

Still, she surprised me.

As she always seemed able to do.

Though it was obvious she had never walked a red carpet, she was elegance personified on my arm as I led her to the photography points and smiled for the cameras. It was a short carpet with few paparazzi, mostly for local news outlets, but she was still blinking owlishly and adorably by the time we entered the palace.

Her Italian was much better than I had given her credit for, and the week of immersive language classes had only honed it further. When we engaged in conversation with the mayor and his wife, she was able to understand the flow of conversation and respond charmingly, if a bit slowly, in kind.

By the time we moved on from the Moris, they were utterly charmed by the *bella donna Americana*.

As was I.

The entire central piazza of the palace had been transformed into an extravagant outdoor ballroom, complete with a tiled dance floor overseen by a sixteen-piece orchestra. They had transported some of the more recognizable statues from the galleries into the courtyard, so I had the pleasure of teasing my date about her resemblance to a marble nymph with flowers in her hair. It was a warm evening, the sky gone to ink, with pinpricks of barely visible stars and a full-bellied moon I found Guinevere peering at as if they were a work of art framed in the rectangular silhouette of the buildings.

"It's beautiful," she admitted when I caught her, as if it was a secret.

"Do not be embarrassed by your enthusiasm for life," I told her, dredging up an old quote from Ivern Ball that suited her so well. "'Knowledge is power, but enthusiasm pulls the switch.'"

"I haven't heard that before," she said with a shy smile. "But I love it."

"You should. It is true in general and for you. It is one of my favorite things about you."

We had a quiet moment without an audience, tucked behind the statue of the nymph in a pocket of shadow.

"Oh? What else do you like?" she asked coyly, leaning back against a pillar and touching the low neckline of her dress. My mouth watered.

I stepped forward, curving around her to shield her from view as I moved her hair off one shoulder and placed a kiss there.

"It would be more sensible to ask what I do *not* like about you, *cerbiatta*," I murmured against her throat, touching my tongue to her pulse point to feel it pound. "To tell you everything I admire would take too long."

"Flatterer," she teased, but clutched me closer and arched into my mouth.

"Ah, Signore Romano, I should have known I would find you in some dark corner, feeding on a woman."

The Neapolitan dialect made me tense even before the words landed. I turned to face the unwelcome intruder, keeping Guinevere at my back.

Sansone Pucci stood before me with a grim smile.

"Usually, people in dark corners do not like to be disturbed," I pointed out to him coolly.

The last time Ludo reported to me, Sansone had been in the south, wrapping up a drug seizure off the coast of Calabria.

And suddenly, he was here in my city.

"I find things are always best brought into the light," he countered with that smug superiority I had sensed in him from afar. "We have not officially met, but I had to introduce myself to the famous Raffaele Romano. Sansone Pucci."

I inclined my head but said nothing, as he clearly already knew my name and was trying to set into motion a game of cat and mouse. He would come to understand that I was neither. The symbol of the Romano family had always been a wolf, a reference to Romulus, the founding father of Rome. And wolves did not play games with their enemies or their prey.

"You know, I once met your father," he continued. "I believe we were questioning him about fraud."

"Which you were never able to prove," I reminded him curtly. "Do not speak ill of the dead, Pucci. Whatever our differences, he was still my father."

Sansone peered at me as if trying to read the truth in my implacable veneer. The history of my falling-out with Aldo Romano was legendary in the right circles, those in the underworld and those in high society. I had refused to take over the business as his only son and so had been cast out. From the ages of twenty-one to twenty-nine, I had not set foot in Tuscany because of the man who ruled it.

It was the only reason I had been able to come home after his death and take over as *capo dei capi* as seamlessly as I had. Everyone knew I had sworn never to follow my father, and when I moved back to Tuscany, I set up my own wealth management firm instead of taking over as CEO of the Romano Group, leaving it in the capable hands of Tonio and Leo.

It seemed my plausible deniability was coming under scrutiny now.

"And who, may I ask, is the lovely lady?" he had the audacity to ask, peering around my shoulder to smile at her.

I forced myself to stay calm even though I wanted to gouge his eyes out for even daring to look at her.

"Guinevere," I said, pulling her in close at my side. "May I introduce the deputy director of the police, Signore Pucci."

"Pleasure," he said in perfect English, stepping forward to take her hand and bring it just short of his mouth in a facsimile of a kiss. "How did a foreigner come to be on the arm of Signore Romano tonight?"

She cocked her head slightly, considering him with none of her usual cheer. I watched as she managed to look down her nose at the much taller man.

"How does any woman end up on the arm of a man? He wins her favor."

"Ah, and how did he win yours?" He stepped closer with a plastic smile I wanted to break into pieces.

"By being a perfect gentleman," she replied smoothly, not realizing her unintentional reference to my nickname, Il Gentiluomo.

Sansone's smile sharpened. "How wonderful for you both. I had heard from mutual acquaintances that you were prepared to be married to Stefania Burette."

Guinevere did not shift one inch at his insinuation, and the last vestiges of my defenses against her crumbled like old stone.

"I am not," I replied coldly.

"Obviously," Guinevere added, turning to wind her arm through mine and beam up at me. "You promised me a dance, darling. Don't make me wait any longer?"

I bent to press a kiss to her nose, oddly grateful for her staunch support in the face of the mysterious animosity between Sansone and me. The faith she had in me was so misplaced but felt like absolution.

"*Certo, piccola,*" I agreed. "Excuse us, Signore Pucci. I hope you have a pleasant time in my city."

He nodded, pushing his hands into his pockets as I took Vera to the dance floor and spun her into my arms. I could feel his eyes on us long after I lost sight of him in the crowd and knew with certainty that somehow we had gotten on his radar.

Porca Madonna.

"You seem very angry," Guinevere said softly, running her fingertips from my shoulder to my neck in a comforting caress. "Who was that arrogant ass?"

My bark of laughter was so loud, it drew attention from the partygoers around us.

Guinevere smiled in triumph at the sound.

"You are the most surprising girl," I told her as I led us around the black-and-white floor. "I knew you would animate my life in ways I could hardly fathom, but the reality is much better."

"For a grump, you can be very romantic."

"I am Italian," I reminded her.

She hesitated. "I'm sorry he was so rude about your father."

"Do not be. He was a *pezzo di merda.*"

Her dark eyes searched my face, so soft and warm, inviting me to trust her enough to explain. For one heart-stopping moment, I wanted to lay all my awful history at her door and beg her to let me stay.

"May I cut in?"

I swallowed my sigh, wishing the night could have been about enjoyment instead of riddled with irritation.

"No," I told Stefania without looking at her.

Guinevere stayed in my arms, but her gaze tracked the woman behind me. I danced us farther away.

"She looks like she swallowed a lemon," she told me.

"That is just the way her face is."

"Raffa," she scolded, but she was biting back a smile. "Don't be rude."

"Why not? It was rude of her to interrupt our dance."

"Is she a friend? I assumed so because she seemed comfortable enough to ask for a dance in the first place."

"She used to be," I confessed flippantly, though something in my gut clenched as I continued to say, "though lately she has confessed to wanting . . . more. Marriage and the like."

Guinevere's lovely face cycled through expressions before landing on something like amused bewilderment. "Can I ask . . . why does she seem to think you want to marry her?"

I enjoyed the way she framed the question because it spoke of her resolve to believe that I had never intended to and never meant to give Stefania that idea. There was no insecurity in her tone or judgment, just that brand of Guinevere Stone curiosity.

"Our families run in the same circles, and my mother has always thought Stefania would make a good wife for a man in . . . my position. She comes from a good family with wealth and connections." I shrugged.

"And she's beautiful."

I shrugged again. "There is beauty in everyone. It does not mean you are attracted to everyone."

"So you have never . . ." She flushed, and I chuckled warmly, touching her cheek with my knuckles to feel its heat.

"No, I have never wanted to. And if you do not mind, I would prefer to think about sleeping with the *donna accattivante* in my arms."

We finished out the dance like that, flirting and laughing as if the deputy chief of the anti-Mafia commission was not watching me like a hawk, and as if Stefania was not eyeing me like a praying mantis.

At some point, I spun her dramatically and reeled her back into my arms, bending her back to place what was meant to be a playful kiss on her mouth. But the moment our lips met, I was lost to the taste of her tinted in sweet white wine and some kind of berry lip gloss.

Everything fell away.

Sansone.

Stefania.

The rising threat against my outfit and the pressures of my position, the responsibility to my family.

Nothing existed under the black-velvet sky except Guinevere and me, safe inside our globe.

"Come with me," I whispered against her damp mouth when I realized I was dangerously close to indecency.

In answer, she took my hand and let me lead her from the well-lit dance floor back into the shadows of the columns and then out into the Boboli Gardens. The gravel crunched under our feet as I took her up the left path bracketing the planted terraces and fountains into the lantern-lit side garden behind rows of hedges. We walked for another minute until we found a stone bench I could pull her down onto, pressing my mouth to hers before she was even fully seated.

She hummed her pleasure onto my tongue and sank her hands into my hair, nails scratching at my scalp.

"I want to touch you here," I told her, voice already raw with want, my hand slipping from her throat to span the width of her upper breasts exposed by the low cut of her gown.

"Yes," she hissed, tipping her head back to give me better access, wanton as a nymph from Roman legends and just as ethereal. "Every night I've gone to bed without you, I've imagined how you might touch me next."

I groaned as I brought my face to her chest, kissing along the neck of the dress until goose bumps blossomed on her skin. I couldn't resist the urge to bite a bruise into the flesh beside her *cornicello*, and when I was done, I rubbed the pink skin with my thumb.

"Now everyone who doubted will know just how much you are mine."

"*Io sono tua*," she breathed, pushing down the cups of her dress so that her pretty breasts were bathed in moonlight. "Please, Raffa."

I complied with her silent plea and ducked to lave her nipple, using my fingers to twist the other tight in my grip. Her cry was choked off, hips squirming against the bench as she sought pressure to satisfy the ache growing between her thighs.

"Are you already wet for me?" I asked against the bottom curve of her pale breast, biting into it because I liked the look of her ringed in teeth marks. "The only romance I am willing to give is this moonlit garden. What I want to do to you would make your virgin ears blush."

Her breath caught before she said, "I want you to tell me. I want to be shocked. I want you to break open this locked box inside me filled with fantasies I don't know how to voice."

I lifted her other breast to my mouth and sucked a bruise beside her nipple before giving it the attention she begged me for with wordless moans.

"I want to taste your sweet *figa* again. Lick you until you are leaking down both thighs and screaming for me to ease the ache in your pussy needing to be filled." I raised my fingers to her mouth and rubbed my thumb over her bottom lip so it fell open at my touch and then slowly slid one finger, then two and three, over her tongue as I spoke. "I would start with one and then work you open on my fingers to train your untried pussy to take my cock. I think you would start to cry, pretty tears leaking down your face as you begged shamelessly for me to fuck you. Would you cry for me, *cerbiatta?*"

"Yes," she gasped around my fingers before sucking them harder into her mouth, rolling her tongue around the tips.

"And I would fill you up, but first, I would fuck this lovely mouth and teach you to take me deep into your throat, so I would show you how to take my cock the way I like. Rough and deep."

She groaned around my fingers. I took her hand and laid it against the thick ridge of my trapped cock. "Can you imagine taking all this inside you? In your mouth and your throat and your delicious pussy?"

"Yes," she said again when I removed my fingers, lifting her head from its supine position between her shoulders to reveal blown-out pupils, eyes glazed as if she was high off my dark fantasies and desperate for another hit. "You'd have to teach me. I've never done that before."

"I can do that," I promised, gripping her chin hard to punch a kiss to her lips before I stood up and took off my jacket.

She watched, panting, breasts wet and limned in silver light as I placed the inside of my blazer on the grass beside the bench.

"On your knees, pretty fawn."

Our eyes collided like two cars, the sensation crashing through my body, rearranging my molecules until I was someone else entirely than I had been before. I watched as her trembling hand raised to her damp mouth, and I thought for one moment it was fear that moved her.

But then she was almost falling in her haste to drop to the ground on the jacket, arranging her skirt around her knees so that she was not tangled before she looked up at me and slowly licked her red mouth.

Cazzo, she was like something out of a Titian painting, at once innocent and powerfully erotic. For all her lack of expertise, she was eager and excited by the dark side of pleasure.

I stepped close to her, pinching her chin so her face was lifted to mine and I could gauge her expression. "What do you want?"

"You," she said instantly, tongue dipping out to tap my thumb.

I wrapped her hair in my fist and used it to press her cheek to the swell of my dick behind my trousers. She rubbed against it, then turned her face to mouth the shape of my shaft with her lips.

I groaned and decided she was owed my honesty. "You are the sexiest woman I have ever known."

Her little moan vibrated through the cloth to my cock.

"Take it out," I told her, because I wanted to watch the excited flutter of her hands at my fly as she unzipped it and pulled me out through the gap in my boxer briefs so quickly that the shaft slapped across her cheek, smearing precum there.

She did not laugh or recoil. Instead, she tilted her head back and opened her mouth.

"Feed it to me?" she asked quietly, just a hint of nerves.

I fisted the base and painted the center of her tongue with my precum.

"*Divino*," she murmured before chasing after me when I moved away. "I want to take more. I've thought about drinking straight from your dick since I tasted you at Fattoria Casa Luna."

I palmed one of her cheeks, hooking a thumb inside her mouth alongside my shaft as I fed more into her hot, wet mouth. Her tongue flicked against the underside of my cock and thumb, lips tightening, sucking as if she would not be satisfied until my entire length was buried inside her.

"That is such a good girl," I praised her, voice wrecked with the pleasure searing through my hips, up and down my body to curl my fingers and toes. "You look so *bella* with my cock stretching your lips."

She moaned, lashes fluttering against her cheeks as she pushed forward to take even more of me. When she gagged, she frowned, pulling off and then replacing her mouth with her hand.

"Can you teach me how to take you deeper?" She licked her swollen mouth. "Into my throat."

My low spine tingled, balls drawing tight at that sweet voice asking for such filthy pleasures.

"*Si, piccola*, open your mouth and take a deep breath. When you want to gag, swallow around my cock until the feeling passes."

She tugged me closer by the shaft and licked, kittenish, at the pearls of seed dripping from the end of me before sinking straight down my length. Pleasure cut through me like a knife to the belly. I folded over slightly, hand tightening in her hair as I helped thrust her along my shaft. The feel of her swallowing around me, the sight of saliva pooling at the edge of her mouth and sliding down her chin, and the way her eyes flicked up to look at me, wet with effort from taking me so deep, had me on the edge faster than ever before.

"Fuck, Guinevere, you are going to make me come too quickly. Yes," I hissed as she swallowed again and the last of my shaft was wedged down her throat. I pressed a palm to her throat gently just to feel the way I filled her up.

I jerked out to the head, her gasp cool and wet against my skin as she sucked in more air.

"Again," she demanded, lifting her hands to wrap them around my hips, fingers digging into my ass to thrust me forward.

How was I supposed to survive her?

She took me harder this time, a tear trickling down her cheek as she moaned at the thick stretch in her throat. I held her there for a moment, long enough to say, "With practice, I will fuck your face just like I can fuck your pussy. Fast, hard, your nose bumping against my groin. I will come straight down your throat like that."

I released her, but she only took a quick breath before diving back down, hungry for me in a way I had never imagined. She continued, sucking wetly, uncaring of the mess I was making of her, just desperate to make me come.

"Please," she said finally, "I want you to come in my mouth."

I used my hand in her hair to tilt her head back farther and then leaned down to spit in her waiting mouth. "Hold on, then," I warned her.

She shivered, clenching her hands around my ass and tugging me forward.

This time I pumped straight to the back of her throat. I set a rhythm she could follow to time her breaths and shallowly fucked her pretty face. One of my thumbs dragged through a tear on her cheek and brought it to my mouth.

"Even your tears taste sweet," I told her, voice stripped bare as pleasure seared down my spine, threatening to turn it to ash as soon as I gave in to the fiery heat of lust Guinevere was stoking with her mouth. "Going to come. Be a good girl and lick every last drop."

She hummed in agreement, and it was the last straw.

I pulled out of her throat and rested on her tongue. "Open wide."

Fisting my cock hard and tight, I grunted as my atoms collapsed in on themselves, an implosion of pleasure that whited out my vision. I opened my eyes to watch cum stripe her tongue before she sealed her lips over the sensitive head of my cock and suckled out every last ounce of seed.

"*Madonna santa*," I cursed, loosening my hold on her hair and stroking it instead.

She pressed her cheek to my trouser-covered thigh and planted a dainty kiss on my wet, spent cock.

"I loved that," she admitted, her voice roughened by the face fucking and all the sweeter for it.

"Clearly, I did as well," I mused dryly before sinking to my knees in front of her. "Are you a soaked mess beneath these skirts?"

She bit her lip but nodded as she raised her eyes to mine. "Yes."

"Do you need my help to come?"

"Please."

I stroked her cheek and lifted her skirt with my other hand until I found the bare skin of her thigh, tracing it up to her sex. She was drenched straight through the silk of her panties, thighs damp with it.

"What a dirty, filthy, beautiful girl you are," I told her proudly, kissing her. "Now do you want to ride my hand?"

She gripped my wrist to keep my hand against her pussy and rose to her knees, spreading them slightly to give me better access. I slipped two fingers beneath the edge of the silk band and groaned at the slick, hot feel of her cunt against me.

"*Così perfetta*," I told her as I lightly pinched her clit, and she gasped sharply, dropping her forehead to my chest in surrender to the pleasure. "How quickly can I make this pretty cunt come for me?"

She panted as I sank two fingers inside her, using the heel of my hand to press against her swollen clit.

"Ride them," I said in that cold voice I'd grown to know she loved.

Slowly, her hips started dancing, rocking back and forth as she fucked herself on my fingers. After a moment, she whimpered, hands clutching at my hair.

"Not enough?" I crooned. "Do you need more?"

"I want *you*," she said, words almost slurred with pleasure.

As much as I would have loved to fuck her in the grass, there was no way I was going to take her virginity in the Boboli Gardens. Instead, I pressed another finger and then another inside her so she could feel the stretch and ache.

That was when she came to life.

She tossed her head back, nipples still lifted out of her dress and pebbled in the cool night air as she rocked her hips against me. Her eyes were closed, face tipped to the moon, and I knew I had never seen anything so beautiful.

"*Vieni per me, cerbiatta*," I ordered, bending to fix my teeth to her neck in a sharp bite.

She shuddered against my thrusting fingers, grinding into the heel of my palm as she cried out. Her hand clutched so hard in my shirt she popped a button, but I barely noticed, transfixed by the noises she made as she wrung every last drop of her climax against me.

"*Bellissima*," I told her, pressing a soft kiss to her throat before running my nose to her jaw and kissing that too. "How are you feeling?"

She sighed and laughed at once, opening lazy lids to grin tipsily at me. "One of the best moments of my life, I think."

"*Bene*, then we agree," I said, kissing the little moue of shock on her mouth before carefully moving my hand from under her skirt. "Now all I want is you in my bed."

CHAPTER SIXTEEN

Raffa

We collected ourselves as best we could, using my silk pocket square to clean up her smeared lipstick and beneath her skirts, but there was no doubt we would leave the party immediately. The idea of being inside a crowd with her now seemed abrasive, the bond between us too open and raw to handle scrutiny or company. My mistake came when Guinevere excused herself to the bathroom as we moved through the courtyard and I did not accompany her. I was caught up in conversation with one of Florence's most well-renowned historians, excited about the prospect of her return so I could introduce them because I knew how much she thirsted for Italian antiquity, when I heard the choked-off cry.

I knew it was her immediately, the hairs on the back of my neck standing on end, my heart in my throat.

My head snapped up from where I had bent it to speak with the older man, and I surveyed the crowded courtyard, searching for the woodland creature in the dewdrop dress.

I found Stefania instead by the bar, lip pulled back over her teeth.

"*Scusi*," I said to the gentleman and cut through the bodies between us like a knife through butter.

The last people divided in front of me, revealing Stefania towering over Guinevere with an empty wineglass and an ugly sneer.

While Guinevere, my beautiful fawn in her dream dress, was covered neck to waist in red wine.

Anger possessed me like a demon, immediate, irrevocable.

"Stefania," I growled, stalking forward to put myself between them. "What the hell do you think you are doing?"

"This slut," she spat in Italian, "claims she is your woman."

"That is right. She is," I said, the words cold enough to stick to my tongue.

Stefania glowered at Guinevere over my shoulder, but I snapped my fingers to draw her attention back to me. "Eyes on me. It seems I am the one you have a problem with, so you should have taken it up with *me*. It is ugly of you to be so childish."

She flushed beneath her tan, and if Guinevere was right and Stefania was a beauty, I could not see it now, and I doubted I would again.

"She is too young for you," she leered. "A child."

"I'm twenty-three," Guinevere stepped in to say with haughty disdain, and I was so proud of her gumption I almost kissed her right then and there.

"We have an understanding," Stefania had the audacity to begin.

I snarled, stepping forward into her space to glare down into her eyes. "Listen to me well, because this will be the last time I speak with you. We have no understanding. You had a wish that would never come true. I felt sorry for you before, but not now. Do not contact me again, Stefania, or you will not like the man you receive."

"I don't like him now," she snapped, then leaned in close to hiss in my ear. "You forget who my father is. You need my family's support."

I did.

Capo Burette was in charge of our two largest factories in Lombardy and had enough wealth and influence to sway the rest of the outfit if he was angry enough to turn against me.

It would be prudent to make nice with her, forgive and forget and kiss her curved ass so that she would go home to Papa and tell him how good a man I was.

But I would not.

Not only because Burette was enough of a man to make his choices without his manipulative, bratty daughter's influence but also because she had brutally embarrassed Guinevere in front of all these guests.

And that was unforgiveable.

"I do not need anyone," I promised, turning my head to speak directly into her ear, watching the way she shivered at our closeness. "I am Raffaele Romano, Il Gentiluomo di Toscana, and you would do very, very well to remember who you are speaking to before I become any angrier."

I leaned back to show her the hellfire in my gaze and then turned sharply on my heel to go to Guinevere. She was standing with her hands fisted at her sides, chin tipped pugnaciously, eyes narrowed at Stefania.

I bent my knees to be closer to eye level to examine her expression, my hands gentle on her shoulders. "Are you okay?"

She sucked in a deep breath before looking me in the eye. Something wicked lit in that brown gaze, and a moment later she was lifting a hand to pull me in for an open-mouthed kiss.

It was not long or overly erotic, but it delivered her point well.

She was mine and I was hers.

I grinned down at her, wildly enjoying the show of possessiveness and aggression. "Should we go home?"

She took my offered arm, head held high, and followed me out of the hushed courtyard.

It was only when we were safely ensconced in the car again and pulling away from the valet station that she sighed wearily and slumped in her seat.

"I much preferred when it was *you* pouring wine all over me," she mumbled.

I couldn't help but laugh, even though fury still tingled in my fingertips. "Me too. I am sorry that happened. It was not quite the night I had envisioned."

"Maybe not. But I would take countless glasses of wine to the chest if it meant even one more orgasm like the kind you've given me."

I laughed again, reaching over for her hand because I could not sit there without touching her. "I do not think you will have to pay that price again, thankfully."

"I just want a long shower and to crawl into bed with you." She hesitated, sliding me a look. "Er, assuming I'll be sleeping with you and not in my old bedroom."

"You assume correctly."

She hid her smile behind her hand, but I could see it in her profile all the same.

My phone rang, Ludo's name flashing across the car system display. I pressed Answer and said, "*Pronto?*"

"Raffa, the police are at Guinevere's apartment," he said in Italian.

Guinevere gasped, so I did not need to translate.

I sped past the turnoff for my place and headed across the Arno toward Fortezza da Basso.

"Why?"

"Someone called and reported a possible break-in twenty minutes ago. The pigs are there now looking everything over."

My mind whirred.

I did not believe in coincidences. What was the likelihood that I would show up at the function with Guinevere and hours later someone had broken into her apartment?

"Find out what happened *exactly*," I ordered. "We are on our way now."

"Martina is two minutes out. She will meet you there."

I cursed after hanging up, my thoughts so preoccupied I almost snarled when Guinevere reached out to touch my arm.

"I really can't afford to lose all my possessions twice in one trip," she tried to joke, the concern on her face for *me* when she had been the one broken into. "Are you okay?"

I grabbed her hand, brought it to my mouth, and kissed the center of her palm before curling my fingers around it. Touching her grounded me like a lightning rod.

"No, I do not like the idea of a strange man in your space." I could barely say the words without my teeth grinding. "I do not like that it seems they waited for you to be gone, which means they were probably watching the apartment."

"Oh my God."

"I am not saying that to scare you, only to explain why I feel like breaking something."

"That is so creepy," she murmured, gaze going vacant out the window as she thought about it. "I will definitely have problems sleeping after this."

"You will not be doing it under that roof," I declared. *"Assolutamente no."*

Absolutely not.

"Raffa," she started, but I raised our joined hands to my mouth and gently bit her finger to stop her.

"No. On this, you must agree with me, Guinevere. You cannot expect me to sleep knowing my worst nightmares have come true and someone has broken into that apartment. I am too far away to make it to you if something happened. Please," I said, even though I had not begged anyone for anything since well before my father died. "Come stay with me for the rest of your time here. Even without this danger, I would want you under my roof."

She was silent for long enough that I dragged my gaze from the road to see she was chewing her lower lip.

"I don't want to be a burden," she said finally.

My laugh was a short, sharp exclamation. "Guinevere, I dream of you nightly. It will not be a hardship to wake up and realize reality is far better than the dream."

We drove onto her street to see blue police cars blocking the entrance to the apartment. I pulled up behind one and got out, ignoring the way one cop yelled that I could not park there.

"Take this," I said, yanking off my jacket to help Guinevere into it. If she held it closed over her breasts, it would hide the worst of the wine stain.

"Thank you," she said, surprising me by taking my hand as we moved forward.

I should have let go, but I did not want to.

Martina was waiting by the front door with a strained look on her face. If Guinevere was shocked to see her in a designer suit and high heels when she had only seen her in workout gear, she didn't blink an eye.

This Martina was my lawyer, the future consigliere of the northern Camorra.

"What is it?" I asked.

"Deputy Chief of the DIA Sansone Pucci is upstairs with the police," she explained. "He arrived just after me, still in his party clothes."

"*Merda*," I muttered, running a hand through my hair. "Okay, thank you for the heads-up."

She nodded, then turned to Guinevere. "How are you faring?"

"I've had an eventful day, and all I want to do is sleep," she admitted.

Martina's gaze dipped to the blazer and the stained dress beneath. "I bet. Okay, let's get this sorted so we can all go home."

We followed her up the stairs past a few police officers and a noticeably distressed Signora Verga, who started weeping again when Guinevere lifted a hand at her in greeting.

The door to the apartment was smashed at the handle, huge splinters of wood in the door and the frame like bared teeth. Guinevere's hand tightened in mine, so I tugged her closer.

Inside, the apartment had been ransacked.

Absolutely nothing was left unturned.

The drawers were ripped out, clothes on the floor and tossed over the unmade bed, the mattress sitting at an odd angle to show they had searched beneath it. Guinevere let out a choked noise, our joint hands moving to her mouth to cover the way it dropped open in shock.

Rage burned through me. I wanted to let go of her hand, banish her to the car, and tear into the policemen about what the fuck had happened. Demanding answers or bribing for them until I knew exactly who had been in my woman's room.

But she was there by my side, leaning into it like she needed me to balance her, and I could do nothing but calm down enough to see to her needs before my own.

I released a careful breath through my teeth and went straight to Pucci.

"Ah, Signore Romano, we meet again so soon," he greeted me jovially as I approached, gesturing with one hand for the forensic tech to leave.

"*Non dirmi cazzate*," I warned. Cut the bullshit. "What happened here?"

His mouth turned down at the corners as if he was hurt by my tone, but he knew well enough not to play anymore. "Signora Verga called because she heard the crash of the door. The other tenant on this floor and the other two were out for the night, and Verga did not feel safe exploring the noise herself. By the time the first police arrived on scene, the invader was gone." He ignored my growl of frustration but accepted a sealed plastic bag from a tech and handed it to me. "Do you recognize this?"

It was a small, carved wooden statue of a lion with wings, like the emblem for Venice. Only inside the mouth of this figurine was a wolf pup limp with death.

I looked up at Martina before handing it over, acid surging up my throat.

The man who had organized my assassination attempt had called himself San Marco, like the famous piazza in Venice, and now this. The symbol for Florence was a lion, too, but wingless, and my family had used the symbol of the wolf long before we'd come up north.

The threat was as clear as if they had left a severed head on her desk.

This unknown threat linked to the northeast was officially coming for us, and they would not stop until they owned what the Romanos had had for decades, the Camorra's seat in the north.

Fortunately, Signora Verga had arrived, and Guinevere's attention was captured by consoling the older woman, so I could speak without worrying if she would understand me.

"Is anything missing?" I asked.

"No, they left only destruction and this symbol." Pucci stepped closer, voice lowering, his eyes on Guinevere over my shoulder. "You clearly know what it means."

A muscle in my jaw popped as I ground my teeth.

"No, it feels like a child's game," I said finally, letting my posture loosen. "There is a group of teenage wannabe thugs that loiters out front. You should check in with them."

"Yes, it could have been some initiation," Martina added with a wolfish grin. "Kids these days."

Pucci blinked blandly at us both before huffing, "I could help, if you were honest with me."

I blinked blandly right back at him.

He sighed. "Listen, I don't know if you've truly given up the ways of your father or if you're much cleverer than people have given your playboy stereotype credit for, but whatever this is reeks of gang activity. You wouldn't want your sweet young American girl getting hurt because of the mistakes of your father, would you?"

Martina's subtle hand on my arm was the only thing grounding me. I breathed in through my nose and fixed my coldest smile between my cheeks.

"If you mean to worry me with mentions of my father, you are missing the mark, Pucci. When he died, I did not shed one tear. Everything about him was rotten through to the core, and if this *is* tied to him, I expect the *police* to do their job and discover that for themselves before they bring whoever did this to justice."

"I don't suppose you would tell me the truth if I asked if your . . . family still had any business interests in Livorno?"

"I do not know the specifics of the Romano Group. Not to mention, again, that we are here for a very specific reason about which you are not being helpful at all. Perhaps I should call the mayor—I was just with him an hour ago—and complain to him about the efficacy of the DIA?"

The ground between us seemed to shake with thunder, the air static with impending lightning. One strike and it would be over, but both of us held precariously still, unwilling to concede victory to the other.

"Does she know the truth?" Pucci asked softly, still trying to lure me into striking him so he would have a reason to cuff me.

"She knows the truth about me," I said, and it felt honest because it was mostly true.

Guinevere might be missing huge chapters of my life's work, but she understood the underlying principles and themes of my identity better than people closer to me who had known me my entire life. She could see the duality in me and accepted it. I just had to believe that she wouldn't care how deep that darkness went if she ever had occasion to find out.

"This is a simple breaking and entering case." Martina stepped forward to draw his attention, squeezing my arm in a silent gesture to take Guinevere out of there. "Why don't we focus on that instead of a ghost story, hmm?"

I left the deputy chief in Martina's capable hands and went to Guinevere, who was talking with a local officer and Signora Verga. Her expression was one of relief when I slid an arm around her waist and accepted her weight against my side.

She gestured limply at the cop. "Apparently, I can't take any of my things yet because it's a crime scene, but he said that nothing was taken." She snorted. "Probably because I had nothing of value to take. Though some of the purses and shoes you bought me could have been sold secondhand for a decent amount of money." I rubbed her frown away with my thumb. "Anyway, I gave my brief statement about being at the party, and they said they would contact me. Can we go home now?"

I fought a smile because it was inappropriate given the circumstances, but the sound of *home* in her mouth was almost as pretty as her moans in the Boboli Gardens.

Instead, I kissed her temple. *"Certo, andiamo, cerbiatta."*

Before we cleared the door, I turned to look at Verga, whose small eyes were wet and red. It went against my usual character to offer aid, but British Raffa would not have thought twice about helping.

"Guinevere is breaking her lease. I will pay the rest of the month and have someone here on Monday to install a better security system for the foyer."

Signora Verga gaped at me, but when Guinevere giggled softly, the sound stirred her enough that she waved her handkerchief at me in thanks before pressing it to her leaking eyes.

"That was very nice of you," Guinevere murmured as she pressed more and more of her weight into me while we walked down the stairs and out to the car. "Sweet, some might say."

"Quiet, you. You are obviously in shock," I mocked, flicking her lightly on the nose before helping her into the car.

I thought she had fallen asleep on the way to my house when she suddenly murmured, "Just my luck, someone breaking into my place. Much more my speed than literally running into my Italian dream man."

When I looked over at her at the next red light, she was asleep, mouth open and soft with sleep. I carried her inside when we arrived, hushing Renzo when he greeted us so that I could get her situated in my bedroom. She was limp as a doll and heavy while I took off her ruined dress and settled her under the covers.

I leaned over to kiss her forehead and murmured my truth into her ear so that it might affect her dreams. "I never expected to run into my dream American girl. Now that I have, I am not sure I will be able to let you go."

CHAPTER SEVENTEEN

Raffa

Everyone gathered in the study while Guinevere slept. We waited until Martina arrived to begin, but the atmosphere after I briefed them on the situation crackled with tension, and everyone was palpably on edge.

"I need to know why this happened," I began slowly, so the anger bubbling lava hot in my gut would not spill onto the people who did not deserve it. "Did Pucci overstep and send someone to break into her place to find something on me, even knowing it would not be admissible in court? Did this San Marco lion-bullshit enemy decide to threaten Guinevere to get to me? Or was this truly a random break-in and the timing is insanely coincidental?"

"The Grecos have ties to Venice," Carmine admitted, shifting forward in his chair to run a weary hand over his face. "Angela Greco was married off to the Tancredi family there, and her mother was originally from Murano."

"Fuck," Renzo and I said simultaneously.

"Ludo, have you found out who the Albanians are using in Livorno now? My bet is on the Grecos or Pietras because they both have access to the coast around the area." I flipped the stone wolf figurine in my hand as I spoke, unable to get the image of the wooden lion with the wolf pup in its mouth out of my head.

Seeing it induced a vivid nightmare of Guinevere just as limp and cold in the arms of my enemies.

Why did that image tear through me? Not with a clean slice but in a great sundering, as if I were being ripped in two. I had known her for three weeks. *Three weeks.*

But what weight did time hold over the human heart?

Because despite having spent the last four years believing that I had become a machine, more metal than bone, I felt alive and completely defenseless sitting in that chair, knowing that my actions could bear consequences for this woman.

This woman I wanted to shield at any cost and keep at my side for . . .

Well, for much longer than the three weeks we had left together.

"I have the shipping manifests from the port authority," Ludo explained, interrupting my thoughts. "But there are thousands of them. I would have asked some of our men to help look through the figures, but . . ."

"But we do not know who we can trust when there is obviously a traitor in our depths," I concluded. "Fine, we do not leave this room until we find evidence of whoever is working with the Albanians. Unless—Carmine?"

He shook his head with a wince. "Drita caught me fucking Regina again. Let's just say we are not on good terms. I doubt she would tell me anything other than a creative way to cut off my own balls."

Renzo snorted, but then, he had always found his brother's womanizing ridiculous.

"Then, we look," I declared warily, thinking of Guinevere alone in my bed. "I refuse to believe these incidents are not tied together. Pucci fucked up tonight asking if the family had ties to Livorno. It proves that someone turned them on to us, and that party clearly has ties to the region."

I pulled out my phone to update Leo and frowned when I saw a new text from him.

Leo: Sorry about being rude to your friend. Bad day, but it isn't an excuse. How long is she in town for?

It had been sent a few hours ago, when I was still at the Pitti Palace, but as I stared at the screen another text came in.

Leo: Did she mention if she had a sister at all?

Raffa: Why the fuck are you so interested in Guinevere?

He responded immediately.

Leo: She reminds me of a girl I used to know. She wasn't good news. Bad memories. I'll stop.

Instead of responding, I put the phone down on the table, irritated with his bad opinion of Guinevere when he did not even know her.

"Okay, email sent," Ludo announced a second before everyone's devices pinged with the new message.

"Good, get to work," I commanded, pulling up the files on my computer and resigning myself to a very long night.

We worked for so long, the sun was a blush on the horizon by the time someone knocked at the closed door.

"Come in," I beckoned in Italian, assuming it was my housekeeper or Servio.

Instead, Guinevere stuck her head through the door, hair tousled from sleep but face washed clean of last night's makeup. She was wearing one of my button-up white silk shirts, and I bemoaned the fact that I could not take her back to my bed and remove it with my teeth.

"Well, this is one boring after-party," she quipped, noticing Martina in her dismantled suit sitting shoulder to shoulder with Renzo on the couch, a tablet in her lap and a computer in his. Ludo was where he most liked to be, on the floor, back pressed to the bookshelves, his phone, tablet, and computer open around him. Carmine had fallen asleep some time ago in the chair across from my desk, mouth open for a trail of drool to leak down his chin.

I smiled tiredly at her, opening my arms in silent appeal. She read my cue and tiptoed across the layered Persian carpets to my side, hesitating only for a moment before climbing into my lap. The feel of her in my arms dragged the chaos of my brain down to the depths of my gut like an anchor so that for the first time in hours, my mind fell quiet. I pushed my nose into her hair to seek out the rosemary scent of her shampoo and kissed her head because my lips were already there.

"You should be asleep," I murmured.

She snorted. "Pot, meet kettle. What are these?"

Her fingers were shifting through the papers I had printed out and laid over my desk, the white littered with red as I tried to look for patterns.

"Shipping manifests," she muttered at the same time I did. "Why would an investment banker be looking at these?"

"A company we have in our portfolio has been accused of committing fraud using shell companies," I lied smoothly, letting my hands wander to her hair, then braiding it before I was even aware I was doing so. It was soothing to have that thick silk in my fingers, mundane work to busy my hands so my brain could take a moment.

"Mmm," she hummed, but her eyes were flying over the pages as she spread them out over my palatial desk. "Do you have a pen somewhere?"

I finished the braid and handed her a pen in exchange for the hair elastic she pressed into my hand. She returned to her task, and I leaned back in the leather chair to watch mildly as she scoured the figures. It would do no harm for her to see the details when she had no clue what we were looking at them for or how we planned to use the information.

In fact, if I had been thinking clearly, I might have asked her to take a look. She had proven herself more than capable at Fattoria Casa Luna with the Zhang-Liu Imports debacle. Guilt screeched across my bones like nails over a chalkboard. Thanks to Guinevere's aid, the CEO was currently food for the fishes at the bottom of the Shanghai harbor and the entire company had been dissolved after the COO admitted to fraud after I had sent men to politely suggest prison was a better sentence to serve than an eternal sleep.

It was not right to involve my innocent American girl in my underworld, however tempting it might have been to utilize her smarts and take comfort from her company in the shadows. This was why I was a reluctant mafioso, because the King Below did not deserve a woman wreathed in sunlight and daydreams.

She was too good for this world, and her association with me was enough to taint her without my exposing her to the violence, retribution, and lies of *la mafia*.

"What did you say you studied in university?" Renzo was asking her when I clued back into the conversation around me.

"I have my MBA with a concentration in finance," she mumbled around the lid of the pen, shifting papers and circling names without any obvious reason. "I'm good with numbers and finding patterns."

"You do not need to help us. It is late, and you had an . . . eventful night. You should sleep," I declared, a little too forcibly because it was so easy to give in to temptation with the weight of her in my lap and the sight of her wildly intelligent brain sifting through this problem like a threshing machine, separating the wheat from the chaff.

She paused, looking over her shoulder at me for a moment before taking the pen lid out of her mouth and sticking it on the end of her pinky as if she was afraid to lose it. Only then did she curl into me, hand to my cheek, nails scratching lightly through the stubble as she searched my face.

"I can, if you want me to. But you are tired, Raffa, and clearly unsettled. I want to help, if you'll let me. You have come to my aid so many times, it's really the least I can do."

"You do not need to pay me back for anything," I reminded her sharply, because she was right—I was tired and stressed, and my filter had burned down to the stub.

"This isn't about payback," she promised me softly, tilting her forehead against mine so that those *occhi di cerbiatta* that had first caught my attention were all I could see. "This is about me doing something for you because I care about you. If I can ease some of the weight on your shoulders, I'm happy to. I'm honestly honored I'm in a position where I'm allowed to help you."

"Because—"

She pressed the hand with the pen lid on her pinky nail to my mouth to stop me.

"Because you matter to me," she concluded with a brisk nod before turning in my lap to address the papers once more, popping the lid into her mouth again as if she needed it to think.

I stared at her as emotion moved through the rusty joints of my body, easing the weight of responsibility and the resulting loneliness I had not realized I felt before now.

I knew Guinevere had the kind of soul that complimented old women on their beauty and smiled at strangers just to brighten their day for a single moment. I knew she was driven and determined; planning a solo trip to Florence after being sheltered her whole life was hardly for the faint of heart. I knew she was the loveliest creature I had ever had the privilege to touch. That I could close my eyes that moment and perfectly reconstruct the pale lilac of her eyelids and the bend in her soft brows, the way her long neck sloped into a slim shoulder.

She was the kind of woman who had inspired artists in Italy throughout the centuries. Dante's Francesca, Petrarch's Laura, and Botticelli's Simonetta. A fleeting force of beauty in their lives, like a shooting star whose impression lingered in their souls forever, leaving an indelible mark. Even a kind of insanity that would not diminish with time.

I thought, sitting there watching Guinevere circle her own patterns in blue ink, her mind working furiously behind those dark doe eyes, that I had found the star that had lit up my own life and unwittingly changed it forever.

And any resistance I had to her involvement evaporated in the heat of that starlight.

"Do you see?" she asked me, bouncing in my lap in excitement.

I leaned over her back, pretending as if my entire world had not just shifted slightly on its axis with the simple act of having her sit on my lap in the early hours because she wanted to help carry the weight of my world.

I wondered dangerously if she would feel the same way after knowing exactly what it was we were doing here.

"You see," she said again when Renzo, Martina, and Ludo had crowded around behind us to look at her discovery. "There are only two discernible patterns. The first is the names of the companies. Do you see how they all reference the one before? They cycle every month, but the basic principle is the same. It's a kind of cipher."

She laid out three pages from the month of May to show us the pattern with a tap of her pen by each company listed for the shipment.

"It's a bastardized anagram mixed with a Caesar shift." She spoke so quickly her tongue almost tripped over the words. "So they start with the first shipment of the month. Here it's Porca Pronto exporting pork products from Livorno, and then a week later, Capitale dell'Olio importing bottles of olive oil from Greece, and then ten days after that Itauba Construction with a shipment of construction materials. Do you see it?"

"No," Renzo grunted.

But my mind was whirring because I did.

"They use three letters from the first business in the next, starting from the fourth letter," I explained before Guinevere could.

Her response was to absolutely *beam* at me. "Exactly. It's obviously used as a signal to whoever is receiving shipments for them at the port authority. I mean, they have to be doing something more than money laundering with a scheme like this. It's fairly brilliant, even, but I would have to see how far back it goes because these are only for May and June."

So obviously the Albanians had set up shop with new contacts when we'd first told them we were breaking our contract in April and then implemented a new process with whoever was bringing in their drugs. It wasn't as sophisticated as our scheme, which relied heavily on submarines and technology to cover our tracks and to limit human error at the port authority, but it was still clever.

And my girl was shrewd as hell for figuring it out with just a glance at the papers on my desk at six in the morning.

"I can find the origin company much better now," Ludo muttered, already moving to grab his computer, then resting it on one forearm as he typed with the other hand on his way back to my desk. "It will take time, but they have given many more data points that can be traced to them."

"*Eccellente*," I told him, but I was staring at Guinevere, honestly a bit in awe of her.

"*Ottimo lavoro*," Renzo bestowed on her, lifting a big hand to clamp it over her shoulder, then giving her a little shake the way he would have done to Martina or Carmine.

Guinevere basked in the praise, her smile almost dopey. "Thanks, Renz."

I lifted my brows at the nickname, but my taciturn right hand only lifted his chin at her and went back to the sofa to continue his work with our new information.

"I knew I wasn't the only one with beauty and brains in this place," Martina complimented her, pressing her cheek to Guinevere's in a rare gesture of intimacy. "This is a big deal for us."

My fawn lifted and dropped her shoulder as if she wasn't sure what to do with the kind words from my crew. Her eyes dipped to mine when Martina moved back to the couch.

Carmine, still out cold in his chair, snored on.

"*Magnifico*," I told her when it was just the two of us behind the desk, palming her entire face in my hands. "Absolutely magnificent."

Her flush was the prettiest swipe of vermilion along her cheekbones. "It wasn't anything."

"It was everything," I corrected, then said, softer, "That is twice now you have come to my financial aid. Even if you had not found anything, it means everything to me that you wanted to help."

Her bashfulness melted away, leaving behind an expression of mingled wonder and tenderness that made the spot behind my sternum ache. I thought perhaps it was because each time she did something to move me, her name was carved into the walls of my chest.

"I may not be strong enough to break a man's finger when he insults you or wealthy enough to fill your closet if you lose all your clothes, but I can protect you in the ways I know how."

I fingered the *cornicello* around her neck and wondered aloud, "Have you heard of the saying '*sfortunato al gioco, fortunato in amore*'?" She shook her head. "It means 'unlucky at cards, lucky in love.' You cannot have good fortune in all things, and so you have to choose, or maybe fate chooses for you. Either way, perhaps you have spent your life until now saving up all your good fortune for a truly worthy love story."

I looked up into her eyes to find them dark as lake water at night, the impact of my words rippling across their surface. We were suspended in the moment, but under the silence I could see that we were breathing in tandem, and I knew without checking that our hearts would be beating the same notes.

"Maybe," she whispered, the word almost sick sounding with hope.

"Boss, I found something," Ludo called out from the floor.

I nodded, drawing my thumb along Guinevere's suede-soft cheek. "It bears repeating—thank you."

"No thanks necessary," she mumbled, getting off my lap as Ludo came around the table with his computer once more. "I'll leave you to sort out the rest, but have any of you eaten?"

"Are you offering to cook?" Martina asked, perking up. "Because Servio won't be in to start breakfast for another two hours, and I'm *starved*."

"Coffee," Renzo added.

"I'll see what I can do," Guinevere said, winking at me over her shoulder as she rounded the desk.

She hesitated beside Carmine, peering at me with mischief in her eyes. When I nodded, she dropped the pen lid that had found a place on her pinky again straight into Carmine's open maw.

He woke up spluttering, everyone enjoying a good laugh after a long night.

Guinevere left bouncing on her tiptoes, grinning ear to ear.

There were still too many unanswered mysteries, but thirty minutes later, one thing had become clear.

The Grecos had taken over operations for the Albanians, and a handful of the shell companies had linked back to some of the higher-ups in their organization.

"What are we going to do?" Martina asked as the scent of frying pork filtered through the room.

I leaned back in my chair, staring into the distance, trying to sort through the threads of information we had and plait them into something we could use to bind the Grecos to the stake and burn them for their betrayal.

"Carmine," I said slowly. "Do you think Drita would forgive you if you took her some choice information? Like perhaps that the Grecos have informed about their previous transactions with us to the DIA?"

Understanding and dark glee suffused his handsome face. "I think she could be persuaded."

"Right, then we contact the Albanians and offer the information without a price. They won't want to lose their ties to Italian trading ports, so we suggest that we will step in again. If they are hesitant, point out that one of our men deciphered their code in under five minutes."

Not one of my men. My woman. But still.

Merda, she was phenomenal.

"I thought we wanted to phase out the drug trafficking?" Martina reminded me. "We've shifted a lot of those old resources into the wind business."

Green tech was a new and burgeoning industry in Italy and across Europe that we had jumped into on the ground floor. We had earmarked half a million euros to bribe local officials to get permits for even more wind farms this year after grossing over thirty million euros off them last year. The lack of government regulations and increasing need for green energy made it a perfect business for the family.

And it was considerably less harmful than the drug industry.

But this could not be helped if we wanted to get the DIA off our backs.

"We outsource it," I explained. "Pull Clan Burette in to take over the operations. Get them set up with the mini submarines in Genoa with Gerlando. He still runs the x-ray machines at the port? Perfect. We connect them. Then the Albanians owe us a favor, the Grecos are fucked, and we toss Burette a bone after I publicly set down his daughter last night in front of half of Florence. Three birds, one stone."

"Stealing the Albanians' business back from the Grecos isn't enough of a punishment for those motherfuckers," Ludo grunted.

Which was true.

"We could—" Renzo started.

"No, we are not killing any of them." I shot my bloodthirsty enforcer a look. "We are trying to get off police radar, not invite further scrutiny."

"It's not like the Gentleman not to send a message," Martina mused, staring at me shrewdly. "Do you have another idea?"

The Grecos had tried to undercut my authority by planting an earworm with the DIA that I had secretly taken over my father's illegal enterprise and was smuggling drugs into Livorno. It was only fair to turn that police attention back on them.

"Call Drita," I told Carmine, grinning like the cat who ate the canary. "Set a meet and explain things to her. I think she can be convinced that the Grecos need further punishment, too, and what better way to do that than getting the DIA's eyes on someone else?"

Martina laughed, bright and happy and edged with evil intention. It had always been one of my favorite sounds, and I grinned at her then. It was in moments like this, problem-solving, maneuvering the constant moving parts of an illegal empire, that made me forget why I had ever shunned this way of life.

It was dangerous, yes, but at the end of the day, it could also make you feel something more than just alive. It could make a mortal man feel like a god.

But when Guinevere popped her head back into the room and announced she had made us all an American breakfast, I realized that my little fawn had the very same effect.

"*Cerbiatta mia*," I said as we moved out of the study toward the sumptuous scents from the kitchen and terrace, my arm around her waist. "How would you feel about visiting an Italian beach one day?"

CHAPTER EIGHTEEN

Guinevere

Living with Raffa was both incredible and frustrating.

Incredible, because his palazzo was a work of art and history that his cook, Servio, and housekeeper, Annella, had countless stories to tell me about. It had originally been constructed in the sixteenth century by Gherardo Silvani for one of the wealthiest merchants in the city and later sold to a local eccentric art lover, who had commissioned Il Garofalo to paint on the ceiling in the living room a mural depicting a woodland setting besieged with wild animals and a naked nymph hiding in the greenery, the goddess Diana painted beside a huge buck in the foreground.

It made me wonder if Raffa had drawn inspiration for my nickname from the otherworldly imagery.

So living in a breathing testament to Florentine history was amazing daily, as was getting to know the motley crew Raffa seemed to have at his beck and call. Despite my negative first impression of him, Carmine proved to be almost ridiculously charming and an incredible storyteller. He regaled me with stories about his youth trailing after Raffa; his older brother, Renzo; and Leo in the Tuscan countryside. The games they would play and the trouble they got into—apparently Leo almost got them all suspended for a rude prank he pulled on one of the nuns at their primary school. He was just as chatty as I could be, and I found myself seeking him out whenever the villa was too quiet and Raffa was busy with work.

I already knew and liked Martina, though her ruthless teasing never failed to make me blush. She was incredibly smart and had taken to furthering my Italian-language education by giving me actual homework and quizzing me over mealtimes.

"If you want to be with a Romano, you must speak Italian," she had explained seriously.

"I leave in three weeks," I'd reminded her, but she had only sniffed and continued with our lessons.

I was grateful.

It made it easier to speak to Ludo, who did not speak English as well as the others but whom I liked the best. He was quiet and unassuming, not particularly handsome but with a set of the sweetest brown eyes I'd ever seen. When Raffa was too busy to go on my runs with me, Ludo would come. They were often silent journeys, but I enjoyed his peaceful energy and occasional keen observations.

He was also happy to aid me in my search for Italian relatives. I figured if anyone could find information on my family tree in Tuscany, it was the man who ran investigations for Raffa's investment firm. We didn't have much more to go on than the fact that my father had immigrated to the United States twenty-six years ago and was born somewhere in the countryside close to Florence. He had changed his name when he immigrated, but I knew he was born with the first names Mariano Giovanni.

Italian recordkeeping was notoriously unorganized and not digitized, most of the information kept on handwritten papers in local record offices, but Ludo promised to do his best with such solemnity that it made me believe he'd make more progress than I ever had.

I only spent time with Renzo when Raffa was around because the two were constantly locked in the study together, working on whatever they'd been dealing with at the firm. But it meant a lot to me when he thanked me for my help because I thought he wasn't the kind of man to give praise easily.

I did not miss my lonely apartment across the river. It had seemed like a symbol of my independence, but it took even more strength of character to live in a house of foreign strangers than it did to live on my own in a little bubble.

But it was frustrating, too, because for the last five days, Raffa had been run off his feet with work.

In fact, he'd left Florence entirely for two nights on a work trip to Switzerland and returned home in the middle of the night on the third. I tried to stay awake for him, but Martina and I had gone to Volterra to see the Etruscan ruins that day, and I was exhausted from the walking, fresh air, and early start.

Which meant I had been living with Raffa for five days and I was still, technically or not, a virgin.

And it was driving me crazy.

Fortunately, I had my period during that hectic stretch. It was over now, and I would be spending the entire day with Raffa.

So I decided to start it off on the right foot by joining him in the shower. The tiles were cold and hard beneath my knees, but the feeling of his heavy shaft stretching my lips more than made up for it. When he came, he fisted one hand in my hair and jerked himself off on my face before hoisting me to my feet and getting me off with his fingers.

"Tonight," he promised before sucking a bruise into my throat. "I will finally teach you how to take every inch of my cock in this snug little pussy."

With a smug grin, he left me panting against the wall of the shower to finish dressing for our day in the ocean.

I was just stepping out of the shower myself when my phone rang. My mind was still trying to reanimate after my orgasm, so I answered it without thinking, assuming it was one of my friends from language school.

"Guinevere." My dad's voice crackled through the microphone like a lightning bolt. "I called six times."

"Oh, I'm sorry. I was sleeping and then in the shower." I put the phone on speaker so I could wrap myself in a huge terry cloth robe I'd found in one of the guest bathrooms and then started to moisturize my face. "Is everything okay?"

"No," he said darkly. "Everything is *not* okay because it appears my daughter has been lying to me about where she is."

My pot of moisturizer fell into the sink with a clatter, my hand hanging numbly in the air.

"Guinevere?" he snapped.

"What are you talking about?" I asked, trying to salvage the situation, but my scrambling brain could find no lie to cover my first one.

"Are you in France?" he demanded point blank.

I chewed my lip. Raffa appeared in the reflection of the mirror, standing at the entrance to his palatial bathroom with a frown fixed to his brow.

Something about the sight of him, that expression of concern and the fact that he had obviously come in a silent show of solidarity, gave me the courage I needed to be honest.

"No," I said, but my voice quavered. "I am not."

I'd never known before that a silence could be deadly, but this felt like a religious shunning or a banishment. This felt like the end of a relationship I'd never thought *could* end.

"Where are you?" he asked quietly, his own words trembling with the brutal force of his anger.

"Florence," I whispered back, my eyes pinned to Raffa as he strode forward with purpose and then gently, *so* gently, pulled me back against his front, wrapping his arms around my belly. "I'm in Florence, Italy."

A beat of silence like the deepening quiet before you know a storm is about to hit.

"What the hell are you doing there?" he roared, the words echoing through the stone-walled bathroom. "You *promised* me you would not

220

go. What the fuck were you thinking? Did the promise you made to me mean so little? Did you think I was asking you to stay away out of sport? This was fucking important to me, Guinevere."

His anger wrapped a hand around my throat and squeezed until my eyes burned and my head throbbed. The only thing keeping me from crumbling under the weight of his censure was Raffa, stalwart and strong at my back.

"Of course it was important. You and Mom are the most important people in my life."

Dad scoffed. "You clearly have no respect or love for us if you could lie to us for *weeks* about your life. What the hell are you doing there? Why would you disobey us like this, Guinevere? I would expect it from Gemma, but you . . ." He trailed off as he realized how he had spoken of my sister, as if she was still here, as if it was okay to speak ill of the dead.

"I lied because I needed to come here," I tried to explain, voice plaintive, nails digging unconsciously into Raffa's forearms at my belly. "It was hardly even a lie because I've been honest my whole life about loving this country. I felt . . . I felt *called* to come here, Dad, and if you want to bring Gemma into this, she's the one who encouraged me to come even though you told me not to."

"Do not speak about your sister. This is about you and your dishonesty. How are we ever going to trust you again? I thought we raised you to be a good, honest person."

A whimper lodged in my throat, and I choked on it as I struggled not to cry. Raffa pushed me into the cabinets at my hips, and it was oddly comforting, being pressed between immovable objects. I could trick my body into thinking it was safe while my mind and heart remained under siege.

"I am a good person." The words were more breath than voice. It eviscerated me to hear him suspect my basic human decency because it was the foundation Dad and Mom had always laid thickly for us. Be good, do good, and good things will come. I didn't believe in the ethos as much as I had when I was a girl. I had been good all my life, but unlucky in the extreme. Gemma had been a good person, despite her lies and manipulations, and she was dead.

I wasn't sure being good got you anything.

"But this was something I needed to do for *me*. Not for you and Mom."

"You've never even been to Italy before. What could have been calling you? What reason could be good enough to explain betraying your parents like this?"

"You never explained to me why you hate it here so much," I countered, voice rising as my temper did. "I asked you all the time, and you always shut me down. I'm a grown woman, and I'm just supposed to trust your opinion about an entire country? About a place that is in my blood *through you* whether you like it or not?"

"Trusting me should be enough," he retorted, his tone matching mine. "If you care at all about us, you'll come home right now. Enough is enough. We can talk about the consequences of your irresponsible actions when you get back."

Behind me Raffa's body shifted just slightly, a tensing in every muscle he tried to curb so I wouldn't detect the way those words affected him.

He didn't want me to go.

And neither did I.

Staring into my own face as if I were staring down my father, I declared, "I am not coming home. I have three weeks left here, and I'm going to enjoy them."

"Guinevere, honey, please come home." The sudden shift from fury to pleading derailed me. "After everything we've been through when you were young and now with . . . with losing Gemma. Your mother and I can't handle this."

"Does she know?" I asked, thinking about how devastated my mom would be with me for lying, but especially for lying about this. Even though it was Dad's hang-up about his homeland, Mom had always supported his aversion completely, and she hated to see him upset.

The sigh that unspooled over the phone was so weary, it made my heart ache. "No. When a friend sent me a photo of you with some man on a red carpet outside Pitti Palace, I thought it might have been a very good resemblance. Even when I called . . . I honestly never thought you would defy me. I-I was hoping I could convince you to come home, and she never needed to know. You must, Jinxy. It's not safe in that godforsaken country."

I winced, realizing how stupid it had been to be photographed together, even though I never could have assumed a random society page article would get back to my dad. I didn't even know he *had* friends in Florence to keep in touch with.

Raffa had turned into something carved from marble, a cage around me instead of a comfort. I looked at him in the reflection, but his gaze was pinned somewhere I couldn't follow.

"Can you explain why you think that is?" I asked Dad softly, because I wanted to understand. I always had. I just needed more to go off than "because I said so."

The silence was telling, filled with anger and fruitless frustration on both ends.

"I'll see you in three weeks," I said, silk over steel because I hated that he was hurting, that I had been the one to make him hurt, but I was not giving up on this dream because it would have been giving up on myself. "I'm still coming home, Dad, and you'll still see me every day at work in the fall. I just . . . I can't give up on this. Not yet. Not now."

Maybe not ever, a cruel voice at the back of my mind whispered. *How will you ever get over this place and this man?*

As if privy to my thoughts, Raffa softened, dipping his head to press a kiss to the mark he'd made sucking into one side of my neck.

"Guinevere, if you stay, there won't be a job waiting for you when you come home because we will not have a relationship," he threatened.

My heart, so full of new experiences and new people, withered in my chest.

"Fine," I whispered as tears finally fell down my cheeks. "If that's the way it has to be, I'll live with the consequences of my actions. What I can't live with is giving up on what I want just to keep you happy."

Silence met me on the other end because he'd hung up.

I squeezed my eyes shut at the burn of hot tears springing from the backs of my eyes and let the waves of sorrow take me under, somewhere dark and deep and lonely.

Distantly, I was aware of Raffa gently pulling the phone out of my grip and lifting me into his arms as he took us from the bathroom into the bedroom and sat carefully on the bed, arranging me in his lap with his back against the headboard. I was crying hard, but silently, soaking Raffa's bare chest and the hem of the fresh pair of shorts he'd put on.

He didn't seem to care.

He held me in his arms as I cried until there was no water or salt left for my body to produce and my head throbbed like an open wound. One of his hands was in my hair, stroking it back from my wet face, and the other was rubbing soothing circles into my thigh.

"I am sorry it came to this," he said finally, when my sniffles had subsided and I lay there in recovery. "It is the worst kind of grief when we cut the final strings of filial responsibility to our parents in order to carve out our autonomy. Our own futures separate from their vision."

There was silence, but I could almost hear the words unspoken in his mouth.

"I am very proud of you for standing up for yourself," he admitted into the top of my hair. "And I do not mean that to be condescending. You are one of the bravest people I have ever known." He chuckled softly. "You throw yourself into life and adventure with such a pure enthusiasm and confidence, it inspires me to seek the pleasure in life as well."

I tipped my chin up to peer at his face, my fingers trailing the furred line of his jaw because they could. "And what brings a man like you pleasure?"

"You," he said simply. "In all your iterations. A goddess on my arm at a party, charming everyone we meet; a genius perched in my lap at my desk, finding something my men, Martina, and I could not find for hours; a little fawn stranded on the side of the road, looking at me with much too trusting eyes. I like them all."

"You make me sound so much better than I am." I rubbed my salt-crusted cheek against his chest hair and listened to the steady thud of his heart.

He snorted. "Oh, I like the girl who curls up on my chest in her sleep and leaves a little puddle of drool and the girl who leaves her clothes on the floor and the one who teases me when I have never enjoyed being teased very much. You must remember my definition of *perfect*, Vera."

I did remember. It wasn't something I was likely to forget, because I wanted to make it my definition too.

"It means something so captivating that you can't help but find it beautiful, flaws and all."

"*Molto bene*," he praised. "Exactly."

"And you feel that way about me?" I asked just to clarify. "Even knowing I lied to my parents about where I was. That I can be that selfish and reckless and stubborn as a mule."

"Especially knowing all that. How boring you would be without those wicked little habits and flaws."

I had never considered it like that before, but he did have a point. "I did always find heroes a little dull."

Raffa laughed from his belly, the sound vibrating through his skin into mine. "And who are your favorite villains?"

"I think I would call them antiheroes over villains. They occupy that murky zone between good and bad that most of us battle to stay out of at all costs. Achilles with his unforgiving pride and rage that ultimately led to his avoidable death. He is flawed and wrong more often than he's right, but we still talk about him as a hero. Scarlett O'Hara in *Gone with the Wind* is one of the most obviously manipulative women in literature, and I cry every time Rhett leaves her without a moment's hesitation."

"'Frankly, my dear, I don't give a damn.'" Raffa surprised me by quoting those cruel parting words. When I laughed, he shrugged a shoulder. "My sisters love any movie, in any language, that will make them cry."

"I think it's easier to empathize with people who aren't all good," I realized. "It's even easier to love them. We can't relate to perfect heroes because none of us are as good as we want to be."

"*Ben detto*," he agreed, but there was a knot in his brow I had to reach up to erase with my thumb.

"I wish I was a better person," I confessed with a sigh as I snuggled closer against his chest. "But I also want to be happy, and those two things always seem to be at odds."

Raffa didn't smile at my joke. Instead he seemed almost upset about it. His voice, when he spoke, was dry with self-mockery. "Ah, that is the difference between you and me, Guinevere. Sometimes I feel like I should wish the same, but at the end of the day, I know I am not capable of being better, and I am happy with where I am."

It was my turn to frown. "Are you? Because even though you keep implying you're a bad guy, you've played the hero very well for me."

"I am a very good actor," he said, deadpan, and I laughed as I was sure he meant me to.

Even after a brutal fight with my dad, this man could make me smile.

CHAPTER NINETEEN

Guinevere

"Have you ever driven a Ferrari?"

I blinked at Raffa as we emerged from the side entrance of the pala-zzo into the courtyard, where a gleaming vintage red Ferrari convertible was waiting for us.

Behind me, Martina was laughing, and Carmine was muttering about never being allowed to drive Raffa's cars because he'd crashed one when he was fourteen.

"Are you serious?" I asked. My mouth dropped open at the prospect.

My dad loved cars in the kind of obsessive way only an Italian immi-grant to the United States would love cars. His garage was his haven, filled with paraphernalia from all the top Italian car companies and even a select few American ones. We weren't wealthy like Raffa—I wasn't sure many people *were*—but John Stone was proud of his collection.

But he would have sold his soul to clap his eyes on the Ferrari NART Spyder Raffa was offering to let me drive.

Only ten of them were ever made, and the last one had sold for something like $30 million.

"Just how rich are you?" I asked him, fisting my hands on my hips. "Because I have to tell you, this is getting a little absurd."

Even Ludo laughed at that, and Renzo bumped my shoulder companionably as they moved past me to the more sensible SUV waiting at the gates.

"Do you want to drive it or not?" Raffa asked with that haughty raised brow, arms crossed so all those muscles bulged in his white linen shirt.

I knew now how he kept so fit: a gym in the basement of the palace that included an actual fighting ring.

"Yes, please." I practically skipped to his side by the car and opened my palm for the keys. "Speed limits in Italy are just suggestions, right?"

He gripped my wrist and used it to pull me forward so I fell into his chest. "Watch yourself, *cerbiatta*. You would not want to hurt another one of my cars."

"Well, you have to admit, the first time kind of worked out for me." I flashed him a cheeky grin and rose to my tiptoes to kiss the corner of his jaw.

"Here," he said, reaching into his pocket to produce a silk Dolce & Gabbana scarf. "This will save your hair from becoming Medusa's snakes."

I laughed but turned obediently and lifted my hair off my shoulders so he could tie the scarf around my head.

"Do I look like Sophia Loren?" I flirted, batting my lashes dramatically.

"No," he said, too quiet for a joke. "You look like you, which I much prefer."

"A hundred euros she crashes," Carmine said just loudly enough for me to hear from where he was glaring at me beside the other car. "No way a little thing like her can handle a car like that."

I stiffened a bit, always self-conscious about my slightness because my lack of musculature and height were a consequence of my medical condition. When I was growing up, some of the kids in my class had called me Sticks until Gemma gave one of them a black eye.

"One thousand euros says we not only make it there in one piece," Raffa drawled, and I knew he was defending me in his own way. When I looked sharply up at him, he winked, handing me the keys and then patting my ass as he crossed to the passenger seat. "But we also beat you to Livorno."

"You're on," Martina declared, grabbing the keys from Renzo and pushing him out of the way before running to the driver's seat.

I looked at Raffa over the hood of the low-slung convertible and watched as he slid the designer sunglasses out of his hair onto his nose. My grin reflected back at me in the lenses.

"And a private bet," he added. "If you get us there first, I promise to eat your sweet *figa* later until you forget every language but the sound of 'Raffa' in your mouth."

I shivered. "*Andiamo!* I have a race to win."

◆ ◆ ◆

We won.

Raffa didn't even seem surprised by the way I handled the car on the busy highway out of Florence toward the coast, and he only whistled through his teeth when I had fun taking the curving side roads on the way to the marina just outside Livorno.

When I told him my father had taught me how to drive in a Maserati, he just laughed at me, grabbed my hand, and kissed my palm.

"Of course he did. The only thing that surprises me about you now, Guinevere, is that I am still surprised when you reveal yourself to be the most remarkable woman I have ever known."

I added it to the list of impossibly sweet things Raffa had said to me.

When Martina had pulled up at the marina, we were making out against the car. She'd honked in a way that felt like a swear word, Renzo had thrown an empty bottle of water at Raffa's head, and Carmine was still pouting.

Only Ludo gave me a fist bump.

Now we were on a beautiful sailboat motoring out of the harbor into the Ligurian Sea. The water was aquamarine close to the shore but deepened into azure beneath the boat as it cut south along the coastline. The rooftops of the passing city were red and orange, the rocky cliffs yellowed to gold by the afternoon sunshine. Everything was so bright it felt like the imagery was seared into my corneas, but I wasn't upset by the idea. I hoped it meant that for the rest of my life, when I closed my eyes, I would conjure up this image of Livorno's cityscape giving way to green hills descending into white sugared beaches and outcrops of rocks fit for Ariel to sing atop of.

It was completely different from the pervasive cultural majesty of Florence, the sense that every cobblestone and doorway had seen millions of lives pass through before your own. This setting was wild and freeing, the briny slap of ocean spray across my face as I sat alone at the bow while Raffa put the others to work behind me, the tangle of foliage that tumbled down the cliffs, and the wet crash of waves into the coastline.

I closed my eyes, dragged a deep breath of sea air into my lungs, and cast my face to the sky.

This was, quite possibly, heaven.

It could have been minutes or hours later that shade over my face roused me from my meditation. Crying had left me exhausted, but I didn't want to sleep when I could be enjoying the sound of the waves and the demanding cry of seabirds, so I had let my mind float like the boat did on the sea.

Now I cracked open an eye and peered at Raffa above me.

His shirt was unbuttoned, revealing the tanned expanse of his tightly muscled torso, and his hair was alive with filaments of bronze, copper, and obsidian under the glaring sun. He was grinning down at me, more carefree than I had ever seen.

"The sea suits you," I told him. "You look like a modern-day pirate."

He laughed a little too hard at my quip, but I figured it was just the brightness of the day and the fact that we got to spend it together after barely any quality time since the Pitti Palace gala.

I moved over a bit so he could sit beside me on the blue-cushioned daybed built into the bow of the boat beneath the swollen sails.

"So you have a boat."

"I have a boat," he agreed, leaning back on his palms to tip his face into the sun the way I had.

"A very large, lovely boat named *Salacia*," I continued.

A minute Italianate shrug. "She was Neptune's consort, goddess of the sea. Only fools name their vessels after him. Anyone who has ever spent any time on the ocean knows she is and could only be a woman."

I laughed at his drollness. "This is my first time on the ocean, so I'll take your word for it."

"You seem very at ease for your first time," he said and then rolled his eyes at my eyebrow wiggle and added, "First time *at sea*."

"Lake life," I explained. "My parents have a boat, nothing like this, just a ski boat we keep on Gun Lake during the summers. It's beautiful there. In fact, before I came to Italy, it was my happy place."

He hummed, eyes closed, and my breath caught at how beautiful he was, sitting on the gently rocking boat with his throat bared and his hair falling back from his tipped forehead in perfect waves. I gave in to temptation and drew the line of his Roman nose with my fingertip and then pressed it into the divot above his lips. He shocked me into laughter by snapping his teeth at me.

"My happy place was Villa Romano," he said without opening his eyes, and I froze, afraid that if I moved I would scare him into stopping. He revealed so little about his life that every kernel felt like gold. "I grew up running barefoot through the acres of trees, and each orchard was its own oasis. We played *nascondino*, like tag, in the olive grove because it had the best hiding places, and *gioco delle biglie* in the barn beside the vineyard. In the summer we were constantly trying to keep up with the ripening fruit, visiting every day to fill baskets and bowls with plums, peaches, and apricots. Sometimes, we would lay under the trees and gorge ourselves until we were sick." He made a face. "I did not eat apricots for two years after I turned twelve."

My laugh was soft because I didn't want him to stop talking.

"My mother was the ultimate host, and we always had people over for every meal. Sometimes, I was sure even she did not know where they came from. But it was fun as a boy to meet strangers from all over Italy and beyond." He cracked a lid open. "Did I tell you that I speak German, Spanish, and Greek as well?"

"Show-off," I muttered with faux bitterness.

His lids lowered, and he grinned again. When he lay down, he tugged me into his side, running his fingers idly through my hair.

"You speak about the villa like it isn't your happy place anymore," I noted, tracing the boxed muscles of his abs to watch the way his belly contracted at the ticklish sensation.

There was such a long pause, I thought he wouldn't go on.

But then, "I did not have a father like you do who cared about my health and safety. If I was not his puppet, I could not be his son."

I winced, both because the sentiment was horrible and because it underscored the fact that my dad, while controlling and specifically insensible about Italy, had only ever wanted me to be happy and healthy.

"What happened?" I asked, because there was more story there, buried in the bitter dregs of his tone.

Raffa sighed, eyes popping open to stare into the vast, cloudless sky above us. "I did much as you did with your father, only I did it a lot less politely."

"You told him to fuck off," I guessed.

His smile was broken at the ends. "Yes. I had a full ride to Oxford to study business. It was my dream to go there, and I could not give it up, even when I tried. I was cut off from the family, not allowed contact with my sisters or my mother, with no access to my inheritance." He shrugged, but it was not something he could play off. "I moved to wet, dreary England and pursued what made me happy at the cost of everything I had ever known."

There were parallels there to my own situation that astonished me but also made me feel petty. My parents had refused to pay for my trip, which had seemed unfair when they had paid for all of Gemma's, but the privilege of growing up as I did with enough money and more than enough love was glaringly obvious.

I would take my dad's hugs and pep talks before every surgery and medical appointment above any palazzo. My mother's homemade pasties and summer cherry pies, eaten with forks straight from the plate on the back deck of our lake house, above any Ferrari or designer dress.

It made me ache for Raffa. I had the absurd thought that I wanted to fuse my heart with his so that he would know, even long after I left, that he would never be alone so long as my heart still beat.

"How long?" I asked instead.

"Until he died four years ago. I lived apart from my home for nine years."

Nine years.

"Oh, Raffa," I murmured, unable to stop myself from moving so I could lay my body flat against his, as if I could imprint myself on his skin. "I'm so sorry."

He wouldn't meet my eyes, but one hand continued to play through my hair, tangling in the wind-blown strands.

"Carlotta married her high school sweetheart and had three children. Stacci married a stranger I had never met and had two of her own. Delfina took over the vines I had loved to help my mother's brother tend as a boy, and my best friend, Leo, took over the business from my father."

The words lay unsaid in the air after he spoke: *They all moved on without me.*

"Why did you come back?"

"Why does anyone do anything? For love. I had missed them every day, and when I could return, I did." Something in his tone said he was holding back, a lingering bitterness I couldn't make sense of.

But he had shared a massive piece of his painful history with me, and I was not going to linger over the details. Not when I only had three weeks left to bring this man enough joy to last him for the rest of his life.

Not when I could spend the last of our time together loving him enough to fill the abyss that nine years without love must have left in his chest.

And there was no doubt then, the two of us pressed chest to chest under the wide Italian sky on the Ligurian Sea, that I loved Raffa.

The kind of all-consuming, life-ruining love that had plagued Dante and Petrarch and Botticelli. An undying love that would never be returned.

It didn't matter, I told myself as I cupped Raffa's face and dragged myself farther up his torso so I could kiss his mouth, soft, feathering brushes like a healing touch on a wound. It didn't matter if he never wanted this gift I'd made of my heart. It would always be his.

What I had told my father was true. I felt called to Italy, and I had since I was a girl lying awake and terrified in the hospital, pretending not to hear my parents weep.

And now I knew what had been calling my name.

Him.

"I hate that you've suffered to get to the man you are today, but the man you are? He's spectacular," I said against his mouth. "And I hope you know that you have left an indelible mark on my life. It feels like everything I wanted to be was just below the surface of my skin, and no matter how hard I tried, I couldn't shed my old skin to find it. You helped me do that. You make me feel like every version of myself is a gift, when before, I thought I would never be good enough. And I might not be good in the traditional sense I always thought was so important, but maybe I am my own version of perfect. Your version. Flaws and all."

"There is no maybe about it," he told me, finally shifting his gaze to mine, eyes fierce with conviction and a yearning that made my teeth ache. "I know you believe you are unlucky. *Sei nata sotto una stella sfortunata.* Born under the wrong star. But to me, *sei la stella cadente che illumina la mia vita.*"

But to me, you are the shooting star that lights up my life.

He cupped my face then, so we were a closed circuit, something I was too scared to call love ebbing and flowing between us. Then he kissed me, a warm, open-mouthed kiss that made my toes curl.

And I wondered clearly for the first time if this moment and this man were enough to make me give up everything I had ever known.

We spent the day anchored off the shore of a public beach with no land access, a tiny strip of U-shaped sand surrounded by craggy rocks on either side of the cove so that the water within was as clear and steady as lake water without wind.

I had a diving competition with Martina and, of all people, Renzo, who actually ended up being voted the winner by the others through their sheer incredulity that he could make his enormous body slip beneath the water with hardly a splash.

Carmine produced a packet of Italian playing cards that went to forty instead of fifty-two and taught me the rules of tresette, which was a surprisingly complicated game played in partners. Luckily Raffa was mine, and he was a shark, because I definitely needed more practice.

I got the start of a sunburn across my nose, and Raffa insisted on lathering me in sun cream even though I'd already reapplied.

We had lunch together at the back of the boat, and Raffa handed me a liter jug of filtered water instead of a glass of wine, which oddly made me want to cry.

Because he was taking care of me in a way that did not seem overbearing or make me feel like a child. Just giving me silent, observant care, like bringing my meds to me from my bag in the cabin after the meal.

Yes, I loved him.

It pulsed in my chest like a lighthouse beacon.

By the time the sun set over the cerulean waters, we were all pleasantly sun drunk and sleepy. Martina was napping with her head in Renzo's lap while he read a German spy thriller, and Ludo and Carmine were bickering softly over another card game.

"Take a swim with me," Raffa murmured into my ear.

I was lying between his legs at the bow, listening to his sweetly accented English as he read from Dante's *Inferno*. We were almost at the end, and I hoped we would finish *Purgatorio* before I had to leave.

I was sleepy, muscles lax from hours in the salt waters, but I was not in a mood to resist anything Raffa wanted, so I stood up and took his hand when he offered it. We stood at the side of the boat, and he grinned.

"*Insieme?*"

Together?

I nodded, and in tandem, we arched over the lines and plunged into the cold sea. When I broke the surface, Raffa was already cutting through the water with clean, powerful strokes, aimed toward a smooth configuration of rocks on the outer ridge of the cove.

I swam in his wake, thinking I would follow him, like Eurydice, blindfolded and trusting through the underworld.

He was standing on the rocks, dripping water out of his hair, when I arrived, and he offered his hand to me. I laughed when he tugged me too hard, pulling me tight against his chest.

"From this angle, they can't see us," he whispered in my ear before nipping it.

I tilted my head and found he was right. Though I could see the boat slowly turning with the tide on its anchor chain, a huge outcropping of white-gold rock meant if we lowered ourselves to the sun-warmed rock below, we would not be seen.

"Why, Raffa, what are you thinking?" I teased, linking my arms around his neck.

"I am thinking I cannot wait until tonight."

He kissed me as soon as the words were out of his mouth, lifting me into his arms with his hands on my ass, pressing me to his groin, where I could already feel the hardening line of his dick. I groaned into his mouth and slid my hands into the wet strands of his hair, holding on as he kneeled on the rock and laid me gently against it.

"You taste like salt and sunshine," he muttered against my mouth between succulent kisses. *"Divino."*

I moaned when those talented lips trailed down my neck, pausing to kiss my *cornicello* before nipping each peak of my breasts through my wet bikini.

"You look like something from another time or another realm," he said as he nosed the fabric aside and sucked my nipple into his hot mouth, shocking after the temperature of the sea. "A woodland nymph, a Renaissance princess, one of Salacia's Oceanids. Sometimes, I cannot believe you are real until I touch you like this."

The scrape of his stubble against my delicate skin lit fires in each breast that merged and raced toward my groin. I was wetter than the ocean had left me when he moved farther down my body and undid the tie of my bottoms with his teeth. The fabric gaped, revealing my bare mound to his gaze and the orange-pink sky.

"Una fragola così bella," he praised, placing an open-mouthed kiss on my clit and then licking me off his lips. *"E altrettanto dolce."*

Such a beautiful pussy, and just as sweet as a strawberry.

I moaned, lifting my hips to give him better access. He took control by cupping my ass and canting my pussy to his mouth as if he wanted to drink straight from the well.

He feasted just as he had promised he would if I won the race to the coast. Long, wet swipes of his tongue from the top of my clit to the furl of my ass, again and again, until I was thrashing against the rock, shamelessly begging for more.

He obliged, twisting a finger into my aching pussy while he sucked at my clit.

My orgasm crashed over me like an errant superwave, drenching Raffa's tongue and hand, dragging me under so that I could not see or hear the scenery, only feel the sensation of him taking me apart at the seams.

The next time, he pinned my hips to the rock with one hand, cheek resting on my inner thigh, and used his other hand to expose my clit from its hood completely, his thumb strumming back and forth gently but insistently over the bundle of nerves. My entire body jittered as if I was being slowly electrocuted by pleasure, the pressure growing into something so sharp and bright, I was almost scared of it.

"Please, Raffa," I cried out, unsure if I wanted him to continue until the end of time or stop immediately before my heart gave out.

"Hush, *piccola*. You can come for me like this. *Lasciati andare e inzuppa la mia mano in quella dolce crema.*"

Let go and drench my hand in that sweet cream.

The sound of his filthy words in the round vowels of his accented English and purring Italian cranked the dial so high, I screamed as bolts of pleasure shot through my pussy, curling my fingers and toes until they cramped.

I was as limp and pliant as kneaded dough for the next orgasm, the one I wasn't sure I could take but Raffa insisted I needed.

"I want you to feel every inch of me as I push into your cunt for the first time," he told me, ruthlessly pressing two fingers into the front of my pussy and rubbing at a spot that made me see stars across the pretwilight sky. "I want you to shiver and shudder with every press. I want you shaking and ready to come the moment I am seated to the root inside you."

"God, Raffa, yes," I moaned, my mind lost to the currents of lust, embarrassment left behind on the banks somewhere like my discarded clothes. "I need to feel you stretch me open. I've been dreaming of it for days. Please, please, please."

"*La mia dolce cerbiatta*," he murmured before he lightly flicked his tongue over my highly sensitized clit with just enough pleasure to take me gently over the edge, pulling this orgasm out of me in sweet, pulsing strokes.

He bit and sucked a mark into each inner thigh to count off each orgasm.

I was still gasping from the aftershocks when he covered me with his sun-hot body, his cock a searing brand as it smeared through the wetness between my thighs.

"So swollen and wet," he murmured, peering between us as he fisted his cock and stroked it through my folds. "It will be hard to take me, but I want you to have every inch."

"Yes," I agreed, clutching at him, then raking my nails down his back in an effort to bring him even closer, though his lightly furred chest was already tight to my breasts. "I want to be impaled on you."

He groaned, dropped his head, and said through gritted teeth, "I want to be rough with you."

"Yes," I hissed.

"I want to fuck you so hard and so often you will feel me every day for the rest of the time we have together. The echo of me inside you when we are apart, aching to be filled up again."

"Fuck, *yes*," I cried as he slotted the head of his wide cock at my entrance and thrust, one smooth, hard glide.

I was too swollen, still too untried, to take all of him in one, but I loved the sensation of him working me open, pulling back and then pulsing forward inch by inch until I could feel his balls pressed to my wet pussy.

"There," he said, triumph rich in his voice, arms wrapped around my torso so I felt utterly consumed by him. "*Il mio posto felice.*"

My happy place.

His words tied all the pleasure oversaturating my body into bows around my heart, the one I wanted so desperately to carve out of my chest and hand to him.

Before I could say anything, though, he was lifting me, sitting back on his heels so that I was balanced entirely in his lap, one of his hands braced at the curve of my spine to keep me upright and the other twisting my wet hair into a rope to use as reins.

"Hold on," he warned me before he started thrusting up into me as he simultaneously brought me down using his hold on my back and hair.

Stars exploded behind my eyes, the edge of painful newness eclipsed by the white-bright orgasm already sparking low in my gut. He fucked me on his cock like I was a doll, and I could not believe I had ever objected to the idea because it was the hottest moment of my life. His olive-tanned skin was sheened with sweat and corded with muscle like that of an old warrior from ancient Rome, his legs and arms flexing with tension as he brought me up and down over his dick. The riot of his drying waves had flopped over his forehead into his pale-brown eyes, which were locked on mine without wavering.

"*Cerbiatta mia,*" he grunted as I ground down on his upstroke, using the roughness of his pubic hair to rub against my clit. "*La mia donna. La mia stella cadente.*"

My little fawn. My woman. My shooting star.

I cried out his name over and over, lost to the vast ocean of his sensation, anchored only by his thick cock inside me and his name carved like an ancient secret into the roof of my mouth.

"Raffa," I sang as I came again, arching in his hold so he had to fight to keep me pinned, grunting as he chased his own orgasm inside me and then cursing in Italian as he came seconds later.

I could feel the heat of him and the kick of his cock as it wrung every last ounce of feeling from my body until I lay limp and utterly used in his arms, head to his shoulder, regaining my breath my only focus.

"*Meus Rex Infernus,*" I murmured against his salty shoulder as he stroked my hair and settled back on his ass to stretch out his legs and hold me close.

It felt right to call him that.

My king below.

Below my skin and muscle and bones through to whatever made up the human soul.

"Thank you," he said in a raw voice after a long moment. "For the best gift I have ever had."

My laugh was breathless. "I think it's me who should be thanking you. I gave you one, you gave me five."

"You gave me *you,*" he corrected, pulling my face from his shoulder so he could kiss my sunburned nose. "When you have not given yourself to anyone else. Not just in this way but . . ." He shrugged eloquently. "I may not deserve the light you bring, but I will enjoy the hell out of it while I can."

"Well, the pleasure is still mine," I joked, hoping he didn't hear the break in my voice.

He hummed a noncommittal reply and held me until the last of the jewel-toned hues faded from the sky and cool blues started to set in.

"We should go," he said at last, lifting me in his arms with a little groan as his knees cracked. "I have something to show you."

He touched me constantly as we righted our bathing suits and then matched me stroke for stroke as we swam back to the boat, as if he couldn't bear to be apart.

Everyone was already ready to go when we climbed aboard, the anchor reeled in and the sails lifted. Raffa let Renzo take the helm so he could sit with me in silence on one of the benches across from Ludo, Carmine, and Martina.

I was surprised when they cut the engine as we stopped near an island close to the coastline, by a small collection of other luxury boats moored off the shore for the night, but I was silent as everyone got up as one and stood on the starboard side. Martina handed out binoculars, and we each lifted them toward a jutting cliffside. There was just enough light left to make out three speedboats as they slinked one by one from somewhere amid the rock.

"What—" I whispered.

"Hush," Raffa returned.

I watched as the boats spread out in a V-shaped formation, heading toward Livorno on the other side of the strait, and wondered why this was tonight's entertainment.

Until I heard the *whomp whomp whomp* of a helicopter.

Seconds later, a spotlight snapped on over the water, highlighting the speedboats for a moment before they splintered from each other, trying to flee.

A muffled Italian voice ordered something I couldn't make out over the speakers, and then more lights filled the darkening ocean from the bows of four police speedboats coming from Livorno.

"Oh my gosh," I gasped, pressing my eyes harder to the binoculars as if that would help me make out the details of the *high-speed police chase* I was watching.

The police split off to follow each of the three boats, and the helicopter followed the one traveling farther out to sea. The six of us watched until the lights were pinpricks on the inky horizon and we could no longer hear the sound of the helicopter.

I turned to Raffa, hardly able to make out his features in the dark. "What the hell?"

He laughed, a long string of notes from the belly. Someone snapped on an overhead light and another at the bow of the boat and started the engines again, moving us out from the boats moored for the night and back toward Livorno.

Raffa's face was creased with smug mischief like that of a teenage boy who had pulled off a wonderful prank.

"I thought you would want to see what your help meant to us." He gestured to the place the boats had disappeared. "The company that screwed us over with dishonesty was smuggling into the port of Livorno through those shell companies you found. We turned them in to the authorities and . . . presto."

"Oh my gosh," I laughed as Raffa picked me up and spun me in a tight circle. "That was *insane*. I felt like I was in a spy film. Feel my heart!" I pressed his hand to my chest when he put me down so he could feel it racing. "Wow. How exhilarating."

Renzo clamped a heavy hand over my shoulder and gave me a little shake. "If you ever need a job, *Vera*?"

Raffa shot him an unamused look, but I was too busy grinning at Renzo to note it. "Oh for sure, buddy. I mean, I knew you guys had to be more than just stuffy investment bankers. Look at you."

"I think this calls for prosecco," Martina announced, ducking into the galley to grab it.

"Servio packed sparkling cider for you," Raffa told me, pulling me into his front and then kissing my temple.

Ludo reached over and offered me his fist to bump.

And not for the first time in Italy, but for the first time with Raffa's chosen family, I felt at home.

CHAPTER TWENTY

Guinevere

It was the Feast of San Lorenzo, and all of Florence—all of Italy—was celebrating. Italy had a long history of celebrating its martyrs, and Lorenzo was considered one of the patron saints of Florence. But I still thought the whole thing was a little too on the nose.

The patron saint of cooks, butchers, winemakers, restaurateurs, and basically anyone involved with food or beverage had been essentially barbecued for refusing to hand over goods to Roman officials and instead giving them to the poor. Now Florentines and Italians everywhere celebrated him by hosting barbecues themselves.

It was slightly morbid, but then, much of Italian culture seemed to embrace sin and darkness instead of shunning it the way we often did in the States. I'd grown to love that aspect of Italy most of all. It was hard to feel shame or insecurity when human flaws were so readily accepted.

The festival also had the distinction of being on August 10, the day the *cocomerata*, or Perseid meteor shower, was supposed to peak, which I was thrilled about. Back home, we spent that weekend at Gun Lake every year, lying in the sloping grass yard toward the dock, head to head, holding hands and counting out the shooting stars. It had been a tradition since before I could remember, and this would be the first summer I wasn't at the cabin to do it with Mom and Dad.

The first summer they weren't speaking to either of their daughters, one by choice and the other not.

I had texted my mom and tried to call, but Elizabeth Stone could be just as obstinate as her husband, and the only reply I'd received was make peace with your father.

But with every day I spent in Florence, I seemed to move further away from peace with my father and toward being at peace with myself. The last three weeks had flown by in a watercolor blur of sights and experiences. Running through the streets of the city with Raffa and Ludo, timing our sprints up the hill to Piazzale Michelangelo and seeing if I could beat them both with my quickness despite their longer legs. Admiring the frescos at the Cappelle Medicee while Raffa regaled me with dramatic tales about Florence's most famous family, the Medicis. Getting gelato on the hottest day of the summer, Raffa pretending to trip and spilling his treat on my chest. Pulling me into a dark alley to lick the melting cream off the upper swells of my breasts and fuck me with one hand slipped up underneath my skirt.

We shopped at the famous Mercato Centrale, and Raffa convinced the men at a butcher shop with a sign that said "EAT MEAT—IT'S GOOD FOR YOUR SEX LIFE" to teach me how to cut the perfect *bistecca alla Fiorentina* for our dinner. He knew what foods I avoided for my kidney health without asking when we picked out produce, and he admitted he had done some research on my condition so I didn't have to lay everything out for him. I kissed him so hard he had to brace himself against a display of tomatoes, and he crushed the fruit beneath his hand.

Later, cooking with him as if we'd always occupied the same kitchen, singing to an eclectic mix of Taylor Swift (because Raffa needed to be inducted into the fandom), Sufjan Stevens (my favorite artist), and Pavarotti (Raffa's favorite singer).

When Raffa had to work, I explored alone or spent time in the library beside his offices, studying Italian and writing to Gemma about my adventures. One day, I realized I had never recovered my postcards to her from Signora Verga's apartment, but when I asked Raffa about it, he said Ludo had packed everything the police had not taken that had been left behind.

It was strange, but I quickly forgot about it, throwing myself into every moment so I could pull out my memories like their own postcards, vivid and nostalgic, when I was back in Michigan.

Our sex life was passionate and voracious. I woke up wanting him, already reaching for him, and went to bed tangled in his limbs, sticking to him with sweat and happy about it because I wanted to be that close. But as the days wore on, it took on an intense, almost feral edge.

One morning, I bit the junction of his neck and shoulder so savagely as I came that I broke the skin and drew blood. Raffa was far from angry—in fact, he looked smugly proud—but I wondered at how far I'd come from the shy virgin and considered, almost apprehensively, how far I had to go in falling into the dark heat of eroticism with Raffa.

There was nothing we did, no way he touched me that I did not love. The same silk scarf I'd worn driving the Ferrari now tied around my eyes as Raffa used his mouth on every inch of my skin, front to back, head to toes, for hours. The slick press of a thumb into the tight vise of my ass as he fucked me from behind or the finger that traced the bulge of his cock in my mouth, slipping onto my tongue along with it just so Raffa could see me struggle to take more.

It wasn't right to say I had a submissive streak; I was assertive about my desire. I pushed into the office one day while Raffa was on the phone speaking in German, and I dropped to my knees beneath the desk to suck him off because I'd read about it in a book once and wanted to try. I hopped up onto the kitchen counter while we were cooking, raising my skirt up to my hips to show him I wasn't wearing anything beneath. Asking him to eat the whipped cream we'd made for a strawberry dessert off my skin.

But there was no denying Raffa had been right. I loved being his doll, bending and surrendering to his commands so I could receive the sweet taste of his praise and the even sweeter reward of the orgasm he made me earn.

We fit in this the way we seemed to fit in all things.

By the time August 10 rolled in and I was set to leave in two days, I almost couldn't breathe for missing him, and I hadn't even gone yet.

If I'd grown more morose as the days grew shorter, Raffa had grown more removed. He spent long days in the office, only emerging for dinner and the odd night out to explore nearby restaurants and bars with live music because we both liked to dance.

It was such a strange sensation, to be so in love and so heartbroken simultaneously. To experience the fiercest joy alongside the deepest pit of despair.

"Enough," Martina snapped as we were chopping tomatoes for the caprese salad side by side in the kitchen.

We were listening to Italian pop music Martina had put on the speaker system, and we had been dancing a little around the kitchen until "Si, ah" came on and reminded me of the night Raffa and I had spent at a local club. It was strange to see a man who preferred to live in luxury and speak about Italy's historic culture indulge in something so . . . young and current. He danced to contemporary music like an idiot, and I loved discovering something he wasn't stunning at.

"You honestly *reek* of sadness," she declared, thrusting her knife at me a little because she was scary and vaguely threatening like that. But we had become close over the last six weeks, and the thought of leaving her behind brought tears to my eyes like a struck spring in soft earth.

It was too much an echo of losing Gemma.

I did not have many friends, and Martina, along with Renzo, Carmine, and Ludo, even Servio and Annella, had become my Italian family. Maybe if my parents were currently talking to me, the idea of leaving wouldn't have felt so much like abandonment.

But it did.

"Oh, *tesoro*," she murmured, seeing the tears in my eyes.

The knife hit the cutting board with a clatter, and suddenly her arms were around me.

Martina wasn't a hugger, and she didn't seem to enjoy being touched unless it was Renzo or Raffa doing it. Raffa had explained that she had trauma that made her distrustful and uncomfortable with most people and left it at that.

So the hug felt like a moment.

And I took it for all it was worth, throwing my arms around her and then tipping my head into the crook of her neck.

"I'm going to miss you so much," I admitted wetly, clutching at her back. "I can't stop thinking about it."

"I know." Her hand patted between my shoulders a little awkwardly, but she let me cling to her and sighed, relaxing into it. "We will miss you too. I hope you know."

"I think I do."

But Raffa still hadn't said the words I was waiting for.

Not "I love you."

As strange as it was, I didn't think we needed that. The phrase was overused in English anyway, and there were so many more beautiful ways to express it in Italian. Many ways Raffa had expressed the sentiment to me already over the last six weeks.

Cerbiatta mia. La mia donna. La mia stella cadente.

My little fawn. My woman. My shooting star.

"And what brings a man like you pleasure?" I'd asked him.

"You," he'd said simply. "In all your iterations."

You must remember my definition of perfect, Vera. Enticing, so vibrant you cannot help but find it beautiful, flaws and all.

Il mio posto felice.

My happy place.

Yes, there were so many other ways to say it and infinite ways to *feel* it. In the touch of his reverent hands on my body as if he was Michelangelo awakening David from marble. The way he looked at me, a keen-edged passion as sharp as the tone of Dante writing about his Francesca. How the world seemed to narrow to the two of us, and it was so easy to forget that so much lay between us.

The truth was, we did exist in a bubble. My family did not know him, and aside from the obvious problem of him living in Italy, they would be appalled by the age difference, even though it seemed trivial to me. I did not know his family, and he did not take us to visit Villa Romano even though I kept asking for stories of it when it had been his happy place. I did not tell him about Gemma's complicated life, and he did not tell me why he thought he was so undeserving of goodness in his life.

It was a defense mechanism, I thought. Keeping the last corners of our souls hidden from one another in hopes the pain wouldn't be so great when it was all over.

But still, I waited for those three words.

Not "I love you," but "Will you stay?"

Martina pulled away only to shake my shoulders, clucking her tongue at me in disappointment. "*Uffa!* You are both blind, standing too close to see each other properly."

"Hey," I protested. "I'm pretty sure you're in love with Renzo, and you haven't done a thing about it. So pot, meet kettle."

A reluctant smile tugged her mouth. In many ways, she reminded me of Raffa. Both of them used their good looks and sharp wit to draw attention away from their soft spots. They had the typical Italian characteristic of saying what they thought even if it wasn't very nice or diplomatic, and they both refused to suffer fools.

But Martina was a woman, and therefore she understood me in ways Raffa probably could not.

"You could tell him," she suggested, moving back to her tomatoes.

Servio came into the kitchen then and hummed under his breath as he checked the beef slow roasting in the oven. When he noticed we were having a heart-to-heart, he covered his ears, then zipped his mouth closed and mimed throwing away the key. I watched him for a moment as he moved to the countertop lined with watermelons we had to cut up after the tomatoes. Apparently, lasagna or pasta with meat sauce, steak, and watermelon were the traditional offerings on San Lorenzo

Day. They even had a free dinner and party with live music in the city, but Raffa had insisted we host a party. I thought it might have been his way of giving me a going-away party too. A chance to celebrate with all the people I had met in Florence while I still could. Even Signora Verga was coming. My meager guest list was amplified by Raffa's, Martina's, Renzo's, Carmine's, and Ludo's friends as well. Servio had told me earlier he was preparing to feed sixty people.

"I've thought about it," I admitted, turning back to Martina. "But I keep telling myself there is no point. So what if I . . . care about him? My life is in Michigan."

"For the last six weeks, your life has been here," she pointed out dryly. "And as a very entertained spectator, I have to say, it seems to be going very well."

"Six weeks is still a vacation. We haven't been living in reality."

She planted a hand on her hip and leveled me with a look that reminded me of my mother. "Why does it feel like you are reading these issues off cue cards?"

I flushed and shrugged. "I may have made a list. I like to be organized. So sue me."

"*Chi non risica non rosica*," she said. "She who does not risk does not get the rose."

"No risk, no reward?" I snorted. "Really, Marti?"

She glowered at my use of the nickname, but I thought she secretly liked it, because she hadn't told me to fuck off yet.

"Fine, do what you want. Mess up both your lives and mine by extension because I'll have to be the one to deal with his mopey ass when you leave."

"Are you almost done with the salad?" Carmine asked, coming into the kitchen in a vest, button-up, and trousers like he was about to walk the Versace runway and not cook in the kitchen with us. "Raffa gave me permission to duck out of work and focus on what really matters." He pointed at me. "Tiramisu."

"The key is making the ladyfingers from scratch." I echoed the words he had been telling me since last week, when I'd agreed to help him make dessert for the festivities. "I know. I took a peek in the pantry, and they turned out really well."

We had left them overnight so they could dry out, all the better to absorb the coffee-and-liquor mixture.

Carmine pressed a hand to his heart. "My angel."

"Stop flirting with *cerbiatta mia*, Carmine," Raffa drawled as he came into the kitchen in bare feet. "I gave you permission to cook with her. Not to try to steal her away."

Next to Carmine's trussed-up finery and grooming, Raffa looked casual in his black trousers and thin knit sweater with the sleeves pushed to his elbows. His hair was still a bit mussed from the make-out break we'd taken a couple of hours ago, and I hoped he hadn't had a Zoom meeting because he also had lipstick on his throat.

"Ha! Like I'd ever leave you for the likes of Carmine," I scoffed, leaning back into Raffa as he pressed up behind me and planted a kiss on my bare shoulder. "If you're going to be jealous, I'd worry most about Servio."

The eighty-year-old cook froze in the act of making six batches of lasagna, eyes wide.

"What?" I said into the silence. "Any woman in her right mind would consider being with Servio for his tortellini alone."

Martina snorted, and Carmine made an insulted noise in the back of his throat.

But Raffa laughed into my hair.

"Are your friends coming?" he asked, kissing my neck.

I squirmed. Even though I'd woken up to his mouth between my thighs while I lay on my stomach in the bed and then come twice when he canted my hips up and fucked me into the mattress, I was still on edge with lust. Knowing I only had two more days to take my fill was definitely a factor.

251

"Yes," I breathed before clearing my throat. "Bibi and Ramesh asked if they could bring a Guyanese dish, and I said of course. I hope that's okay."

"Of course. They are welcome here, and it will be interesting to have something other than the usual spread."

Servio grumbled at that, but we both ignored him.

"I made my mom's recipe for potato salad," I told him. "She makes it every summer for the Fourth of July, and obviously I missed that because I was here, so I thought it might be nice to add to the celebration."

I turned my head to catch Raffa looking into the distance, and I wondered if he was imagining spending the Fourth of July with me in some alternate reality where we could have that kind of future.

He blinked, and the moment was gone.

"What did you think of the Corteo Storico della Repubblica Fiorentina?"

Ludo, Martina, and I had gone to the parade in front of the Basilica of San Lorenzo that morning while Raffa worked with the others. I'd hoped he would go with me, but I knew before he made an excuse that he wouldn't.

It was like he was trying to ease us apart by degrees.

I wanted to shout at him that it wouldn't hurt any less to rip the bandage off slowly.

"It was amazing," I breathed. "The historical outfits, the suits of armor, the drummers and the trumpeters. I honestly didn't know where to look."

"She was like a kid in a candy store," Martina teased. "I was almost embarrassed by her enthusiasm."

"You were the one to first shout 'Viva San Lorenzo,'" Ludo reminded her.

She threw a slice of tomato at him.

The atmosphere in the kitchen stilled for one vibrating moment.

"No," Raffa told me, stepping away from me.

Carmine held up his hands to shield his fine suit. *"Assolutamente no."* Martina and I shared a look before both reaching for the huge bowls of sliced tomatoes in front of us.

"Food fight!" I hollered, turning to hurl a handful of tomatoes at Raffa.

They landed with a splat on his back as he twisted away from me. He froze, staring in shock at the hit, before lifting his gaze to mine.

"You will regret that," he promised.

"You'll have to catch me first," I declared, grabbing the bowl and then running away with it.

Behind me, I could hear Ludo and Carmine hurling insults at each other in Italian and Martina's wild cackle of delight.

A second later, the steady fall of Raffa's feet as he chased after me.

"Attenta, cerbiatta, il cacciatore viene a prenderti," Raffa called after me.

Careful, little fawn, the hunter is coming for you.

I hid behind the corner at the entrance to the music room, trying to calm my breathing so he wouldn't hear me as he approached.

He stalked into the room like the hunter he'd claimed to be, so I should have known I couldn't catch him by surprise, but I tried anyway.

I jumped out, trying to lift the bowl of tomatoes over his head, but he caught me around the wrist and wrenched it down so the bowl wavered and fell between us, coating our torsos in multicolored heritage tomatoes.

Raffa blinked at the mess I'd made of both of us and the terra-cotta tiles at our feet before sighing dramatically. "I warned you, little fawn."

I screeched as he ducked, the steel bowl falling with a clang to the floor. He put a shoulder to my belly and lifted me in a fireman's carry before taking off on firm strides down the corridor to our bedroom.

I banged on his back. "I'm needed in the kitchen, Raffa."

"You're needed over my knee, Vera," he corrected. "Thanks to your little stunt, I now have an insatiable need to see this fine ass as red as a tomato."

"People will arrive soon," I argued, even though something in my belly heated at the idea of being spanked. It wasn't something we had done yet, but it was a fantasy I'd had for years, touching myself at night and imagining what some faceless, handsome older guy might do to me if I acted out.

Probably a classic fantasy for a repressed good girl like me to have, but that didn't make it any less sexy.

Raffa tossed the door shut behind us and dropped me gently to my feet, immediately stepping out of my reach.

"Hands on the door, feet shoulder width apart. Tilt those hips to present that beautiful ass for me," he ordered in that fire-and-ice voice that made shivers pour down my spine.

I hesitated for only a moment, because I was covered in tomato gunk, before I did as he asked. Being in that position alone was so erotic, arranging my body to his liking, obeying his orders even if it meant pain because I knew, always, in the end he would make it worth it.

There was a sudden slap a split second before I felt the impact sink sharp roots into my backside. He had spanked me through my skirt, but the blow still left a mild heat in its wake.

"How is that?" he asked, running his nose down the shell of my ear.

"Good," I said, but my mouth was suddenly too dry, so it didn't come out right, and I had to try again. "Good."

"*Va bene*. Because that was only a little taste," he muttered darkly before he grabbed the bottom of my ruined shirt and pulled. "Arms."

I raised them so he could rid me of the material, my damp nipples beading in the air-conditioned room. With another quick tug, my apron and skirt fell to the floor at my feet.

"Step out."

When I did, he reached for the garments and tossed them somewhere behind us. I waited for him to touch me again, but he didn't. For a long moment that felt like minutes, I stood still, almost trembling with anticipation. A faint sound like a choked-off moan made me wonder if he was . . . touching himself to the sight of me presented like that.

Heat sluiced over my skin and pooled low in my belly.

Just when I was going to cave and look over my shoulder, his naked body pressed into my back and his hand was at my sex, cupping it in one palm.

"Already wet just from the anticipation of a good spanking and standing so pretty for me. I could have come just from looking at you, painted my load on this pretty ass and left you wanting. That would have been a better punishment for my greedy girl. But alas, I am too addicted to the way you moan when you come to leave you without an orgasm."

I panted as his fingers moved over my clit, dragging my wetness from my center up to the bundle of nerves.

"Do you want to say something to me?" he asked pleasantly.

"Thank you, Raffa," I said instantly, because it felt natural to thank him for indulging me. "Spoiling me."

He hummed with pleasure. "Such a good, sweet girl. I wonder if you will say that when I'm done with you."

His words were followed swiftly by the hit of his other hand against the underside of my ass cheek. The skin was tender, and I jumped in surprise at the sting.

"Count for me," he commanded, nipping at my neck as I arched it back on a moan because his other hand was still playing in the increasing wet heat of my pussy.

"One."

"Parla in Italiano."

"Uno."

His hand disappeared from between my legs.

Smack.

The same place on the other cheek. My toes curled into the floor, and I pressed my hot cheek to the cool wooden door.

"Due."

His hand was back, playing at my swelling clit, pinching it and then soothing it with circles of his thumb. I panted and canted my hips back even more.

Another smack.

"Do not move."

"*Tre.*" I moaned around the number.

The heat of the slaps built on itself as we continued in this rhythm, the burn digging roots that alchemized into pleasure as they reached my pussy. Raffa continued to play with me randomly, almost bringing me off before spanking me, harder and harder, and then playing with me again.

By the time I choked out "*venti,*" I was sweating, my skin too tight for my body so I felt I would burst.

I was achy all over, not just my bottom burning like banked coals, a deep fire I knew would last through the night, but also my pussy. It throbbed around an emptiness that obsessed my mind. All I could think about was the need for impact there too. A slap, a cock, a tongue.

Anything to provide the friction I needed to get off.

"I need," I tried to say, but a frustrated whimper interrupted my speech as Raffa cupped my entire soaking cunt in one hand with just enough pressure to make me crazy. "I need more. Please."

"Where do you need it?" he asked coolly, because somehow, he always knew how to read my body. "Another set to this sweet pink ass, or something here, where you really ache?" A finger moved infinitesimally over my clit.

I ground my teeth in order to stay still.

"Such a beautiful, obedient girl," he said, voice thick with desire. "I think you deserve a treat now that you've taken your punishment so well."

He stepped even closer, bringing our hips together so the hot, thick line of his cock rested in the crease of my ass. The hand that wasn't cupping my pussy went to my neck, cupping it in the same way, from pulse point to pulse point, his thumb under the hinge of my jaw to push my head back into an arch. My whole body was bowed like that, quivering with tension. All I needed was one sweet piercing arrow of pain or pleasure to trigger the release of all this tension at my core.

"I am going to spank your swollen *figa* now," he informed me in that haughty voice that made me want to crawl for him. "Five strikes, and if you come before the fifth, we will start from the beginning again and continue until you get it right. Even if it takes all night. Even if guests start to arrive and they can hear your lovely cries through the night. *È chiaro?*"

"*Capisco*," I returned, the word shapeless in my mouth because I was somehow drunk on the endorphins of being hit in just the right way by just the right man.

He pressed a kiss to my sweaty neck before saying, "Count them off."

Slap.

My body rocked to my toes as sensation rocketed through me, obliterating any notion of remaining calm.

"*Una!*" I cried out, teeth almost chattering as I fought to keep from begging.

Slap.

A sharp cry punched from my throat, and my hips rocked hard back into his hand as he cupped my stinging pussy and rubbed in the ache until it turned to sweet, honeyed pleasure.

"*Due.*" The word fell from my mouth to the floor, my entire focus on the hot spot between my thighs, bracketed by Raffa's big, calloused hand.

"You are so good for me," he praised, pushing me even higher into a space that felt like floating through a light box. "So sweet letting me slap this pussy before I fuck it."

This slap was harder, fingers curling over my clit so that the pain rang through it like a great metal bell.

"*Tre!*" I grunted through my teeth, my legs and arms shaking now.

"So close," he crooned to me. "You can do it. I will be so proud of you if you can wait to come all over my palm on five."

"Yes, Raffa," I breathed, locking down every muscle in my body in anticipation of the next stinging hit.

It didn't help.

The hit felt like fire against my wet skin, the sound of it a gunshot in the quiet room.

I quaked, my legs gone to jelly so the only things holding me up were the hand wrapped like a collar around my neck and the one curved around my cunt.

"*Quattro*," I panted against the door, rocking my forehead against the wood in an attempt to ground myself.

"Last one," Raffa whispered, rubbing my pussy in gentle, firm circles with his palm. "You have been so stunning. Absolutely perfect. This time, if you need to, Vera, you can come for me."

"Thank you," I breathed a second before his hand left my swollen folds entirely only to swing back against me with more force than before.

Air exploded from my lungs, my chest compressed, every atom in my body contracting for one single, brutal moment and then—I screamed—release.

It shot through me like an arrow, shattering the tension so that it broke into pieces and scattered in my bloodstream, carrying heady sensation to every inch of my body.

I was still coming when Raffa switched his hand for his cock and wiped his hand on my hip before grabbing me tight, slanting my ass higher, and *driving* into my clutching heat.

My cry was garbled. I was breathless with shock as the first orgasm nose-dived into a second, this one softer, longer, rippling through me like waves in a pond.

"*Così perfetta*," Raffa growled as he fucked me, the hand around my throat shifting to my shoulder, one arm banded across my breasts so he could thrust me back into him and keep my climax-wrecked body from hitting the door. *"Fatta per me."*

So perfect. Made for me.

"Per sempre," I found the will to say as he gave definition to the phrase "fucking your brains out."

Forever.

When he came, he whispered my name into my ear again and again like a supplication, like his cum was an offering to some ancient pagan goddess.

I added that to my list of ways Raffa Romano said "I love you," and knew in my heart that the other three words would come before the end of my stay.

We were meant to be together, and, climax-drunk, I could see no reasons why we shouldn't be.

CHAPTER TWENTY-ONE

Raffa

Life was better than it had been since I was a boy, too innocent and young to understand the cruelties of the world. Only perhaps it was better because now I was a man who knew just how cruel the world was and how to make myself cruel enough to defend against it.

And even then, I still fell in love with a girl who was made of starlight and sunshine.

That was the only way I knew how to define the feeling that overcame me whenever I was with her or thinking of her. As if a supernova was expanding in my chest.

Nothing had ever felt like it before, but I had read enough poetry to recognize that these symptoms spoke of love.

I had dated at Oxford and in London, beautiful, interesting women who knew nothing about my history, but there was no comparison.

Even though Guinevere did not know everything about me, specifically the nature of my business and the kind of man I had to be to do it, she still knew so much more than anyone else. From the very first, it was like she had sensed the shape of my soul buried six feet deep in the fallow field of my chest and carefully nurtured it back to life.

Her love of Italy lent itself to knowing me the way women before her had not. How could anyone love me without knowing of Italy? The country that had, for better or worse, carved me slowly and irrevocably into the form I took now. No number of years in Britain could rid me of that influence, and I realized, to my surprise, I was pleased by that.

I had been right at the start when I'd told Guinevere she could make me fall in love with my country again. I just had not expected her to make me fall in love with them both simultaneously.

Loving her was the less surprising of the two.

She was everything good I admired, shaded in just enough of her own unique darkness to be three dimensional and vibrant with complexity.

But the fact that she had made me fall in love with myself?

Shocking.

It was hard to look back at the last four years, no, thirteen including the time in England, and see how truly unhappy I had been. First cast out of my family with only infrequent, clandestine communication so that my father would not discover I was still in contact with my mother and sisters. Completely without the comforts of my culture—the only friends who knew who I was straight through to the bone were Martina, who moved to be with me after the death of her husband, and Renzo and Carmine, who visited whenever they could.

Then, when I returned to Italy, a bittersweet homecoming because I had to pick up the dirty mantle of a man I hated in order to safeguard the Romano women from the vultures circling in the wake of Aldo's death.

Even as I adjusted to my new reality, it was with a resignation that tainted me through to the very marrow of my bones. Even as I grew to enjoy aspects of the work and the shadowed corners of my psyche that made me so adept at it, I could not fully rejoice in this new life because it had not been my decision to live it.

Loving Guinevere, though terrifying, seemed like the first decision I had made for myself since I'd left Italy, turning my back on my past to pursue my dream of Oxford and a civilian life.

I wondered what I would do to keep the dream of Vera alive too.

I stood drinking a glass of wine in the corner of the kitchen, watching her. She was laughing, hand on the forearm of her old Scottish friend, Fergus, as if she needed his support to hold her up. Bibi, the beautiful Black woman, flicked her on the nose and made her laugh so hard I could hear the faint strains of it over the music and the other general chatter of the San Lorenzo festivities. She had started to talk more with her hands, especially when she spoke Italian, and they fluttered through the air like pale birds.

It was impossible to look away from her radiance.

"You're completely gone for her," Martina observed as she sidled up beside me, leaning her hip against the counter so we were pressed together.

For someone who usually avoided physical touch, she sought it with Renzo and me whenever she could. I wondered if she was as touch starved as I hadn't realized I was before meeting Guinevere.

I sighed, angling an annoyed look her way.

"Don't sigh at me as if I'm some inaccurate nuisance. I am one of your best friends and, I'll have you know, filled with deep wisdom."

"I think you mean bullshit."

Her elbow dug into my side, but I was ready for her, transferring my glass to the counter so I could pin her in a headlock.

Renzo appeared, blinking at us mildly. "Oh, are we reverting back to the age of eleven?"

"Don't tease him," Martina said as she squirmed out of my loosened hold. "Can't you see he's in love?"

Renzo gave her his best unimpressed stare, which was effective on almost everyone but Martina.

"Don't pretend you haven't noticed." She leveled a finger at him and then swung it into my face. "None of us have ever seen you happier."

I lifted my shoulder in a slight shrug but had to hide the beginnings of a grin behind my wineglass.

"Oh, Raffa," she said, seeing it anyway, softening into my side. "What are you going to do about it?"

My sip of wine turned sour in my mouth, and I had to force myself to swallow it.

Was that not the million-euro question?

"There is a tension between what I want to do and what I know is the right thing," I confessed.

Renzo considered me with the full weight of his keen attention. "You have not hesitated to do what you want for a very long time."

"It is not just about me," I snapped, then sighed. "If I ask her to stay . . . I would have to tell her everything. She either hates me and leaves on the next plane out, or she finds a way to love me still and I subject her to a lifetime of danger as my woman."

"She leaves on a plane in two days whether you tell her or not," Renzo prompted.

"And the man I know would not let anything happen to his woman," Martina decreed with her chin in the air, her eyes flashing with memories.

The night she had finally told me her truth. The night her husband had ended up dead, impaled on the edge of my knife.

I slid my arm around her waist and hugged her into my side. "I would die for her tomorrow if it meant keeping her safe for the rest of time. Loving her like that . . . can you not see how wrong it feels to ask her to stay?"

"She would," Renzo said, looking into the informal living room where Guinevere was still talking with her friends. Ludo was at her shoulder, too, drinking a Sanpellegrino in solidarity with Vera because he was like that. Of us all, he had the best heart, so it did not surprise me that those two had struck up a quiet, lasting bond.

One of my soldiers, Gustavo, whom I had known since our youth, approached Guinevere to introduce his wife, who was a history professor at the university.

Guinevere's face lit up.

"I know," I murmured, because I could feel her love like a light on my face every time she looked at me. "But she thinks I am her hero, a Prince Charming in my red Ferrari saving her on the side of the road. What if she knew I had a body in the trunk, hmm? What if she knew how many people I had killed?"

And how much I enjoyed it, I thought but did not say.

Martina made a sympathetic noise in the back of her throat before dropping her cheek to my shoulder, and Renzo moved to stand on my other side, close enough to bump my shoulder. Sandwiched between the two, I felt grateful that Guinevere had opened my eyes to the beauty in my life that had already existed.

"Thank you," I told them. "For putting up with my miserable ass for all these years. I would not be here without you."

If they were surprised by my uncharacteristic show of effusiveness, they did not bat an eyelid. Instead, Martina lifted her beer toward us both and waited until we raised our wineglasses before saying, "*Per sempre.*"

Forever.

I could toast to that and take comfort in the fact that no matter what I chose to do, I had my *famiglia* to fall back on.

"For what it's worth, though, boss," Renzo said. "I think you should ask her to stay. She thinks you are better than you are, yes, but I think you both believe she is better than she truly is too. She is smart, Raffaele. If she has been looking, and she has, she will have had the opportunity to draw her own conclusions. She just didn't want to."

It was an interesting argument, one I hadn't considered.

Guinevere was darker than she appeared. She adored the harsh crack of my voice commanding her to do things her sweet, dirty mind had only dreamed in her most depraved fantasies. Admitted that she felt safe when I broke the finger of the *stronzo* who had called her a whore outside Fortezza da Basso. Crowed with glee watching as the trap she had helped lay for the Grecos snapped into place around their necks in the Ligurian Sea.

Oh yes, she had a dark side, and it called out to me like whispers in the night. I could even believe it was one of the reasons she was so drawn to me.

But self-perception was such a tricky business, and I should know that best of all.

Guinevere's parents had told her to be good and do good her entire life. They had reinforced that she was the good sister, the good daughter, so heavily that I could feel the physical tremors of joy when I called her a good girl in the bedroom.

Now *good* was a label she had given herself as much as anyone else had.

And I was not sure anything or anyone could change the way she thought about herself except for Guinevere.

She had found fertile soil here in Florence to dig her roots into, soaking up nourishment she had been looking for all her life, tipping her head to the sun until she blossomed. Her confidence grew every day, and along with it her sense of self.

It was gorgeous to behold.

There was a difference, though, between growing from what you were and changing entirely. And she would have to do that if she wanted to stay and be my woman.

She would have to become the Queen Below to my King.

The thought of her royal and clothed in shadow by my side, Proserpina to my Pluto, made my throat tight with a hope so big it threatened to choke me.

I was about to open my mouth to declare I would tell her at the end of the night, after our guests had left, when Carmine entered the room looking slightly disheveled. He immediately made for a carafe of wine on the counter and poured himself a large glass.

A moment later, a friend of Martina's appeared, a small bruise at the hinge of her neck and shoulder.

Martina, Renzo, and I chuckled, ignoring Carmine's smug grin. He swallowed a hefty gulp of expensive wine and wiped his mouth with the back of his hand.

"Dehydrated?" Martina teased.

Carmine winked. "I hope you don't mind, Raffa. We used the bench in the gym for some X-rated exercise."

I rolled my eyes at him, but my mood was so good I couldn't be even slightly irritated.

"Oh," he mentioned. "You should fire whoever you used for the flowers, boss. They left an arrangement of chrysanthemums in the foyer."

He made a sign to ward off the devil, but I was too preoccupied with his words to pay it any mind. Annella, my housekeeper, had hired people to decorate the house for the party, but the decorations were mostly Florentine banners and huge urns filled with white and red flowers.

Not chrysanthemums.

They were only used on graves and at funerals in Italy, and as a superstitious people, we avoided them on any other occasion.

"Show me," I demanded.

Carmine set his wineglass on the counter, sobering instantly. Martina and Renzo followed behind me as we moved through the first floor and down the stairs to the foyer.

The flowers were in a large, low bowl on the marble table at its center.

I searched the blooms and came up with a small card perched on the edge of the bowl.

"I did not die, yet I lost life's breath."
You will not die. You will not go gently.

So I will take your breath instead and watch you suffocate.

San Marco

As if the quote from Dante's *Divine Comedy* made it so, I could not breathe.

Terror was a noose cinched too tightly around my neck, all my blood rushing to my head and inducing dizziness so severe I had to brace my hand on the table.

Of course, there was only one choice for who my breath could be. And she was laughing upstairs with her friends at a party.

Renzo plucked the card from my hand and read it before cursing savagely and passing it off to Martina.

"She leaves in two days," Carmine soothed after reading it himself. "You just have to be careful until then."

I could not speak, muted by that ever-closing noose.

"He was going to ask her to stay," Martina murmured, her hand soft against my forearm.

"This is why I never could." The words almost wheezed out of me, wrung from my air-deprived lungs. "She has already survived so much. I will not ask her to survive this."

"Whoever the fuck San Marco is, we will find them eventually," Renzo swore. "We have suffered worse fools than these. The Pietras are a shell of what they once were before we broke them apart for taking Aldo. Eight Greco members are rotting, awaiting prosecution from the DIA, because they dared to turn against us. We will end this poetic motherfucker's threat too."

"Yes," I agreed on a hiss as fury worked fingers under the rope around my throat and pulled it loose.

I let the dark joy of violence fill my blood and bring me back from the brink of panic. Il Gentiluomo was a figure spoken about in whispers in dark corners and back alleys. A man so monstrous he had become legend. For a brief moment, I forgot that monster was me, having spent too long in human skin around Guinevere.

But there was no future where I was not both, and there was no future where I could live with Guinevere suffering the consequences of my choices.

"Talk to Annella. Get the name of the decorator or the florist and discover who the fuck sent these," I ordered as the cool mantle of numb cruelty settled back around my shoulders. "Find me the man, find me the messenger, I do not care. Just find me someone to kill for this."

Renzo and Carmine both nodded before taking off back up the stairs to do my bidding.

"Raffa," Martina tried, voice soft, hand still on my arm though I was numb to it.

"Not now. The party is over. Wrap it up without causing alarm in the next hour. I do not want anyone outside the family in this house after that."

The idea of people I did not trust farther than I could throw them being in the same city, let alone under the same roof as Guinevere, filled me with primal rage.

Martina hesitated a moment before her posture changed, shoulders tightening, spine straightening to her normal military bearing. "Yes, boss."

"Nothing touches her," I ground out. "Not so much as a bee stings her in the next forty-eight hours before she is gone. Understood?"

She nodded.

I went to find my woman and install her for the rest of the night within arm's reach of my side. In a way, I was glad for the rage flaming in my rib cage. It almost overwhelmed the crushing grief at my heart.

CHAPTER
TWENTY-TWO

Guinevere

The party was a massive success.

It was incredible to have our friends under one roof for the festivities, eating delicious food and talking about things I never had as a university student. Philosophy, literature, the importance of cultural celebrations like the Feast of San Lorenzo each year, and the relationship Italians had with their food. It was *enriching*. All of it. Rich, verdant earth to dig my roots into so I could suck up all the nutrients of this place and these people before I had to leave.

If I had to leave.

Raffa was aloof for the first half of the party, but he spent the last two hours with me, a hand around my low back sewing me into his side. He spoke to my friends in slow, patient Italian so they could understand him, and even indulged Fergus in a debate about the Italian football league.

At one point, Greta had leaned into me and whispered, "Good job, Guinevere. He is an Italian dream."

Now everyone had gone, leaving only the mainstays in the palazzo. Servio and Annella were already at work cleaning the space even though it was after midnight, but they refused to go to bed before it was done.

I would have liked them to join us, but it was enough to have the others.

They were gathered in a loose knot in the study, speaking quietly, when I found them after setting everything up for my Perseids tradition, but they went quiet as soon as I entered.

For some reason, I was nervous, hands wringing together, damp fingers tangling. Maybe because I was homesick twice over, for the family I had back in Michigan that wasn't speaking to me and the family I'd made here that I had an uncertain future with.

"Back home, my family spends most of the summer at our cabin in Gun Lake," I explained in Italian, because it was natural now after weeks of practice. "During the meteor shower, we lay in the grass together and make wishes on shooting stars."

I could feel Raffa's gaze on me like warm hands, sliding over my face and body possessively. His look said, "I love you." It said, "You are my shooting star."

"Will you come and lay with me on the terrace and make a wish with me?" I asked softly, feeling slightly childish but pushing past the embarrassment because I knew how to do that better now.

Ludo moved first, walking toward me and then beyond, straight out the door.

I knew he was going to the terrace, and his action was his response.

A smile pulled through my mouth as I looked back at the others.

"Is there a limit on wishes?" Carmine asked as he walked to the door too. "Because I can think of five or six."

I snorted. "No, Carm, I don't think there is a limit on wishes. It's a galaxy, not a genie. The scale is a little different."

Martina and Renzo followed close behind him. The latter bumped his arm gently into mine as he passed, but Martina hesitated to brush a sweet kiss along my cheek.

Which left Raffa leaning his narrow hip against his desk, arms crossed, brow raised in a facsimile of the way he'd been before I knew who he was under that cool look and expensive armor.

I tiptoed over to him in my bare feet and offered him my hand in question.

He stared at it for a moment before raising his own, gently engulfing it in his much-bigger palm. When he looked back up at me, there were lines of strain beside his eyes and a wealth of disquiet in the autumnal brown.

"I could use a wish or two," he confessed.

I squeezed his hand in answer and led him quietly through the house out onto the big terrace off the kitchen. I had cleared some space on the corner of the deck, laying down thick blankets and a few pillows because the flagstone was not as comfortable as grass.

Ludo, Martina, and Renzo were waiting, heads tipped back to look at the milky spill of bright stars tossed on the black-velvet night sky.

"Um, we usually lie head to head," I mentioned as I stepped on the blankets and folded to my knees, tugging Raffa down with me.

There was zero hesitation as everyone stepped forward and lay down with me. Martina on my right, Renzo beside her, and Carm beside him, and then Ludo on the other side of Raffa on my left. The moment we were all settled, I sucked in a deep breath, feeling the closed circuit of our energy wash over me.

Raffa inhaled deeply, too, as if he hadn't had a breath of fresh air in much too long. He brought our tangled hands to his chest and pressed them over his heart.

I could feel his heart thump beneath my palm.

"Ah! Did you see that one?" Carmine exclaimed, raising his hand to point at a spot in the sky. "My first wish is about a brunette I met in Pistoia."

"You aren't supposed to share wishes," Ludo muttered. "It is unlucky. They won't come true."

"I make my own luck."

A touch to the *cornicello* charm around my neck that I never took off. I looked down from the sky to see Raffa's other hand reaching across to finger the pendant.

"Promise me you will wear this forever," he said quietly but strangely intensely.

"I didn't know you were such a superstitious Italian," I teased, but the graveness of his expression made my smile wane. *"Certo, Raffa, se desideri."*

Yes, Raffa, if you wish.

"I do." His hand dropped away, and he propped it behind his head to stargaze once more.

"Oh, that one looked like it would crash into the Duomo," Martina exclaimed as a large streak of white exploded across the sky.

We spent at least an hour out in the dark, counting our lucky stars, before people started to trickle off to bed. Martina stood first, pausing briefly before offering her hand to Renzo to help him up. He took it and did not let go when they walked into the house.

Carmine left next, face splitting in two around his yawn, complaining that a dalliance from earlier that night had worn him out.

When Ludo left, he did it quietly, only stopping to knock his foot against mine in good night.

He closed the balcony doors behind him.

Leaving Raffa and me under the blanket of starlight.

We turned our heads to each other simultaneously, and the next moment, we were kissing. He took my mouth like a man dying of thirst, sipping at my lips, drinking deeply from me as if he would not survive without my lips on his. He tugged me onto his body without breaking our contact, pressing my lower back to flex his hardening cock against my belly.

I moaned, sinking my hands into his hair as I shifted to straddle his hips so I could grind down on him properly.

When we broke apart, we were both panting.

He pushed a hand into my sternum, so I sat up, and then he gathered my short dress in his hands, pulling up until I had to curve my body and raise my arms as he took it over my head.

"*Così bella immerso nella luce della luna*," he murmured as he studied me with black, sparkling eyes, as if chips from the star-strewn sky had fallen into them.

So beautiful bathed in moonlight.

"*Voglio bagnarti di sborra*," he continued in that same silky voice that wound around my body like bondage.

I want to bathe you in my cum.

His hand collected both my wrists behind my back so that my chest was arched, nipples pebbled in the cool night air. He knifed up to suck hard at each and then blew cooler air over them so that I shivered.

He continued his smoky refrain, explaining everything he was going to do to me under the face of the moon as he alternated between sucking and biting my breasts. The flesh turned red, ringed in teeth marks I could see even in the dim light spilling out from inside and the silver glow of the sky.

I wished I could have his teeth marks on my skin every day for the rest of my life.

"*Ti scoperò ovunque.*"

I am going to fuck you everywhere.

I gasped as his free hand slid between my breasts down to my belly, delving beneath my thong to cup my pussy. It was one of his favorite moves, curving that big hand around my sex in a display of total ownership that always made me leak into his palm.

"*Ti scoperò la bocca. La tua figa. E il tuo culo stretto*," he continued, the words guttural now as he worked two fingers inside, twisting them into that sensitive ridge on my inner wall that made my vision produce its own stars.

I am going to fuck your mouth. Your pussy. And your tight ass.

My hips rocked unconsciously against his fingers as he added another and fucked me harder.

"Would you like that, *cerbiatta*?" he murmured against my throat, nipping the skin there, too, so I knew in the morning I would be decorated in the jewelry of his lust. "Would you like me to own you everywhere?"

"Yes," I hissed instantly, bending to try to catch his lips. "I want you everywhere. I do not want a single inch of my body to belong only to me when we are done."

The thought of taking his big shaft in my ass was darkly alluring. I'd fingered myself there before back in the States, curious about the tightly furled entrance, shocked by the swell of wet that pooled in my pussy from the illicit contact. In my room, alone at night with my fantasies, I was free from the shackles of being the good girl, and I could indulge in all the ways I secretly was not.

I gasped as Raffa flipped me suddenly onto my back, his hand breaking my fall so I landed gently. He knee-walked up my body even as his hands went to his pants, deftly undoing his belt and fly until he was free to take his cock from the tight confines.

It looked *beautiful* painted in silver light, the veins raised and mouthwatering around the wide shaft, the precum on the head the same color as the moon.

"Open wide for me."

I shivered at that biting tone and let my mouth drop open, tongue peeking out to greet his skin as he slid straight into my opening. My eyes fell softly closed as I hummed around the salt bite of his taste. I relaxed my jaw instinctively, used to this now. He had taught me well how to take him deep and hard and often.

One of my favorite feelings was the wedge of his cock impaled balls deep in my mouth and throat. The triumph of taking every inch soared through me straight to my groin so that I squirmed and rubbed my thighs together, desperate for friction.

Sensing my rising desperation, he tore his shirt off and leaned back, bringing my hand to the abdominals cut starkly into his skin. I groaned when he cupped my head in one hand to raise it higher and used the other to slap my legs apart so he could dip fingers into my slick folds.

"You look so pretty with your lips stretched tight around my cock," he told me in growling Italian. "Like you were made to suck me. Made to take my cock."

He groaned when I sucked him on the backstroke, flicking my tongue over his slit to gather the cream spilling out. His fingers curled inside my pussy, and the heel of his hand ground down on my clit so that my legs started to shake.

"Yes, little fawn, come with my cock down your throat," he ordered.

As in everything with Raffa, I had no choice but to obey. My cries were muffled by his shaft, and I gagged once, so his cock slid even deeper, and he moaned at the way my mouth gripped tight around his driving dick. My orgasm was sharp and short, an exclamation point at the end of my lust that only made it stronger.

Raffa pulled out of my mouth a moment later, squeezing a big hand around the root of his drool-slicked, reddened cock to curb his climax.

"Take off your panties and get on your hands and knees," he instructed as he stood. "Wait for me like that and do *not* touch yourself."

I let loose a slight whimper at that order but did as he asked while he went to the doors, peered inside to make sure everyone was in bed, and disappeared inside.

When he returned, I was in position, my *figa* and *culo* framed high in the air between my spread legs.

"*Così carina,*" he praised as he dropped to his knees on the blankets behind me, and a glass bottle landed next to me. Olive oil.

I turned my head to watch as Raffa lifted the bottle, uncapped it, and poured some into his palms. He rubbed them together to warm the liquid and then smoothed his rough-slick hands over the globes of my ass until they gleamed with a high shine under the starlight.

"*Che bella,*" he murmured, his voice almost punch drunk with lust, taking in the sight of his oiled hands on me.

I gasped, head dropping between my shoulders as the head of his cock kissed my entrance and then slid smoothly into my pussy, the way eased by his thick fingers so I could take him all in one stroke. I thrust my hips back into his, grinding down, but he only moved in deep, slow circles that shuddered desire through my hips in shocky waves.

He was too preoccupied with massaging his oiled thumbs over my crinkled hole, pressing deeper and deeper on each pass until one sank inside. I jumped at the unfamiliar burn, but his other hand held me steady at my hip and hushed me with soft, nonsensical praise in Italian.

"Be good for me," he intoned, and I realized I was panting, working my hips in useless palpitations because sensation was bombarding my body.

I could feel it in the curling ends of my toes. At the roots of my hair and the base of my teeth. It was everywhere, around me and inside me.

Raffa, Raffa, Raffa in my mouth like the only word I knew in any language.

He replaced his thumb with a finger and then slowly worked another one inside the rim, stretching me enough to make me hiss before I sank into the burn.

"I know my girl loves pleasure," he said as he pumped those fingers into my ass, holding me still and open with his other palm, and I knew without looking that his eyes were fixed on the way he split me open on his cock in one hole and his fingers in the other. "But she loves some pain too."

I couldn't disagree. Mostly because my brain had short-circuited and my mouth had stopped working except to form the shape of his name and the occasional plea.

"Do you want my cock here, *mia dolce cerbiatta*?" he cooed to me, a third finger pressing, massaging at the tight clutch of my hole until it gave way and closed tight around the added digit.

I cried out, head snapping up as my back bowed and unexpected pleasure knifed through my pussy and ass, the edge meeting in the middle and driving deeper so that I shook and shook and shook with climax. My teeth snapped together with the force, and all I could see behind my wrenched-closed lids was the night sky imprinted in my brain, a galaxy of pinprick color.

"So good," he crooned as I spiraled back down into his grip like a feather. "I am going to fuck you here and own this piece of you. No matter where you go from here, your first moments of pleasure will always be mine."

I opened my mouth in lazy protest, to tell him the only place I wanted to go was to bed in his room—our room—for the rest of forever.

But then his fingers were leaving me, except one hooked into my slightly stretched hole as if to hold it open for the press of his searing cock. I held every muscle so still, I seemed to vibrate as he gradually stuffed my tight hole full with his steely length.

I cried out softly, head limp on my neck as his balls pressed to my soaking pussy and he was finally deep inside me. The heat and burn of him in my most forbidden place felt like a brand of ownership on the inside of my skin. It made me feel his in a way I never had before.

His hands cupped the flare of my ribs and traced them to the small of my waist and up over my ass to hold my hips.

"I am going to fuck you hard, now, *mia stella cadente*," he warned me, voice threadbare with the same longing I felt coiled around my hips and soul. "Going to own you now and forever."

"Yes," I gasped, tipping my hips even higher so he notched deeper and made me shiver. "Own me forever."

The way he fucked me then was as savage as he promised. Pulling himself slow and smooth to the hottest, tightest point of my entrance in a way that made saliva pool behind my teeth and then snapping his hips hard to drill back into my depths.

Over and over.

Harder and harder.

The hands on my oiled hips slipped under the intensity and became claws, fingertips stamping oval bruises and nails giving me half-moon scratches that I would wear as if on a gemstone Renaissance belt.

I locked my elbows so I could drive back against his thrust, falling deeper and deeper into the debauched act, lost to the all-consuming feel of the deep, earthy pleasure.

And when he reached down with his cleaner hand to thrust two fingers into my steadily leaking, swollen cunt, I threw my head back and howled my orgasm to the moon.

Seconds later, he came, too, pulling out carefully before fisting his cock until he rained hot seed over both my holes.

And when he came, he shouted my name to the same moon as in a pagan union, a marriage under the stars that felt more eternal than if we had signed any kind of legal document and binding code.

I was his.

Completely, unutterably, until my dying day.

After, when he cleaned me up as best he could with his discarded designer shirt, ruining it without a thought, he collected me in his arms and carried me through the dark, quiet house to his palatial bedroom. He got into bed without allowing me to the leave the circle of his arms and then settled me curled up on his torso like a kitten.

I was completely exhausted, but I clung to wakefulness, waiting to hear those three little words I was now so certain he would ask me.

Will you stay? Will you stay? Will you stay?

I repeated them in my mind like a spell, and when he spoke, at first, I thought he himself had spoken them.

But no.

"You are brighter than any star we saw tonight," he confessed as he stroked my hair with one hand and my hip with another. As if he couldn't bear for any inch of me to be unloved for even a moment. "Please, promise me something."

"What?" I whispered around the hope lodged in my throat.

"*Segui la tua stella,*" he murmured. "It means 'follow your destiny.' Do not go home and let your parents dictate your life any longer just because you feel guilty about their loss of Gemma. Just because you feel you should be able to make their lives easier by being good at the cost of your dreams. Whatever wishes you made in the safety of your head tonight, follow them for me, even when I am not there to show you how much I am cheering you on."

I blinked at the flood of tears that attacked my ducts, trying to keep them back through sheer force of will.

The only wishes I had made tonight were to stay here with Raffa forever, but it seemed he didn't have the same dream.

"Your dreams mean more now to me than my own," he said quietly before kissing the top of my head.

A few minutes later, his hands went limp on my body as sleep swept him and my hope for those three little words away forever. When I was sure he was deeply asleep, I turned my face into his chest and let myself anoint him with my tears as I whispered, "I love you, Raffa. In any language, across any distance. And I always will."

CHAPTER TWENTY-THREE

Guinevere

I woke up with a gasp because there was a hand over my mouth.

My eyes flew open, torso knifing up only to be gently pushed back down. Raffa was leaning over me, the whites of his eyes gleaming in the dark room.

"Hush," he insisted quietly, sharp urgency in every line of his coiled body as he hunched over me like a shield. "Someone is in the house."

Fear tied my belly into tight knots. He removed his hand to press a finger to his lips.

I nodded, heart moving to hammer in my throat so hard I thought I would vomit around it.

A light was flashing on Raffa's bedside table like a silent alarm, throwing red light into the room every few seconds. It was a security system, I realized with relief.

The police were on their way.

The door to the room creaked open.

Raffa pushed me into the mattress, straddling my body, facing the door with a *gun* raised in the direction of the entrance.

But it was only Ludo, his own handgun in both hands. He jerked his head at Raffa and made a hand gesture toward the hall before disappearing again.

Raffa nimbly climbed off the bed and grabbed for my hand.

"Hide in the closet while I go sweep the house," he ordered me softly in Italian. "Do not make a noise and do *not* come out unless you recognize the voice of whoever is in the room."

When I didn't say anything, gaze fixed to the dark metal of the gun in his other hand, he shook me slightly by the shoulder.

"Guinevere," he snapped quietly and raised the gun to point the barrel at his eyes as if he wasn't even aware he had a loaded gun between his fingers. "Eyes here. Do you understand me?"

I nodded, but when he tried to move away, I clutched harder at his hand.

Raffa's features softened slightly as he looked down at my nails digging into his skin. He pulled me into his arms and pressed a long kiss to my temple.

"You will be safe, little fawn. Do you trust me?"

I was nodding before he had finished asking the question. "I'm not scared for me. I'm scared about you going out there. Please, stay in here with me. Let Ludo and Martina handle it. They were in the army!"

Raffa's smile was a thin slice of white in the dark. "Do not worry about me, Vera. Whoever has broken into my home should be much more afraid of me than I am of him. Now, do as I say. *Hide.*"

I rose to my tiptoes to press a hurried kiss to the side of his mouth and then turned to run across the wood floors to Raffa's walk-in closet, the door closest to the windows overlooking the inner courtyard. There were slats in the wood so I could see out if I pressed my face to the door.

I didn't hear Raffa leave, but I knew when he did because fear gripped tighter at my throat. My heart raced so hard, I thought it would give out, and I felt dizzy from the strain.

Long minutes passed, and nothing.

I was almost relaxing slightly when I heard the creak of the old wood door opening again to the bedroom.

My heart stopped, slamming into an impenetrable wall of fear.

Because I knew somehow that it was not Raffa.

Or Martina, or Renzo, or Ludo, or Carm.

Somewhere deep in the palace there were a shout and the concussive bang of a gunshot indoors.

Through the slats in the door I saw a shadow detach itself from the wall and freeze in the middle of the room at the sounds from the second floor.

My hand slowly went to my mouth as if I could press my too-loud, panicked breath back into my body.

A second later, the dark form moved again, crossing to the bed. I watched as it seemed to check the sheets and then crossed to the bathroom diagonally across the room from where I hid.

Thumps echoed throughout the palace.

The shape of a man reappeared almost instantly, walking faster now.

Coming straight for me.

I swallowed my scream and threw myself backward, my bare toes silent on the carpet. My back hit the end of the closet, ten feet from the slatted door.

I pressed my spine hard to the wood as if it could absorb me and keep me safe.

But it couldn't.

A moment later, the door swung out on quiet hinges, and a tall, lean body filled the gap.

I was trapped.

Fear clogged every pore so completely I could not even scream. Every scary movie I had ever seen where the heroine didn't call for help suddenly made sense.

I was frozen in terror and faced with a man who stepped forward just slightly, so the moonlight fell through the slats onto a face wearing a Venetian mask.

And the dark metal of a gun raised to point at me.

"*Mi dispiace, ma tu sei il suo respiro e lui deve morire,*" came the muffled words from the man who clearly intended to kill me.

I am sorry, but you are his breath, and he needs to die.

Oh my God.

Time slowed to a molasses drip while thoughts flew through my head like shooting stars.

My parents back home, aching from betrayal, not knowing they would ache so much more when I never came home at all, lost to the evil Italy they had warned me about.

Raffa, somewhere in the house, without knowledge that I loved him with every single thing inside me.

The life I could have lived if I'd only been brave enough to take a risk when I could have.

All of it gone in the single press of a finger around a trigger.

The masked man took three big steps forward and aimed the long barrel of the gun at my forehead.

I couldn't close my eyes or look away.

I wouldn't be a coward in this final moment before the end came.

So I was watching him as the BANG screamed through the tiny closet, deafening me momentarily, making me flinch. My face seemed to break open, sharp pinpricks of pain punching into my skin, moving hot and wet across my forehead, my cheeks and chest.

I took in a shuddering breath and realized, *I am not dead.*

But the masked man before me had the entire front right of his face blown clean away, only crumbled bone and wet, bleeding muscle and tissue left in its place as his body swayed and then fell forward into me.

I scuttled to the side, avoiding his collapse, pressing myself into the corner of a row of suits.

Without the man between me and the door, I could see who stood there.

The perpetrator of that vicious, life-ending BANG.

Raffaele Romano, arms still raised, locked and steady, a curl of gray smoke shimmering in the moonlight over the cocked gun. As I watched, he took a step forward and drilled three more bullets into the body at my feet without flinching.

I opened my mouth, and finally, I screamed.

CHAPTER TWENTY-FOUR

Guinevere

I ran.

The basic human response to a terrifying situation is fight or flight, and I knew, even in my stupefied horror, that there was no way I could ever fight Raffa.

So I leapt over the body—*the body*—like the fawn Raffa had accused me of being and darted past him before he could even lower the gun.

The gun!

There were people I could go to inside the house. Martina was my first thought, ex-military and badass, but logic ripped the thought into pieces.

Everyone in this house was unequivocally *his*.

So loyal to him, they could not be trusted to help me even under the best circumstances.

And these weren't that.

Because that same level of loyalty that made them a family meant only one thing.

They knew.

They knew Raffa was a monster masquerading as a man.

They knew, they knew, they knew.

I was still screaming.

The sound echoed off the high ceilings of the house as I raced through the first floor and stampeded down the stairs in my bare feet, slipping slightly on the marble because they were slick with blood.

Blood.

By the time I made it to the bottom, I was going so fast, I could not have stopped if I'd tried. Voices were starting to sound behind me, but I couldn't focus on those.

I had to keep my eyes trained on the doors at the end of the huge foyer, and when I reached them, I threw myself against the heavy wood while I twisted the knob, forcing it open faster than the old, ornate hinges wanted to move.

They screeched painfully, but I was still screaming, so I didn't notice.

Cool night air hit my face, shaking some clarity back between my ears.

The police.

That was where I needed to go, to the police station.

I couldn't think beyond that to what I would say, what I would do, once more caught without a phone or ID, in a little nightgown the same maple-brown shade as Raffa's eyes.

The cold eyes of a *killer* that I had stared into countless times, believing they were the windows to the soul of a man I loved.

I ran.

Turning on my heel on the pavers, I sprinted toward the Arno. The sun was just a faint glow on the horizon, so I wasn't sure if the police station would be open, but I remembered where Raffa had taken me to make my statement in Santa Croce.

There were a few people in the streets. A small group of drunk youths around my age who laughed when I passed in my silk nightie at a sprint. An older man, his dog peeing against a graffitied wall.

I kept running.

All the way across the Arno and to the left down to the police station.

It didn't look open to the public, but there were lights on within, so I raised my fist to pound on the empty door . . .

. . . and found I could not bring my fist to connect with the glass in the frame.

I stood there, swaying slightly, as I sucked in deep, long inhales, and the lack of motion, the time to breathe, cooled the hot rush of panic in my blood until I was as inert as volcanic rock. Trapped in my body while my thoughts battled each other.

As much as instinct urged me to knock on that glass and report a murder, I physically could not bring myself to turn Raffa in.

It was more than the simple fact that, in however brutal a way, he had saved my life.

It was every moment that had led to this one, every moment where I had believed the very best of him. His touch on my shoulder when he was retying that red dress, his mouth on my breasts through the wine-soaked gown, and the feel of him inside me under the starlit night only a handful of hours before this. The way he'd made me fall in love not only with this country and him but also with myself. Exactly how I was.

After years of my being sheltered and controlled for my own good by my parents as we all fought to discover how to live with my primary hyperoxaluria type 1 diagnosis, where it felt as if my condition defined me more than any of my other characteristics did, it had been such an overwhelming blessing to have someone like Raffa admire and care for me. He had made me feel safe and strong, smart and captivating. Worthy of the kind of love I had only ever read about in epic poems.

I sobbed right there in the street, catching it in one hand like I'd thrown up my sickly, bleeding heart.

Raffa was not the kind of hero from those poems, and clearly, I was too silly and naive to be any kind of heroine.

Because seeing Raffa kill that man so coldly had locked a pattern into place I had been too blinded by rose-tinted love to ignore.

The broken skin on his knuckles when we danced in the restaurant, the way he'd threatened Wyatt at the winery, the two different companies trying to steal from his investments, and the calm, eerily cold way he'd reacted and then exacted retribution, at least against the latter. I shuddered to think what he might have done to the people at Zhang-Liu Imports, but part of me knew he hadn't just turned them in to the police.

Even the scene where he'd confronted and broken the finger of the driver who had called me a whore took on a new light. What once had almost aroused me now seemed to be one scenario in a pattern of violent behaviors.

Raffaele Romano was not the man of my dreams.

He was the stuff of nightmares.

A dangerous criminal who was so inured to violence, sabotage, and death that he didn't blink an eye at taking justice into his own hands. With Zhang-Liu, with the shipping company, with the driver who had called me a whore, and finally, with the man who had broken in tonight and ended up with four bullets through his body on the floor of the closet.

That man was no random thief.

He was there with a gun searching for something. No. Someone.

Raffa had enough enemies to rival James Bond.

It was too surreal to comprehend, but the only thing that continued to rise to the surface of my murky thoughts was this: *You do not know Raffaele Romano.*

He is not the man you thought he was.

You are a silly girl in love with a dream you projected onto a man who was probably laughing at your naivete this entire time.

Shame and heartbreak and horror soured my gut so that this time when I sobbed, I gagged, bile having surged up my throat.

"Posso aiutarla?"

Can I help you?

An officer in the standard blue uniform stood at the door, a cell phone held to his ear. He peered at me through the murky glass and then unlocked and opened the door.

My fist fell to my side listlessly as panic followed swiftly on the heels of the bile at the back of my tongue. I did not want to speak to the police. Even if I didn't know Raffa, even if I'd loved a mirage, there was no way I could turn him in.

Not after everything that had happened.

My heart simply wouldn't allow it.

"No, I mean, *yes*," I amended, holding up my hands as I backed away slowly. "I'm fine, thank you."

When he only frowned and stepped forward, I repeated myself in Italian, adding, "Really, I'm just great. I got a little lost, but I know my way home now."

The officer glowered at me, murmuring something too low and fast into the phone in Italian for me to discern before he hung up and stuffed it in his pocket. When he moved forward this time, I wasn't expecting his swiftness, and he caught my wrist with a painful grip.

"You are covered in blood," he informed me, as if I wasn't aware.

And truly, in the chaos of it all, I had forgotten. Now that he mentioned it, I could feel the dried gore tightening my skin, making it itch. When I gave in to the impulse, my fingers came away flaked in dried blood.

"Come with me," he said, tugging me inextricably into the station.

Alarm cracked through my cool resolve, lava hot once more and flooding my entire nervous system.

"No!" I almost shouted, trying to wrench my arm out of his hold without any progression. "NO. I do not have to go inside. There is nothing. I just hurt myself."

"I would like to hear why you are covered in blood and bone," the officer demanded as he opened the door and hauled me inside the cold reception area.

I shivered violently, but it had nothing to do with the air-conditioning.

"You can tell me why a young tourist arrives at the police but does not want help," he continued with narrowed eyes before taking my arm again and leading me through a mostly empty bullpen to a side room with a metal door.

"I wouldn't want to waste your time," I tried again, my heart beating so loudly I couldn't focus, vision swimming. Oh my God, I thought, I was going to get Raffa arrested when all I wanted to do was just get away. "I'm an American. I have rights, and you can't just—"

The metal door banged shut in my face, and there was a rusty whoosh as he slid a lock into place. When I tested the handle, I was not surprised to find it locked.

"Fuck," I murmured, curling my arms around myself, blood flaking off my arms as I did and falling like macabre confetti to my feet. "What have I done?"

Half an hour later, I was in a private room in the station, wrapped in a shiny emergency blanket with a lukewarm paper cup filled with thick espresso. The officer, Domani Lastra, was middle aged, with a soft, open face and big gray eyes that looked at me with sympathy as I spun a yarn about the events of the evening. When I was finished, he looked at me for a long, silent moment, then sighed and reached over to pat my hand on the table before he told me he would be right back.

There was a metal cabinet in the corner of the room, just clean enough for me to make out my warped shape and the vivid red of blood still splashed across my face and chest.

I shuddered as I thought about red being Raffa's favorite color.

Revulsion rolled through me, and I gagged into my hand, breathing hard so I wouldn't throw up on the table. Blood was gross enough to have all over me. I didn't want to add vomit.

I closed my eyes when the nausea passed and focused on fighting the tears that burned in the back of my nose.

I would not cry over Raffa.

I refused to soften myself toward the man who had been my first and only lover.

The least of his crimes was lying to me blatantly, intentionally, for the last six weeks, so why did it hurt more than any of the others?

I felt more alone than I ever had before when just hours ago, I had thought I'd finally found a home where I could thrive, with people who understood and loved me.

Who I had thought I understood enough to love in return.

So then why hadn't I told Lastra explicitly that Raffa had killed the intruder?

Why, when the time came, had my mouth opened and silence spilled out?

I knew his name more intimately than I knew my own. My mouth had formed those consonants and vowels when I was moved to tears, to pleasure, to laughter. It would, even now, I knew, be the last thought stuck in my head if I ever suffered from dementia.

So. Why. Could. I. Not. Speak. It?

Instead, I'd told Lastra that someone had broken into my room at the palazzo and threatened me. Someone in the house had killed him before he could hurt me, a murder of self-defense, but I'd run away from the scene before I could get a clear grip on the details. When he asked me why I'd run from the people who saved me, I told him the truth. I'd grown up in small-town Michigan, where the most violence I had ever witnessed was when my neighbor hit her husband with a rolled-up newspaper after discovering he'd had an affair. Running had been a survival instinct I had no experience to curb within myself.

The point was, I told Lastra, there had been a murder.

I told him the address and insisted he send help even though, obviously, the threat had passed.

He assured me dryly that, as he was a police officer, he would send help to the scene.

I wondered if Raffa and the others were okay.

I tried again not to cry.

Shock was setting in, quaking under my skin like shifting tectonic plates, redefining who I was and what I knew for the second time in six weeks.

Because if this was all a *lie*, then who was this new Guinevere Stone?

There was a brief knock on the door, Lastra's deep baritone asking in Italian if he could come in.

I called out my agreement, curling the crinkly blanket tighter around my shoulders as if it could shield me from the events of the night.

Lastra opened the door and stepped into the room.

But he did not close it behind him.

Instead, a familiar face appeared around the door, followed by a body I had spent hours worshipping.

Raffa Romano. Dressed in a three-piece suit like those Carmine favored, his hair perfectly in place, not a speck of blood on him.

I shot out of my chair, the metal screeching across the floor, then banging onto its side. As Raffa moved farther into the room and Lastra closed the door, I pressed myself into the corner across from them and fought the primal urge to hiss.

"What are you doing here?" I shouted in Italian, looking wildly at Lastra. "This man! You can't—! Please, take him away."

Raffa had tensed midstep, staring at me like he had never seen me before.

Lastra sighed deeply and patted Raffa's arm. *"Buona fortuna, capo."*

Capo.

Boss.

The last threads of my sanity and understanding snapped under the shears of that one telling word.

"What the hell!?" I yelled as Lastra slipped out the door. "Who are you?"

Raffa walked over to the table, his movements stilted, almost robotic. "Will you sit?"

"No," I snapped, my stupid hands trembling so that the blanket crinkled constantly. "I don't want to sit with you. Why the hell are you here? I-I didn't say you were the one to kill him when I gave my statement. I won't." I swallowed thickly, fear a sour tang on my tongue. "You don't need to worry about me telling anyone about anything. I wouldn't ever turn you in, e-even now."

"Guinevere." His head slumped forward on his neck, his voice ragged around the sound of my name. "*Dio mio*, I would never harm a hair on your head. Please, sit down so I may explain."

I shook so hard, the blanket wouldn't stop rustling, so I threw it to the floor and went to the chair. I placed it in the far corner and sat there with my arms and legs crossed. His eyes on my skin *hurt*, and I wished he would not look at me.

"You just blew a man's brains out without blinking an eye," I said, reliving it again and again.

Because that was the craziest thing about it all.

Not that Raffa had a gun when they were legal in Italy. My father was strictly antigun and could argue for hours with the television about the lack of strict gun control in America, but I could understand the need to have one to protect the palace, or maybe when Raffa traveled through the country as one of its wealthiest citizens.

But to use it like that?

No hesitation. No qualms whatsoever, even after the man had fallen brainless at my feet. When I'd looked up into those whiskey-brown eyes and been met with cold ruthlessness.

"You've killed before," I whispered.

Of course he had.

It matched the pattern I'd refused until now to piece into shape at the back of my mind.

Raffa did not disagree.

"The man was there to hurt you, Guinevere. Someone sent you flowers. Chrysanthemums. In Italy, you only buy chrysanthemums to bring to a funeral or lay on a gravestone. They were not a gift. They were a warning. And tonight, that man came to see it through."

"Who was he?" My voice was losing steam, fading as I was into a specter of myself.

I was cold, quaking, and utterly alone. The reality of my situation, of how stupid I had been to throw in with a stranger so completely, living with and loving him when I didn't even really *know* him or this country . . .

God, it was sick how stupid I had been.

How right my father was, and how angry it made me to think that.

Raffa huffed a frustrated breath and ran both hands through his hair. "I do not know yet. Now that you have the police involved, it will be easier to identify him but harder to discover who he worked for."

"You have multiple enemies." I thought back woodenly on my earlier suspicions about who Raffa might be. "Who *are* you?"

There was blood on my hand, smeared on the insides of my thumb and forefinger.

I wondered how difficult it would be to get it off. Books and movies always spoke about how hard it was to get bloodstains out of skin.

Red handed and all that.

"Guinevere."

I hated that the sound of my name in his mouth could cut through anything, even shock. My head snapped up, and I was looking into his eyes before I remembered why I shouldn't.

They were absolutely wrecked.

The emotion I had been looking for after he pulled the trigger had surged back in, turning the flat black to warm copper again. I had never noticed the lines beside his eyes so much, heavy folds that made him look tired and pained. For the first time, he looked every inch of his thirty-four years, every one of those eleven years older than me.

"I would *never* let anything hurt you," he said slowly, as if he was afraid I would not understand my own language. "I would kill a thousand men who tried, and I would sleep like a fucking baby knowing I did the right thing every time."

I shivered so violently, my tooth tore across my bottom lip and made it bleed.

Raffa leaned over the table, hands flat to the top, face broken open with sincerity. "I know I am not the hero you thought I was, the hero I warned you I could never be. But I am not quite the villain either. I know that because you showed me all the goodness I had to offer. You shone your starlight on my fucking soul when I thought I had compromised that a long time ago, and you brought everything I have to offer to the surface again. You proved to us both I can be kind and generous." He sucked in a sharp breath and wrenched his eyes from me to stare at a spot on the floor as he whispered fiercely, "You proved to me I am more man than metal when you reminded me I had a heart and I could love with every goddamn piece of it."

"Don't you dare," I mouthed, breathless with rage. "Don't you dare tell me you love me now when you couldn't say it before!"

"I could not say it before because you did not know the truth," he growled. "How could I tell you I loved you, ask you to stay, when you did not know?"

"Then why didn't you tell me?" I shouted, slamming my hand against the wall. "Why the fuck did you spend six weeks making me fall in love with you if you were just playing games?"

To my horror, I started to cry. As if unleashing my fury was the key to unlocking the depths of my pain, I wept. Short, soft hiccuping sobs I tried to catch in my hands, dropping my head to hide the way tears sluiced down my face.

"*Cerbiatta mia*," he murmured, voice thick with his own despair. "No, no. Please, do not cry. *Porca puttana*, I did not set out to hurt you like this. How could I ever have expected to meet the light of my fucking life after hitting her with my car? How could I have braced for the impact of knowing you and how it would crash through me, changing everything I thought I knew about my life? About myself?"

I couldn't stop crying, and his words weren't helping.

"Just." I gulped down a sob. "Just tell me the truth. It's the l-least you can do now."

He sighed again, but the sound seemed torn out of him. "I think you know who I am, Vera. I think a part of you has wondered for a while now."

"No," I said, even though the truth was a heavy weight in my stomach. "I don't."

He looked at me for a long moment, and I let him, arrested in the spotlight of his gaze. The same gaze that used to make me feel invincible, like I could be any me and he would love her.

Something pinged behind my breastbone.

Hadn't I thought I could love any iteration of Raffa the same?

But no. Not like this. Not this man who murdered and lied like some people drank coffee.

"No?" he asked finally, wearily. He dragged a hand over his face and let it drop with a thud to the table. "You do not remember the blood-stain on my shirt the day I danced with you in the trattoria? I had just finished in the basement with Galasso, the *sacco di merda* who tried to rape you your first night in the country."

I gasped, hands covering my mouth even though my tears had trickled to a stop. "What?"

Raffa nodded, and something dark curled the edge of his ruddy mouth. "Ludo found the *figlio di puttana* and brought him to the basement. Umberto's is one of our restaurants, and we use it for business sometimes."

"What did you do to him?" I asked, but I knew.

Of course I did.

I would never let anything hurt you. I would kill a thousand men who tried, and I would sleep like a fucking baby knowing I did the right thing every time.

"You killed him," I whispered into my hands.

When Raffa didn't respond, I looked up to see his grim smile of acknowledgment.

"I drugged him and then beat him to death with my own hands. Ludo took him into the countryside and made it look like a car accident. You can look it up if you want. The crash was in the local news."

"The company you 'invested' in," I said, the dots already connected, the image clearer than I'd ever wanted to see it. All I could do now was validate my findings. "How legal was your investment?"

"Very good, Vera," he said smoothly, the same way he might have praised me for staying very still when he spanked me. Even now, it made my heart stutter. "A rival . . . business was making a play for my company. They turned the deputy chief of the DIA, Sansone Pucci, on to me."

"That's why he was such an asshole at the party."

He inclined his head. There was something different about him now, like he had lowered the partition between who he claimed my Raffa was and the man he'd truly been. He looked more wolf than man, with those sharp canines glinting in that tight, mean little smile and his eyes darkened by the heavy ridge of his frowning brow.

Like another man entirely.

"To be fair, I was not doing what they accused me of, but . . ." He opened his palms in a mock show of innocence. "I could not let that stand. You found the shell companies that revealed which family was working behind my back, and we took care of them."

"The police raid on the boats. You even took me to *watch* it," I said, shocked by his audacity.

It spoke of a certain kind of joy in his work, and that, more than finding out the extent of his crimes, hardened my heart toward him. How could I believe such a man would love me when he was capable of such lies, corruption, and enjoyment of it all? How could I believe he wasn't lying about what mattered most, the shattered heart lying between us?

He sneered. "You enjoyed it, Guinevere. The clues were there. You just did not want to acknowledge them. Do not do us the injustice of pretending I did not give you the real me. I know I did—I *feel* that I did because my heart is no longer inside my chest. You took it when you ran, and I will not get it back unless you come back with me."

He stood up abruptly and crossed to me on swift legs, only gentling slightly when I recoiled. Dropping into a crouch so we were eye level, he slowly lifted a hand to show me he meant no harm and laid it, whisper soft, against my chest.

"Can you feel it beating against your own?" he asked in a thread-bare voice. "I know I do not deserve a second chance, but I am not too proud to tell you I will spend the rest of my life working to earn it. Let me ask you to stay. Stay now that you know and get to know the real me. The man you once aptly called Rex Infernus. Stay forever, because I promise, Guinevere, no one will ever love you as much as I do."

"You're a mafioso," I said into the pause, determined to have it all out between us. With each piece of the puzzle slotting into place, it felt as if I'd erected a shield between myself and him. I was numb beneath it, growing colder and colder. It was much better than the lava-hot rage and pain of before. "Am I right?"

His sigh was answer enough.

"You lie, steal, cheat, assault, scam, and *murder* for a living." The words cut coming up, causing wounds I knew would leave permanent scars. "How can I ever love a man like that?"

Raffa flinched as if I'd hit him with the full weight of my body, face turning away from me, cheeks flushing scarlet. He sucked in a quaver-ing breath and nodded slowly.

He did not realize it was a genuine plea for help. That if he could only convince me and teach me, the way he had taught me so many other things, perhaps I could find a way to rewire my brain, to make sense of his darkness, and the dream of us wouldn't have to die.

What an impossible hope, one more to add to my silly, girlish heart.

"Right," he whispered to himself in Italian. "Of course."

I curled tighter in on myself, hating how hard it was to see him in such pain when he was the cause of my own.

He stood suddenly and turned on his heel to walk toward the door. A pause, his shoulders tense and unmoving, before he twisted back to look at me.

An implacable expression was fixed to his face. It made him look like a total stranger.

"I will have Martina pack your things for you," he said in a perfect monotone. "If you can just text her where you will be, she will get them to you before you leave tomorrow."

"Okay." I swallowed hard around the words that clawed their way up my throat.

Why did you do this to us? To me?

Knowing all this, I still don't think it's enough to kill the love that's overgrown inside me.

We stared at each other for a long time, and I pretended I wasn't cataloging everything one last time. Even though he'd become the villain, he had still left a massive impression in my life and my soul, and now I would have to learn to live around it.

"For what it is worth." He paused. "For what *I* am worth, I may have lied about what I do and how I do it, about my family and our history. But I never lied about anything else. Honestly, no one has ever known me better than you do."

"Frankly, *caro mio*." I bastardized the quote from *Gone with the Wind* with Italian, so cruel it hurt my teeth as the words passed them. It calcified that armor around my heart and gave me the strength to look him right in those cold black eyes. "I don't give a damn."

Raffa rocked back on his heels, mouth parting slightly as my final shot found its mark.

Suddenly exhausted beyond all reasoning, I closed my eyes and wished on one last shooting star that when I opened my eyes, he would be gone for good.

And when I did, he was.

The end . . . for now.

ACKNOWLEDGMENTS

This book is an embodiment of so many themes and topics that I love. My mother's father was Italian, and I've always held Italy and Italian culture dear to my heart. In fact, I have visited countless times and seen so much of the gorgeous country, but it is still not enough to satiate my love of Italy. Guinevere's journey closely mirrors my own experience of moving to France for the summer when I was nineteen. I was from a small city where I had friends I had known most of my life, and moving abroad completely blew open the doors on everything I had previously known about myself and my world. Traveling teaches you so much about yourself, so this story is not only an ode to my love of Italy but also an homage to the value of exploring new horizons, both within and outside ourselves.

I have to start my acknowledgments by thanking my absolutely wonderful agent and publicist, Georgana Grinstead, without whom my dream of writing for Montlake would never have been realized. Thank you, Georgie, for always advocating for me, loving me, and supporting me no matter what. I am so blessed to have a friend like you in my life, and there isn't a moment I am not grateful for you and what you do for me.

Next, of course, to Lauren Plude at Montlake, for being as excited to work with me as I was to work with you and the Montlake team. This process has been a dream because you are at the helm. Thank you for loving my words and giving me this opportunity.

To Sasha Knight, my absolutely exquisite editor, who polished my diamond in the rough until it gleamed like a jewel of the Nile. Thank you for making this experience so collaborative and positive. It was truly the best experience I have ever had working with an editor, and I am so grateful I got to work with you.

To Annie, my copy editor, who polished this manuscript into a true diamond.

To the rest of the team at Montlake who worked tirelessly to package, market, and perfect *My Dark Fairy Tale* into the product it is today. I thank you from the very bottom of my heart.

As always, I have to thank my beloved assistant, Annette, who redefines what it means to be a ride-or-die friend. Thank you for always having my back and for loving me so purely. I'll adore you and admire you forever.

To my other assistant, Jess. Working with you fuels my creative engine and frees up so much time for me to write more words. Thank you for being an OG Giana Darling fan and for always bringing light, productivity, and innovation into my life.

My Baby Darling, Miss Valentine Grinstead, you are one of my dearest friends, and it doesn't matter that we have an age gap or live on opposite sides of the continent from each other. Your humor, style, kindness, and wit always make me laugh and feel seen and heard. Love you forever.

Sarah Kleehammer, my Aussie bestie, I adore you, and I am so thankful my words brought us together to form this iron bond. I admire you so much for always finding the beauty and humor in life and sharing that with me.

To my content team, ARC team, and street team, I am unutterably grateful for everything you do for me and all the ways you spread love for my books! Without you, no release would be successful, so thank you for your constant support.

To the members of "Giana's Darlings," my safe, sweet corner of Facebook where we get to talk about all the bookish things. Every single one of you means so much to me. I still remember when I had four hundred readers in there and couldn't believe my luck. I hope you know how much I love every single one of you.

For Becca, who would fly to me in a heartbeat if I needed her. You are the kind of friend every girl needs in her life.

Brittany, my fellow forbidden soul sister, the friend who is always there to root for me, I am so freaking lucky to know you and love you.

Kandi, even when I disappear into the ether, you find a way to connect with me and make me feel like I am not alone or forgotten. You have the kind of energy that brings joy to every life you touch, and I'm so lucky you touch mine.

Emilie, the CEO of Giana Darling fandom, for everything you do to support and uplift me, I love you always.

To my girls, Armie, Madison, Fiona, and Lauren, who have taught me the beauty of female friendship. Your support, guidance, and genuine joy for my successes always awe and humble me. I love you all so much.

To my sister, Grace, who is as independent and supportive as Gemma is to Guinevere. Since I was a little girl, you and Dad were the only two people to believe I could be a writer, and I know I wouldn't be here without you both today.

To my boys, Al, Devo, Kev, Sam, Spencer, and Noah, there are shades of you in almost every book I write because I can't help but include groups of men—like Renzo, Carmine, and Ludo—who support, tease, and love the hero and heroine the way you have done for Mr. Darling and me most of our lives. I wouldn't be me without you, and I love you to the depths of my soul.

And finally, last as always because we always save the best for the last note, to the love of my life, my husband. I sit here typing this on your birthday, feeling overfull with gratitude and awe that I get to spend this life as your best friend and wife. You inspire me to write every word of romance and passion I have ever written or will ever write. Loving you is the best thing I will ever do.

ABOUT THE AUTHOR

Photo © 2024 Paige Owen

Giana Darling is a *USA Today*, *Wall Street Journal*, and Amazon Top 40 bestselling Canadian romance writer who specializes in the forbidden and angsty side of love. She currently lives on an island in beautiful British Columbia, where she spends time riding on the back of her husband's bike, baking pies, and reading while snuggled up with her golden retriever, Romeo.

To get the latest info on her books, upcoming events, bonus content, and more, visit Giana's website at https://gianadarling.com, where you can also sign up for her newsletter. Connect with the author on social media via Instagram (@GianaDarlingAuthor), X (@GianaDarling), or YouTube (@gianadarlingauthor). You can also find her on Facebook (check out her readers group, Giana's Darlings), TikTok, Goodreads, and BookBub.